BESTIARIES
AND THEIR USERS
IN THE MIDDLE AGES

BESTIARIES AND THEIR USERS IN THE MIDDLE AGES

RON BAXTER

SUTTON PUBLISHING
COURTAULD INSTITUTE

First published in the United Kingdom in 1998 by
Sutton Publishing Limited · Phoenix Mill
Thrupp · Stroud · Gloucestershire · GL5 2BU

in association with the Courtauld Institute, Somerset House, Strand, London WC2R 0RN

British Library Cataloguing in Publication Data
A catalogue record for this book is available from the British Library

ISBN 0 7509 1853 5

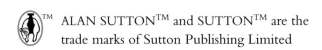

™ ALAN SUTTON™ and SUTTON™ are the
trade marks of Sutton Publishing Limited

Typeset in 11/14pt Bembo Mono.
Typesetting and origination by
Sutton Publishing Limited.
Printed in Great Britain by
WBC Limited, Bridgend.

CONTENTS

FIGURES AND PLATES

COLOUR PLATES

Between pp. 114 and 115.

1. Bourges Cathedral, Resurrection window, detail of lion and pelican scenes.
2. St Petersburg, Saltykov-Shchedrin Q.v.V.1, f. 9r opening of Bestiary text.
3. New York, Pierpont Morgan M.81, f. 8r opening of Bestiary text.
4. St Petersburg, Saltykov-Shchedrin Q.v.V.1, f. 20v *simia*.
5. New York, Pierpont Morgan M.81, f. 19v *simia*.
6. Westminster Abbey 22, f. 1v monstrous races.
7. Oxford, St John's College 61, f. 103v *ex-libris*.
8. Oxford, Bodleian Bodley 764, f. 12r *elephantus*.
9. Oxford, St John's College 61, f. 1v Creation scenes.

TABLES

PREFACE

This study investigates the connection between changes in the organization and content of the text and illustrations of Latin Bestiaries, and changes in the ways they were used.

An analysis of the narrative of the *Physiologus*, the Greek text upon which all Bestiaries ultimately rely, reveals it to be a structured treatise on virtue and vice. The changes and additions made to this in England in the twelfth and thirteenth centuries continually acted to disrupt this structure, substituting for it one based on the organization of the natural world as recounted in the Genesis creation myth. An investigation into the centres of use of Bestiaries in the Middle Ages, and their popularity among the different religious orders provides a geographical, temporal and institutional framework for these changes. The question of what kind of book the *Physiologus* had become is addressed by a study of the institutional context of Bestiaries: where they were shelved in monastic libraries, and the kinds of texts with which they were regularly bound. Studies of three cases of Bestiary consumption provide examples of the new kinds of use to which the books could be put.

Finally, I look into the question of *narration*, the ways in which the *Physiologus* and Bestiaries based on it were read. This involves the study of verbal structures in the texts themselves, and the identification of clues pointing to public (oral) or private consumption.

The first three years of this research were funded by a grant from the British Academy. I am grateful to the staffs of the manuscript libraries in this country and abroad who have been unstinting in their help with my research into the Bestiaries in their collections. Particular thanks are due to William Voelkle of the Pierpont Morgan library, who generously allowed me to examine MS M81 while it was in London for the exhibition *English Romanesque Art, 1066–1200* in 1984.

From the many people who have freely contributed their expertise, I should like to single out the late Mr Christopher Hohler whose approach to manuscripts, always firmly rooted in the conditions of their consumption, taught me what questions to ask; the late Professor Julian Brown, who instructed me in the practicalities of examining manuscripts; Professor Robin Cormack, who was always ready to offer valuable guidance on the theoretical implications of my work; Dr John Lowden and Mr Michael Evans, who supervised the thesis on which this book is based, and who were unstinting in their support and advice; Mr Nicholas Orchard, who read parts of the work in draft and acted as Devil's advocate to some of my wilder flights of theoretical fancy; and Mr Geoffrey Fisher of the Conway Library, whose experience in obtaining photographs was invaluable. Above all, I should like to thank my wife, Kathryn Morrison, without whose encouragement and criticism the book would never have been written.

CHAPTER ONE

THE STORY OF A DISCOURSE

I shall take as my starting-point whatever unities are already given . . . but I shall not place myself inside these dubious unities in order to study their internal configuration or their secret contradictions. I shall make use of them just long enough to ask myself what unities they form; by what right they can claim a field that specifies them in space and a continuity that individualizes them in time . . . I shall accept the groupings that history suggests only to subject them at once to interrogation . . . [1]

Michel Foucault

Between 1851 and 1856, Charles Cahier and Arthur Martin published editions of three Latin *Physiologus* texts,[2] the French prose Bestiary of Pierre le Picard, and the French verse Bestiary of Guillaume le Clerc, illustrating them with plates taken from one Latin *Physiologus* (Brussels Bibl. Roy. MS 10074) and three French Bestiaries (Paris, Arsenal MS 283; Bibl. Nat. MS Fr. 7534; and Bibl. Nat. MS Suppl. Fr. 632). This was by no means the only publication of *Physiologus* textual material in that period,[3] but its significance to art historians lay in the juxtaposition of text and illustrations that it provided. It was this juxtaposition that led directly to a view of Bestiaries which still pervades art historical writing in this country.

The earliest published expression of this view that I have found appears in Charles C. Perkins's *Italian Sculptors*, published in 1868, and takes the form of an excursus on animal symbolism awkwardly appended to a chapter on sculpture in Apulia.[4] Perkins's

---

1. Foucault (1974), 26.

2. Cahier and Martin (1851–6). The three texts were Brussels, Bibl. Roy. MS 10074 (the A text), dated there to the end of the tenth century, and here to the early eleventh; and two MSS in the Burgerbibliothek in Berne, MS 233 (B text) of the eighth to ninth century, and MS 318 (C text) of the ninth.

3. Editions of Latin text include the eighth-century alphabetical fragments of Mai (1835), Heider's (1850) edition of a recension entitled *Dicta Iohannis Chrysostomi de naturis bestiarum*, which he found in a Gottweih codex and, most usefully, Mann's (1888) edition of the English Latin Bestiary, British Library MS Royal 2.C.XII. Greek texts included Pitra (1855), Lauchert (1889) and Karneev (1890 and 1894). The last named included an edition of Moscow 432 (π text), the Greek recension from which the Armenian, Younger Syriac and Latin A and B texts derived. Tychsen (1795) and Land (1875) published two different Syriac texts, the latter printed with a Latin translation; Hommel (1877) is Ethiopic; and Marr (1904) Armenian and Georgian. More complete surveys of the early literature may be found in Sbordone (1936.2), pp. 30–40, and in Perry (1937).

4. Perkins (1868), 7–9.

argument was that in Christian symbolism natural forms are the signs of hidden religious meaning, and that the Bestiary was a codification of animal symbolism:

This habit of looking for a symbol in every created thing, led to a system of mystical zoology contained in the *Physiologus* or Bestiary, a work which explains the now forgotten meaning of many of the strange forms carved about the facades of mediaeval churches.[5]

For a fully developed expression of the paradigm, we must turn to the work of John Romilly Allen. The last of his 1887 Rhind Lectures was entitled 'The Mediaeval Bestiaries', and dealt with the symbolism of animal imagery in ecclesiastical carving.[6] Allen attempted to answer two questions:

(1) whether there is any evidence in contemporary literature that a system of symbolism, founded upon the characteristics of the animal world, existed during the Middle Ages; and (2) whether it can be proved that such a system was applied to the decoration of Christian monuments and buildings.[7]

As an answer to the first question, Allen proposed that such a system was codified in 'the Bestiary, or book of beasts',[8] thereby imposing a spurious unity on the mass of different texts and following Perkins in labelling the result 'a system of mystic zoology'.[9] His approach to the second question was to start from cases of clear-cut Bestiary symbolism, as in the stained glass in the ambulatory of Bourges Cathedral. Here a central image of the Resurrection of Christ is surrounded by four types of the subject; two from the Old Testament and two found in Bestiaries (colour plate 1). The stories of the Pelican piercing her breast so that her blood revives her dead chicks, and the Lion breathing life into his stillborn cubs are both explicitly related to Christ's Resurrection in the *Physiologus* text. Allen's illustrations in this category were all continental.[10] From these he passed to his best English example, the south doorway of the church at Alne, Yorkshire, a unique instance which was to be used again and again to bolster the case for unity.[11] At Alne, the model for the imagery was certainly a Bestiary. Not only are the subjects of eight of the *voussoirs* identified by inscriptions,

5. Ibid., 9.
6. Allen (1887), 334–95.
7. Ibid., 335.
8. Ibid.
9. Ibid., 341.
10. Ibid., 341–3.
11. See also Allen (1888).

but the compositions of all nine, although Allen did not note this, are almost identical to those in Oxford, Bodleian Library MS Laud Misc. 247 (compare plates 1 and 2). What Allen failed to point out was that there is nothing in the arrangement to show how the doorway was meant to be understood. He was content to conclude:

> We have now succeeded in showing that the system of mystic zoology contained in the mediaeval Bestiaries was not only recognized by the Church as a means of conveying religious instruction as far back as the eighth century, but also that animal symbolism, corresponding exactly with that of the MSS, was used for the decoration of ecclesiastical buildings of the twelfth century, side by side with scenes from Scripture and such sacred devices as the Agnus Dei.[12]

Two points must be made. First, Alne was the only twelfth-century monument he mentioned, and second, while he demonstrated the presence of animal imagery there, he was unable to justify any reading of animal symbolism, or to synthesize any meaning in the combination of those particular animals. He simply assumed that a symbolic reading was expected. When he turned to the manuscript Bestiaries themselves, he found himself unable to detect the nature of the systematization: 'In the bestiary the stories about the various animals do not seem to be arranged on any definite plan as regards the order in which they come.'[13] This failure was a direct result of the assumption of discursive unity: the assumption, in other words, that all Bestiaries are the same kind of book, fulfilling similar functions. In chapter two I shall show how the *Physiologus* was organized in well-defined groups of chapters along Christian ethical lines, and in chapter three how changes in the chapter order and textual content eroded this coding and substituted another. By investing Bestiaries with a false homogeneity, Allen ignored the specificity of each individual manuscript. Such followers of Allen's method as Druce and Collins were if anything even less successful. Both writers betrayed a heavy reliance on Alne,[14] both inferred Bestiary symbolism when confronted with Bestiary imagery, and both developed their arguments simply by juxtaposing examples of church sculpture with chapters of Bestiary text. It is not my prime concern here to point out the weaknesses inherent in such an approach, but to indicate an important mechanism by which Bestiaries came to be regarded as a unity, in this case a 'system of mystic zoology'. An interesting by-product of this was that Allen found it difficult, and Druce impossible, to resist the attempt to reconcile this mystic zoology with the more rational modern variety. Allen pointed out that

12. Ibid., 357.
13. Ibid., 380–1.
14. See, e.g., Druce (1912); Collins (1940).

Plate 1. Alne (Yorks) St Mary, south doorway showing, in the outer order, vulpis, pantera, aquila, hiena, caladrius *and* caper.

Plate 2. Oxford, Bodleian Library Laud Misc. 247, f. 149r. Vulpis the fox attacked by birds who think it is dead.

to anyone holding the view that this life is chiefly a preparation for a better one to come, modern science, which seeks to classify and arrange objects according to their physical properties, must seem little better than elaborate trifling unless some spiritual advantage is to be gained thereby.[15]

But he did not seem to doubt that they were wrong and we are right: 'the bestiary contains many mistakes due . . . to confusing one animal with another from want of zoological knowledge'.[16]

Druce, on the other hand, was prepared to credit the compilers of Bestiaries with a surprising level of zoological knowledge, identifying the *amphisbaena*, described in some Bestiaries as a dragon with a head at each end, with a specimen of the worm *amphisbaena alba*, which he discovered in the South Kensington museum.[17]

15. Allen (1887), 337.
16. Ibid.
17. Druce (1910).

The tendency to identify the Bestiary as a work of zoology, mystic or otherwise, has gone a long way towards establishing its discursive unity. T.H. White has asserted that it is, 'a serious work of natural history, and one of the bases upon which our own knowledge of biology is founded'.[18] And the same view seems to be shared by the ornithologist Brunsdon Yapp,[19] and by Wilma George, who undertook an exhaustive analysis of texts and images of the *yale*, ultimately concluding that it was either a Cape buffalo or an Indian water buffalo.[20]

Bestiaries, then, were constructed by Allen as uniform in meaning and a source of visual symbolism. The final threads in the fabric, establishing a time span and a geographical framework in which the paradigm operated, were to be woven in by Joseph Anderson, to whom Allen acknowledged his debt for suggesting 'the line of enquiry to be followed'.[21]

As his introduction to Allen's encyclopaedic *The Early Christian Monuments of Scotland*, Anderson contributed his Rhind Lectures for 1892. In this we find two significant assertions. First, on the subject of the *Physiologus*, that: 'though translated into many languages . . . its essential substance remained the same from the fifth to the fifteenth century'.[22] This formulation gave the timespan to the currency of the system of mystic zoology found in the Bestiary. Although the passage is specifically about the Physiologus, Anderson had already made it clear that he considered 'Physiologus' and 'Bestiary' to be practically interchangeable terms:

the system of animal symbolism which was such a prevalent feature of the Christian art of the early Middle Ages was derived, for the most part, from an anonymous treatise on the nature of beasts, originally known by the name *Physiologus*, and later in its adaptation to the system of Christian symbolism as *The Divine Bestiary*.[23]

His second assertion was to provide the geographical framework: '. . . the Bestiary was known and used in Britain as well as on the Continent, where there are early manuscripts of it in all the great libraries.'[24] The logical connection is somewhat tenuous. If there were early manuscripts of it in all the great libraries on the Continent in 1892, that proves nothing about its geographical spread in the Middle Ages, either

18. White (1954), 231.
19. Yapp (1981).
20. George (1968).
21. Allen (1887), 334.
22. Allen (1903), xli.
23. Ibid., xl.
24. Ibid., xli.

in Britain or in Europe in general. Nevertheless, we find similar assumptions about the universal availability of Bestiaries either implicit or explicit in much subsequent writing. The four examples below span the period from 1932 to 1960.

The manuscripts (Bestiaries) . . . were at hand in every monastery . . .[25]

the library of any cathedral or large monastery would have possessed a copy (of the Bestiary).[26]

at least one copy (of the Bestiary) seems to have been present in most twelfth-century libraries . . .[27]

a recent book has named the *Physiologus* . . . as among the usual contents of an English mediaeval library, and this is doubtless true of continental libraries also.[28]

George Druce was one of the most prolific and influential writers on the subject.[29] Some idea of his continuing prestige can be gauged from the short bibliography of Morgan's earliest volume in the recent and important *Survey of Manuscripts Illuminated in the British Isles*,[30] which lists nine entries under his name. Most of Druce's articles were monographs on individual animals. His usual approach was to supply translations of Bestiary chapters on his chosen subject, taken from both Latin and French Bestiaries, to extract from them any symbolic meaning and indications of possible zoological identity, and to reproduce a few Bestiary miniatures. The bulk of the text would then comprise a survey of ecclesiastical stone and wood carving of the subject.

A recurring complaint was that it was often difficult to be sure exactly which beast was intended by the carvers, particularly in the case of serpents and dragons. This difficulty led him to produce many highly speculative identifications, but he never doubted that some specific creature was intended in every case, and that its Bestiary symbolism was intended to be recalled by the carving. One of the most dubious, and paradoxically one of which Druce himself seemed most confident, was of two corbels high on the west front of Kilpeck church which appear to represent dragon's heads

---

25. Saunders (1932), 63.
26. Anderson (1938), 11.
27. Stone (1955), 245 n. 6.
28. McCulloch (1960), 44.
29. See bibliography for Druce's main articles on Bestiaries. Towards the end of his life he frequently corresponded with M.D. Anderson, then Lady Cox, to whom he gave considerable guidance in the identification of Bestiary subjects found in church sculpture. Some of this correspondence is preserved in the Book Library of the Courtauld Institute of Art.
30. Morgan (1982), 42–4.

with their mouths open, revealing long, spiralling tongues (plate 4). He considered this motif to represent a crocodile swallowing a *hydrus* (plate 3), and with the aid of Bestiary texts took it to symbolize the mouth of hell.[31]

Francis Bond's *Wood Carvings in English Churches: 1. Misericords*, published in 1910, went a long way towards establishing Allen's Bestiary discourse as the major key to the imagery of misericords. The book is organized largely according to the subject matter of the carvings, and the *Physiologus* material occupies by far the largest part.[32] This is subdivided into the classifications suggested by Allen,[33] that is, into Birds, Beasts and Fishes; Imaginary Birds, Beasts and Fishes; and Composite monsters. These distinctions, found nowhere in the *Physiologus* itself, betray an attempt to superimpose the criteria of modern zoology on material quite foreign to it. In his preface, Bond was explicit about his view of animal symbolism, and it differed little from Allen's. After alluding to the wealth of animal imagery in churches he rhetorically asked, 'what does it all mean? How did it get into churches of all places? And where did it come from?'[34] We do not have to wait long for the answer, 'to deal with it adequately would be to write a complete History of Ecclesiastical Zoology as it is set forth in the Bestiaries, the popular text-books in the Middle Ages'.[35] The discourse, then, was well established by the first decade of this century, and it would only be tedious to trace its transmission in detail through the works of writers like Prior and Gardner, Saunders, M.D. Anderson and Collins.[36] I shall return to assess the effects of the discourse on more recent literature, but first I must turn my attention to two early writers whose work seems to stand outside it.

Emile Mâle's *L'art religieux du XIIIe siècle en France* was first published in 1898. Like Allen, Mâle demonstrated a familiarity with published editions of *Physiologus* texts.[37] Unlike Allen, however, he also displayed a wide reading among other medieval texts which relied on Bestiary and *Physiologus* material, and he was therefore able to assess the sources of the pictorial material he examined with greater precision. A case in point is a window in the apse of Lyon Cathedral, whose juxtaposition of *Physiologus* and scriptural imagery had already been pointed out by Cahier.[38] Three of the five scenes show New Testament episodes accompanied by *Physiologus* types: the

31. Druce (1909:I), 324–5.
32. Bond (1910) chapters III to V (pp. 19–64).
33. Allen (1887), 381.
34. Bond (1910), vii.
35. Ibid.
36. Prior and Gardner (1912) especially pp. 27–32; Gardner (1951), *passim*; Saunders (1928 and 1932); Anderson (1935 and 1938); Collins (1940).
37. Mâle (1898), 50.
38. Ibid., 55.

fluenſ illud a facie lauarec .Vnde otaci poeta. Scercore
fuicac° crocodrilli. Oua ſua incerta fouec .maſculuſ
& femina inceſ fouendi ſeruanc. hunc hydruſ deglun
tuſ dentib; & unguib; incerunc . & uiuuſ inde exit .

hidruſ 7ợm deglurac
ẽu corerodiluſ.

Eſ ſ AHIWAL quod grece dicic dorcon· launc uero

Plate 3. Oxford, Bodleian Library Laud Misc. 247, f. 152r. The hydrus *kills a crocodile by crawling into its mouth and eating its way out.*

Annunciation with the unicorn trapped by a virgin; the Resurrection (signified by the scene of the Holy Women at the Empty Tomb) with the lion breathing life into a dead cub; and the Ascension with the *caladrius* and the eagle, which both fly to heaven to restore life (plate 5).[39] While Cahier had assumed that the scheme resulted from the familiarity of the designer of the window with Bestiary material, Mâle was able to show that the entire programme, which includes Old Testament as well as Bestiary types, was taken from the *Speculum Ecclesiae* of Honorius Augustodunensis.[40]

Mâle was concerned to counteract the tendency current among archaeologists to overstate the influence of Bestiaries on medieval imagery, and was only able to cite two cases of direct borrowing from this source in France: a capital with an owl surrounded

39. The window is divided into seven central fields with borders on either side. The Ascension occupies the top three fields with below it, from bottom up, the Annunciation, the Nativity, the Crucifixion and the Holy Women at the Tomb.
40. Ibid., 54–9. This is also true of the Bourges window discussed above.

Plate 4. Kilpeck (Herefs.) SS Mary & David, corbel on the west front of a dragon's head with curling tongue (identified by Druce as hydrus *and* crocodile*).*

by other birds at Le Mans, and another at Troyes showing the Peredixion Tree with birds in its branches and two dragons waiting to eat them if they strayed out of its protective shade. On Bestiary symbolism he was even more scathing.

> Mais nous voici en présence de la faune et de la flore si riches de Reims, d'Amiens, de Rouen, de Paris, et du monde mystérieux du gargouilles. Y chercherons-nous aussi des symboles? Quel livre nous en expliquera le sens? Quel texte nous guidera? Avouons-le: les livres ici ne nous apprennent plus rien; les textes et les monuments ne concordent plus. En les rapprochant les uns et les autres on n'arrive a aucun conclusion certaine . . .[41]

Mâle confined his study to French art, but was not without influence in this country.

---

41. 'But here we are in the presence of the rich fauna and flora of Reims, Amiens, Rouen and Paris, and the mysterious world of gargoyles. Shall we also look for symbols? Which book will explain their meaning? Which text will guide us? Let us admit it: here the books will tell us nothing, the texts and the monuments no longer agree. Comparing the one with the other we arrive at no clear conclusion.' Ibid., 64.

Prior and Gardner followed his lead in using the classification made by Vincent de Beauvais in the *Speculum Maius* as the matrix for their treatment of iconography.[42] Within this framework, however, their handling of Bestiary symbolism reveals that they had not taken Mâle's warning to heart, preferring to follow the lead given by Allen and Druce (both of whom they cited in footnotes) in reading sermons into carved stone and wood. In their description of a misericord at Chester, showing a hunter distracting a tiger with a glass ball in order to steal its cub, a plate illustrating the carving was juxtaposed with a summary of the Bestiary story from an unspecified manuscript, ending with the moral to be drawn from the image:

> So we are warned not to be like the tiger-mother, but to keep watch over our cubs, that is our souls, nor to be deluded into losing them: for the hunters (i.e. the Devil) would deceive us with mirrors, viz. the delights and luxury of the world.[43]

Mâle's appeal for caution was no competition for the allure of Allen's system of mystic zoology which held the key to medieval imagery. By and large, it was simply ignored by British writers.

Unlike Mâle, M.R. James did not oppose Allen's paradigm, unassumingly presenting his own work on text as marginal to the discourse. It is only relatively recently that the value and implications of his approach have begun to be recognized. *The Bestiary* of 1928 opens with an introduction on the history of the texts of the *Physiologus*, which relies on Cahier and Martin, Lauchert, Hommel and James's own research. There follow short descriptions of thirty-six English Bestiaries and briefer notices of five (including Migne's printed text) which James considered foreign. Each entry contains a short codicological description, usually detailing the number of leaves, the number of lines to a page and the type of illustration, if any. This is followed by indications of medieval ownership where this is known. The bulk of each entry is given to an analysis of the text, including any opening title, the opening words of the book, the order of the first few chapters and the main textual divisions. The forty-one Bestiaries are grouped into four families according to their textual organization. The bulk of the book is a facsimile of Cambridge University Library MS Ii. 4. 26, and this is immediately preceded by an analysis of the immediate sources of almost every line of the text of this Bestiary; details of its provenance; and a description of its miniatures.

Throughout his survey, James was concerned to record any details of medieval consumption or production specific to individual Bestiaries. Under both Bodleian MS

---

42. Prior and Gardner (1912), 27.
43. Ibid., 30.

Laud Misc. 247 and BL MS Stowe 1067 he compared the script to that of Christ Church, Canterbury, and elsewhere he noted any *ex-libris* inscriptions or other indications of early ownership.

James's own view of the nature of the Bestiary was set out straightforwardly enough on the first page of the introduction:

> It is a Bestiary: and those who know the name will have at least a rough definition of a Bestiary in their minds, as a sort of moralized Natural History illustrated with curious pictures. That is so far correct. Indeed, the Bestiary may be reckoned as one of the leading picture-books of the twelfth and thirteenth centuries in this country . . . Leading and influential: for researches such as those of Cahier and Martin in the last century and of Mr G.C. Druce in this, have shown how widely images and ideas taken from it have permeated medieval art. But for its pictures I do not think that the Book could possibly have gained or kept any sort of popularity. Its literary merit is *nil*, and its scientific value (even when it had been most extensively purged of fable, and reinforced with soberer stuff) sadly meagre.[44]

James's acceptance of Druce's work; his summary of the Bestiary as 'a sort of moralized Natural History', recalling Perkins's 'system of mystical zoology'; his disparaging comparison with modern science, all these place him within the discursive unity I have been at pains to identify. His own contribution to the discourse, however, was a marginal one. He accepted that the value of the book lay in its pictures, yet he expended all his greatest efforts on text, notably in the classification of manuscripts and the source analysis. He may simply have been doing what he did best, but it is at the margins of a discourse that deconstruction begins,[45] and James's perverse concentration on what seemed unimportant was ultimately to render Allen's paradigm untenable. 'Ultimately' because it is only in the last ten years, notably in Muratova's writing, that much attention has been paid to the implications of the textual and pictorial differences between Bestiaries.

James's work might have been expected to bear a more rapidly ripening fruit in the area of dating. His assertion that Bestiaries were books of the twelfth and thirteenth centuries was based on the observation that of the forty-one manuscripts he examined, only four fell outside that period. Nevertheless, as late as 1955, we still find Gardner attributing Bestiary symbolism to carvings on fifteenth and sixteenth-century bench ends.[46]

44. James (1928), 1.
45. See Derrida (1972), especially pp. xv–xix.
46. Gardner (1955).

Plate 5. Lyon (Rhône-Alpes) Cathèdrale Saint-Jean. Detail of Redemption window, showing a group of apostles witnessing Christ's ascension, flanked by Bestiary subjects. Caladrius (left) cures a sick man by absorbing his disease and flying into the sun. Aquila (right) the old eagle renews himself by flying into the sun.

The first art historian to take any serious account of James's work was Florence McCulloch. Her *Mediaeval Latin and French Bestiaries*, published in 1960, included a reorganization of James's four family classification involving the subdivision of the First Family.[47] I shall show in chapter three that the new categories she introduced were ultimately unhelpful and even misleading. In relation to the discourse I have been at pains to examine, McCulloch's book seems curiously retrogressive. She added fifteen Latin Bestiaries to James's list, but made no attempt to address differences of text between individual manuscripts in each family. Indeed, by treating each grouping as a unity, and simply listing its members with no indications of medieval ownership, or even nationality, she went some way towards undermining the value of James's careful research.

Unlike James, McCulloch appeared totally unconcerned with the precise conditions of production and consumption of Bestiaries. A key to the reason for this may be that she

47. McCulloch (1960), 25–44.

was unable to examine many of the manuscripts themselves, but relied heavily on photographs, facsimiles and, above all, microfilms. In her acknowledgements she recorded five grants: three for the purchase of microfilm; one for a summer's work at the Harvard University Library; and one to cover publishing costs.[48] She made no mention here of any grant for travel to Europe. Although she thanked several European libraries for letting her illustrate her book with tracings from their manuscripts, it seems clear that she did not visit the libraries and make the tracings herself.[49] Among the libraries she listed were the British Museum, the Bibliothèque Nationale in Paris, and the Danish Royal Library in Copenhagen. Elsewhere, in a footnote, she mentioned that she had only seen specific manuscripts from those institutions on microfilms.[50] It seems possible that she wrote the book without handling any Bestiary outside the United States.

Well over half of *Mediaeval Latin and French Bestiaries* is taken up by a chapter called *General Analysis of the Principal Subjects treated in Latin and French Bestiaries*. This takes the form of a dictionary of Bestiary subjects, each entry giving versions of the Bestiary story and moralization found in various texts; describing a few illustrations and suggesting possible identifications of the subject.[51] This approach only differs from Druce's in failing to record instances of the occurrence of each subject in architectural sculpture and woodcarving, and indeed for subjects treated by Druce she relied heavily on his articles.

In the same year that McCulloch's book appeared, the Metropolitan Museum of Art in New York published *A Cloisters Bestiary*, a slim, heavily illustrated volume primarily intended for the museum bookshop.[52] It opens with a preface, describing a Bestiary as:

> . . . a form of natural history that was widely read and respected in the Middle Ages. Although it was intended as a serious and factual commentary on the animal kingdom, the medieval Bestiary presented an enchanting mixture of fact and fancy, often enlivened by illustrations that spurred the imagination to its own devices.[53]

Once Bestiaries are presented as serious works on natural history, there is little alternative but to point out their shortcomings in this respect (although Druce, as we saw in the case of the *amphisbaena*, and, in particular, White sometimes took the line that the zoological information they gave was not always as far-fetched as it might appear).

---

48. Ibid., 8–9.
49. Ibid., 9.
50. Ibid., 75, n. 17.
51. Ibid., 78–192.
52. New York (1960).
53. Ibid., 1.

The body of the text of *A Cloisters Bestiary* begins with a chapter on the creation of birds, fish and animals, comprising Genesis text illustrated by a detail of a fourteenth-century Spanish altarpiece. There follow fifty-one chapters on individual creatures. Each chapter consists of Bestiary text, usually taken from White (1954) but with moralizations largely omitted, illustrated by photographs of objects in the Cloisters Museum. None of the illustrations are from a Bestiary: the objects shown range from a German fifteenth-century silver beaker cover, engraved with a hunting scene, for the chapter on the bear, to a Spanish thirteenth-century stone relief of a lion. The chapters themselves follow the order of no Bestiary I have encountered. The first twenty-one are on quadrupeds. Within this grouping no distinction is made between wild beasts, domestic animals and small animals: divisions found in Bestiaries of James's Second Family, which had some meaning for twelfth and thirteenth-century readers. The next nine share only the anachronistic property of being considered fabulous today. Next follow two reptiles and a group of fifteen birds, oddly interrupted by four chapters on fish.

The omission of moralizations reinforces the representation of Bestiaries as inaccurate works of natural history, as does the re-ordering of the chapters into groups based on modern zoological taxonomy. Equally misleading is the choice of illustrations. The juxtaposition of Bestiary text with non-Bestiary imagery is a device we have seen at work in the hands of Druce, Bond, Prior, and Gardner and Mary Anderson, with the purpose of assigning Bestiary symbolism to beast imagery. This is clearly not the chief intention here, since the moralizations have largely been edited from the text.[54] Its effect can only be fully appreciated when it is considered alongside such disparate elements as the title of the work, the intended consumer and the wholesale reorganization of textual material.

A Cloisters Bestiary was intended as a popular book, aimed at the general reader. The preface ends with the hope that it will, '. . . help the reader to appreciate better the variety of fascinating animals that abound in medieval art'.[55]

It lacks the specificity of a Bestiary, in that its bowdlerized text relies on a variety of sources, including White's idiosyncratic translation of Cambridge University Library MS Ii. 4. 26, Rendell's translation of the rhymed *Physiologus of Theobaldus*,[56] and several manuscripts, including New York, Pierpont Morgan Library MS M81 and 'Bodleian Manuscript 601',[57] (presumably a misprint for Bodleian Library MS Bodley 602). The

---

54. Ibid., 4. Of the three natures of the lion, all of which are moralized in the *Physiologus* and in Bestiary texts, only the third (the vivification by the parent of cubs born dead on the third day) is given its moralization here (Christ's Resurrection on the third day).
55. Ibid., 2.
56. Rendell (1928).
57. New York (1960), 2.

choice of four Bestiaries of different textual recensions was doubtless deliberate: its implications are far reaching.

All these factors taken together disclose not merely a representation of Bestiaries as a discursive unity, but a conception of 'The Bestiary' as something other than a collection of manuscripts: in effect as the mass of medieval zoological knowledge and imagery. This notion was by no means new. Something of the kind lurks behind the widely espoused notion of the 'system of mystic zoology', but it received explicit expression in Barbier de Montault's *Traité d'iconographie chrétienne* (1890), a widely used iconographic reference book noted in the bibliography to Bond (1910):

> comme au moyen âge, nous comprenons tout ce qui a vie sous le nom générique de bêtes: quadrupèdes, poissons, reptiles, insectes, oiseaux. L'ensemble fait ce qu'on appelait autrefois le *Bestiaire*.[58]

It is now worth turning to two books, both appearing in the 1950s in important series on the History of Art, and both still included on reading lists. T.S.R. Boase's *English Art, 1100–1216* was volume III of the *Oxford History of English Art*, which Boase edited himself. On sources for the repertory of images in the twelfth century, he tracked through the source material leaving the Bestiary, 'in the end most potent', until last.[59] Although he footnoted James (1928), his main point, about the reading of animal imagery, could easily have been written by Druce.

> The antelope caught in the bushes is an appropriate tanglewood tale: the crocodile that devours a man and then weeps for him or the hyena plundering a grave are good horror stories: the *caladrius*, the white bird that cures jaundice, perches on the sick bed and foretells recovery by looking at the patient or death by averting its head: to each a moral application is applied, which increases the puzzling nature of visual references on capitals or in initials. Thus the lions which pervade Canterbury manuscripts may be the Devil roaring for his prey, the symbol of St Mark, or, from the Bestiary, a type of the Resurrection because the lion cubs were said to be born dead and to come to life on the third day.[60]

This passage appears in a chapter devoted to art in Reading and the West Country in the reign of Henry I. The Bestiaries with which Boase was dealing he explicitly stated to

---

58. 'As in the Middle Ages, we include all living things under the generic name of beasts: quadrupeds, fish, reptiles, insects, birds. The collection is otherwise called the Bestiary.' Barbier de Montault (1890), 126–7.
59. Boase (1953), 85–9.
60. Ibid., 88–9.
61. Ibid., 88.

be Latin texts.[61] It is worth looking, with these two facts in mind, at some of the Bestiary stories quoted above. The story of the crocodile weeping for its prey appears in the French verse Bestiary of Philippe de Thaon, originally composed shortly after 1121, but surviving only in three later copies, the earliest of which, British Library MS Cotton Nero A.V., dateable after 1152, is un–illustrated.[62] Of the two surviving Latin Bestiaries produced in the reign of Henry I, Laud Misc. 247 contains no chapter on the crocodile at all and Stowe 1067 includes a chapter taken from Isidore, which does not contain this story. In fact, the story is found in no Latin Bestiaries at all, although it is mentioned by Druce.[63]

The story of the *caladrius* curing jaundice is even odder. This chapter appears in the *Physiologus*, but no disease is specified, the text referring only to the bird's ability to tell whether a sick man will live or die, and to heal him if he is curable. The specific reference to jaundice comes from Pliny's chapter on the *icterus*, a bird with similar diagnostic powers.[64] Again, jaundice is specified in Migne, but not, so far as I have found, in any surviving English Latin manuscript Bestiary. In Migne, the debt to Pliny is acknowledged, but Boase's immediate source was probably Druce, who provided a translation of the relevant passage.

> Suidas (calls it) charadrus, who tells us that it is a maritime bird great and greedy, and possessed of such power that if those afflicted by jaundice gaze at it, they are freed (from their complaint), as Pliny has asserted about the bird (called) 'icterus'. . . [65]

Elsewhere Boase repeated Druce's curious identification of the crocodile and hydrus on the west front of Kilpeck.[66] Alne appears once more, described as a 'careful programme', but again without any indication of how it is to be read.[67] Finally, the Bestiary is again seen to fall short of modern standards of zoology: 'As it purports to be a work of natural history, it should be here that the new exactness of observation should have the widest scope . . .',[68] but by and large, according to Boase, it does not.

Lawrence Stone's *Sculpture in Britain: The Middle Ages* appeared in the *Pelican History of Art* series two years later in 1955. It has been mentioned above that Stone followed Joseph Anderson's lead in asserting that Bestiaries were to be found in most twelfth-century libraries. Otherwise, he made only one mention of Bestiary imagery in sculpture, inevitably Alne. Again he had no doubt that a symbolic reading was intended: 'the beasts are depicted in attitudes and shapes which conform to the

---

62. For the dating evidence, see McCulloch (1960), 47–9.
63. Druce (1909.I), 316.
64. Pliny xxx, 11, 28.
65. Druce (1912), 402.
66. Boase (1953), 114.
67. Ibid., 239.
68. Ibid., 293.

symbolic meaning attached to them in the manuscript commentaries'.[69] He did not try to unravel any meaning beyond retelling some of the stories in juxtaposition, so to speak, with the portal sculpture which he illustrated. Stone's footnotes to his remarks on Bestiaries do not reveal the sources of his ideas, but an examination of his bibliography is instructive. James (1928) does not appear, but we do find Gardner (1951), Prior and Gardner (1912), Anderson (1935), Allen (1903), Boase (1953) and Bond (1910).

Recent writing on Bestiaries has been dominated by the work of Xenia Muratova.[70] As a Russian writer based in Paris, she stands very much in the European tradition. She is not concerned with the issue of Bestiary symbolism in sculpture, and tends not to refer to the work of Druce and Boase. A great deal of her work has been devoted to the tracing of sources for Bestiary illustrations, an area with which I shall not be concerned.[71]

The direct relevance of her work to my own falls largely under the heading of localization. In contrast to writers in the English tradition, she does not accept that Bestiaries were universally popular in this country. Instead, she has attempted to establish a 'cultural milieu in which this kind of illustrated scientific and moralizing literature found favour'.[72] Her ideas on this were stated as early as 1977, but a more recent formulation is to be found in 'Bestiaries: an Aspect of Medieval Patronage' published in *Art and Patronage in the English Romanesque* in 1986, and originally given as a paper at a symposium held to coincide with the 1984 Arts Council exhibition, *English Romanesque Art, 1066–1200*. A detailed examination of this paper will give a fair idea of her approach to the question of consumption.

It opens with a quotation and a translation of the long inscription on f. 1v of the Bestiary, New York, Pierpont Morgan Library MS M81, recording the donation of this book, four others, and a *Mappa Mundi* to the Augustinian priory of Radeford (now Worksop) by Philip, a canon of Lincoln Cathedral.[73] She takes this *ex-libris* to be:

important evidence for the presence of an illuminated Bestiary in this area, for the circulation of models for Bestiaries, and probably that Philip's manuscript was produced in this area. But it also gives us an idea of the cultural milieu in which this kind of illustrated scientific and moralizing literature found favour. It allows us

69. Stone (1955), 80.
70. See bibliography. Her more recent views, with which I shall be most concerned, are most conveniently found in Muratova (1986.I).
71. e.g. in (1984.I), (1984.II) pp. 32ff. and (1977).
72. Muratova (1986.I), 120.
73. See chapter four for the full text of the inscription.

to suggest that a cultured élite centred on Lincoln and on its cathedral school was one of the likely promoters of the production of illuminated manuscripts of Bestiaries, providing a close integration of text and illustration. The fact that a bestiary, together with other books, was donated to an Augustinian house *ad edificationem fratrem* is also significant. It can be interpreted as indirect proof of the importance, for the Augustinian order in Lincolnshire, of the Bestiary as an instrument of moral education.[74]

From this single *ex-libris* she has deduced three things: production of Bestiaries in the Lincoln area; a group of consumers to supply the demand for production; and consumption by Lincolnshire Augustinians in general.

Her next step is to extend the 'cultural milieu'. The French verse Bestiary of Philip de Thaon was dedicated to Aelis, Henry I's queen from 1121. From this Muratova deduces a general interest in Bestiaries among the royal entourage.[75] She now turns to the ubiquitous south doorway of Alne, but not to assert Bestiary symbolism, as have so many before her. Her aim is to extend the cultural milieu into Yorkshire, and in doing so she suggests a mechanism by which the dispersion might have been accomplished:

It is tempting, remembering the important rôle played by Bestiaries in Cistercian teaching in this region, especially in the work of St Aelred of Rievaulx, to link the appearance of representations from the *Physiologus* cycle in the sculptural decoration of Yorkshire with the influence of the Cistercians, perhaps from Rievaulx.[76]

She has thus set up a field of Bestiary consumption covering Yorkshire, Lincolnshire, the Cistercians, the Augustinians and the royal entourage, relying on primary evidence from only two Bestiaries. It is a common complaint among medievalists that the primary sources are rare, but for Bestiaries a great deal is available which Muratova has chosen to ignore, notably *ex-libris* inscriptions in other Bestiaries, and book lists from medieval libraries. There is enough of this class of material available to allow the kind of statistical analysis which must be the basis for any generalizations about consumption by area or by class of user.

Instead of this, Muratova has preferred to support the conclusions of her examinations of single manuscripts and secondary material by amassing quantities of circumstantial evidence which lacks specific reference to Bestiaries, much less to any

74. Ibid.
75. Ibid., 120–1.
76. Ibid., 121.

individual example. Thus, in support of her assertion that Lincoln was a major centre of production and consumption, she puts forward first, 'the flowering of Lincoln Cathedral's theological school which enjoyed close connections with the theological school of York and with Oxford scholars, and extended its influence to the neighbouring monasteries'.[77] Next, Gerald of Wales's retirement to Lincoln *c.* 1192–4;[78] and finally the arrival in 1186 of the swan-loving St Hugh of Avalon.[79] Only later and in passing does she mention that the twelfth-century book-catalogue of Lincoln Cathedral listed no Bestiary.[80] The fifteenth-century catalogue does not list one either, but she has not seen fit to record this at all.[81]

Similar arguments are used to support her assertions about royal consumption of Bestiaries. She admits that, 'We do not find direct evidence for the possession of Bestiaries by members of the royal family in the twelfth or beginning of the thirteenth century,'[82] but presses on nonetheless. This time her circumstantial evidence is centred around 'the interest of English kings in natural history',[83] an implicit assertion that all Bestiaries were perceived to be natural history texts. Her data includes Robert Cricklade's dedication of a volume of Pliny to Henry II; the latter's tutelage by William of Conches, 'a philosopher inclined towards metaphysical speculation on nature';[84] King John's ownership of a copy of Pliny; and the decoration of the painted chamber at Westminster with Bestiary images of dogs[85] (a subject taken from Pliny and introduced to some Bestiaries via Solinus).

On the question of consumption, then, Muratova is concerned to attach Bestiaries to well-defined social groups and geographical areas. As to how they may have been used, she has performed valuable work on variations in textual organization, particularly in analyzing differences in the prefatory material to the Pierpont Morgan and St Petersburg Bestiaries,[86] which she recognizes as being connected to the special needs of different users. It is unfortunate that her conclusion to this analysis, 'that the same treatise could serve different purposes, according to the wishes of the client and the destination of the book'[87] is not examined in any detail, especially since a great deal is known of the destination of the Pierpont Morgan Bestiary. Instead she returns to the

77. Ibid., 131.
78. Ibid.
79. Ibid.
80. Ibid., 134.
81. Woolley (1927), x–xv.
82. Muratova (1986.I), 136.
83. Ibid.
84. Ibid.
85. Ibid.
86. Ibid., 122; Muratova (1984.II).
87. Muratova (1986.I), 122.

generality of the cultural milieu, and deduces 'a constant reworking of the bestiary in the circles in which these two manuscripts were produced'.[88]

Muratova's observations on use by Cistercians are based largely on Friar Morson's careful analysis of Bestiary material in the sermons of Aelred of Rievaulx and Gilbert of Holland.[89] For the classes of user she has herself added to the cultural milieu, she is less precise: 'Bestiaries were used as teaching aids by two of the important intellectual agents responsible for education in England in the second half of the twelfth century: the secular and the regular canons.'[90] While for the court, 'the Bestiary served as entertaining and moralizing reading for the royal ladies'.[91]

The extensive influence of Muratova's speculations on localization may best be gauged from their effects on the literature of the two major medieval exhibitions held in this country recently, and on the authoritative *Survey of Manuscripts Illuminated in the British Isles*. Nigel Morgan's *Early Gothic Manuscripts [I]*, published in this series in 1982, includes four of the 'early series of luxury Bestiaries', which have been Muratova's chief concern: St Petersburg, Saltykov-Shchedrin Library MS Lat. Q.v.V.I.; Aberdeen University Library MS 24; Bodleian Library MS Ashmole 1511 and Cambridge University Library MS Ii. 4. 26. In his entry on the Ashmole Bestiary, Morgan accepts Muratova's North Midlands provenance for the entire group.

It has recently been suggested (Muratova, 1977) that the early series of luxury Bestiaries (nos 11, 17, 19, 21) have sufficient links to imply production in the same region, possibly at the same centre, perhaps Lincoln. There seems little doubt that evidence from both style and ownership of some members of the group indicates a North Midlands or Northern provenance.[92]

The style evidence is Morgan's own. As for medieval ownership, this can only refer to two members of the group: New York, Pierpont Morgan Library MS M81, with the combined *ex-libris* and book list mentioned above, which appeared in the previous volume of the *Survey*,[93] and the Cambridge Bestiary, which James linked to Revesby Abbey on the grounds of the first three letters of an *ex-libris* which is no longer legible.[94]

---

88. Ibid.
89. Morson (1956).
90. Muratova (1986.I), 120.
91. Ibid., 120–1.
92. Morgan (1982), 65.
93. Kauffmann (1975), 126–7.
94. James (1928), 35.

Muratova's involvement in the symposia associated with the exhibition *English Romanesque Art, 1066–1200* has been examined above. It remains to analyze the extent to which her ideas on localization have been incorporated into the catalogues of this exhibition and its successor, *Age of Chivalry: Art in Plantagenet England, 1200–1400* (London, Royal Academy, 1987). The Romanesque exhibition included three Bestiaries, two of which, New York, Pierpont Morgan MS M81 and Aberdeen University Library MS 24, belong to Muratova's 'early series of luxury bestiaries'. For both of these books, Muratova (1977) is one of only two bibliographic references given, the other in both cases being to the relevant volume of the *Survey of Manuscripts Illuminated in the British Isles*.[95] In the short entry on the Morgan Bestiary, space is given to repeat her assertion that, 'because the whole group is so closely related, it has been suggested that all these Bestiaries were produced at one centre, possibly at Lincoln, where there was an important cathedral school'.[96]

In the entry on the Ashmole Bestiary in the *Age of Chivalry* catalogue, Morgan again accepts Muratova's grouping, and repeats her suggestion that: 'these manuscripts (i.e. Pierpont Morgan MS M81, St Petersburg, Aberdeen MS 24, and Ashmole MS 1511) were produced in the North Midlands or Lincolnshire'.[97] The bibliographic reference is now to the more recent publication discussed at length above.[98]

Since this chapter was written Debra Hassig's *Medieval Bestiaries: Image, Text, Ideology* has been published.[99] This book is much more limited in its coverage than its title implies, since the author has chosen to restrict herself to the twenty-eight Bestiaries included in four volumes of the *Survey of Manuscripts Illuminated in the British Isles*.[100] In fact, the bulk of the text comprises twelve chapters, each dealing with a single animal, and in this it reads like a series of separate studies of the type pioneered by George Druce.

Before summarizing my own approach, it will be worthwhile to set down the main premises which make up the Bestiary paradigm reviewed above. I have tried to unlace five main strands that have gained currency largely through repetition. These may be summarized as follows:

1.   There is a discursive unity called 'The Bestiary'. This may comprise the entire body of textual recensions, Latin and French, or, in its broadest interpretation, the medieval understanding of the animal world.

---

95. Exh. Cat. Hayward (1984), 132–3.
96. Ibid., 132.
97. Exh. Cat. R.A. (1987), 304–5.
98. Muratova (1986.I).
99. Hassig (1995). See also my review (Baxter (1996)).
100. Kauffmann (1975), Morgan (1982), Morgan (1988) and Sandler (1986).

2.   The Bestiary is a medieval encyclopedia of zoology, with moralizations.

3.   Its moralizations were so widely understood that Bestiary imagery could be taken to imply symbolic meanings when it occurred in stone sculpture and woodcarving.

4.   Bestiaries were to be found in every monastic library of any size.

5.   Their currency extended to the fifteenth century. Although this was explicitly denied by James (1928), Gardner was still able to write about the symbolism of Bestiary subjects in fifteenth-century woodcarving as late as 1955, implying not only that the images were still familiar but that the associated text was still widely read.

The first and last points, as we have seen, were tackled by James (1928). By and large the first is no longer a live issue in scholarly writings, and McCulloch's modifications of James's Four Families provide an almost universally used system of classification.[101] The broad notion of 'The Bestiary' as a kind of medieval zoo, however, exemplified by *A Cloisters Bestiary*, has attained a metaphoric status in the English language uncommon in other European tongues. In the English translation of Sauerlander's *Gotische Skulptur in Frankreich 1140–1270* we read that: 'The sensations aroused by the contemplation of the Rheims Visitation and a Romanesque Bestiary pillar are of a different order . . .'.[102]

No clue of what a Romanesque Bestiary pillar might be is given by the surrounding text. Perhaps the author had the trumeau from the dismantled portal at Souillac in mind (plate 6), although this could hardly stand as the representative of a class of objects, 'Romanesque Bestiary Pillars', since it is unique of its kind.[103] When we turn to Sauerlander's own German text, however, we find that he originally wrote 'Vor der Riemser Heimsuchung entstehen andere Empfindungen als vor einem romanischen Bestien pfeiler . . .'.[104]

Not a 'Bestiary pillar', but a beast pillar, which makes a lot more sense. The identification of beasts with Bestiaries is revealed to be the English translator's responsibility. It is difficult to resist finding out what the French translator made of it: 'La Visitation de Reims éveille en nous d'autres sentiments qu'un pilier roman orné d'animaux entrelacés . . .'.[105]

---

101. See, e.g., Kauffmann (1975), 76, 126; Morgan (1982), 57, 60; Morgan (1988), 86; Muratova (1986.I), 121, 139, n. 29.

102. Sauerlander (1970), English translation (1972), 8.

103. The only comparable object is, to my knowledge, the trumeau of the south portal of the abbey of Saint-Pierre at Moissac. The front face of this has addorsed male and female lions with their bodies crossed. Jeremiah and St Paul appear on the east and west faces, and the back is carved with a fish-scale pattern.

104. Sauerlander (1970), 6.

105. Ibid., French translation (1972), 6.

This translator also seems to have thought of Souillac, but here too there is no mention of Bestiaries. It was only in English that they were equated with medieval animal imagery.

James's observation that most English Latin Bestiaries were produced in the twelfth and thirteenth centuries is now largely accepted, although there has been a tendency to date individual manuscripts later than he did, sometimes by as much as half a century.[106]

The third premise, on the symbolism of Bestiary imagery when it is divorced from its text, has always been an Anglo-American preoccupation. Mâle rejected it in 1898, and Muratova has never addressed it, but it was still argued strongly by Boase in 1953 (and in the corrected edition of 1968), and by McCulloch in 1960. Its persistence in writings in English seems to be bound up with the crab-like entry of Bestiaries into art historical literature in this country. Nineteenth and early twentieth-century writers were only concerned with Bestiaries insofar as their imagery found its way into carved wood and stone. Even James was apologetic in presenting his study of the texts of the manuscripts themselves, and we have seen that until McCulloch's *Medieval Latin and French Bestiaries* appeared in 1960, the significance of James's catalogue was largely ignored by art historians.

The situation in Europe has always been different. We have seen that Cahier and Martin (1851–6) provided the material for the appropriation of Bestiary texts by English writers on sculpture. Since then, the most important studies on the text itself have come from the Continent,[107] almost the only exceptions worth mentioning being the work of the American scholars, Francis Carmody and Ben E. Perry (see bibliography). Apart from James (1928), almost no textual work of any significance has come out of this country since Thomas Wright's publication in 1841 of an edition of Philippe de Thaon's Bestiary in BL MS Cotton Nero A.V.[108]

The two remaining postulates, points 2 and 4 in my list, are still live issues in art historical writing. Point 2, concerning the status of the Bestiary as a work of natural history, is still largely accepted. Point 4, on the geographical spread of Bestiaries, is very much under discussion, despite Muratova's strenuously argued case for Lincoln. The analysis of these two, together with point 5, on the timescale during which Bestiaries were produced – handled only in the most general terms by recent writers – will be the main concern of this study.

---

106. e.g., James dated BL Add. MS 11283 to the early twelfth century, whereas Kauffmann (1975), 125 gives the currently accepted date of *c.* 1170. Similarly James dated MS Bodley 764 to the late twelfth century while recent writers agree in dating it *c.* 1240–60 (Morgan (1988), 53; Baxter (1987), 196).

107. Pre-eminent is the work of the Italian scholar, Francesco Sbordone (1936.I and II), (1949). More recent work of value on the Greek text has been published by Offermanns (1966) and Kaimakis (1974). See also Maurer (1967) and Henkel (1976).

108. Wright (1841).

How, then, is one to interrogate this discourse? Despite the work of James and Muratova in questioning the assumptions about Bestiaries written into the history of art towards the end of the nineteenth century, it is still common for academics to refer to Bestiaries as if they all filled the same purpose. Such references are often incidental to the main lines of argument, and are so loosely phrased that they might mean anything. The introduction to Morgan (1982), for example, includes a section on the main types of books produced in the period.[109] Bestiaries are described as 'the books of animal lore'[110] but no clue to their use is given. The reason for this is that Morgan's study is chiefly concerned with production, and specifically with the production of miniatures, rather than with the consumption of books. Hence he tends to sidestep the historiographic issues I am concerned to address. I shall have more to say on the question of evidence of consumption and production in the preamble to chapter four.

The issue of consumption can only be examined by a painstaking analysis, mainly of text but also of illustrations when they occur, and such an analysis is attempted in chapters two and three of this book. Having established the structure of the *Physiologus* text that formed the original book, together with a cycle of images associated with that text, it is then possible to identify changes made to the structure of the book. It is assumed that both the original structure and the modifications answered the needs of users of the Bestiary: consumers not usually identifiable by name, but often enough by date, geographical location and social class or religious order. Chapter four is an attempt to provide a geographical and temporal framework of patronage for the changes descibed in earlier chapters.

Chapter two is concerned with the way the *Physiologus* was organized. The chapters are found to be ordered, not by any zoological taxonomy of the creatures that are their ostensible subjects, but according to the Christian ethical themes contained in the moralizations of each chapter. This structure implies a particular type of didactic purpose, which is shown to be at work in both text and accompanying miniatures.

This superficial level of organization is the key to the way the *Physiologus* was used to teach Christian ethics. It cannot explain either the ideological messages underlying the individual lessons, or the way in which these are taught by a structured corpus of animal stories. To do this, a different kind of analysis was needed. Gerard Genette has proposed a useful distinction between three meanings of the word *récit*, or 'narrative'.[111] The first is the narrative statement, or 'text', an oral or written account telling of events in particular words. In the case of the *Physiologus*, this signifier is represented by the text and images of a specific manuscript. The second meaning he called *histoire* or 'story', the

109. Morgan (1982), 15–25.
110. Ibid., 23.
111. Genette (1986), 25–7.

Plate 6. Souillac (Lot) Abbey church, trumeau of dismantled portal carved with entangled, biting animals.

succession of events and collection of characters taking part in the narrative: in other words, the signified to which a particular text refers. The third meaning is the act of narration itself: the performance, either public or private, through which a story is told.

My analysis of chapter organization in the *Physiologus* in chapter two is thus, according to Genette's distinction, an analysis of 'text' (even though images are considered as well). A method for the analysis of 'story', which reveals how the *Physiologus* operated to convey a particular ideological message, was suggested by the work of A.J. Greimas.[112] In this, attention is focussed on the characters, or actors, taking part in the stories of a corpus.

The *Physiologus* text contains a large number of animal, vegetable, mineral, human and superhuman actors who play a limited number of roles. There are several stories of predators and their prey, for example, including the *aspidochelone* or whale, which lures fish into its open mouth, and the *vulpis* or fox, which traps birds by pretending to be dead. In the moralizations of these stories, the predator is always found to correspond to the Devil and the prey to humanity. The wide range of actors can thus be identified with just a few symbolic roles, which Greimas called 'actantial functions'. The significance of Greimas's model is that it provides a structure of relationships between the actantial functions that is useful in identifying the way the *Physiologus* operated to convey a specific ideological message to its audience. Again, this message was legible in both text and images.

The *Physiologus* text that formed the basis of the Bestiary was thus geared to a highly specific group of consumers with shared ideological assumptions. Changes in the structure of the book: rearrangements of chapter order, additions and deletions of textual material and changes in the way the miniatures related to the text, all eroded the potency of the message, substituting another which was at once less precise and more adaptable to different requirements. In chapter three, various modifications of these kinds, which took place in England in the twelfth and thirteenth centuries, are broadly examined. It is not to be supposed that these changes formed a linear development in the Bestiary. Although it is often the case that some changes took place on the backs of others, it is also true that Bestiaries of an earlier type continued to be produced, and must therefore have still been found useful.

In chapter four, evidence of consumption from the Bestiaries themselves and from medieval book lists is used to identify times, centres and classes of user for whom these books were useful. Such evidence is scarcer than one would like, but enough is available to identify a few important centres of use, and even to identify classes of consumer interested in specific forms of the book.

Consumption involves more than simply matching users to products. The question

---

112. Griemas (1986), especially pp. 172–91.

of how the products were used is equally important. Chapter five thus attempts both a synthesis of the conclusions from the two preceding chapters, and an analysis based on both internal and external evidence of the uses to which Bestiaries were put by different users. For the latter, internal evidence is tied to Genette's concept of *narration*, keys to the performance of which are provided by the text itself. It is possible, for example, to identify features of composition which imply that some texts were intended to be read aloud to an audience rather than consumed in private by individuals. Evidence external to the text is found both in borrowings from the Bestiary used in other texts of known application, and in the other texts with which the Bestiary was regularly associated, in the hands of individual users, within sections of medieval libraries and within the boards of the same original binding.

CHAPTER TWO

NARRATIVE IN THE
PHYSIOLOGUS

THE LATIN B TEXT

The starting point for the study of Latin Bestiaries must be the *Physiologus* text on which they are based. Indeed, the earliest surviving Bestiaries are almost indistinguishable from the *Physiologus* without close textual analysis. At first sight, too, the *Physiologus* text appears no more than a collection of chapters on real and imaginary animals and stones, put together completely at random. My aims in this chapter are to show that the *Physiologus* was not arbitrarily but systematically arranged; that the various animal stories worked together to send an ideological message to their audience; and that, in one case at least, this ideological message could be reinforced by a cycle of illustrations.

The Latin Bestiaries produced in England between the twelfth and the fifteenth century had as their basis the *Physiologus* B text.[1] This is known in three ninth-century continental manuscripts: Bern, Burgerbibliothek MS Lat. 233, from the Loire region; Oxford, Bodleian Library MS Auct. T.II.23, from Tours; and Montecassino MS 323, probably French.[2] The Bern and Oxford manuscripts have only thirty-one chapters,

---

1.   The Latin B text was a translation from the Greek π text, itself one of several recensions of the original. Dating the Greek text and the Latin translation is problematic since the earliest surviving Greek *Physiologus* (New York, Pierpont Morgan Library MS 397, known by the siglum G) dates from the tenth or eleventh century, while the oldest Latin B text (Bern, Burgerbibliothek MS 233) is an early ninth-century manuscript. Lauchert (1889) dated the composition of the original text before 140 AD on the basis of internal correspondences with elements of Gnosticism, especially the account of the Incarnation as a katabasis through the celestial hierarchies in *leo*; and on reflections of *Physiologus* material in other Christian writers, of whom Justin Martyr (100–65 AD) was the earliest. At the other extreme, Wellman (1930) accepted no internal evidence of dating and was extremely cautious about external evidence, accepting nothing but direct quotations as proof of borrowing. His earliest examples all come from the end of the fourth century, and he concluded that the work was composed *c.* 370. For a discussion of these issues, see Sbordone (1936.2), 154–9. The Latin translation must predate the *Decretum Gelasianum*, normally dated to 496, which includes in a list of prohibited books a *Liber Physiologus qui ab haereticis conscriptus est, et beati Ambrosii nomine signatus apocryphus*. Ambrose is also involved in a piece of disputed but probably valid evidence indicating a much earlier date. There is a correspondence totalling ninety words between the Latin B text chapter on *perdix* and a passage in the Hexaemeron (6.13:3). Although Ambrose was capable of reading the Greek text, the word-for-word correspondence, extending at the most to a continuous passage twenty-two words long, makes the probability of independent translation extremely remote. Orlandi (1983) has suggested that the translator of the *Physiologus* could have copied Ambrose as easily as the reverse, but a little reflection will show that this is most unlikely. Why should a translator with the Greek original before him take the trouble to turn to Ambrose for this one passage? The translation, then, must predate the composition of the *Hexaemeron* in 386–8 AD.

2.   The Bern and Oxford manuscripts were edited by Carmody (1939) under the sigla B and Z respectively. Montecassino MS 323 has not, to my knowledge, been edited, but was noted by Orlandi (1983).

the former ending incomplete, the Montecassino manuscript has thirty-two. The evidence of later manuscripts, however, points to a full B text structure of thirty-six chapters, arranged in the order of Laud Misc. 247.[3]

TABLE 1. CHAPTER ORDERS OF B TEXT AND LAUD MISC. 247

	BERN LAT. 233	**LAUD MISC. 247**	**B TEXT (PRESUMED)**
1.	*Leo*	*Leo*	*Leo*
2.	*Antalops*	*Autalops*	*Autalops*
3.	*Lapides Igniferi*	*Lapides Igniferi*	*Lapides Igniferi*
4.	*Serra*	*Serra*	*Serra*
5.	*Chaladrius*	*Caladrius*	*Caladrius*
6.	*Pellicanus*	*Pelicanus*	*Pelicanus*
7.	*Nycticorax*	*Nicticorax*	*Nicticorax*
8.	*Aquila*	*Aquila*	*Aquila*
9.	*Phoenix*	*Fenix*	*Fenix*
10.	*Uppupa*	*Huppupa*	*Huppupa*
11.	*Formica*	*Formica*	*Formica*
12.	*Sirena et Onocentaurus*	*Syrene et Onocentauri*	*Syrene et Onocentauri*
13.	*Herinaceus*	*Herinacius*	*Herinacius*
14.	*Ibis*	*Ibis*	*Ibis*
15.	*Vulpis*	*Vulpis*	*Vulpis*
16.	*Unicornis*	*Unicornis*	*Unicornis*
17.	*Castor*	*Castor*	*Castor*
18.	*Hyaena*	*Hiena*	*Hiena*
19.	*Hydrus*	*Ydrus*	*Ydrus*
20.	*Caprea*	*Caper*	*Caper*
21.	*Onager*	*Onager et Simia*	*Onager et Simia*
22.	*Fulica*	*Fulica*	*Fulica*
23.	*Panthera*	*Pantera*	*Pantera*
24.	*Aspidochelone*	*Aspis chelone*	*Aspis chelone*
25.	*Perdix*	*Perdix*	*Perdix*
26.	*Mustela et Aspis*	*Mustela*	*Mustela et Aspis*
27.	*Asida*	*Aspis*	*Assida*

3. Mann (1888) includes an edition of London, BL MS Royal 2.C.XII, a Bestiary textually identical to Laud Misc. 247. Carmody (1939) produced an edition from thirty manuscripts, many of them only loosely connected with the B text. Some, like Bern, Burgerbibliothek MS 318, represent translations from different Greek texts. Others, like Cambridge, Corpus Christi College MS 22, contain considerable modifications to the Latin text. One result of this is that his edition contains an extra chapter (37. *Lacerta*) never found in the B text. Laud Misc. 247 actually contains thirty-seven chapters because *mustela et aspis*, which as a single chapter in the early B text manuscripts, has been split into two chapters.

	BERN LAT. 233	LAUD MISC. 247	B TEXT (PRESUMED)
28.	*Turtur*	*Assida*	*Turtur*
29.	*Cervus*	*Turtur*	*Cervus*
30.	*Salamandra*	*Cervus*	*Salamandra*
31.	*Simia*	*Salamandra*	*Columba*
32.	*incomplete at end*	*Columba*	*Peridexion*
33.		*Peridexion*	*Elephans*
34.		*Elephans*	*Amos*
35.		*Amos*	*Adamas*
36.		*Adamas*	*Mermecolion*
37.		*Mermecolion*	

Note. In this and other tables giving lists of chapters, the chapter names follow the rubrics in the manuscripts. Hence spellings of chapter names may vary considerably.

A glance at the B text chapter order (Table 1) reveals that if any organizing principle is at work, it is by no means taxonomic: birds, mammals and sea-creatures, reptiles, fabulous creatures and stones follow on from one another with a complete disregard of class.

Writers as different in approach as Allen and Sbordone have agreed that there is no logic in the order of the chapters in the *Physiologus*, simply because the kind of order they were looking for was one based on the kind of taxonomy they themselves were used to. Sbordone denied the existence of any logic in the chapter order,[4] giving as evidence the variations of chapter order in various Greek texts. Production considerations make this difficult to accept: if the order of the chapters was not important, why would a copyist take the trouble to alter it?

Allen, failing to detect any logical arrangement in the texts,[5] reorganized the chapters for his own convenience as follows:

I. Representations, more or less conventional, of creatures which really exist, under the subdivision of (a) beasts; (b) birds; (c) fish; (d) reptiles; (e) insects.

II. Fabulous creatures and sea monsters, chiefly derived from classical sources.

III. Mystical creatures from the visions of Daniel, Ezekiel and St John.[6]

His system, in other words, was a zoological taxonomy with categories added to account for creatures which fell outside it. A passage from Borges, quoted by Foucault, repeats 'a certain Chinese encyclopaedia' where it is written that:

---

4. Sbordone (1936.2), 29.
5. Allen (1887), 380–1: 'In the Bestiary the stories about the various animals do not seem to be arranged on any definite plan as regards the order in which they come.'
6. Ibid., 381.

animals are divided into: (a) belonging to the Emperor, (b) embalmed, (c) tame, (d) sucking pigs, (e) sirens, (f) fabulous, (g) stray dogs, (h) included in the present classification, (i) frenzied, (j) innumerable, (k) drawn with a very fine camelhair brush, (l) *et cetera*, (m) having just broken the water pitcher, (n) that from a long way off look like flies.[7]

Borges's enumeration helps us to understand that scientific taxonomy is not the only possibility. To go further, that such an organization is unable to provide a picture of the natural world which is of any value outside its own artificial limits. After all, there is nothing wrong with any of Borges's categories: on the contrary, each of them suggests an alternative to scientific taxonomy, just as valuable within its own boundaries. Furthermore, the fact that the categories may (but do not necessarily) overlap while retaining their own specific applications points to the futility of any attempt to devise a universal taxonomy.

Nevertheless, Borges's taxonomy fails to work as a system because the animals it includes are categorized according to different criteria, and to the medieval reader of the *Physiologus*, Allen's system would be just as puzzling because it contains precisely the same category mistakes. Creatures of fable and those mentioned by classical writers may be (but are not necessarily) beasts, birds or fish. More crucially, creatures which 'really exist' are privileged in Allen's classification (in the same way as those 'belonging to the Emperor' are given first place in Borges's), but they are distinguished from those whose existence would have been perceived as more 'real' to a medieval cleric since it was revealed by God to Daniel, Ezekiel and St John.

Once we have jettisoned the idea that neither the *Physiologus* nor any of the recensions of Bestiary which depend on it is a treatise on zoology, we are left free to examine the texts on their own terms, and make our own decisions about their nature. It is at once apparent that the organization of the animal world represented by the arrangement of the contents of these books was subject to periodic and extensive changes. The chapters were grouped and regrouped, new text and whole chapters were added, the accompanying images and their relation to the text were transformed. The broad outline of these changes was charted as long ago as 1928.[8] In chapter three I shall trace them in more detail, but before this the structure of the *Physiologus* B text must be examined.[9]

---

7. Foucault (1974.1), xv.
8. James (1928), 7–26.
9. The text of Carmody (1939) has been used, supplemented from Mann (1888) for the chapters on *Amos, adamas and margarita* which Carmody did not edit, and omitting the irrelevant chapter on *lacerta*. Where Carmody's edition is quoted, no reference is given. Biblical quotations are given as they occur in these texts, with references to Biblical book, chapter and verse.

Each of the thirty-six chapters is structured in exactly the same way. In the first part, some characteristic of behaviour or appearance of the chapter's subject is described, and in the second a Christian moral is extracted from it. In chapters like *leo*, the lion, and *formica*, the ant, where more than one characteristic is assigned to the creature, this structure is repeated several times. It has been suggested (though not recently) that this strict separation of the literal and the moralizing indicates that the *Physiologus* was originally a zoological text to which the morals were added later,[10] but in fact it proves precisely the opposite. It was a deliberate textual strategy intended as an object lesson in the non-literal interpretation of the Old Testament.

The entire text is heavy with Biblical quotations, but it is striking that the first, or literal, section of each chapter tends to include passages from the Old Testament while the second, or moralizing, section relies on the New.[11]

A chapter list is to be found in table 1. In the course of this analysis, reference is also frequently made to table 2, which summarizes the moralizations contained in the thirty-six chapters. Alongside this text I have placed the images from Brussels, Bibl.Roy. MS 10074, the eleventh-century *Physiologus* from Saint-Laurent, Liège.[12] This is the illustrated Latin *Physiologus* most closely preceding the earliest English Bestiaries in time. It is illustrated with drawings for the first twelve chapters only, but these drawings show formal relationships with English Bestiary illustrations, which will be explored in the next chapter. Finally, although its text is not identical with the B text throughout, it only deviates from that in the last twelve of its thirty-six chapters, and that to no great extent.[13]

10. Tychsen (1795) was the first to take this position, which was broadly followed by Pitra (1855), Land (1875) and Hommel (1877). Lauchert (1889) demonstrated on the basis of a methodical analysis of Greek, Latin and other texts that the *Physiologus* was compiled in its present form.

11. Old Testament passages appear in the Latin *Physiologus*, not as quotations from the Vulgate but as direct translations from the Septuagint used in the compilation of the Greek original. These sometimes differ significantly from the Vulgate text with which the readers were familiar, especially in the names of the animals, but no attempt seems to have been made to reconcile the two. In *hyaena*, for example, the B text reads: *De qua etiam per Hieremiam prophetam dictum est: Spelunca hyaenae hereditas mea facta est.* This may be compared with the English translation of the Septuagint (see bibliography): *My inheritance has become to me as a lion in a forest; she has uttered her voice against me; therefore I have hated her. Is not my inheritance to me a hyaena's cave, or a cave round about her?* (Jer. 12, 8–9). In the Vulgate, on the other hand, no mention is made of the hyena, and the same verses are rendered: *Facta est mihi hereditas mea quasi leo in sylva; dedit contra me vocem, ideo odivi eam. Numquid avis discolor hereditas mea mihi? numquid avis tincta per totum? Venite, congregamini, omnes bestiae terrae, properate ad devorandum.* In translation this becomes: *My inheritance has become to me as a lion in a forest; it cries out against me; therefore I have hated it. Is not my inheritance like a bird of the wrong colour? Come, gather round all the beasts of the earth, prepare to eat.*

12. Silvestre (1979), 152–3. For a bibliography of this manuscript, see Fraeys de Veubeke (1981), 28, n. 27.

13. Cahier and Martin (1851–6) edited the text of the Brussels *Physiologus* under the siglum A, which it has retained in subsequent discussions. Sbordone (1936.1), lxxiii, identified the chapters where A deviated from B, as did Carmody (1939), 7, without acknowledging Sbordone's work. This lapse was commented upon by the latter in his fuller treatment of the Latin texts ten years later (Sbordone (1949), 248–9).

TABLE 2. STRUCTURE OF THE B TEXT

GROUP	CHAPTER	THEME
1.	1. *Leo*	Christ's divinity
	2. *Autolops*	} Avoidance
	3. *Lapides Igniferi*	} of vice
	4. *Serra*	}
2.	5. *Caladrius*	Christ's rejection by the Jews
	6. *Pellicanus*	} Jews
	7. *Nycticorax*	} and
	8. *Aquila*	} Gentiles
3.	9. *Fenix*	Christ as fulfilment of the Law
	10. *Upupa*	}
	11. *Formica*	} Letter
	12. *Sirena et Onocentaurus*	} and spirit
	13. *Erinacius*	} of the
	14. *Ibis*	} Law
	15. *Vulpis*	}
4.	16. *Unicornis*	Christ's renunciation of the Devil
	17. *Castor*	} Human renunciation
	18. *Hyaena*	} of the Devil
5.	19. *Hydrus*	The Harrowing of Hell
	20. *Caper*	} The community
	21. *Onager et Simia*	} of the
	22. *Fulica*	} faithful
6.	23. *Pantera*	Christ's redeeming mission
	24. *Cetus (aspidochelone)*	} Avoidance of
	25. *Perdix*	} the Devil's snares
	26. *Mustela et Aspis*	} by turning
	27. *Assida*	} to Christ
	28. *Turtur*	}
7.	29. *Cervus*	Christ and the saints
	30. *Salamandra*	}
	31. *Columba*	} The power of Christ

GROUP	CHAPTER	THEME
	32. *Peredixion*	} in the community
	33. *Elephantus*	} of saints
	34. *Amos propheta*	}
8.	35. *Adamante*	} The Incarnation
	36. *Margarita*	} of Christ

THE STRUCTURE OF THE B TEXT

1. DOUBLE CHAPTERS

A key to the organizing principle around which the *Physiologus* is structured is to be found in the two chapters containing pairs of animals: 12. *Sirena et Onocentaurus* and 26. *Mustela et Aspis*. It seems logical nowadays to consider sirens and centaurs together since neither of them exist: Allen's creation of a group of 'fabulous creatures and sea monsters' from within the Bestiary material is an example of just this kind of unreflective common sense. A medieval European reader, on the other hand, could not be so certain. Only a handful of the creatures of the *Physiologus* were native to Europe, the remainder only being known from written reports. There was no more reason to doubt the existence of sirens and centaurs than of lions, ostriches or salamanders. The association of weasels and asps is even more puzzling from a zoological point of view, and it is clear that a different kind of connection must be found.

Chapter 12 of the *Physiologus* opens with Isaiah's prophecy of the desolation of Babylon (Is. 13, 21–2):

Isaias propheta dicit: Sirena et Daemonia saltabunt in Babylonia, et herinacii et onocentauri habitabunt in domibus eorum.[14]

(The prophet Isaiah says: Sirens and Demons will leap in Babylon, and hedgehogs and centaurs will live in their houses.)[15]

Three creatures are mentioned by name: sirens and centaurs, which are the subject of this chapter of the *Physiologus*, and hedgehogs which are dealt with in the next. This

---

14. The Vulgate gives: '*et habitabunt ibi struthiones, et pilosi saltabunt ibi: et respondebunt ibi ululae in aedibus ejus, et sirenes in delubris voluptatis.*'
15. The English translations of *Physiologus* text are my own unless otherwise stated.

suggests immediately that animals were grouped together in the *Physiologus* for what might loosely be called theological, as opposed to zoological, reasons.

The text goes on to make several points about sirens and centaurs. Both are half human and half wild. Sirens lure sailors by their sweet music, lulling their willing ears and senses into sleep before tearing their bodies to pieces. Centaurs are like senseless and treacherous unformed people,

> *Habentes promissionem pietatis, virtutem autem eius abnegantes.*[16]
> (Promising piety, but denying its power).

They represent the other side of the coin. While sirens are animals in human form, centaurs are men made like senseless animals. Together they form a warning against being deceived by the allurements of the world.

> *Sic igitur et illi decipiuntur qui deliciis huius saeculi et pompis et theatralibus voluptatibus delectantur, tragediis ac diversis musicis melodiis dissoluti, et velut gravati somno sopili efficiuntur adversariorum praeda.*
> (Thus, therefore are they deceived who are entranced by the delights of this world, and by displays and theatrical performances, by tragedies and various licentious musical tunes, and as if lulled into a deep sleep they become the plunder of the enemy.)

The weasel and the asp combine in a similar way to press home a different message. Again the moralization is founded on the Bible, but in this instance two quotations are used. The chapter opens with the bald statement that the weasel is an unclean beast.

> *De mustela praecipit lex non manducare; quia immundum animal est.* (cf. Lev. 11, 29)
> (The law prescribes that the weasel should not be eaten, because it is an unclean animal.)

And at the start of the section on the asp, we read:

> *Isti tales non solum mustelae comparantur, sed etiam aspidi surdae, quae obturat aures suas et non audit vocem incantatis.* (cf. Ps. 57, 5–6)
> ((The wicked) are not just like weasels, but also deaf adders, which plug their ears and will not listen to the voice of the enchanter.)

16. cf. 2 Tim. 3, 5.

The *Physiologus* tells the story that the weasel reproduces unnaturally, taking in semen through the mouth and giving birth through the ear. This practice is compared with the disobedience of those who accept the Word of God but fail to disseminate it correctly. Likewise the adder, who resists the snake-charmer by pressing one ear against the ground and blocking the other with its tail, is compared with those who close their ears to the words of the preacher. As in the case of the siren and the centaur, we are presented with an agent and the recipient of an action: in this chapter an ineffective agent is coupled with an unreceptive recipient. The two combine to stress the importance of the true dissemination and reception of the Word.

There is a third pairing of this type not to be found in the B text, but present in Laud Misc. 247, and in another of the Carolingian texts, Bern Burgerbibliothek MS 318, known as the C text. This links *onager*, the wild ass and *simia*, the ape. Both are taken to signify the devil. The *onager* is said to bray on the spring equinox, when the day becomes as long as the night, just as the Devil howls when he sees that the people of light, the faithful, have become as numerous as those who walk in darkness, the sinners. The ape has a head but no tail in the same way as the Devil had a head, it is argued, in that he was originally an angel in heaven, but has no tail because he will perish entirely at the end of the world. It has been asserted that this somewhat unwieldy analogy is reinforced by a pun on the words *cauda* – tail and *caudex* – scripture,[17] but if such a pun was intended it is nowhere brought out in the text.

Analysis of these pairings leads inevitably to the conclusion that in the Carolingian *Physiologus* animals were grouped by the lessons they were employed to teach rather than by any zoological consideration. In the next section we shall see that this organizing principle extends to the entire structure of the book.

2. GENERAL ORGANIZATION OF THE B TEXT

Ten chapters interspersed through the text concern animals identified with Christ (see table 2). Generally these chapters contain no lesson for the reader, but concentrate instead on one aspect or more of Christ's Incarnation. These chapters form introductions to groups of chapters, linked by a common theme, which follow them.

GROUP 1: *LEO, AUTALOPS, LAPIDES IGNIFERI, SERRA*

The opening chapter on *leo*, the lion, is an introduction to the whole work, as well as to group 1. Christ is first identified with the Lion of Judah, that is as a fulfilment of Old Testament prophecy, by means of a quotation from Genesis:

17. White (1954), 34.

Etenim Iacob, benedicens filium suum Iudam ait: Catulus leonis Iudas, filius de germine meo, quis suscitabit eum. (cf. Gen. 49, 9)
(For Jacob, blessing his son Judah, said: Judah is a lion's whelp, the son of my seed, who will rouse him?)

Three characteristics of the lion are then described. First, when it smells the hunter while walking on the mountains, it covers its tracks with its tail so that the hunter should not follow it to its den and capture it. The moralization of this passage was important to Lauchert's argument that the *Physiologus* was associated with the Gnostic heresy (see n. 1). Christ's Incarnation is described in terms of a *katabasis*, or descent through the celestial hierarchy.

Sic et salvator noster . . . missus a superno patre, cooperuit intelligentibus vestigia deitatis suae, et est factus cum angelis angelus, cum archangelis archangelus, cum thronis thronus, cum potestatibus potestas, donec descenderet in uterum virginis.
(Thus our saviour . . . sent from above by his father, covered the traces of his divinity from understanding, and was made an angel among the angels, an archangel with the archangels, a throne with the thrones, a power with the powers, until he should descend in the virgin's womb.)

Christ's concealment of his divinity during the *katabasis* is asserted through a gloss on Psalm 23, which is quoted:

Quis est ipse rex gloriae? Dominus virtutum ipse est rex gloriae. (cf. Ps. 23, 10)
(Who is this king of glory? The lord of the virtues is the king of glory.)

In glossing this passage, the *Physiologus* text attributes the question to angels in heaven who failed to recognize Christ during his ascension because he had concealed his divinity from their understanding in the course of his descent. The reply is given by the angels accompanying him in his ascent.

The lion's second characteristic is that it sleeps with its eyes open. Again the Psalmist provides the parallel.

Ecce non dormitabit neque dormiet qui custodit Israel. (Ps. 120, 4)
(Behold he who guards Israel neither slumbers nor sleeps.)

Although Christ's body died on the Cross, his divinity did not.

Finally the cubs of the lion are said to be born dead, and vitalized on the third day by the breath of their father. The comparison, of course, is with Christ's Resurrection, and the Father is presented as the agency of this in a closing repetition of the Genesis passage which opened the chapter.

Dormitabit tamquam leo, et sicut catulus leonis, quis suscitabit eum? (cf. Gen. 49, 9)
(The lion will seem to fall asleep, and the lion's whelp, who will rouse him?)

In this opening chapter, then, Christ is identified as the fulfilment of Old Testament prophecy, a theme which is to recur throughout the work; and his divinity and Resurrection are asserted.

There follow three moralizing chapters on the avoidance of vice. *Antalops*, the antelope, provides a warning against intemperance; *lapides igniferi*, the fire-stones, a warning about the danger of women; and *serra*, a sea-monster, a general injunction to remain steadfast in faith, and avoid being conquered by:

cupiditate, superbia, ebrietate, luxuria, ac diversis vitiorum generibus.
(lust, pride, drunkenness, wantonness, and the other types of vice.)

GROUP 2: *CALADRIUS, PELICANUS, NYCTICORAX, AQUILA*

Caladrius returns to the theme of Christ, opening the second group.[18] Two main points are made. It is a totally white bird, and whiteness is equated with sinlessness through quotations from John and 1 Peter:

Venit ad me princeps huius mundi, et in me non invenit quicquam (John 14, 30). *Qui peccatum non fecit, nec inventus est dolus in ore eius.* (1 Pet. 2, 22)
(The prince of this world comes to me, and finds nothing in me. Who did no sin, neither was guile found in his mouth.)

Secondly it is said to act as diagnostician and physician. If someone is taken ill, the

---

18. I have referred in chapter one to attempts to identify Bestiary creatures with living animals, based on the assumption that the *Physiologus* is a work of zoology. *Caladrius* provides an example both of the effort which can be expended on such an exercise, and of the ultimate futility of it. Druce (1912), 397–407 went into the question of the bird's identification at great length, and demonstrated that, at least as far as the illustrators of Bestiaries were concerned, there was no agreement about what a *caladrius* looked like. From references in classical sources, and in Leviticus and Deuteronomy, he could only conclude that it was a water-bird. The story of its healing powers led him tentatively to identify it with Pliny's *icterus*, which cured jaundice in anyone who looked at it. The problem here is that the cure is sympathetic, relying on the bird's yellow colour, while the *caladrius* is specified as all white. This objection he disposed of by suggesting that the symbolism of the bird (as Christ) could not be founded on it unless it was white, 'and it seems very probable that the author made it out to be whiter than in nature for this purpose'. This is only ridiculous if one accepts Druce's assumption that the Bestiary was a serious work of zoology. Later writers have largely followed Druce while ignoring his uncomfortable conclusions (see, e.g., McCulloch (1960), 100–1). Only White (1954) among modern writers has expressed a firm opinion of the bird's identity, ignoring Druce's analysis of classical, medieval and modern usage entirely, and suggesting that it was 'a white wagtail (*Motacilla alba Linn*) for wagtails are still regarded in Ireland with a superstitious dread'. (Ibid., 115, n. 1). Yapp (1981), perhaps wisely, did not tackle the question at all.

caladrius will either avert its face from the patient or look towards him. In the first case the patient will die, but in the second the disease is absorbed by the bird, which then flies into the sun to disperse it. In the moralization, the moribund patient is identified with the Jews, from whom Christ averted his face because of their unbelief. The Gentiles, on the other hand, are saved, and their sins taken away by his ascent on the Cross. These two themes, the rejection of the Jews, and the sacraments of baptism and eucharist instituted by the Crucifixion, are the subjects of the next three chapters.

The chapter on the pelican, probably the best known of the *Physiologus* stories, describes how the young birds attack their parents who strike back, killing them. On the third day, their mother revives them by piercing her flank to spill her blood on their bodies. A prophecy from Isaiah is used to relate the chicks' attack on their parents to the rejection of Christ by the Jewish nation.

Filios genui et exaltavi, ipsi autem speuerunt me. (Is. 1, 2)
(I have nourished and brought up children, and they have rebelled against me.)[19]

The subsequent revival of the dead chicks by the blood of their mother is paralleled by the piercing of Christ's side on the cross: the blood and water which flowed stand for the sacraments of eucharist and baptism,

in salutem nostram et vitam aeternam.
(for our salvation and eternal life).

The argument in *nycticorax*, the night-raven, turns on the bird's nocturnal habits, contained in its name,[20]

tenebras amat magis quam lucem
(it loves the darkness more than the light),

and on the proscription against eating its flesh found in Deuteronomy.[21] Just as

---

19. Authorized Version (revised).

20. Again a problem of identification has been perceived. Yapp (1981), 42 considered the Greek *Physiologus* to refer to an owl on the grounds that Aristotle used the name for the horned owl, but thought that the identification was no longer made in the Latin Middle Ages, when owls were known under the names *noctua* (the little owl) and *bubo* (the eagle owl). In the earliest surviving English Latin Bestiary, Laud Misc. 247, f. 143v the illustrator has drawn an unmistakeable owl which is rubricated *Nicticorax que et noctua dicitur*. A different model was used in Cambridge, Corpus Christi College MS 22, f. 166v and this rather resembles a hawk, but may be intended for a raven since, in this manuscript, textual additions identify the *nicticorax* with '*corvus noctis*'. Stowe 1067, f. 8r includes drawings of both types side by side.

21. The *Physiologus* text gives *nycticorax immunda avis est*. The Vulgate does not mention *nycticorax*, but since both Leviticus (11, 15–16) and Deuteronomy (14, 14–15) proscribe both *noctua* and *omne corvini generis* this is no help in deciding what sort of bird the *nycticorax* was thought to be.

whiteness was equated with sinlessness in *caladrius*, so darkness and ritual uncleanness are equated with ignorance here, in this case the ignorance of the Jews, who repulsed Christ saying:

Nos regem non habemus nisi Caesarem. (John 19, 15)
(We have no king but Caesar.)

Quotations from Psalms and the prophets are then used to illustrate God's rejection of the Jews in favour of the Gentiles.

illuminavit nos: Sedentes in tenebris et in regione umbrae mortis (Is. 9, 2); *et in regione umbrae mortis lux orta est nobis. De hoc populo salvator per prophetam dicit: Populus quem non cognovi servivit mihi.* (Ps. 17, 45); *et alibi: Vocabo non plebem meam plebem meam, et non dilectam meam dilectam.* (Hos. 2, 2 quoted in Rom. 9, 25)
(He has illuminated us, who sat in the darkness and in the land of the shadow of death; and in the land of the shadow of death light has shined on us. Of this nation the saviour said through the prophet: The people whom I have not known will serve me; and elsewhere: I will call them my people which were not my people: I will call beloved those who were not beloved.)

The chapter on *aquila*, the eagle, synthesizes the two previous chapters in a call to baptism addressed to Jews and Gentiles alike. The Biblical basis of the moralization is taken from Psalm 102:

Renovabitur ut aquilae iuventus tua. (Ps. 102, 5)
(Your youth shall be renewed like the eagle's.)

This is expanded into the story of the old eagle who removes the mistiness from its eyes and the heaviness from its wings by flying into the sun and then plunging into a well. Jews and Gentiles are urged to follow the example of the eagle, renewing their hearts, through the sacrament of baptism, in the spiritual well of the Lord.

GROUP 3: *PHOENIX, UPUPA, FORMICA, SIRENAE ET ONOCENTAURI, HERINACIUS, IBIS, VULPIS*

The long third group takes as its theme the letter and spirit of the law. The opening chapter, *phoenix*, relates the well-known story of the bird's immolation and rebirth to Christ's Resurrection, but the bulk of the exegesis is concerned with the synthesis of Old and New Testament teaching. Hence the spices with which the phoenix coats both wings in order to kindle fire are equated with the words of the two testaments, contained in Christ, seen as the initiator of the new law and the fulfilment of the old.

Non veni solvere legem, sed adimplere (Matt. 5, 17). *Et iterum, Sic erit omnis scriba doctus in regno caelorum, qui profert de thesauro suo nova et vetera.* (Matt. 13, 52)
(I have not come to destroy the law but to fulfil it. And again, thus is every scribe instructed in the kingdom of heaven, that he should bring out new and old things from his treasure.)

The concordance between the testaments is an important theme for the whole work, but especially, in view of its concern with the relationship between the new law and the old, for this group of chapters.

Chapter 10, *upupa*, the hoopoe, is a straightforward injunction to follow the Fifth Commandment. The chicks of the hoopoe are said to soothe the eyes of their ageing parents, and to pluck out their oldest feathers, to repay them for their upbringing. If irrational birds behave in this way – it is asked – why do rational humans fail to fulfil their duty to their parents?

The long chapter, *formica*, which follows, is ostensibly concerned with the feeding behaviour of ants. A parallel is drawn throughout between the Word of God and the grains of wheat that constitute the ants' food. The chapter is in three sections corresponding to three habits which are described. In the first, ants are said to seek food in an orderly file, returning by the same route and thus laying a trail for each other to follow. All an ant has to do in order to find food is to follow the ant in front. The moralization is curious in that a parallel is drawn with another story which is itself parabolic: that of the Wise and Foolish Virgins (see Matt. 25, 1–13). Both stories are admonitions to prudence: 'Watch, therefore, for ye know neither the day nor the hour wherein the Son of man cometh. (Matt. 25, 13 AV.)' Superficially this would appear to bear little relation to the theme of the Law which characterizes this group, but as was the case with the Psalmic basis of the first part of *leo*, the Biblical quotations used are to be understood in terms of their context. The parable of the Wise and Foolish Virgins forms part of Christ's address to his disciples on the Mount of Olives, a passage rich in Old Testament quotation, on the subject of the coming of the Son of man, which is intended to establish Christ as the fulfilment of Messianic prophecy. In this it relates directly to the chapter on the phoenix that opened this group.

The second nature of the ant teaches the way in which the Old Testament is to be understood. When ants store the grain they have collected, they divide it into two parts so that if the rain gets into their nest, the entire food store is not spoilt. The words of the Old Testament should similarly be seen in two ways.

id est secundum historiam et secundum spiritalem intellectum.
(that is as history and as spiritual knowledge.)

This division of the Old Testament into spiritual and literal aspects as a basis of Christian apologetic is first seen in its developed form in the work of Origen, who knew the Greek *Physiologus*, but ultimately derives from Jewish commentators such as Philo Judaeus.[22] As an exegetical technique, it retained its vitality throughout the Middle Ages.

The third nature contains a caution against heresy that has been used by Lauchert in dating the Latin translation of the *Physiologus*.[23] The ant is said to be capable of distinguishing between wheat and barley by their smell, and to reject the barley in favour of wheat. Barley is identified with heresy: the false food becomes the false Word.

The theme of the corruption and rejection of the Word is continued, as we have seen, in the next chapter, *sirenae et onocentauri*. *Herinacius*, the hedgehog, which follows, repeats the admonitions to avoid temporal pleasures found in *sirenae et onocentauri*. Hedgehogs are said to scale vines when the grapes are ripe, knocking the fruit onto the ground and rolling on it to impale it on their spines. They then take it away to feed their young. In the moralization, use is made of the image of Christ as the true vine, and the Christian community as its branches which can bear no fruit without him. The hedgehog, of course, is the Devil who bears away this spiritual fruit.

et fiat anima tua nuda, vacua et inanis, sicut pampinus sine fructu.
(and makes your soul naked, empty and vain, like the vine tendril, without fruit.)

Again, any suspicion that the text is straying from the theme is banished by an examination of the scriptural context. Christ compares himself to the true vine in a long address to his apostles after the Last Supper. The explanation of this image includes Christ's commandment, 'that ye love one another, as I have loved you (John

22. Origen is the earliest writer on record as referring explicitly to the *Physiologus* (see Sbordone (1936.2), 162, 174). Wellman was able to ignore this piece of external dating evidence on the grounds that the two passages in Origen are known only in Latin translation, and the references could have been inserted by the translators, in one case Rufinus, and in the other, Jerome. For Sbordone (1936.2), 158, '*l'intrinseca omogeneita col pensiero allegorico di Clemente e di Origene*' was one of the considerations which led him to date the composition of the Greek text between the end of the second century and the first decades of the third.

23. Several heresies are listed as follows, '*fugi igitur Sabellium, Marcionem, Manichaeum; cave Novationum, Montanum, Valentinum, Basilidem, Macedonium, cave Donatianum et Photinum, et omnes qui ex arriana stirpe*'. Lauchert (1889) suggested that the omission of the Nestorians from the list indicated a date before 431. It does nothing of the kind, of course. First, the list in Bern 233, of the ninth century may not be an accurate copy of that in the original Latin translation. Even if it were, nothing can be proved from an omission, which may be deliberate or accidental. The only evidence of dating provided by this list is the approximate *terminus post quem* supplied by the earliest currency of the latest heresy. In this case, the heresy of Macedonius, created Bishop of Constantinople in 341–341, who died in 360. The heresy was condemned several times in the Theodosian Code, the earliest canon using the name dating from 383 (16.5.59). Even this is not much help, because there is nothing to prove that the list of heresies was not constantly modified according to the concerns of the day.

15, 12 AV.)' understood as a summary of the Mosaic code. Finally, in case the major theme should have been obscured by the injunctions to avoid carnal pleasure, the chapter ends with the assertion,

> *Congrue igitur Physiologus naturas animalium contulit et contexuit intelligentiae spiritualem scriptuarum.*
> (Rightly therefore has *Physiologus* brought forth the natures of animals and preserved the spiritual knowledge of the scriptures.)

The chapter on the ibis is founded entirely on its ritual uncleanness (see Lev. 11, 17; Deut. 14, 16). Early Alexandrian understanding of the food laws, expressed here and in Philo and Aristeas, saw them as allegories of virtues and vices.[24] Carnivorous and especially carrion-eating birds were considered unclean because they persecuted the weak or, as here, because their diet was seen as unwholesome.[25] In the *Physiologus* text the ibis is said to subsist on the corpses of fish which it finds on the shore, because it dares not enter the water. In the explanation, the waters are described as:

> *intelligibiles et spiritales aquas, id est in altitudinem ministrorum Christi,*
> (waters of understanding and spirituality, that is to say the depths of the teachings of Christ)

and the food to be found there provides,

> *spiritales et mundissimos cibos,*
> (spiritual and most purifying meals)

which are identified with the fruit of the spirit described in the previous chapter. In returning to the underlying theme of vice and virtue that occupied the two previous chapters, the opportunity is taken to list the spiritual fruits (stolen by the Devil in the guise of the hedgehog, and avoided by the ibis):

> *fructus autem spiritus est caritas, gaudium, pax, patientia, longanimitas, bonitas, benignatis, mansuetudo, fides, modestia, continentia, castitas* (Gal. 5, 22–3)
> (The fruit of the spirit is charity, joy, peace, patience, long-suffering, generosity, benevolence, gentleness, faith, modesty, self-control and chastity)

24. Douglas (1978), 43–4, 46–7.
25. Ibid., 47.

and the works of the flesh,

> *immunditia, adulteria, fornicatio, impudicitia, luxuria, idolatria, ebrietas, avaritia, cupiditas* (Gal. 5, 19–21)
> (uncleanness, adultery, fornication, immodesty, lechery, idolatry, drunkenness, greed and ambition),

both taken from St Paul.

Although it is based on the food laws, the moralization of this chapter has shifted entirely to the theme of avoiding the snares of the world, which informs the entire text. Despite this progressive shift, the group has a coherence born of continuity: each chapter takes up and amplifies some point from the one before. The same is true of the final chapter in the group: *vulpis*, the fox, is in its moralization identical to *ibis*, but it is approached from the opposite direction. *Ibis* and *vulpis* present opposite sides of the same coin in much the same way as the pairs *mustela et aspis*, and *sirenae et onocentauri*. The ibis is an eater of dead flesh, which is the work of the Devil: the fox is the Devil himself pretending to be dead flesh. He smears his body with red earth, lies on the ground and holds his breath, so that birds believe him dead and alight on him, then he rapidly kills and eats them.

GROUP 4: *UNICORNIS, CASTOR, HYAENA*

This group of chapters takes up the theme of vice as the snare of the Devil from the previous group, and confronts the problem of avoiding the snare. Again it is introduced by a chapter presenting Christ as an exemplar: the well-known story of the unicorn. The unicorn is a small animal, like a kid but with a single horn in the middle of his forehead. He is very speedy so that no hunter can catch him, but he is captured by a trick. A virgin girl is led to the place where he lingers, and as soon as the unicorn sees her he leaps into her lap, and is easily taken.
Christ is identified with the unicorn at some length. Old and New Testament references to unicorns and horns are interpreted as prefigurations.

> *et dilectus sicut filius unicornis* (Ps. 28, 6)
> (and he was esteemed like the son of the unicorn),
> *et exaltabitur sicut unicornis cornu meum* (Ps. 91, 11)
> (and my horn shall be raised like the unicorn's),
> *suscitavit eum cornu salutis in domo David pueri sui* (Luke 1, 69)
> (he raised up a horn of salvation in the house of his son David),
> *primitivos tauri species eius, cornua eius tamquam cornua unicornis* (Deut. 33, 17)
> (his form is of the firstborn of the bull, and his horns like the horns of unicorns).

The single horn of the unicorn is taken to signify Christ's saying, reported in John's gospel,

ego et pater unum sumus (John 10, 30)
(I and the father are one),

while the unicorn's speed is equated with the inability of the members of the celestial hierarchy to identify Christ,[26] and the inability of hell to hold him.

Next, the smallness of the unicorn is compared to the lowliness of Christ's Incarnation:

dicente ipso: Discete a me, quia mitis sum et humilis corde (Matt. 11, 29)
(as he said of himself: Learn from me, one who is mild and humble of heart).

Like the unicorn, Christ was not trapped by the hunter or devil, but descended into the Virgin's womb of his own free will for the salvation of mankind. That this was an act of self-sacrifice refers back to the description of the unicorn as 'like a kid',

quod autem est similis haedo unicornis – et salvator noster secundum apostolum: Factus est in similitudinem carnis peccati, et de peccato damnavit peccatum in carne. (Rom. 8, 3)
(that the unicorn is like a kid is because according to the apostle our saviour: Was made in the likeness of sinful flesh, and from sin he condemned sin in the flesh.)

This complex and coherent piece of exegesis was evidently satisfying to its author, since, like only five other chapters, *unicornis* ends with the statement,

bene ergo dictum est de unicorne.
(therefore it was well said of the unicorn.)[27]

The next two chapters are concerned with human renunciation of the Devil, through temperance and through constancy to Christ. *Castor*, the beaver, is hunted for his testicles, which have medicinal uses. When he sees that he is being hunted, the beaver bites his own testicles off and throws them in the face of the hunter to preserve his life. If he has already done this during an earlier hunt, he displays his rear to show that he is not worth chasing. Testicles provide the symbol for

---

26. The same parallel was used to relate Christ to the lion covering his tracks to confound the hunters in *leo*.
27. The other chapters with similar endings are *herinacius, ibis, vulpis, caprea* and *panthera*.

omnia vitia et omnis impudicitiae actus
(all vices and lewd acts),

and should be thrown in the Devil's face. If the Devil sees that his human prey has nothing of his, i.e. no vices, he will give up the chase. This chapter and the next advocate giving the Devil his due, and this advice is supported by quotations from Paul and Matthew.

reddite omnibus debita, cui tributum tributum, cui vectigal vectigal, cui timorem timorem, cui honorem honorem (Rom. 13, 7)
(repay to all their dues, tribute to whom tribute is due, tax where tax is due, fear where fear is due, honour where it is due),
non potestis duobus dominis servire, id est deo et Mammonae (Matt. 6, 24)
(you cannot serve two masters, that is God and Mammon).

The moralization in *hyaena*, the hyena, is again based on the animal's ritual impurity, here attributed to a supposed ambiguous sexuality:

aliquando quidem masculus est, aliquando autem femina, et ideo immundum animal est
(for it is sometimes male and sometimes female, and therefore it is an unclean animal).[28]

Sexual ambiguity is then compared to ambiguity of faith: with the Jews, who were first faithful and afterwards idolatrous, and with members of the Christian community, who are devoted to sensuality and greed. Like the beaver, the hyena teaches that faith is impossible without a complete rejection of the Devil's works.

GROUP 5: *HYDRUS, CAPER, ONAGER ET SIMIA, FULICA*

This group is concerned with the church, the community of the faithful. *Hydrus*, which opens the group, is an animal living in the Nile whose deadly enemy is the crocodile.[29] When it sees a crocodile sleeping on the river bank with its mouth open, the hydrus rolls in the mud to make its body slippery, then it slides into its enemy's

---

28. The Vulgate does not mention the hyena as an unclean beast in either Leviticus or Deuteronomy, but its uncleanness must be due to its failure to fit the model of the cloven-hoofed, cud-chewing ungulate established by pastoralists who habitually ate sheep, goats and cattle (see Douglas (1978), 54–5).
29. For White (1954), 179 n. 2, the hydrus is 'clearly a water-snake'.

mouth. This rouses the crocodile, which immediately swallows it whole. Once inside the crocodile, the hydrus tears apart the viscera of its helpless prey, emerging unscathed through the stomach. This savage disembowelling is compared in the moralization with the Harrowing of Hell, which Christ tore apart from within. Emphasis is laid on Christ's rescue of the saints from hell:

et monumenta aperta sunt, et resurrexerunt multa corpora sanctorum. (Matt. 27, 52)
(and the graves were opened, and the bodies of many saints were resurrected).[30]

Caper, the goat, which follows, describes Christ's relationship with the church. As the goat grazes in the mountain valleys, so Christ grazes in the church, taking as his food,

bona opera christianorum et elemosinae fidelium
(the good works of Christians and the almsgiving of the faithful).

The high mountains, which the goat loves, represent the prophets, apostles and patriarchs beloved of Christ. Finally the goat's good eyesight represents Christ's recognition of good and evil.

sicut et caprea a longe cognoscit venantium dolas, ita et dominus noster Iesus Christus praevidet et Praescivit dolus diaboli
(just as the goat recognizes the cunning hunter from afar, so also our lord Jesus Christ foresees and foreknows the cunning of the devil).

Onager et simia is the next chapter, and I have already shown that both the wild ass and the ape represent the Devil. It will also be remembered that the specific aspect of the Devil described in this chapter is his howling over the souls of the faithful prophets and patriarchs lost to him. We find here resonances of the content of the two previous chapters: the release of these very souls from hell, in *hydrus*, and the love which Christ feels for them, in *caper*.

Fulica, the coot, ends this group.[31] It is said to be the most prudent of birds, remaining in the same place for its entire life:

---

30. Within the context of this group of chapters, the Harrowing of Hell is presented as the institution of the Church. In the text of Matthew quoted above, however, the resurrection of the saints followed the destruction of the temple which broke open their graves.

31. Yapp (1981), 11 stated that the Bestiary *fulica* is not the modern coot, known to zoologists by the Latin name *fulica atra*, but did not offer an alternative identification.

fulicae domus dux est eorum (Ps. 103, 17)[32]
(the coot is the master of its home).

The moralization complements that of *caper*, which started the group. The wild goat grazes in the mountain valleys as Christ is sustained by the church: the coot keeps to one nesting place as the faithful stay within the church.

et ibi quotidianum panem immortalitatis, potum vero pretiosum sanguinem Christi; reficiens se sanctis epulis et, super mel et favum, suavissimus eloquiis domini
(and there he daily takes the bread of immortality and drinks the precious blood of Christ, reviving himself with holy food and with the words of the lord, sweeter than honey and the honeycomb).

GROUP 6: *PANTERA, CETUS, PERDIX, MUSTELA ET ASPIS, ASSIDA, TURTUR*

The theme of this group is the avoidance of the snares of the Devil by turning to Christ. *Pantera*, the panther, opens the group and is said to be an animal whose only enemy is the dragon. When the panther wakes from sleep after a meal, it roars loudly, emitting a sweet odour from its mouth. The roaring and the sweet smell attract all the other animals except the dragon, who shrinks with fear at the noise, and hides underground in a cave, numb with shock and still as death, while the other animals follow the panther wherever it goes.

The panther is associated with Christ by means of a prophecy from Hosea:

ego sicut panthera factus sum Effrem, et sicut leo domui Iudae idolis serviebat (Hos. 5, 14)[33]
(I was made like the panther to Ephraim, and like the lion to the house of Judah which was serving idols).

The moralization is quite straightforward. Christ is the true panther, who draws to himself the human race, which was held captive by the Devil. This is supported by Old and New Testament quotations:

captivam duxit captivitatem (Eph. 4, 9)
(he led captivity captive),

---

32. The Vulgate gives '*Herodii domus dux est eorum*'.
33. The Vulgate gives '*Quoniam ego quasi leeana Ephraim, et quasi catulus leonis domui Juda.*'

ascendens in altum coepisti captivitatem, accepisti dona in hominibus (Ps. 67, 19)
(ascending on high you have laid hold of captivity, you have accepted gifts among men).

This is the main moralization of the panther story, but it occupies only the first third of the chapter. The remainder is taken up with various aspects of the panther's appearance and behaviour: with its variegated colour, which is linked to Christ's manifold wisdom; with its handsomeness and gentleness; with its habit of sleeping after hunting, which is related to Christ's death after the sports of the Jews (*a Iudaeicis illusionibus*); with its waking after three days; and finally with the sweetness of its breath, which is related to the persuasiveness of Christ's words:

quam dulcia faucibus meis eloquia tua, domine, super mel et favum ori meo (Ps. 118, 103)
(how sweet are your words to my taste, lord, sweeter than honey and the honeycomb to my mouth).

The following chapter describes two characteristics of *aspidochelone*, or *cetus*, the whale, one of which may be seen as forming a dipole with the main moralization of *pantera*. While Christ, the panther, attracts the faithful with the sweet odour of his words, the Devil, in the form of the whale, lures into his mouth those lacking in faith – the little fish, again by means of a sweet-smelling odour. Just as a Biblical quotation was found to relate sweet smells to the words of Christ, another is available to link them to the lures of the flesh:

unguentis et variis odoribus delectantur, et sic confringitur a ruinis anima (Prov. 27, 9)
(by oils and diverse perfumes they are allured, and so the soul is brought to ruin).

This is the second characteristic of the whale. In the first, we are told that its huge body floats on the surface of the sea, deceiving sailors who think it is an island. They moor their ship to it, disembark and light a fire to cook a meal. When the whale feels the heat of the fire, it dives, pulling the ship and the sailors down to the bottom of the sea. This behaviour is taken to exemplify the cunning of the Devil in ensnaring the faithless – who pin their hopes to him and his works – and pulling them down to hell with him.

The Devil is constantly scheming to carry off souls but, as we saw in *pantera*, Christ is on hand to confound his tricks with his sweet words. The next chapter, *perdix*, brings this out, synthesizing the two previous chapters. *Perdix*, the partridge, steals the eggs of other birds and hatches them out, hoping to rear them as its own. When the nestlings hear the voice of their true mother, however, they desert the partridge and return to their natural parents. The warmth that the false mother offers is compared to the allurements of the flesh, and the song of the true mother to the voice of Christ. Likewise, when the spiritual weaklings who have allowed themselves to be deceived by the Devil hear Christ's voice,

> *sumentes sibi alas spiritales per fidem evolant et se Christo commendant*
> (assuming their spiritual wings by faith they fly away and commend themselves to Christ).

There follows the chapter on *mustela et aspis*, discussed above. Again the subject is the divine Word, or voice of Christ, but this time the concern is with its dissemination and reception.

The conclusion of the argument of this group is that the man of God must ignore earthly concerns, which are simply the snares of the Devil, and dedicate himself to Christ. This message is contained in the two chapters that close the group. *Assida*, the ostrich, like *perdix*, deals ostensibly with a bird's treatment of its eggs. The ostrich, knowing that it is naturally absent-minded, and will forget to sit on its eggs, notices when the Pleiades are rising in the sky, then lays its eggs and buries them in the sand. This is in the summer,

> *id est quando messes florent, et aestas est, circa mensem iunium*
> (that is when the harvests bloom, and it is summer, around the month of June),

and the warmth of the sun on the sand incubates the eggs and hatches the chicks. The moralization is that people, like the ostrich, should ignore earthly things and turn their eyes to heaven. Three New Testament quotations are included to press home the lesson:

> *quae retro sunt obliviscens, ad destinatum contendo bravium supernae vocationis* (Phil. 3, 13–14)
> (forgetting the things that are behind, I strive toward the prize of the high calling),
> *qui diligit patrem aut matrem aut filios plus quam me, non est me dignus* (Matt. 10, 37)
> (whoever follows his father or mother or children rather than me is not worthy of me),
> *dimitte mortuos sepelire mortuos suos, tu autem veni sequere me.* (Matt. 8, 22)
> (let the dead bury their dead, but you come and follow me).

It can hardly escape notice that the burden of this chapter is directly opposed to the lesson taught in *upupa*, in group 3. As we shall see in chapter three, it only becomes possible to include the two birds in the same section of a Bestiary when the organizing principle has changed from a moralizing to a pseudo-taxonomic one, based on the Creation myth.

The chapter on *turtur*, the turtle-dove, which ends this group, repeats the injunction to remain faithful to Christ and the church, adding a call for chastity. The hen turtle-dove takes only one mate, remaining faithful to him even if he is taken by a hawk or a bird-catcher. Likewise the church remained faithful to Christ after his crucifixion and ascension to heaven, and the individual Christian must do the same:

qui perseveraverit usque in finem, hic salvus erit (Matt. 10, 22)
(he that endures to the end shall be saved).

Both this and the quotation in *assida* from the same chapter of Matthew are taken from Christ's sermon to his apostles, when he sent them out to preach to the Jews. The main purpose of their preaching is given in Matt. 10, 7:

euntes autem praedicate dicentes: Quia appropinquavit regnum caelorum
(go and preach saying: the kingdom of heaven is at hand),

which, in brief, summarizes the teaching of this group.

GROUP 7: *CERVUS, SALAMANDRA, COLUMBA, PEREDIXION, ELEPHANTUS, AMOS*

This group deals with the whole community of the faithful in all the races of the world. The opening chapter, *cervus*, the stag, forms a bridge with group 6, in that it falls into two parts, the first concerned with Christ and the Devil and the second with Christ and the prophets and apostles. The chapter opens with the following Psalmic quotation,

sicut cervus desiderat ad fontes aquarum, ita desiderat anima mea ad te, deus (Ps. 41, 2)
(as the hart panteth after the water brooks, so panteth my soul after thee, O God),[34]

and passes to the story that the stag, when it notices a serpent, fills its mouth with water and expels it into the serpent's hole, forcing it out in order to crush it underfoot. The stag's recognition of the serpent is compared to Christ's recognition of the Devil in the races of man, whom he expels with a stream of divine wisdom:

cuius non potest antiquus draco suffere sermones
(the old dragon which cannot stand his words).

34. Ps. 42, 1. (AV).

The story of the Gadarene swine (see Matt. 8, 28–34; Mark 5, 1–16) is then told at some length, repeating the lesson that Christ can recognize the Devil and expel him.

The text then turns to another Psalmic quotation,

montes excelsi cervis (Ps. 103, 18)
(the high mountains of the stags),

and compares these mountains with the apostles, prophets and priests on whom the faithful may stand to attain the recognition of Christ:

levavi oculos meos ad montes, unde veniet auxilium mihi (Ps. 120, 1)
(I will lift up mine eyes unto the hills, from whence cometh my help).[35]

In the next chapter, *salamandra*, the salamander's ability to survive in the fire, and indeed to extinguish flames, is compared with the miracles performed by the saints. The obvious parallel is drawn, with the three men cast into the fiery furnace by Nebuchadnezzar (Dan. 3, 19–30), and the moralization is pressed home with quotations from Paul and Isaiah:

fide omnes sancti extinxerunt virtutem ignis, ostruxerunt ora leonum (Heb. 11, 33)
(by faith all the saints quenched the violence of fire, stopped the mouths of lions),
si transieris per ignem, flamma te non comburet (Is. 43, 2)
(if you pass through the fire, the flames will not burn you).

The long chapter, *columbae*, the doves, which follows, relates the varied colours of doves in general terms to the races of the world, and in particular to various prophets and martyrs. In the opening, ten colours are listed, ending with red (*rufus/rubeus*) which is,

super omnes primus, qui omnes regit et placat, et quotidie etiam agrestes congregat in columbario suo
(the first above all, which rules and appeases all, and so daily the flock gathers in its dovecote).

The red dove is identified with Christ,

qui nos pretioso sanguine redemit et intra unam ecclesiae domum de diversis nationibus congregavit
(who redeems us with his precious blood and brings the different nations together within one church).

35. Ps. 121, 1. (AV).

The universal church of Christ is thus compared to the dovecote presided over by the red dove.

In the second part of the chapter, specific interpretations are given for nine of the colours listed in the opening. *Niger* (black) stands for the Law, which is obscure and needs interpretation; *struninus* (speckled) for the diversity of the twelve prophets; *aerius* (sky blue) for Elijah, who was carried to heaven in a chariot (Kings 2, 11); *cinericius* (ashy) for Jonah, who made penance with ashes (Jonah 3, 6); *aurosus* (golden) for the three mentioned in *salamandra* who refused to worship Nebuchadnezzar's golden image (Dan. 3, 18); *melenus* (yellow) punningly for Elisha, who caught Elijah's mantle (*melotis*);[36] *albus* (white) for John, who cleansed by baptism; *stephanitus* (silver), again punningly, for Stephen, the first martyr; and finally *rubeus* (red) for Christ. This was indicated in the opening, but here Old Testament prophecies are assembled to add force to the image of the blood of the Passion.[37]

Columbae is followed by *arbor peredixion*, the Peredixion Tree, which also deals with doves, and which continues the theme of the church as protector of the faithful. Doves are said to congregate in this Indian tree, attracted by the shade and the sweetness of its fruit. While they are in the tree or its shadow, they are safe from the predatory dragon: if they leave it, the dragon will eat them. The doves stand for the faithful, the tree is the church, and the shadow is the Holy Spirit:

umbra vero arboris spiritus sanctus est, sicut dicit Gabriel Sanctae Mariae: spiritus sanctus superveniet in te, et virtus altissimi obumbrabit tibi (Luke 1, 35)
(the shadow of the tree is the Holy Spirit, as Gabriel said to blessed Mary: the Holy Spirit will come upon you, and the power of the highest will overshadow you).

The dragon, of course, is the Devil who lies in wait for all who stray outside the church:

cave ergo quantum potes ne extra hanc domum foris invenieris et comprehendat te ille draco serpens antiquus, et devorat te
(therefore beware all you can lest you are found outside that house and that old dragon catches you and devours you).

I know of no Bestiary in which *arbor peredixion* is not treated as a separate chapter, but there is evidence that it was originally the last part of *columbae*. Apart from the

---

36. The Vulgate account uses *pallium* throughout for Elijah's mantle.
37. Cant. 4, 3; Is. 63, 1; Gen. 38, 28–30; Cant. 5, 10.

shared subject matter and theme, there is an indication to be found in the text, whose opening words,

> *item aliud dictum est de ipsis columbis*
> (another thing is said of these doves),

point to a continuation rather than a fresh start. Why, then, was it found necessary to detach *arbor peredixion* from *columbae*? The two together would constitute a very long chapter; slightly longer than *pantera*, and almost as long as *margarita*, the pearl, otherwise the two longest in the work. Unlike these two, however, *columbae* provides a textual opportunity for a break through the introduction of new characters: the Peredixion Tree and the dragon. This, in turn, presents new illustrative possibilities. The text of *columbae* proper contains no narrative, and illustrating it is difficult for that reason. *Arbor peredixion*, on the other hand, provides a scene which can be dramatically illustrated. *Arbor peredixion* miniatures can be among the most effective in a Bestiary (plate 7), whereas *columbae* miniatures, often simply showing a row of identical birds, tend to be unsuccessful, especially, as in the case of most of the earlier books, when little or no colour is used (plate 8). The chance to include a dramatic image does not, however, constitute a sufficient motive for breaking up a chapter, and the main reason for this must lie in the great length of the original chapter. I shall suggest in chapter five that these early Bestiaries were designed to be read aloud, and a disproportionately long chapter could present both institutional problems, related to the amount of time available for reading such extracts, and didactic ones, concerned with the attention span of the listeners.

In the next chapter, *elephas*, the elephant, we read a very similar story of protection from a dragon. The elephant gives birth in a pool so that the vulnerable mother and baby are safe from the waiting dragon, who dares not enter deep water. Two subsidiary stories are also included: the first relating the elephant's sexual habits to the Fall, and the second comparing the potency of burnt elephant bones against poisonous reptiles to the purifying power of God, which protects the hearts of the faithful against the intrusion of evil thoughts. This last can be read as a reduction to a personal level of the main arguments of this and other chapters in the group. In each case, protection is offered against the Devil, who takes the form of a dragon or serpent.[38] In *arbor peredixion*, protection is offered by the church, which is twice referred to as a house:

> *(deus) qui habitare facit unanimes in domo* (Ps. 67, 7)
> ((God) who makes the solitary dwell in a household),[39]

---

38. In *cervus*, the Devil is represented by a serpent. The equivalence of 'serpent' and 'dragon' is implied by the reference to the Devil as *antiquus draco* in the same chapter. In this case, protection is given by the power of the words of Christ.
39. AV gives 'God setteth the solitary in families' (Ps. 68, 6).

Plate 7. Oxford, Bodleian Library Laud Misc. 247, f. 162v arbor peredixion *miniature. The doves are safe from the dragon as long as they remain in the tree.*

cave ergo quantum potes ne extra hanc domum foris invenieris
(therefore beware all you can lest you are found outside that house).

In the story of the burnt elephant bones, protection is actually offered to a house,

nam et ossa et pellis de elephante in quocumque loco vel domo fuerint incensa, statim odor eorum expellit inde et fugat serpentes
(the bones and hide of the elephant, when burnt in any place or house, at once give off an odour so that serpents flee),

which is then compared to the heart of the faithful. An analogy is being drawn between the apostolic church, repository of the faith and protection of the international community of the faithful, and the heart of the individual believer, purified by the works and commands of God.

The inclusion of an allegory relating to the Fall in this group must be seen as a prologue to the recital of Christ's saving mission to the whole human race, found in the next chapter, *Amos*. We are told that elephants are intelligent, but possess very little physical lust, and that when a pair want to produce young, they go,

ad orientem . . . usque in proximum paradisi
(to the east, to the neighbourhood of paradise),

Plate 8. Oxford, Bodleian Library Laud Misc. 247, f. 161v columbae *miniature. The artist has attempted to make the row of doves more interesting by showing them in different poses.*

where they find a tree called *mandragora*, or mandrake. The female eats the fruit of this tree and persuades her mate to eat too, after which they copulate, and the female conceives immediately. To give birth, she enters a pool of water, as described above. In the moralization, the parallel with the Genesis myth of the Fall is developed, in which the pool is compared to the world, into which the progenitors were cast after their expulsion from Paradise (Gen. 3, 23–4):

cuius hic mundus figuram habet propter multas eius fluctuationes et communicationes, et innumerabiles eius voluptates et passiones

(which stands for this world because of its many changes and interactions, and its countless lusts and passions).

This can only be seen as an alternative to the moralization discussed above, wherein the water signifies a refuge from the Devil rather than the site of his snares. By means of this dual connection, a parallel is made between the Fall and the protection offered by Christ to sinners in the church. The link is made explicit in the following chapter, Amos, which ends the group.

This chapter takes its name from the quotation from the book of Amos with which it opens:

item Amos propheta dicit: non eram propheta, neque filius prophetarum, set eram pastor caprarum (Amos 7, 14)

(Amos the prophet says: I was not a prophet, nor the son of prophets, but a herdsman of goats).

The reason for using a chapter heading different in kind from all the others in the work was presumably that a chapter on goats already existed. A passage from Matthew 16, 13–16 is then paraphrased in order to relate the Amos quotation to Christ:

neque filius prophete, set filius Dei vivi
(not the son of the prophet, but the son of the living God).

Christ was a herdsman of goats in that he assumed human form to take care of the whole human race turned to sin. Those who received him were made sheep; those who did not, and those who persisted in sin remained goats, grazing in the desert. Such are the Jews today (cf. Matt. 25, 32–3). Christ's Incarnation is thus explained as the result of the Fall, which drove mankind to sin.

GROUP 8: *ADAMANTE, MARGARITA*

The final group deals with Christ's Incarnation itself. It contains just two long chapters, which treat the theme in different ways. *Adamans*, the diamond, discusses the Incarnation as the fulfilment of prophecy, establishing Jesus as the Messiah, while *margarita*, the pearl, describes the historical version contained in scripture. *Adamans* thus relies heavily on Old Testament, and *margarita* on New Testament quotations.

The moralizations in *adamans* are founded on four sources: three observations on the properties of the stone, and one prophetic quotation. The diamond is found in a high mountain in the east; it is sought by night, because in the daytime the sunlight outshines its brightness; and neither iron, nor fire, nor any other stone can prevail against it.[40] Finally we read:

---

40. The diamond prevails (Latin *prevalere*) over iron and other stones in the sense that it is the hardest naturally occuring substance. The empirical scale devised by Friedrich Moh in the nineteenth century grades minerals from 1 (talc) to 10 (diamond). Substances in the scale will scratch minerals of a lower hardness number, and are scratched by those of higher hardness. Iron (6.5) and other stones (e.g., quartz (7) and topaz (8)) are thus scratched by diamond. As for fire, diamonds will not melt unless heated in the absence of oxygen to 3,500 degrees centigrade. Being composed of elemental carbon, however, they can be oxidized at lower temperatures. This reaction merely produces a very gradual reduction in size and a slight smell, and was not noted until the late seventeenth century.

de hoc lapide adamante dicit propheta: Vidi virum stantem super murum adamantinum et
in manum eius lapidem adamantem in medio populi Israel
(of this stone diamond the prophet says: I saw a man standing on a wall of
diamond, and in his hand a stone of diamond in the midst of the people of Israel).
(Amos 7, 7–8)[41]

The high mountain in the east signifies God the Father,

ex quo omnia oriuntur
(from whom all things originate).

Christ's origin is the Father, but quotations from John's gospel are used to emphasize
his identity with the Father:

Christus in pater et pater in me est (John 14, 11)
(Christ is in the father and the father in me),[42]
qui me videt, videt et patrem (John 14, 9)
(whoever sees me sees the father also).

In the opening chapter of the *Physiologus* text, the lion's love of mountains was
explained in a similar way, and a further comparison may be made between the
obscurity of the diamond, leading to its being sought by night, and the lion's habit of
covering its tracks with its tail. It will be recalled that this was explained in terms of the
failure of the company of heaven to recognize Him in His descent to earth. This
exegesis was based on a reading of Psalm 23, 10, which is again quoted here:

quis est iste rex glorie
(who is this king of glory?)

In *adamans*, therefore, we see evidence that the text is being brought to a conclusion
by means of an explicit return to matters introduced at the outset. Further evidence
that this group is in part a summary is seen in the reintroduction of three further
themes to which the text has returned time and again. The nocturnal brilliance of the
diamond is compared to Christ's illumination of the people of darkness:

41. The Septuagint (see bibliography) gives, 'Thus the Lord showed me; and behold, he stood upon a wall of adamant,
and in his hand was an adamant', which is substantially what is quoted here except that it is God who stands on the
wall. In the Vulgate, we read, *Dominus stans super murum litum et in manu ejus trulla caementarii* (The Lord stood on a
rendered wall, and in his hand a mason's trowel).
42. The Vulgate gives *non creditis quia ego in patre et pater in me est*, as a reported speech of Christ (Believe me that I am in
the father and the father in me) (AV).

sicut dicit David propheta ex persona totius humani generis: quoniam tu illuminas lucernam meam, Domine, Deus meus, illumina tenebras meas (Ps. 17, 29)
(as the prophet David said in the person of the whole human race: for you light my candle, lord, my God, lighten my darkness).

Likewise the supremacy of the stone over all other materials, and over fire, is compared to Christ's dominion over death and hell; a theme previously explored in *phoenix*, *hydrus* and *salamandra*. A quotation used in *hydrus* is repeated here:

devicta est mors in victoria. Ubi est mors contentia tua, ubi est mors aculeus tuus? (1 Cor. 15, 55)
(death is swallowed up in victory. Death, where is your opposition, where is your sting?).

Finally the vision of a man standing on a wall of diamond is compared to John's vision of the Heavenly Jerusalem (Rev. 21, 10–27), which is similarly described as constructed of precious stones. A reader familiar with the passage could not fail to recognize the implied parallel between the diamond, glowing with its own inner light, and the Heavenly City, which: 'had no need of the sun, neither of the moon to shine in it: for the Glory of God did lighten it, and the Lamb is the light thereof. (Rev. 21, 23 AV.)' The wall of diamond is thus composed of

sanctos et vivos lapides, de quibus edificatur celestis Ierusalem. Hi sunt apostoli, prophete, martires quibus neque ignis, neque gladius, neque bestiarum dentes prevalere potuerunt
(the holy and living stones of which the heavenly Jerusalem is built. These are the apostles, prophets and martyrs over whom neither fire nor the sword nor the teeth of beasts can prevail).

The image of the church of Christ, supported by the saints, previously drawn in group 7 is produced once more here.

The man in the vision holds a diamond in his hand which, by an exegetical tour de force almost incomprehensible to the modern reader, is made to symbolize both Christ's divinity and his assumption of human form. In order to gain some insight into the argument, it must first be accepted that the term *adamans*, here translated as diamond, was freely applied to any hard mineral.

The argument starts from the description in Daniel of 'a certain man clothed in linen, whose . . . body also was like beryl'. (Dan. 10, 5–6 AV.) Divinity is implied by the precious stone (beryl and diamond were equally *adamans*), and humanity by the linen garment – like grave clothes:

lineum . . . id est indumentum, quod de terra nascitur
(linen . . . that is a pall, which is born of the earth).

It is thus possible to conclude that:

virum stantem super murum adamantinum . . . in manu eius adamas, id est filius Dei et
filius hominis, qui in utero Mariae carnem assumere dignatus est.
(the man standing on the wall of diamond . . . with a diamond in his hand, is the
son of God and the son of man, who assumed flesh in Mary's womb).

The final chapter, *margarita*, draws a parallel between the production of a pearl in an
oyster and the Incarnation of Christ. The oyster is said to rise from the bottom of the
sea in the morning and open up when it reaches the surface. There it absorbs the rays
of the sun and turns them into a splendid pearl. The oyster is taken to stand for the
Virgin, who ascended from her father's house to the temple at the time of morning
prayer. The production of a pearl is compared to the Annunciation. The opening of
the oyster stands for Mary's receptiveness, expressed in the words spoken to the angel
Gabriel:

ecce ancilla Domini, fiat michi secundum verbum tuum (Luke 1, 38)
(behold the handmaid of the lord; be it unto me according to thy word).[43]

The dew signifies the words of Gabriel, in which are contained the seed of Christ.
Support for this parallel is provided by the blessing of Jacob by his father (again
pointing to the closing of the text by referring back to its opening),

det tibi Deus de rore coeli (Gen. 27, 28)
(God gave you the dew of heaven),

which is read as a prophecy that Christ would be born of Jacob's seed.

The second component in the production of a pearl, the light of the sun, is equated
with the purifying power of the creator, expressed in terms of light in the opening
chapter of John's gospel. Christ, of course, is compared to a pearl in the parable of the
merchant and the pearl (Matt. 13, 45–6), and the remainder of this long chapter is
devoted to an exegesis of the parable:

43. Luke 1, 38 (AV).

simile est regnum celorum homini negociatori querenti bonas margaritas. Inventa autem una
bona margarita vendidit omnem substantiam suam et possedit margaritam
(the kingdom of heaven is like a merchant seeking good pearls. Finding one good
pearl he sold all his goods and bought it).

The gospel text itself gives no explanation of the parable, but the meaning is
apparent enough. The *Physiologus* text adds an important ingredient by comparing the
merchant, not to an individual seeking salvation, but to the company of apostles, to
whom the parable is addressed, and by implication to Christian communities engaged
in the religious life. This important closing passage returns to the theme of the
salvation offered to individuals by the religious life developed previously, notably in
group 1. This will be discussed more fully in chapter five, but it is worth noting here
that the theme is contained in the discussion of a parable from Matthew 13, a chapter
that includes, alongside a long series of parables, a justification of the parabolic method
of teaching on the grounds that,

it is given unto you to know the mysteries of heaven, but unto them [i.e., those
who are not apostles] it is not given. (Matt. 13, 11 AV.)

This is no less than a vindication of the *Physiologus* text itself, which is constructed in
the form of a series of related sets of parables, carefully interpreted for the use of
religious communities.

READING THE IMAGE (I)

In order to concentrate the discussion for a preliminary reading of the use of
illustration in the Brussels *Physiologus*, I shall try to summarize the main
conclusions to be drawn from the analysis of the text. First, there is an organizing
principle which is not rooted in any notion of zoological taxonomy, but can
loosely be called moralizing. That is to say, the chapters are grouped according to
Christian ethical themes (see table 2). It follows that the work's purpose is a didactic
one, aimed at members of religious communities. It has been observed before that
the *Physiologus* text provides examples from the natural world as guides to human
behaviour, but the real teacher is Christ. His explicit teachings are reiterated
throughout the text, and the typological weighting of the work allows him to
subsume the teachings of the prophets too. More than this, Christ's didactic role is
encoded in the very structure of the text, in that he provides an example in the
first chapter of each group, which the reader is taught to follow in subsequent
chapters.

The Brussels *Physiologus* contains fifteen pen-drawn miniatures, illustrating the first twelve chapters,[44] each drawing following the portion of text to which it refers. Spaces have been left for illustration after the remaining chapters, but the programme was never completed.

The choice between placing illustrations before or after the text to which they refer depends on two considerations. One is compositional, relying on the exemplar, and the other functional, depending on the intended use. When a book is copied, it is usual to follow the arrangement of the exemplar unless powerful user constraints demand a change. In this case, the only surviving illustrated *Physiologus* older than the Brussels manuscript, Bern Burgerbibliothek MS 318, has miniatures preceding the relevant text,[45] but it was certainly not the exemplar for the Brussels *Physiologus*, and since it is a ninth-century book, it can hardly be taken as a guide to normal illustration practice in the eleventh century. For manuscript books in general, Weitzmann gave examples of both systems of illustration placing, but only for ninth-century books.[46] If we turn to books approximately contemporary with the Brussels *Physiologus* and from the same general area, we can easily find examples of both methods.[47] On balance we must assume that user considerations determined the decision to place the miniatures after the relevant text rather than before it, if not in this manuscript, at least in an exemplar.

In deciding to position the miniature after the text, the compiler of the Brussels *Physiologus* has subordinated the image to the text: the reading of the image is conditioned by the text which precedes it. More than this, individual miniatures are profusely rubricated, to allow for no mistake in their reading.

The most striking difference between the illustrations of the Brussels *Physiologus* and later Bestiary cycles is that an attempt is made to illustrate the moralizations as well as the animals or stones which represent the ostensible subject matter of the work. Despite the difficulties inherent in such a project, all of the miniatures except *serra* illustrate the moralization in some way. Four methods are used, either singly or in combination. The first is to show Christ as teacher, the second is to show Christ's Passion, the third makes use of the typological parallels drawn in the text, and the last shows the practical or institutional operation of the textual lessons. All four approaches are, of course, closely linked to the teaching methods employed in the text itself.

The first method, used in *autalops*, is the most discursive, in that this part of the image would be completely obscure without the accompanying rubric. Plate 9 shows

44. *Caladrius* has two miniatures and *formica* three.
45. Steiger and Homburger (1964), *passim*.
46. Weitzmann (1947), 72–3.
47. Brussels, Bibl. Roy. MSS 9987–91, a Prudentius from Saint Amand, has miniatures generally preceding the relevant text, while the first illustrated *Life of Saint Amand* (Valenciennes Bibl. Mun. MS 502), dateable between 1066 and 1090, has miniatures following the chapters to which they correspond.

f. 141 r with the end of the chapter followed by the accompanying miniature. In the upper register, the antelope is shown with its horns trapped in the shrub (*autalops firmatum cornua sua in arborem*), while the hunter (*venator*) kills it with his spear. Below, Christ is shown in an attitude of teaching, a book in his right hand and the left outstretched towards a receptive listener. The rubric, *Homo dei abscide omnia vitia mala a te ut non comprehenderis a diaboli* (Man of God cut off all vice from yourself, so that you will not be caught by the devil) summarizes the moralization of the text, but has no scriptural justification. The representation of Christ as teacher underlines the didactic function of the work, discussed above. He appears in this form in miniatures to five of the twelve chapters illustrated.[48]

In another of the miniatures where Christ is shown as a teacher, *nycticorax* (plate 10), the dependence on the rubricated text is reduced by incorporating the figure of Christ in a narrative image. At the top left is David surrounded by his enemies (Ps. 101, 9) gesturing towards the bird, shown on the roof of an arched structure, with the rubric:

factus sum sicut nicticorax in domicilio. (Ps. 101, 7)
(I am like a *nicticorax* on the housetop).

Christ stands immediately below David, parallelling him in both position and pose. He points diagonally upwards at Caesar, enthroned under the arch, with the rubric:

reddite quae sunt Cesaris Cesari (Matt. 22, 21)
(give to Caesar what is Caesar's),

reporting his speech. The words are addressed to a group of Jews, all pointing up to the emperor, their words indicated by the rubric:

nos regem non habemus nisi Cesarem (John 19, 15)
(we have no king but Caesar).

Despite the increase in the figural element at the expense of the discursive, produced by the introduction of scriptural narrative, the miniature still depends principally on the rubricated text for its legibility.

The illustration to *pellicanus* shows the use of the second method, the depiction of events from the Passion (plate 11). The Crucifixion image in the lower register is so familiar that no rubrication was thought necessary in this part of the miniature, beyond

---

48. *Autalops, nicticorax, aquila, phoenix* and *unicornis*.

uocem eius uenit et occidit eum · Sic & tu homo quisludes
sobrius ee & castus · & spiritualr uiuere · cuius duo cornua
sunt duo testamta p quas poteris resecare & excidere
abste oma uitia corporalia · hoc e adulteriu fornicatione
auaritia · inuidia superbia · detractione · ebrietate &
omem lubrica huius seculi pompa · tc egaudent tibi angli
& omfm uirtutes celor · Caue ergo homodi ab ebrietate
ne obligeris luxuria & uolutate · & int fruaris a diabolo ·
U mu eru & mulieres · apostare faciunt homines a do ;

Plate 9. *Brussels, Bibl. Roy. 10066–77, f. 141r* autalops *miniature. Above, the antelope has trapped its horns in a shrub and cannot escape the hunter; below, Christ teaches the lesson to be learned from the antelope – that men of God must avoid the Devil's works.*

that naming the figures represented. The two pelican scenes in the upper register are loaded with text, however. The inference is that the teaching of the *Physiologus* could work in either of two ways. Received opinion is that it is 'a compilation of pseudo-science in which the fantastic description of real and imaginary animals, birds, and even stones were used to illustrate points of Christian dogma and morals'.[49]

In this case, however, the crux of Christian dogma is used as an illustration of the way the natural world operates. The distinction, of course, is anachronistic. For the early medieval Christian, the behaviour of the pelican was not simply a reminder of the Passion. Created nature was one means by which eternal truths were accessible to humanity: animals behaved as they did because God created them so. Their observable natures are a cloudy reflection of the will of God, not to be fully clarified until the Day of Judgement.[50]

We have already seen the typological method at work in the identification of Christ with David in the illustration to *nycticorax*. In *lapides igniferi* (plate 12) two Old Testament examples cited in the text are juxtaposed with an illustration of the nature of these stones. In the upper register a woman[51] brings the stones together, clearly identified as male and female by their shapes. Of the two, it is the male stone which is inflamed by the female. The woman presents the flaming stone to a receptive man, armed with a spear, at the instigation of the angel of Satan (*angelus satane*) standing behind her, in an allegorical image of the diabolical nature of female seduction. Immediately below is represented the unsuccessful seduction of Susannah. The two elders (*falsi presbiterii*) are juxtaposed with the angel of Satan and the woman with the fire-stones above, while the virtuous Susannah, whom they confront (Sus. vv. 19–21) stands below the soldier; her gesture of alarm contrasting with his receptiveness.[52]

On the right of the lower register, the same tripartite composition is repeated a third time, in an image of the Fall. Again the two negative figures, the tempters, are on the left, while the tempted Adam on the right indicates his compliance with the same open-handed gesture seen in the soldier above.

A similar approach is used in the second illustration to *caladrius*, which shows the bird's actions confronted with an invalid on the mend (plate 13). The patient lies on his bed while a friend holds the *caladrius* aloft. The bird stares steadily at the invalid, and a

---

49. McCulloch (1960), 15.
50. See Eco (1986), 52–64.
51. The sex of this figure is not entirely unambiguous. The skirt is certainly female in that it lacks the male overskirt. I am grateful to Kathryn Morrison for this observation. The curious headgear, like a Phrygian cap, seems more male than female but occurs on no other figures in the manuscript, even those labelled Jews.
52. Gaspar and Lyna (1937), 23, wrongly described the figures labelled *falsi presbiterii* as Joseph and Samson. They also described the figure at the right of the upper register as '*un spectateur effrayé*': an evaluation at odds with his expressionless face and receptive gesture.

Plate 10. Brussels, Bibl. Roy. 10066–77, f. 144r nycticorax *miniature. Above, David, surrounded by his enemies, compares himself with the night-raven perched on the roof; below, Christ tells a group of Jews to give to Caesar (top right) what is his due. The vertical juxtaposition of Christ and David emphasises the typological link.*

second onlooker raises his arm in a gesture of joy. Above the bed and to the left, the *caladrius* is seen again flying towards the sun, which is shown as a disc containing a half-length figure holding a torch. Four more onlookers crowd around the end of the bed, two of whom are turning to look at a large standing figure of Christ with both arms upraised. The foremost of these, gesturing with his hands, makes the link between the behaviour of the *caladrius* and Christ, who, according to a rubric, is taking our sins to himself. This figure of Christ, in the pose of Crucifixion, is juxtaposed with a drawing of Moses raising the brazen serpent on a tree which runs right down the outer margin of the page: a drawing which is badly damaged owing to the deliberate mutilation of the Crucifixion image on the other side of the leaf. The miniature is thus a very complex one, including the typological Moses scene to press home the point that it is through Christ's Crucifixion that the sins of mankind are absolved.

The illustration to *aquila* (plate 14) shows how the fourth technique for illustrating the moralization, by depicting its institutional operation, is used in combination with images of the bird's nature as reported in the text, and of Christ teaching. At the same time, a typological dimension is added by the rubrication. On the left, the story of the eagle's rejuvenation is shown in three images. At the top, it flies towards the sun, (*ubi aquila comburit alas suas ad radios solis*); at the bottom, it plunges into a well, (*ubi trina vice se fonti mergit*); while to the far left it appears in a tree with its wings displayed (*ubi aquila renovata sede in arborem*).

To the right, in the upper register, a figure of Christ teaching looks over his shoulder at the behaviour of the eagle, while addressing a group of listeners with the words

et tu homo sive Iudeus sive Christianus renovate sicut aquila iuventutem suorum
(and you, O man, whether Jew or Christian, renovate your youth like the eagle).

This is almost exactly the form of words found in the text itself, and is a quotation from Psalm 102. The rubrication of the image thus serves to establish the typological link between Christ and David. In the lower register, we see how this spiritual rejuvenation is institutionally achieved, in an image of baptism. The priest performing the sacrament is juxtaposed with Christ, while the naked figure in the font corresponds to his receptive audience. A direct connection, taken from the text, between the sacrament and the behaviour of the eagle is established by the font, on the same level as the eagle's well and similar in shape.

Evidence of the subservience of image to text in the Brussels *Physiologus* is thus abundant. Further proof may be seen in the way the miniatures are arranged in registers. Division of the illustrated space into horizontal bands was a device commonly used around this period; either to present a continuous narrative, comic-strip fashion, as in the great illustrated Bibles or lives of the saints, like the twelfth-century *Life of St Quentin* in Saint-Quentin Chapter Library (plate 15), or to distinguish between levels in the spiritual hierarchy, as in Ottonian manuscripts like *Henry II's Book of Pericopes* (Munich, Staatsbibliothek Clm. 4452, see plate

Plate 11. Brussels, Bibl. Roy. 10066–77, f. 143v pellicanus *miniature. Below, Christ on the cross; above, the mother is wounded by her chick (left), and after striking back (not shown), she revives her dead chicks with her own blood (right).*

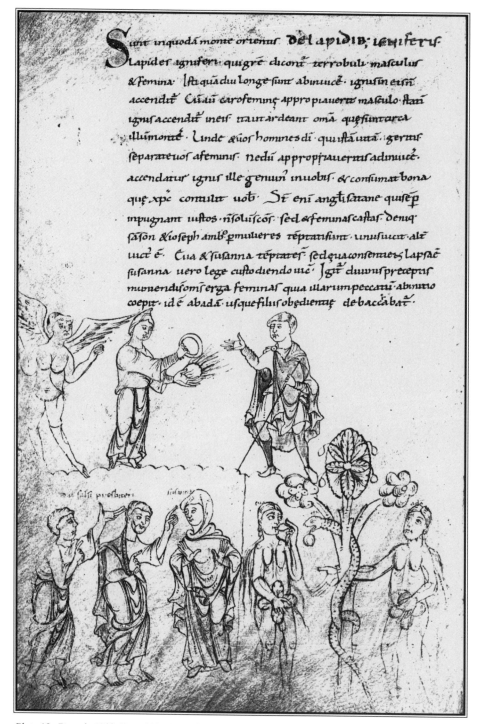

Plate 12. Brussels, Bibl. Roy. 10066–77, f. 141v lapides igniferi *miniature. Above, the male fire-stone catches fire when the female stone is brought near; below, Susannah and the Elders (left), and the Fall (right).*

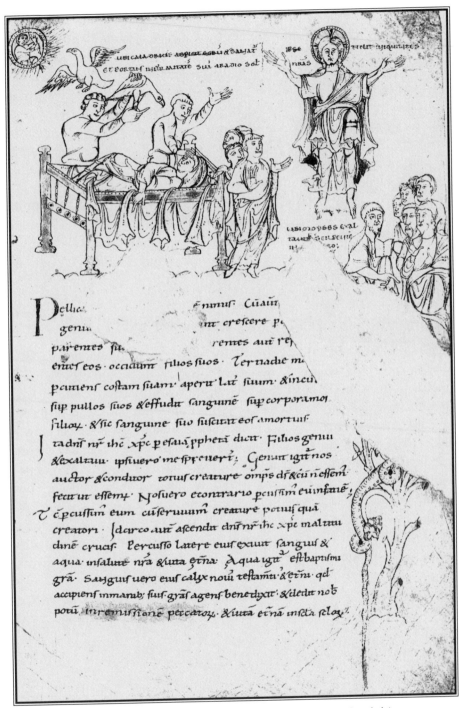

Plate 13. Brussels, Bibl. Roy. 10066–77, f. 143r caladrius, 2nd miniature. The caladrius cures a patient by flying into the sun (top left). At the right, Christ in Crucifixion pose and Moses and the Brazen Serpent are typologically connected.

16). Here Christ crowns King Henry II and Queen Kunigunde between St Peter and St Paul on the upper level, while the personifications of the Empire appear below.

The use of registration in the Brussels *Physiologus* is based on an entirely different premise. The method is seen at its simplest in the illustration to *autalops* (plate 9). The two levels represent neither a continuous narrative, nor a spiritual hierarchy (since Christ appears at the bottom). Rather they serve to distinguish between levels of exegesis, and are thus totally reliant on the organization of the preceding text, in which the literal description of the animal's nature is followed by the moralization. The beauty of the method can be more fully appreciated in a more complex miniature such as that accompanying the chapter on *aquila* (plate 14).

The text, as we have seen, falls into three parts: the Biblical quotation, the description of the eagle's rejuvenation, and the exhortation to baptism. To these three parts correspond the three areas of the image. Furthermore, the textual arguments connecting the three levels of exegesis are made pictorially; by the juxtapositions and formal correspondences described above.

READING THE STORY: THE ACTANTIAL LEVEL

A zoologist's reaction to the *Physiologus* text must be that the information it contains about animal behaviour is both scanty and inaccurate. It could not be based on observation, since the animals in question do not behave like this even when they exist. In fact, the characteristics ascribed to the animals served no other purpose than to justify the moralizations, and the unfamiliarity of a western medieval audience with all but a few of the animals described was one factor in allowing the fabulous stories told about them to persist.

All of this is certainly true. In the narrative corpus that makes up the *Physiologus* text, the animals are no more than actors taking on roles in order to drive home an ideological message. What is more, different animals can take the same role, playing Christ, the Devil, or the Jews, in different chapters of the corpus. The foregoing analysis of the text provides us with no tool for an analysis at this level, and a clue to the reason for this is provided by a distinction made by Gerard Genette[53] between uses of the French word *récit*, rendered here and by Genette's translator, Jane E. Lewin, by the English word 'narrative'. Genette's three senses are *histoire*, *récit* and *narration*, which I shall translate as 'story', 'text' and 'narration'.[54] The text is what we read: in this case

---

53. Genette (1986), 25–7.
54. Lewin prefers 'story', 'narrative' and 'narrating', see Genette (1986), 27, n. 2. I prefer the translation suggested by Rimmon-Kenan (1983), 3, on the grounds of clarity. 'Narrative' is the English word which best expresses the ambiguity of *récit*. It would be confusing therefore (despite Genette) to use it again as an aspect of itself. For *narration*, either 'narration' or 'narrating' would do equally well, and so the French spelling may as well be retained. It seems less confusing to introduce 'text' for Genette's restricted meaning of *récit* than to use the narrative root yet again.

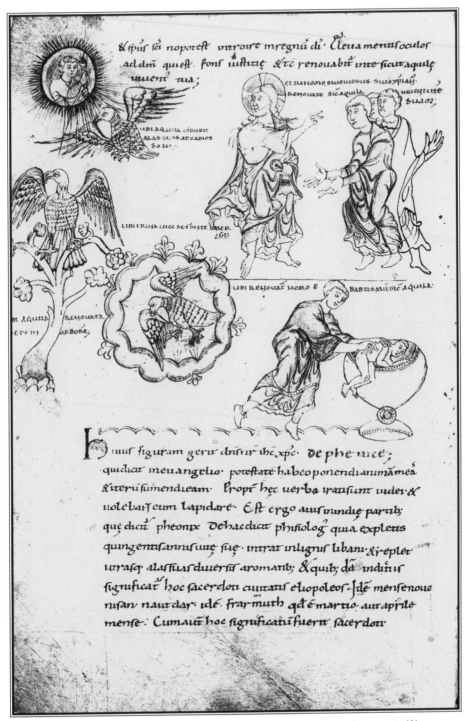

Plate 14. Brussels, Bibl. Roy. 10066–77, f. 144v aquila *miniature. The old eagle renews itself by plunging into a pool and flying into the sun (left). Man is renewed by baptism (right).*

Plate 15. Saint-Quentin Chapter Library, Life of S. Quentin, p. 11. Successive narrative scenes are depicted in two registers.

the *Physiologus* text (and accompanying drawings) in the Brussels manuscript. The story is the succession of events told by the text, together with the participants in these events. The narration is the process of transmission of the text, on which I shall have more to say in chapter five.

The problem which concerns us now, that of analyzing the parts played by the animal, human and spiritual characters appearing in the text, clearly falls into the realm of story. A model which has been found useful in such an analysis is that proposed by A.J. Greimas.[55] This is based on the notion of *actants*, who differ from *acteurs*, or the characters in a story, in that they are general categories underlying all narrative, and are defined not by their individual qualities, but by the narrative function they perform.[56] Thus, *acteurs* are numerous, whereas the number of *actants* in Greimas's model is only six. These are represented schematically in the following diagram.

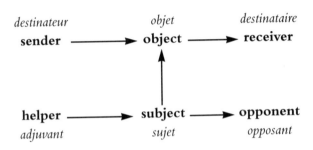

The model was developed from Greimas's criticisms of V.I. Propp's analysis of Russian folktales,[57] and its applicability to such narratives of love and quest is readily understood. The subject is the male hero, or prince, who seeks an object – often a princess – supplied by a sender or donor – usually her father. In this case, the *actants*, 'subject' and 'receiver' are conflated. The subject may receive help or hindrance from other characters or agencies. Within such a tale, *acteurs* may constantly change their actantial roles. The sender, for example, may initially be an opponent (if the prince does not look like a prince). The preliminary quest may be for some object other than the princess, like a magic sword or a ring which, once possessed, becomes a helper in later stages.

The corpus of folktales that form the subject of Propp's study is thus seen to reproduce a single actantial message in a series of different guises. The message itself, embodying such notions as success through struggle, patriarchy and a rigid class structure, gains power through repetition. Greimas has argued that the relationship

55. Greimas (1986).
56. Ibid., 128–30, 174–80.
57. Propp (1958).

Plate 16. Munich, Staatsbibl. Clm. 4456, f. 2r Pericopes of Heinrich II. The earthly and heavenly realms are shown in different registers.

between subject and object, which is manifested in narratives as a relation of quest, is a specialized form of a teleological relationship of desire.[58] That is to say that the actantial functions expressed in narrative are particularizations of power functions in an ideology. Narrative is a product of ideology, and the flexibility of his model is such that it can help to describe the social systems underlying a wide variety of narratives. For a militant Marxist ideology, for example, he proposes:

Subject: Man
Object: Classless society
Sender: History
Receiver: Humanity
Helper: Working class
Opponent: Bourgeoisie

The *Physiologus* text, like Propp's folktales, can be seen as a corpus of stories designed to reinforce an ideology, and a provisional model for the medieval Christian ideology expressed in the *Physiologus* text might first be proposed as:

Subject: Individual Christian
Object: Christ
Sender: God, the Father
Receiver: Mankind
Helper: Saints
Opponent: The Devil

The functions of sender, object and receiver are the easiest to investigate. The relationship is repeatedly rehearsed explicitly, for example in the chapter on Amos:

(Christus) pastor autem caprarum fuit, quoniam missus de sinu patris assumpsit humanam carnem et factus est caprarum pastor, id est totius humani generis in peccatis conversantis; gensque, que eum receperunt et crediderunt in eum, qui misit eum, facti sunt oves; qui vero non receperunt eum remanseruntque in peccatis suis, sunt hedi pascentes in deserto, ut sunt hodie Iudei.

(Christ was a herdsman of goats, however, insomuch as he was sent from his father's loins, assumed human flesh and was made a herdsman of goats, that is the whole human race turned to sin; and the people who received him, and believed him, and

58. Greimas (1986), 180–1.

confessed him, were made sheep; those who did not receive him and those who persisted in sin, they are goats grazing in the desert, just as the Jews are today.)

Similar passages may be found in *leo, caladrius, phenix, unicornis, pantera, adamante* and *margarita*: key chapters in the structure of the text, in that they mark its opening and closing as well as the openings of six of the eight groups into which it is divided.

As well as these explicit statements of the relationship, the functions are encoded in the stories themselves. An example may clarify this. In *formica*, the ability of the ant to distinguish between wholesome and unwholesome foods by the odours they emit is paralleled by the man of God's power to tell between orthodoxy and heresy. The functions may be represented on a diagram.

TABLE 3. SENDER, OBJECT AND RECEIVER ACTANTS IN *FORMICA*

LITERAL LEVEL			MORALIZATION		
Sender	**Object**	**Receiver**	**Sender**	**Object**	**Receiver**
Wheat/ Barley	Odour	Ant	Orthodoxy/ Heterodoxy	Word	Man

It will be obvious from this that the Father/Son/mankind relationship is not the only one encoded in the functions of Sender, Object and Receiver. A fuller picture may be seen with the aid of the table below, that defines these functions in those chapters in the text which contain some story of the transmission of an object from a sender to a receiver.

TABLE 4. SENDER, OBJECT AND RECEIVER ACTANTS IN *PHYSIOLOGUS*

	LITERAL LEVEL			MORALIZATION		
Chapter	**Sender**	**Object**	**Receiver**	**Sender**	**Object**	**Receiver***
Leo	Mountain	Lion	Hunters	Father	Christ	Mankind
Caladrius	Air	Bird	Patient	Heaven	Christ	Mankind
Pellicanus	Mother	Blood	Chicks	Christ	Sacraments	Mankind
Formica	Grain	Odour	Ants	Doctrine	Word	Mankind
Sirenae	Sirens	Music	Sailors	Devil	Pleasure	Mankind
Pantera	Panther	Odour	Animals	Father	Christ	Mankind
Cetus	Whale	Odour	Fishes	Devil	Pleasure	Mankind
Mustela	Male	Seed	Female	God	Word	Mankind
Aspis	Enchanter	Voice	Adder	Preacher	Word	Mankind
Cervus	Stag	Water	Serpent	Christ	Word	Mankind

* No distinctinction has been made between different classes of mankind specified in different chapters, such as 'Jews', 'Gentiles', 'doubters', etc.

Studying the moralization columns of this table it is striking that the function of receiver is always filled by the human race, while those of sender and object fall into two sharply contrasted groups. We receive earthly pleasures from the Devil; and Christ, his sacraments or the Word from God or (in the case of *formica* and *aspis*) the church. In the latter case, where God is the sender, the three possible objects are effectively the same, since mankind receives Christ in the sacraments. Mankind is thus given the choice between just two alternatives represented by the objects on offer, and the aim of the *Physiologus* is to aid the choice by pointing out who the respective senders are.

It will be remembered that Greimas's model was initially developed to study stories of quest, and therefore it would next seem reasonable to investigate the subject/object relationship at the heart of all pursuit narrative, taking as starting point the *Physiologus* chapters that fall into this category. Eleven of the chapters are stories of hunting or pursuit. These are listed below.

TABLE 5. ACTANTIAL FUNCTIONS IN STORIES OF QUEST

	LITERAL LEVEL		MORALIZATION	
Chapter	**Predator**	**Prey**	**Predator**	**Prey**
Leo	Hunter	Lion	Angels	Christ
Autalops	Hunter	Antelope	Devil	Man of God
Herinacius	Hedgehog	Grapes	Devil	Man of God
Vulpis	Fox	Birds	Devil	Sinners
Unicornis	Hunter	Unicorn	Jews	Christ
Castor	Hunter	Beaver	Devil	Man of God
Caper	Hunter	Wild goat	Judas	Christ
Cetus (2)	Whale	Fishes	Devil	Doubters
Perdix	Partridge	Eggs/chicks	Devil	Mankind
Peredixion	Dragon	Doves	Devil	Faithful
Elephas	Dragon	Young	Devil	Mankind

It will first be noticed that at the literal level, the level of *acteurs*, a wide range of predators and prey take part. Only the hunter is repeated more than once as predator, and this is only to be expected in stories of hunting. At the level of moralization, the actantial level, on the other hand, the number of functions are dramatically reduced in agreement with Greimas's conclusions. The Devil operates as predator in all cases where mankind is the prey (men of God, sinners, doubters and the faithful having this in common), while in all the other examples the prey is Christ. These latter cases are interesting in that Christ is sought, not by the faithful, but by some other agency. Thirdly, it will be seen that the appearance of Christ alongside representatives of humanity in the last column of the table establishes a metaphoric relationship: mankind is asked to identify with Christ in some way. The clue to the form of identification is found, for example, in the chapter on the unicorn.

In tantum autem acerrimus, ut nec ille subtilissimus diabolus intellegere aut investigare potuit

(He is so swift, however, that the most cunning Devil could neither perceive nor trail him).

A similar recital of the Devil's impotence against Christ appears in *caper*:

dominus noster Iesus Christus praevidet et praescivit dolus diaboli
(our lord Jesus Christ foresees and foreknows the cunning of the Devil).

I have been careful not to identify the categories of predator and prey with those of subject and object in this discussion. The two alternative identifications of the object actant have already been established as Christ or worldly pleasure in the course of the investigation into the sender/object/receiver relationship. Furthermore, the didactic strategy of the text (that of teaching by example) works best for a human readership if the subject actant is also humanity. A problem seems to arise here in the cases where the Devil is the predator and humanity the prey, because it is clear that mankind is the object in the Devil's quest for souls. The position is not this simple, however, since the Devil habitually behaves not as a hunter, but as a trapper. In other words, his prey is not hunted down, but lured by some bait attractive to humanity: the prey is the subject, and the bait the object. *Cetus*, the whale, is a typical case. The animal catches its prey by luring them into its mouth by means of a sweet odour, as the Devil attracts the faithless with the bait of

voluptatibus ac lenociniis
(sensuality and pandering).

We shall leave aside the final pair of actants in Greimas's scheme – the helper and the opponent – for the moment, since, as we shall see, they stand in a novel mutual relationship which cannot be fully appreciated until the broad outline of the ideological model has been clarified. The identification of the functions in the two sets of relationships studied already has revealed that two connected structures exist, one associated with salvation and the other with damnation. These may be set down as follows.

TABLE 6. SALVATION AND DAMNATION MODELS IN *PHYSIOLOGUS*

	SALVATION	**DAMNATION**
Subject	Mankind	Mankind
Object	Christ	Pleasure
Sender	God the Father	Devil
Receiver	Mankind	Mankind

The picture may now be completed by the addition of the helper and opponent actants. As with the other functions, the number of *acteurs* is great, including, on the one hand, Christ, the saints and scripture, and on the other, the Devil and the pleasures of the flesh, not to mention the animals themselves which operate by example. The problem is not one of selection but one of synthesis, to return to Greimas's definition, '*Les unes (adjuvants) . . . consistent à apporter l'aide en agissant dans le sens du désir, ou en facilitant la communication*,' while, '*les autres (opposants) . . . au contraire, consistent à créer des obstacles, en s'opposant soit . . . la realization du désir, soit . . . la communication de l'objet*'.[59]

At root, subsuming all the individual *acteurs* who aid or oppose humanity, the opposition:

helper *v*. opponent

reduces to:

spirit *v*. flesh

an opposition which is repeatedly emphasized in the text. Each warning against earthly temptation is accompanied by a corrresponding injunction to follow the ways of the spirit. In *vulpis*, for example, we read:

> *qui autem volunt exercere opera eius, ipsi desiderant saginari carnibus eius (id est diaboli), quae sunt: Adulteria, fornicationes, idolatria, veneficia, homicidia, furta, falsa testimonia, et cetera his similia; dicente apostolo: Scientes hoc quia, si secundum carnem vixeritis, moriemini; si autem spiritu opera carnis mortificaveritis, vivetis*
> (those who want to practice his works, they need to be fattened with his meats (that is the Devil's), which are: adulteries, fornications, idolatries, poisonings, murders, theft, lies, and such like; according to the apostle: Because knowing this if you live according to the flesh you die; if, however, with the spirit you slay the works of the flesh and live).

Similar examples could readily be multiplied.

Returning to the two ideological structures already established, the place of this opposition immediately becomes clear. In the 'salvation' model, spirit and flesh take on

59. Ibid., 178.

the respective roles of helper and opponent, while in the 'damnation' model the positions are reversed. Of course, the latter was not intended as a practical guide in the same way as the former, but it was necessary that both systems should be fully developed in order to emphasize the superiority of the 'salvation' model at every point.

Our final ideological model differs from that postulated at the beginning of this analysis in two ways: in the functions of helper and opponent, and in its dual nature. The reason behind this may already be suspected. While the first model, on the lines of Greimas's militant Marxist example, was intended as a description of the world, the second is a guide to behaviour consistent with the preaching function of the work.

READING THE IMAGE (II): THE ACTANTIAL LEVEL

An example of the encoding of the actantial relationships into the images accompanying the Brussels *Physiologus* text may be taken from a more detailed reading of the illustration to *pellicanus* (plate 11). The story, it will be recalled, unfolds in three stages.

1. The pelican is wounded by its chicks. This corresponds to the wounding of Christ by humanity.
2. The pelican strikes back, killing the chicks. No parallel moralization is drawn to this episode.
3. The pelican revives its chicks with its own blood. This corresponds to Christ's sacrifice on the Cross, and to the sacraments of eucharist and baptism thereby initiated.

The miniature is arranged on two registers, with the literal level occupying the upper. Only two stages of the pelican story are illustrated: stage 1, where the adult bird is the object of a wounding by its chick, and stage 3, where it is both the object of its own wounding, and the sender of its blood to the chicks. Stage 2, which has no parallel in the moralization, is not illustrated. The reading of the standard Crucifixion image below is conditioned by these pelican images. The adult bird attacked in the first scene, with its wings spread and head to its right, echoes Christ on the Cross; while in the right-hand scene, the same bird, with the same tilt of the head, is wounded, like Christ, in the right side. The Crucifixion thus takes on the same complex of meanings. Christ is at once the object of wounding by mankind, whose representatives, Longinus and Stephaton, have been deliberately mutilated by a later user; and the victim of self-sacrifice, a reading which could not easily have been illustrated without the second pelican image to reinforce this. He is also the sender of sacraments to mankind, again a point of doctrine that would not normally be made by a Crucifixion image, but which is here insisted on by the spray of blood from his side, duplicating that with which the pelican revives its chicks.

CHAPTER THREE

THE LATIN BESTIARY
IN ENGLAND

THE EARLIEST ENGLISH LATIN BESTIARIES

The *Physiologus* B text formed the basis for the composition of subsequent English Bestiaries. Changes were made, however, in such a way that the encoded meanings were eroded and finally entirely replaced by others. These changes, apparently tentative and superficial at first, were nevertheless systematic and related to a transformation in the function of the book. In the following pages I shall track a sequence of modifications that were made to the text in twelfth and thirteenth-century England, some apparently systematic and purposeful, others more in the nature of failed or abandoned experiments. The result of all this experimentation was not, as we might expect, an improved Bestiary adapted to a new purpose, but a diversity of forms, each answering different needs.

LAUD MISC. 247: TEXT

The earliest surviving English Latin Bestiary is almost certainly Bodleian MS Laud Misc. 247.[1] As well as the *Physiologus* text, it contains short passages from Book XII of the *Etymologiae* of Isidore of Seville, added to the end of all but seven chapters.[2] These additions are invariably prefixed by the rubric, *Ethimologia* or *Ethimologia Ysodori*, in red. This form of the text is an innovation belonging neither to England nor to the twelfth century. An identical text is found in the unillustrated tenth-century continental Bestiary, Vatican MS Palat. Lat. 1074.[3]

The additions from Isidore are quite different in character from the *Physiologus* text. While *Physiologus* presents the animal world as an expression of Christian teaching,

---

1. Dateable *c.* 1110–30 by script and drawings, see chapter four for a fuller discussion. BL MS Stowe 1067 is roughly contemporary, but is so roughly produced that primacy cannot be established on these lines. I agree with James (1928, 7, 10) that both were probably made in Canterbury (but St Augustine's rather than Christchurch), and suggest that the two stages of production of Stowe indicate the exemplary presence of something very like Laud in both text and miniatures.

2. *Autolops, Lapides Igniferi, Serra, Caladrius, Peredixion, Amos* and *Mermecolion.* Isidore's work contains no chapters bearing these titles.

3. After *Mermecolion* the scribe of the Vatican Bestiary has written 'Explicit libri, bene Physiologus arguit. Amen'. followed by the rubric 'De Etimologiarum libro' and then Isidore's chapters on *Psitacus, Ercine* and *Coturnix.*

Isidore relates details of behaviour, appearance and above all etymology, without drawing specific moralizing conclusions.[4] An example will readily show the difference in approach. After the *Physiologus* text of *Unicornis* in Laud, we read,

> It is called Rinoceros by the Greeks, in Latin this is interpreted as 'horn on the nose' (*in nare cornu*). Monoceros, that is to say Unicornis, is the same too. It has four legs and a single horn in the middle of its forehead, so sharp that it will pierce anything which provokes it. For it often fights with elephants, and overcomes them by wounding them in the belly.
> They are said to be so brave that they cannot be captured by any of the hunters' skills. But as those who write about their natures assert, if a virgin girl is displayed, who uncovers her bosom when the unicorn appears, the beast sets aside all its ferocity and lays its head there as if asleep and is captured without weapons.[5]

Isidore begins by demonstrating the aptness of the unicorn's three names. Etymology was the ruling principle of his work, as its title suggests. The preface to Book XII explains the reason for this. All the animals were given their names by Adam, according to their natures.[6] The very names of the animals, therefore, echo the organization of the animal world as seen by the first man, immediately after its creation. In its structure the *Etymologiae* directly follows, not the chronological order of Creation described in the Genesis myth, which in any event is not detailed enough to provide an organizing principle, but the hierarchy of the food laws given in Leviticus and Deuteronomy.[7] Mary Douglas has shown that these laws have their basis in a rule of classification inherent in the Genesis myth: 'in the firmament two-legged fowls fly with wings. In the water scaly fish swim with fins. On the earth four-legged animals hop, jump or walk.'[8]

Broadly, Leviticus deals first with land creatures, then with water creatures, and finally with flying creatures. Within the first category, a division is implied between domestic beasts like cattle (which provide the model for an edible land creature), wild beasts and small animals (which are edible insofar as they conform to the criteria established by the domestic beasts); and finally creeping things, including both reptiles like snakes and terrestrial invertebrates like worms (which are unclean). No subdivision of water creatures is made, but flying things are effectively divided into birds (which are clean if they can fly), and insects (which are clean if they leap rather than crawl).[9] Such

---

4. James (1928), 9, saw the difference as one between 'more or less sober natural history' and the 'purely fabulous'.
5. My translation.
6. Isidore, XII, 1, 1–8.
7. Leviticus XI, 2–47. Deuteronomy XIV, 3–20.
8. Douglas (1978), 55.
9. In effect the distinction is between flying creatures with two legs, and those with more than two legs.

creatures as the locust are thus seen as edible land creatures, incidentally equipped with wings. Isidore follows this order, describing successively domestic beasts, wild beasts, small animals, serpents, worms, fish, birds and flying insects.

Having given an account of the unicorn's names, Isidore goes on to describe it and to list its habits. It will be noticed that he includes here the method of capture related in the *Physiologus* text. Isidore's frequent repetition of *Physiologus* stories demonstrates his reliance on that text, which was certainly available to him in Latin. It is striking, however, that he avoids including the Christian interpretation of the story despite its obvious potentialities. This is another characteristic of Isidore's method: he doggedly refuses to moralize, confining himself to the known facts.[10]

The addition of passages from Isidore therefore indicates a shift in emphasis from Christian moralization towards a description of creation based on the most popular encyclopedic compilation of ancient authorities then available. From the point of view of the use of the Bestiary, this modification would seem to seriously compromise its value as a sequence of didactic moral texts, or sermons, by breaking up the text structure outlined above.

LAUD MISC. 247: IMAGES

A comparison of the miniatures in Laud with those in the Brussels *Physiologus* reveals the same tendency to underplay the moralizations. Comparing the illustrations to *autalops* in the two books (plates 9 and 17), we see that the Laud miniature fails to illustrate either the moralization or the narrative element of the antelope's capture; neither is it rubricated beyond the mere inclusion of the animal's name. What remains is a minimal sign placed before, rather than after, the text to which it relates. The abandonment of the moralization in the image is an index of the loss of interest in the particular didactic purpose revealed in the analysis of the Brussels *Physiologus*, more especially since it necessitates relinquishing the multi-register structure of the miniature which, we have seen, reinforced the reading of the text on many exegetical levels. In this case, what is omitted is not only the image of Christ as teacher enjoining a representative of humanity to abjure all vice in order that he should not be known to the Devil. The visual metaphors between Christ and the antelope, and between man and the hunter also remain unillustrated. So little remains that no rubric is needed, because the image is unreadable in narrative terms.

The stripping of narrative from the image is completed by the omission of the

---

10. Which, as he freely admitted, he obtained at second hand, describing the work as: '*Opus de origine quarundam rerum, ex veteris lectionis recordatione collectum*' (Isidore, Ep. VI). On the authorities consulted by Isidore, see, e.g., Manitius (1911), 60ff; Wittkower (1942), 168.

Plate 17. Oxford, Bodleian Library Laud misc. 247, f. 141r autalops *miniature. The moralisation is not illustrated (compare plate 9).*

hunter, leaving only the beast, its horns entangled in stylized foliage, and its name. Such an image matches the changing structure of the book in the direction of Isidore's description of the organization of creation: the animal itself assumes greater importance, not on its own account, but for its place in the divine order of the world. The movement of the image from the end of the chapter to the beginning is now easier to understand. No longer do we have a miniature subservient to the text, and expressing its moral lessons by means of a heavily rubricated, multi-register composition; the image now serves as introduction to the text, but does no more than indicate its subject matter. In this respect it operates on Genette's level of *narration*, in that it serves as a concise sign to identify the place in the text.[11]

This is not to say that the moral didacticism of the *Physiologus* was abandoned at a stroke in Laud Misc. 247. The additions to the text and the stripping of the image point to no more than a change of emphasis. The process begun here was to go much further.

11. Clanchy (1979), 142–4, 230.

M.R. JAMES'S 'FIRST FAMILY OF BESTIARIES'

James described Laud Misc. 247 as, 'the most representative copy' of his First Family of Bestiaries,[12] in which grouping he included any Bestiary beginning with the two chapters: *Leo, Autalops*. McCulloch divided this First Family into three versions.[13] The first contained books like Laud Misc. 247, which she called the 'B-Is version', because she believed that the text followed the order of the *Physiologus* B text, with additions from Isidore. The second, containing Bestiaries like Cambridge, Sidney Sussex College MS 100, she called the 'H version', since the text is printed in Migne among the works of Hugo of St Victor.[14] The third included books like St Petersburg, Saltykov-Schredin MS Lat Q.v.V.1., which she designated 'Transitional', as representing a stage between James's First and Second Families. I shall show that the approaches of both James and McCulloch represent a considerable simplification of the complex of changes undergone by the Bestiary in the course of the twelfth century, and at the same time provide no rationale by which these modifications may be understood.

James's First Family contains fourteen manuscripts, and McCulloch's B-Is version, seven of these.[15] In fact, only three other surviving Bestiaries known to me follow the text and chapter order of Laud Misc. 247. These are the Bodleian manuscripts Bodley 602 and Douce 167, and British Library MS Royal 2.C.XII. The first is from the Augustinian priory of Newark, Surrey, the third from the Benedictine monastery of St Peter, Gloucester, and all three date from the early thirteenth century. The Royal Bestiary is not illustrated, but the miniatures in Bodley 602 are closely related to those in Laud. Bodley 602's miniatures could not have been copied directly from a Bestiary like Laud, however, since they include details omitted from the latter that are clearly part of the original composition. The two miniatures to *leo* are a case in point. In Bodley 602 (plate 18) all three natures from the *Physiologus* are illustrated in three registers, whereas in Laud (plate 19) the first nature is not represented, and the other two are confusingly conflated. The drawings in Laud are systematically simplified in this way, in comparison with the related Bodley 602 cycle. Despite its late date, therefore, Bodley 602 must be a more faithful copy of a shared source.

---

12. James (1928), 7.
13. McCulloch (1960), 28–34.
14. P.L., 177.
15. James (1928) listed the following as First Family MSS: Bodleian Laud misc. 247★, BL Royal 2.C.XII, BL Stowe 1067★, Bodleian Douce 167★, Bodleian Bodley 602★, BL Sloane 278, Hugo de S. Victor lib. II, Sidney Sussex Coll. 100, Perrins 26 (now Getty, Ludwig XV3)★, Sion Coll. (now Getty, Ludwig XV4)★, Pierpont Morgan MS. 81, BL Royal 12.C.XIX, Trinity R.14.9. (884), Corpus Christi 22★. Of these, McCulloch's B-Is family comprised those asterisked in the list above.

Douce 167 follows Laud closely to the end of the Laud text, after which a chapter on *lupus*, the wolf, is added. As I shall shortly explain, this chapter was among a small group added as early as the first third of the twelfth century, when the reorganization begun with Laud was continued.[16] *Lupus* was certainly added to Douce 167 after the rest of the book was considered complete: it appears on the recto of a leaf that shows signs of having been added to the original quire.[17]

PARIS, BIBL. NAT. MS NOUV. ACQ. LAT. 873

The last Bestiary to be discussed in conjunction with Laud is the late twelfth-century St Augustine's, Canterbury book, Paris, BN. Nouv. Acq. Lat. 873. This was noted by neither James nor McCulloch, but is of considerable interest since its original owner can be identified.[18] From the list of chapters in table 7, it can be seen that the order of the Paris manuscript follows Laud as far as 21. *Onager et simia*.[19] After this, although no new material is added, there is a rearrangement of chapters. At first sight this may seem to indicate no more than inaccuracy in copying, but three observations militate against this. First, nothing has been forgotten. Second, the chapter on *mustela et aspis* has been divided into two parts, which points to deliberate intention. Finally, the resultant order of the last sixteen chapters is not random but systematic. Chapters 22 to 26 fall into Isidore's category of *bestiae*,[20] 27. *mustela* is a *minutum animans*, and the remainder are *aves*, *pisces* or *serpentes*. After the series of beasts which form chapters 15 to 21, it doubtless seemed logical to the compiler to continue with the remaining beasts, which appear in the order they were found in the textual model. *Mustela* followed, but not the serpent *aspis*, which was relegated to the end of the text. Isidore's scheme was not followed in detail, even in these last sixteen chapters, but the change in chapter order is a further move towards a classification in terms of the animals themselves, and away from a system based on moralizations. Nowhere is this clearer than in the separation of *mustela* and *aspis*, which originally formed a didactic dipole intended to compare the true dissemination and rejection of the Word.

---

16. *Lupus* is found, together with *crocodrillus*, *canis* and *ibex* in BL MS Stowe 1067.

17. Douce 167 is a single quire of twelve leaves, the last two of which are additions (i.e., I [14] wants 1, 2 probably blank). It is ruled in two columns of thirty-six lines throughout, except for f. 12v, containing *lupus*, which has forty-three lines.

18. As Adam, the sub-prior of St Augustine's, Canterbury. This is uncommon but not unique, see chapter five.

19. *Onager* and *simia* form separate, successive chapters in Nouv. Acq. Lat. 873. The significance of this will emerge from the discussion in the text.

20. Assuming 26. *Amos* to be treated not as the prophet but as his goats, which form the subject matter of the chapter.

Plate 18. Oxford, Bodleian Library Bodley 602, f. 1v leo miniature. The three natures are illustrated.

Plate 19. Oxford, Bodleian Library Laud misc. 247, f. 139v leo miniature. Only the second and third natures are illustrated (compare plate 18).

TABLE 7. CHAPTER ORDERS OF LAUD, STOWE AND PARIS N.A.L. 873

	PARIS	**LAUD**	**STOWE**
1.	*Leo*	*Leo*	*Leo*
2.	*Autalaps*	*Autalops*	*Autalops*
3.	*Lapides Igniferi*	*Lapides Igniferi*	*Onocentaurus*
4.	*Serra*	*Serra*	*Herinatio*
5.	*Caladrius*	*Caladrius*	*Vulpis*
6.	*Pellicanus*	*Pelicanus*	*Unicornis*
7.	*Niticorax*	*Nicticorax*	*Castor*
8.	*Aquila*	*Aquila*	*Ydrus*
9.	*Fenix*	*Fenix*	*Crocodrillus★*
10.	*Huppupa*	*Huppupa*	*Hiena*
11.	*Formica*	*Formica*	*Onager*
12.	*Sirena et Onocentaurus*	*Syrene et Onocentauri*	*Simius*

	PARIS	LAUD	STOWE
13.	Herinatius	Herinatius	Caper
14.	Ibex (bird)	Ibis (bird)	Pantera
15.	Vulpis	Vulpis	Draco★
16.	Unicornis	Unicornis	Mustela
17.	Castor	Castor	Cervus
18.	Hiena	Hiena	Elephans
19.	Hidrus	Ydrus	Lupis★
20.	Caprea	Caper	Canis★
21.	Onager	Onager et Simia	Ibex (beast)★
22.	Simia	Fulica	Lapides Igniferi
23.	Panthera	Pantera	Serra
24.	Cervus	Aspis chelone	Caladrius
25.	Elephantus	Perdix	Pelicanus
26.	Amos propheta	Mustela	Noctua
27.	Mustela	Aspis	Aquila
28.	Fulica	Assida	Fenix
29.	Aspidochelone	Turtur	Huppupa
30.	Perdix	Cervus	Formica
31.	Assida	Salamandra	Syrena
32.	Turtur	Columba	Ibex (bird)
33.	Salamandra	Peridexion	Fulica
34.	Columbis	Elephans	Aspidochelone
35.	Peredixion	Amos	Perdix
36.	Adamas	Adamas	Aspis
37.	Mermecoleon	Mermecolion	Assida
38.	Aspis		Turtur
39.			Salamandra
40.			Columbas
41.			Peredixion
42.			Amos propheta
43.			Adamas
44.			Mermecolion

STOWE 1067 AND LAUD MISC. 247

James described British Library MS Stowe 1067 as having 'a text either quite or nearly identical with that of Laud'.[21] As I shall explain, this is a long way from the truth.

21. James (1928), 9.

McCulloch similarly classed Stowe with her 'B-Is version', exemplified by Laud.[22] Neither author noted the considerable textual differences between the two books, and more recent writers have been content to follow one or the other.[23] In order to unravel their relationship it will be convenient to look first at the structure of the two books, then at the chapter orders, at individual passages of the text, and finally at the drawings.

STRUCTURES OF LAUD AND STOWE

The Bestiary in Laud is the fourth of eight texts collected in the volume.[24] Although the whole collection may be the work of four scribes, the Bestiary text is continuously written in a single hand. Stowe, by contrast, contains only the Bestiary. It is made up of two eight-leaf quires written by two different scribes. Quire I contains marginal additions by the scribe of quire II, and is illustrated with line drawings (plate 20). Quire II has spaces for illustrations, none of which has been added.

CHAPTER ORDERS OF LAUD AND STOWE

Table 7 compares the chapter orders of the Laud and Stowe Bestiaries. The chapters asterisked in Stowe are additions not found in Laud. The number of chapters has been increased from thirty-six to forty-four. This is achieved by the addition of five new chapters, and the separation of three double chapters.[25] It is significant that all the additions occur in quire I.

The order begins to deviate from Laud as early as chapter 3 where, in place of *lapides igniferi* we find *onocentaurus*. The compiler of quire I of Stowe has systematically gone through the chapters of the model, extracting those on beasts, which appear in the same order as in Laud, and ignoring all other classes of creation. This selection process even extended to the double chapters; hence *onocentaurus* and *mustela* appear, while their respective companions in the *Physiologus* text, *sirena* and *aspis* were set aside. After the chapter on *ydrus*, which deals with that creature's enmity for the crocodile, a

---

22. McCulloch (1960), 30.

23. e.g. Klingender (1971), 384; Kauffmann (1975), 76.

24. Coxe (1853–8), II, 206–7. The Bestiary occupies folios 139r–168v, starting at the beginning of quire XIV and extending into quire XVI, which is completed by the *Sententia beati Augustini de imagine Dei in homine*, written by another scribe.

25. The new chapters in Stowe are *crocodrillus*, *lupis*, *canis*, *ibex* and *draco*. The text of *draco* is identical with the Isidore material added to *pantera* in Laud. The double chapters split up in Stowe are *sirena et onocentaurus*, *onager et simia*, and *mustela et aspis*.

chapter on the latter was added. When the supply of beasts provided by the model was exhausted, three more – *lupus*, the wolf, *canis*, the dog, and *ibex*, the ibex – were added from elsewhere. Returning to the model, a start was made on adding those chapters previously set aside, again following the order of Laud, a process completed by the second scribe. The reorganization carried out by the scribe of quire I therefore involved neither more nor less than the isolation of the *bestiae* at the beginning of the text.[26]

TEXTS OF LAUD AND STOWE

The first scribe also implemented considerable changes to the text, omitting and rearranging passages from the original *Physiologus* and Isidore material, and making additions freely adapted from Solinus and from the text included in Migne with the works of Hugo of St Victor,[27] but speculatively attributed to Hugo de Folieto.[28]

Quire I comes to an end at the foot of f. 8v, part way through the chapter on *upupa*. This chapter was not completed by the scribe of quire II, who began f. 9r with the next chapter, *formica*. Throughout quire II, the text is not the complex compilation of sources found in quire I, but simply follows Laud. Moreover, the marginal additions made by the second scribe to the first quire all constitute parts of the Laud text which the first scribe had omitted. These considerations, added to the observations that quire II has no illustrations, that there are significant codicological differences between the quires (considered more fully below), and that the two quires are in different conditions of wear (quire I being badly browned, while quire II is much cleaner), indicate that the two parts existed separately for some time, and that they were copied from different models.

The model for quire II must have been similar to Laud. Quire I, on the other hand, had no single model. We shall see that the physical appearance of the manuscript points to it having been the original site of the structural and textual experimentation that it embodies. It includes material not to be found in a Laud-type manuscript, but this is all text that occurs, or survives here for the first time. In Stowe, the experiment was abandoned midway through *upupa*, but it was certainly completed elsewhere. Cambridge, Corpus Christi College MS 22 dates from the third quarter of the twelfth

---

26. In Isidore's system, *draco* is not a beast but a serpent, *crocodrillus* is a fish, and *mustela* a small animal. All three were presumably classed with the rest since they walk on land. In the case of the first two, it was probably thought reasonable to place them immediately after the chapters from which they derived: respectively *pantera* and *ydrus*.
27. This is the text printed as book II of *De Bestiis et aliis rebus* in Migne, P.L. 177.
28. Ibid., cols. 9–10.

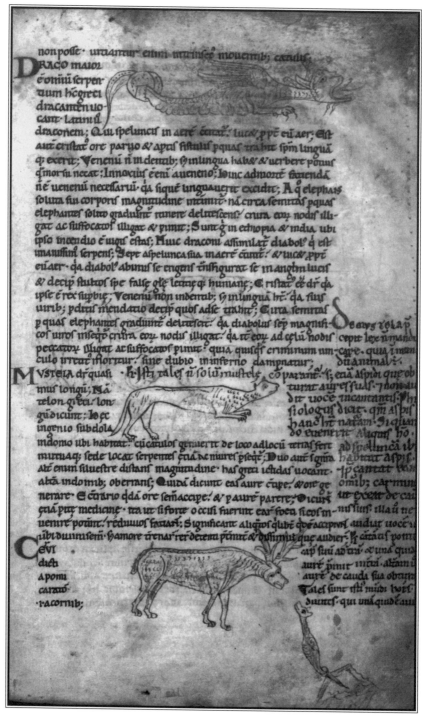

Plate 20. London, BL Stowe 1067, f. 5r draco, mustela, cervus. A sketch for draco *is visible in the margin.*

century,[29] and is incomplete at the beginning and the end, starting part way through *vulpis* and ending in *peredixion*. For these thirty-seven chapters, however, the order follows Stowe, while the text follows Stowe's main text (without the marginal additions) as far as *upupa* (the point where quire I of Stowe ends). Thereafter the Corpus 22 text continues the complex synthesis of sources characteristic of the first quire of Stowe.

An examination of the main text and marginal additions of the first chapter in Stowe reinforces the conclusions drawn from our examination of the chapter order: that the didactic paradigm implicit in the *Physiologus* text was suffering further erosion at the expense of the descriptive Isidore paradigm. The main text of *leo* is given below, with lines numbered as in Stowe (see plate 21).

1. *Leo ex greco vocabulo inflexum*
2. *est in latinum: Leo enim grece latine rex*
3. *interpretatur; Est quisque omnium quadru-*
4. *pedum princeps: Cuius genus trifarium dicitur:*
5. *E quibus breves sunt et iuba crispa et sunt*
6. *longi imbelles et coma simplici; Animos*
7. *eorum frons et cauda indicat; Virtus eorum in pectore firmitas in*
8. *capite; Venabulis septem a venatoribus terrentur; Rotarum strepitus*
9. *timent: et magis ignem et cum ad nullius pavent ocursum: feruntur*
10. *album gallum valde timere; Phisici denique dicunt: quatuor na-*
11. *turales res habere leonem: Prima est quod cacumina montium amat*
12. *ire: Secunda virtus si vero contingerit ut a venatoribus querator corum*
13. *odorem eorum sentit atque sua vestigia cauda sua tegit ut per eius vesti-*
14. *gia: venatores eum investigare nequeunt; Sic et salvator noster spiri-*
15. *talis leo de tribu iuda radix iesse filius david missus a superno*
16. *patre cooperuit vestigia deitatis sue carnem assumens ex maria*
17. *virgine: ut etiam diabolus humani generis inimicum misterio in-*
18. *carnationis eius ignarus quasi purum hominem eum conatus sit temptare;*
19. *Cum enim dominus noster in deserto diu ieiunans pro nostris peccatis esuriret ex*
20. *parte carnis: accessit ad eum temptator dicens ei si filius dei es dic*
21. *ut lapides isti panes fiant; Quando autem voluit pro nobis pati:*
22. *traditum a discipulo in mani iudeorum natus est morte vincere quem*
23. *vivum non valuit superare; Sed cum propria virtute a mortuis resurrecu*
24. *set: non solum ab inferis rediit sed etiam captivam duxit captivitatem*
25. *suam demonstrans deitatem; Secunda vero virtus leonis est: quia cum dormit*

29. Kauffmann (1975), 125.

26.   *oculos apertus videtur; Quod de christo dicitur in canticis canticorum; Ego*
27.   *dormio et cor meum vigilat; Dormivit enim caro in cruce*
28.   *moriendo: deitas vero vigilabat cuncta regendo; Unde psal-*
29.   *mista; Ecce non dormitavit neque dormiet; Tertia eiusdem virtus*
30.   *est; Cum leena parit suos catulos: mortuos gignat; et custodet*
31.   *tribus diebus donec veniens pater eorum in faciem eorum exalet vivifi-*
32.   *centur; Sic omnipotens pater dominum nostrum iesum christum filium suum tertia die*
33.   *suscitavit a mortuis dicente iacob; Dormitabit tamquam leo et sicut*
34.   *catulus leonis suscitabitur; Quarta autem virtus eius est: quod nisi Iesus*
35.   *facile irascitur patet enim eius misericordia quod prostratis*
36.   *partit; Captivos homines obvios repedere permittit et non*
37.   *nisi magna fame interimit; Ad cuius exemplum ratio-*
38.   *nabiles homines respicere debent: quia non lesi irascuntur*
39.   *innocentes obprimunt cum noxios christiana lex dimittere*
40.   *iubeat liberos.*

How does this text compare with that of Laud? In Laud, the *Physiologus* B text is followed by verses 1 to 6 of chapter II of the twelfth book of Isidore's *Etymologiae*, introduced by the rubric, *Ethimologia Ysidori*.[30] The Stowe text opens (lines 1–10) with verses 3 and 4 of Isidore, into which the quotation from Proverbs 30, 30, *cum ad nullius pavebit occursum* (line 9), is interjected. Verse 6 of Isidore appears in lines 34–7 (*quod nisi . . . interimit*). Verses 1, 2 and 5 do not appear. Of the *Physiologus* B text, verses 2–5 in Carmody's edition[31] appear in lines 10–16 of Stowe (*Phisici denique . . . deitatis sue*), and verses 10–17 in lines 25–34 (*Secunda vero . . . suscitabitur*). In both cases, however, the B text has undergone considerable modification. The remainder of the Stowe text (lines 17–25 and 37–40) constitutes the earliest appearance known to me of portions of the text printed in Migne and usually ascribed to Hugo de Folieto.[32] The probable date of Stowe, *c.* 1120–30, renders his authorship unlikely since he was born about 1110, and his earliest works date from the 1150s or 1160s.[33]

What conclusions can be drawn from these changes to the text? First, the extracts from Isidore are not appended but are integrated with the *Physiologus* portions. Most strikingly, the chapter opens with the verse from Isidore that deals with the lion's name. This is verse 3 of Isidore's chapter on the lion: verses 1 and 2, which appear in Laud, may have been left out here since they are not specifically on the lion, but deal

30. Mann (1888), 37–8.
31. Carmody (1939), 11.
32. Loc. cit. (n. 27 above).
33. Clark (1982), 63.

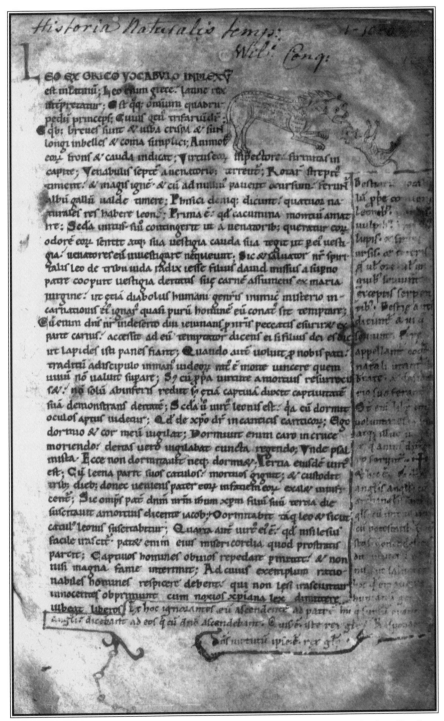

with the definition of a wild beast. Turning to the *Physiologus* extracts, we see that an attempt has been made to renumber the natures of the lion. The *Physiologus* lists three: it covers its tracks with its tail when hunted in the mountains; it sleeps with its eyes open; and its cubs are born dead and revived on the third day. The compiler of Stowe has considered the first of these as two separate natures: liking the mountains (lines 11–12), and covering its tracks (lines 12–14), and thus began by reporting that the lion has four natures (line 10). The scheme went wrong, however. When the next nature, that of sleeping with open eyes, was reached, the scribe was copying directly from the *Physiologus* text and described this too as *secunda virtus* (line 25). His third nature is therefore also the same as in the *Physiologus* (line 29), and the fourth (line 34), that the lion is not easily angered unless wounded, is part of the text added from verse 6 of Isidore. There are thus five natures, numbered *prima, secunda, secunda, tertia,* and *quarta,* the first four from the *Physiologus* and the last from Isidore.[34] The intention of the compiler to synthesize authorities rather than to separate them, as in Laud, is implied not just by the way passages from the *Physiologus* and Isidore were freely combined with new material, and by the omission of rubrication to signal the Isidore material, but also by the suppression of the name *Physiologus.* In line 10, where the corresponding passage in Laud reads, '*Physiologus dicit*' ('*Physiologus* says'), Stowe has '*Phisici denique dicunt*' ('thus scientists say').

It remains to examine how the omissions and insertions described above affect the reading of the text. An indication of what is taking place is given by the renumbering of the lion's three natures. It is important to the structure of the *Physiologus* text that the third of the three natures of the lion parallels Christ's Resurrection on the third day. In the B-text, the closing of the chapter mirrors the opening. The text begins and ends with the quotation from Genesis 49, 9; and the statement of the three natures, immediately following the opening, can be juxtaposed with the statement of Christ's Resurrection on the third day, preceding the closing of the chapter.

The importance of the opening and closing of a text cannot be overemphasized. The quotations from Genesis in the *Physiologus* text establish the lion's relationship with Christ through the typological connection with Judah. They are statements; not about the behaviour or the nature of lions, but about how, through the typological link, lions can signify Christ. In the Stowe text the Genesis quotation

---

34. Paris, B.N. lat. 14429 of the third quarter of the thirteenth century shows evidence of a similar attempt at renumbering. It is similar to Stowe, following the same order for the first six chapters and deviating only slightly as far as the thirteenth. In *leo* the scribe, realizing that four natures was not enough, began by stating that it had five, but again went wrong in numbering them: '*prima*' (*quod cacumina montium amat ire*); '*secunda*' (*sua vestigia cauda sua tegit*); '*secunda*' again (*cum dormit oculos apertos habere*); '*tercia*' (*cum leena parit suos catulos catulos mortuis parit*); and '*quarta*' (*quod nisi Iesus facile irascitur*).

appears only in relation to the reviving of lion cubs on the third day, and the reorganization is such that this now occurs some three-quarters of the way through (lines 33–4). Significantly, the opening passage is concerned with the lion's name (Isidore, v. 3).

The Isidore extracts added to the Laud text appear in full in Stowe, except for the first two verses which do not deal specifically with the lion; and the fifth, which repeats and compresses the purely descriptive parts of the *Physiologus* text. The treatment of the *Physiologus* text itself in Stowe is much freer. As well as the opening quotation, the moralization of the first nature has been entirely changed (lines 16–25). In place of the failure of the angels to recognize Christ on his ascent to heaven, Stowe substitutes the direct confrontation between Christ and the Devil in the wilderness. As I have shown above, such a confrontation has no place in the narrative of *Physiologus*. The two are consistently presented as alternative objects with humanity the subject. While the substitution in Stowe is easier to follow, it seriously compromises the intention of the original text.

The marginal additions by the scribe of the second quire simply reintroduce everything that appears in the Laud text but was not in the main Stowe text. Even this may not be an attempt to revert to the original text, since none of the main text has been erased: it may merely represent the accumulation of as much information as possible.

IMAGES IN LAUD AND STOWE

The drawings in Stowe are less competent than those in Laud but their compositions are usually identical (compare plates 17 and 22). Like the Laud drawings, they precede the chapter to which they refer, although they are invariably indented into the first few lines of text while those in Laud more often than not occupy the whole width of the written space. A consequence of the addition of four new chapters to quire I was the need to find illustrations for the four beasts which did not appear in the model. Two of the four offer interesting evidence of the processes involved. *Crocodrillus* had already been shown in the *hydrus* drawing, and its own miniature is no more than a reworking of this (plate 23 shows both). *Draco* was an entirely new subject, and in the margin alongside the drawing is the vertical impression of a tracing of a dragon in leadpoint, indicating the use of an external model (plate 20). Another significant deviation from Laud, however, is the drawing illustrating *nycticorax*. Laud clearly shows an owl (plate 24), while the Brussels *Physiologus* showed a hawk-like bird (plate 10). Stowe gives both versions (plate 25), which would seem to indicate an interest in the actual appearance of the bird. It is possible that the owl has been added along with the marginal additions to the text, since the drawing is even less assured than in the other miniatures.

SUMMARY

Stowe 1067 is not a high grade production. The membrane is hard and wrinkled, with follicles clearly visible on the hair side. The leaves are irregular in size, particularly in quire II, and the hard-point ruling in quire I moves randomly from recto to verso and from hair side to flesh side (quire II is ruled on the hair side throughout). More obviously, the work of both scribes and of the hand responsible for the drawings is considerably inferior to that in Laud. The book is interesting, however, for reasons closely connected to its unprepossessing appearance. Its physical untidiness and experimental text are two sides of the same coin. The physical and compositional signs of its production provide testimony to influential modifications to the Bestiary taking place in the first third of the twelfth century, the overwhelming evidence that localizes these changes to Canterbury will be examined in greater detail in the next chapter.

PIERPONT MORGAN MS M. 81 AND THE TRANSITIONAL DELUSION

The Worksop Bestiary, New York Pierpont Morgan MS M. 81, stands at the centre of a group of manuscripts that share textual and pictorial features. These manuscripts are:

M. New York, Pierpont Morgan MS M. 81.
P. St Petersburg State Public Library MS Lat. Q.v.V.1.
R. London, British Library MS Royal 12.C.XIX.
A. The Northumberland Bestiary, formerly Alnwick Castle MS 447.

Initially it will be convenient to treat M as representative of the group; differences within the group will be discussed later.

An inscription on f. 1v of M identifies the book as part of a gift of five volumes given by Philippus Apostolorum, a canon of Lincoln Cathedral, to the Augustinian priory of Radeford (i.e., Worksop) in 1187.[35] It was probably produced very shortly before that date, and is, together with P, one of the two earliest survivors from the group. Although the two are closely related, evidence of primacy between them has, in the past, been read either way. I shall show there is strong textual evidence that P preceded M, but in view of my general conclusions about survival rates, it is unlikely that either was the first Bestiary of this type to be produced.

The term 'transitional' was invented by McCulloch to describe manuscripts that

---

35. See chapter four for the full text of the inscription.

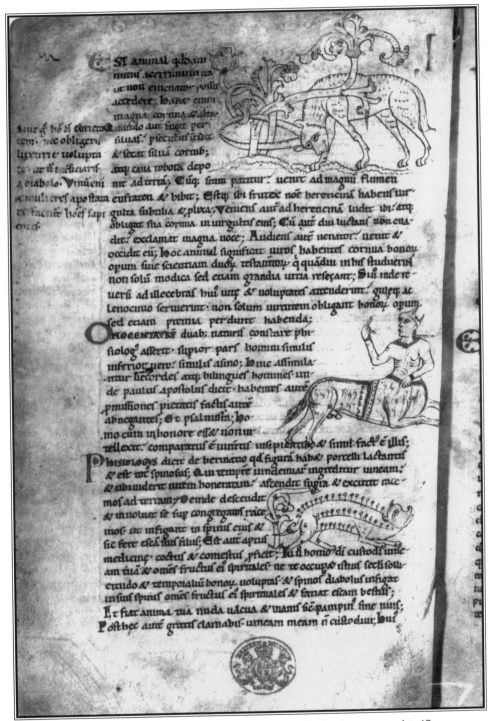

Plate 22. London, BL Stowe 1067, f. 1v autalops, onocentaurus, herinacius, *compare plate 17.*

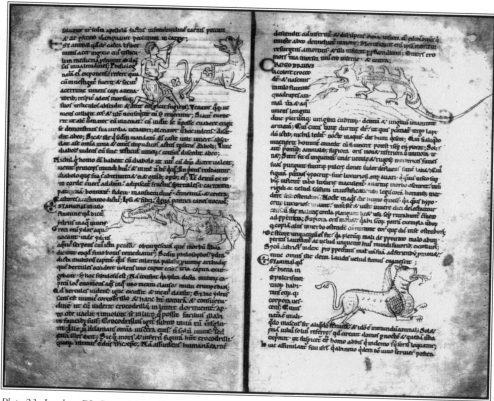

Plate 23. London, BL Stowe 1067, ff. 2v and 3r castor, ydrus, crocodrillus, hiena.

keep the first twenty-four to forty chapters of the First Family, following the order and text of either B-Is (i.e., Laud) or H (i.e., Stowe), and continue with sections taken from Isidore.[36] This grouping is valid as far as it goes, but its failure to distinguish between manuscripts based on Laud and on Stowe limits its usefulness. As well as M, P, R and A, McCulloch included two other books in her transitional group. Cambridge Trinity Coll. MS R.14.9, follows Laud for its first forty-two chapters, omitting the three stones, adding five chapters from Isidore and splitting *elephantus* into two without adding any new textual material. The remaining seventy-seven chapters of the manuscript follow a Second Family sequence.[37] Her other transitional manuscript is

36. McCulloch (1960), 33.
37. Second family chapter orders are extremely variable, especially after the *bestiae*. The closest to Trinity Coll. MS R. 14.9 are found in London, BL MS Harley 3244 and Paris, BN MS Lat. 3630.

Plate 24. Oxford, Bodleian Laud misc. 247, f. 143v nycticorax *miniature. An owl-like bird is shown.*

Queen Mary's Psalter (British Library MS Royal 2.B.VII), which contains no Bestiary text, only a series of marginal illustrations that broadly follow the order of Laud.[38]

A more serious criticism of McCulloch's group concerns her selection of the term 'transitional' as 'the only name that adequately but dully describes these manuscripts which in their appearance are of fine and imaginative execution'.[39]

Her definition, as we have seen, is on purely textual grounds, but by placing the Morgan group in an intermediate position between Stowe (and Laud) and the Second Family books, she implies a linear development in which the Morgan books form the intermediate stage. This paradigm is implicit in the organization of her work (her characterization of the term 'transitional' as 'adequate but dull' reveals the extent of the encoding), but also surfaces occasionally in her text.

The nature of the old *Physiologus* changes sometime during the twelfth century – not beyond recognition because the venerable B-Is (i.e., Laud) chapters can always

---

38. Warner (1912) is a facsimile edition.
39. McCulloch (1960), 33.

Plate 25. London, BL Stowe 1067, f. 8r pellicanus, nycticorax. *Both versions of* nycticorax *are shown, compare plates 10 and 24.*

be perceived within the mass of added material, but the transformation is still very great. Though the analogy should not be pushed too far, the change might be compared to the one taking place in architecture at approximately the same time – from the simpler Romanesque to the more highly developed Gothic.[40]

This is a seductive model of development but it relies on the assumption that the Morgan group preceded the Second Family textually, and this is by no means immediately obvious. The two groups are certainly related in some way: the identity of whole chapters synthesized from a multiplicity of sources rules out the possibility that they were separately derived from common models, but detailed textual examination is needed before it can be decided which of the two recensions came first.

In fact, the evidence of survivals points in the opposite direction. The oldest Second Family survival, London, BL MS Add. 11283, is dateable by minor initials, script and drawings to *c.* 1170, while the Morgan Bestiary must have been produced shortly before its donation in 1187.

McCulloch was not alone in subordinating evidence to the attractions of a model. For T.H. White a constant stimulus of scientific enquiry governed the changes that took place in Bestiary organization: 'the Bestiary . . . began to grow like a living tree'.[41] Commitment to a model based on continuity leads easily to the adoption of such terms as 'transitional' to account for discontinuity and maintain the anthropologizing fiction of a consistent organizing principle. The rupture is concealed under the guise of a passage from one state to another. What is implied is a period of change between two steady states, but the truth is very far from this. The Morgan group represents a condition of remarkable textual stability, extending over a period of some eighty years at a time when other types of Bestiary were subject to considerable reorganization. For a medievalist the term is loaded with extra repercussions of which McCulloch showed her awareness when referring to 'the change . . . taking place in architecture at approximately the same time'. Despite her apologetic presentation of the parallel, there is enough here to invest a population of dispersed events with a unifying spirit, a *Weltanschauung* amounting to a collective consciousness of change, especially in view of the subsequent identification of a contemporary 'transition' in the figurative arts. A demonstration of the persuasiveness of this reassuring model is given in Nigel Morgan's description of R: 'The *series of illustrations* is transitional between the First and Second Families of Bestiaries as classified by M.R. James [my italics].'[42]

40. Ibid., 34.
41. White (1954), 234.
42. Morgan (1982), 60.

TABLE 8. CHAPTER ORDERS OF STOWE 1067 AND MORGAN M. 81

	STOWE 1067	**MORGAN M. 81 (M)**
1.	Leo	Leo
2.	Autalops	Autalops
3.	Onocentaurus	Onocentaurus
4.	Herinatio	Herinatio
5.	Vulpis	Vulpis
6.	Unicornis	Unicornis
7.	Castor	Castor
8.	Ydrus	Hiena
9.	Crocodrillus	Ydrus
10.	Hiena	Hydra
11.	Onager	Sirene
12.	Simius	Caper
13.	Caper	Onager
14.	Pantera	Simia
15.	Draco	Satyrus
16.	Mustela	Pantera
17.	Cervus	Elephans
18.	Elephans	Lupus
19.	Lupus	Canis
20.	Canis	Cervus
21.	Ibex (beast)	Mustela
22.	Lapides Igniferi	Formica
23.	Serra	Ibex (beast)
24.	Caladrius	Lapides Igniferi
25.	Pelicanus	Assida
26.	Noctua (= Nycticorax)	Tigris
27.	Aquila	Pardus
28.	Fenix	Linces
29.	Huppupa	Grifes
30.	Formica	Aper
31.	Syrena	Bonacon
32.	Ibex (bird)	Ursus
33.	Fulica	Manticora
34.	Aspidochelone	Parandrus
35.	Perdix	Eale
36.	Aspis	
37.	Assida	

STOWE 1067	MORGAN M. 81 (M)

38.	*Turtur*
39.	*Salamandra*
40.	*Columba*
41.	*Peredixion*
42.	*Amos propheta*
43.	*Adamas*
44.	*Mermecolion*

STOWE AND THE MORGAN GROUP

The textual dependance of the Morgan group on Stowe rather than Laud is easily seen, both in the chapter orders of the two books and in details of the text itself. Table 8 compares the forty-four chapters of Stowe 1067 with the first thirty-five of the 110 in Pierpont Morgan M. 81. The rearrangement of the early chapters of Stowe is found here too. The first seven chapter headings are identical. Thereafter, as far as 24. *Lapides Igniferi*, the Stowe order is broadly kept, although there are notable omissions and insertions. The omissions, Stowe chapters 9, 15, 23–9 and 36, are all serpents (*draco, aspis*); fish (*crocodrillus, serra, aspido chelone*) or birds (*caladrius, pellicanus, nicticorax, aquila, enix, huppupa, ibex, fulica, perdix*) according to Isidore's classification. The two insertions are also from Isidore. *Satyrus*, the satyr, follows *simia*, as it does in the *Etymologiae*. *Hydra* is inserted after *ydrus* and here again Isidore is followed, although both are found among the serpents in the *Etymologiae*. 25. *Assida* is an interesting case. Alone among the birds, the ostrich has not been moved from the first group of chapters. Looking at the text, we find that it begins, '*Est animal quod dicitur asida* . . . (rather than *Est volatile* . . . as is the rule for birds)'. Furthermore, the ostrich

habet quidem pennas sed non volat sicut caeterae aves; pedes vero habet similes camelo
(has feathers but does not fly like other birds, and has feet like a camel).

Although the ostrich is included among the birds in Isidore, it appears initially under its alternative (Greek) name of *struthio*. Not until the whole Bestiary was reorganized along Isidorean lines (as in James's Second Family books) did the ostrich take its place among the birds. In the meantime, however, the group centred on M represents an attempt to isolate the *bestiae* from a Bestiary like Stowe into the first group of chapters, adding to their number from Isidore only such beasts that had something in common with those already there, and removing to other sections chapters dealing with creatures not classed as *bestiae* in Isidore.

Textual analysis confirms that M was derived from something very like Stowe, and not directly from Laud. The message is not so easy to read, because the M text is greatly expanded, mainly from Isidore, and the Stowe text itself is full of inaccuracies, but the trace is clear enough to leave no doubt. The text of *leo* was used earlier in this chapter to demonstrate the differences between Laud and Stowe. An analysis of the *leo* text of M will take the story a stage further. It is first worth noting that the chapter has been expanded to sixty-six lines (not counting the general introduction to *bestiae* which precedes both text and miniature of *leo*) from the forty lines of Stowe. A line by line analysis would not be especially helpful: I have instead divided the text into blocks to show its composition.

1.	*Leo fortissimus . . . occursum.* (Proverbs 30, 30)	[lines 1–2]
2.	*Leonis vocabulum . . . ignes magis.* (Is. Et. XII, ii, 3–4)	[2–11]
3.	*Leo nature sue iii . . . consortium.* (Ambr. Hex. vi. 14)	[11–14]
4.	*Phisici dicunt . . . in celis.* (Phys. I, 2–5)	[15–23]
5.	*donec missus . . . perierat.* (Phys. I, 7)	[23–5]
6.	*Et hoc ignorans . . . temptare.* (cf. Stowe 17–18)	[26–8]
7.	*Etiam hoc . . . habere viderit.* (Phys. I, 8–10)	[28–32]
8.	*Sic et dominus . . . vigilabat.* (Phys. I, 12)	[32–4]
9.	*Sicut dicitur . . . vigilat.* (Phys. I, 11)	[34–5]
10.	*Et in psalmo . . . suscitabitur.* (Phys. I, 13–17)	[36–44]
11.	*Circa hominem . . . magna perimunt.* (Is. Et. XII, ii, 6)	[44–53]
12.	*Pariter omnes . . . probat dentium.* (Sol. 27, 13–15)	[53–60]
13.	*Leo eger . . . servari.* (Ambr. Hex. VI, 26)	[61–2]
14.	*Leo gallum . . . veretur.* (Ambr. Hex. VI, 26)	[62]
15.	*Leo quidem . . . occiditur.* (Ambr. Hex. VI, 37)	[63–4]
16.	*Adversi coeunt . . . leene.* (Sol. 27, 16)	[65–6]

References to *Physiologus*, Isidore, the *Hexaemeron* of Ambrose, and the *Collectanea* of Solinus are to the editions given in the bibliography.

The passage at (6) appeared, as far as I could discover, for the first time in Stowe (see above). It is certainly not found in Laud, nor in any of the sources used to augment the *Physiologus* text. It will be remembered that I concluded, in view of the internal evidence of Stowe's production, that it may well have been composed by the compiler of the book. This is the strongest purely textual evidence for Ms reliance on the Stowe recension, but several other points provide circumstantial confirmation. Like the main text of Stowe, M omits *Phys.* I, 1 and I, 6 (although it includes *Phys.* I, 7–9, which Stowe omits in the main text). Furthermore, M includes the textual variation *cacumina montium amat ire*, following Stowe, where Laud has *ambulat in montibus* (*Phys.* I, 2). This variation, however, also occurs in Brussels, Bibl. Roy. MS 10074. The additions from

Isidore are also closer to Stowe than to Laud. In Laud, the whole of *Etymologiae*, XII, II, 1–6 was added after the *Physiologus* text. The original scribe of Stowe omitted verses 1, 2 and 5, but the first two were added in the margin by the scribe of quire II (plate 21). The compiler of M used verses 1–2 as an introduction to the *bestiae*, before the *leo* miniature, and, as in Stowe, left out verse 5 altogether.[43]

The *Physiologus* still forms the central core of the chapter, and is the major source in terms of lines, but it accounts for less than half of the text (twenty-seven lines out of sixty-six). Like Laud and the *Physiologus* B text, M opens with a striking Old Testament quotation, but the two quotations are very different in implication.

B text

Etenim Iacob, benedicens filium suum Iudam ait: Catulus leonis Iudas, filius de germine meo, quis suscitabit eum (Gen. 49, 9)

(For Jacob, blessing his son Judah, said: Judah is a lion's whelp, the son of my seed, who will rouse him?)

Morgan

Leo fortissimus bestiarum ad nullius pavebit occursum (Proverbs 30, 30)

(The lion is the strongest of the beasts, afraid of nothing it meets).

The former prepares for a typological comparison of Christ with Judah using the lion metaphorically. The latter is a statement about lions,[44] and is followed in M by further statements of the same type from Isidore and Ambrose, describing the etymology of their name, their disposition (short ones with curly manes are peaceful, tall ones with straight manes ferocious), their fears (rumbling wheels and fire), and their mating habits (monogamous). Not until we reach line 15 is the *Physiologus* material introduced, opening with '*Physici dicunt leonem tres principales naturas habere*' (rather than '*Physiologus dicit . . .*', again following Stowe rather than Laud), and proceeding with the story of the lion covering its tracks when hunted. It is natural therefore to read this too as zoological rather than theological material. No moralization appears until line 21, and in the light of what has gone before, it comes as something of a surprise to the modern reader.

43. This is the section dealing with the three natures of the lion, which Isidore originally took from the *Physiologus*.
44. Read in the context of Prov. 30, the statement forms part of Congregantus's (Agar's) aphoristic personal philosophy. It places the lion alongside the cock *succinctus lumbos* (literally, with girded loins), the ram and the king who cannot be resisted, as four things which move majestically. It may, of course, be suspected that any positive statement about a king was readable by the compiler of M as a statement about God, but two observations may dispel this suspicion. First, the reference to the king in Proverbs was not repeated in M. In fact the same passage appeared in Rhabanus Maurus, VIII, 1, but only after the metaphorical relationship between Christ and lions was well established, not at the beginning of the text and again without mention of the irresistible king. Second, a close contextual reading is almost certainly ruled out by the explicit sexuality of the imagery.

The *Physiologus* text forms the central block of the chapter. The last third, taken from Isidore, Solinus and Ambrose goes a long way towards negating what remains of a narrative already corrupted from Stowe, by returning to the anecdotal zoology of the opening passages.

VARIATIONS WITHIN THE MORGAN GROUP

Of the four manuscripts treated as a unity above, only M and R are truly sisters, and the identity between these two is so close that R must be a direct copy of M. Briefly, not only do the two coincide in every word of text, and in the compositions of their miniatures, they are also ruled with the same number of lines per page (twenty-four), and for the first ninety-seven leaves of Bestiary text had exactly the same words on every page, and almost on every line.[45] The similarity does not extend to the quiring, so presumably M had been bound when the copying took place.

The areas where differences of content are to be found between members of the Morgan group are in the prefatory material included at the start of each Bestiary, in textual variations within the chapters themselves, and in details of the miniatures. The order of the 108 chapters is the same in every case.

PREFATORY MATERIAL

Table 9 below gives the prefatory material found in M.

TABLE 9. PREFATORY MATERIAL IN MORGAN M. 81

Section	Folios	Text	Source
	2r	**De forma mundi**	
I		*Mundus dicitur . . .*	Hon. Aug. I, 2
		De creatione mundi	
II		*Creatio mundi quinque . . . facio omnia*	Hon. Aug. I, 2
	2v	**De etatibus mundi**	
III		*Prima etas in exordio . . . appellavit adam*	Is. Et. V, 39, 1
IV		*Prima etas est ab adam . . . inspicitur*	Is. Et. V, 38, 5–6
V	3r–4r	*Igitur perfecti sunt . . . non erubescebant*	Gen. 2, 1–25
VI	4v	*Homo dictus . . . homo ab humo*	Is. Et. XI, 1, 4

45. The identity extends in M from the beginning of f. 2 to the end of f. 96r, corresponding to f. 1 to f. 79r in R. The discrepancy in the number of leaves is explained by leaves lost from both books: M lacks only two (between f. 66 and f. 67), while R lacks eighteen.

Section	Folios	Text	Source
VII		*Adam sicut beatus . . . quod est ve*	Is. Et.VII, 6, 4–6
VIII		*Adam primus . . . assumptus est rediit*	Hon. Aug. III

LEAF LOST

Section	Folios	Text	Source
IX	5r	*Nam veteres . . . caprarum et ovium*	Is. Et. XII, 1, 6–8
		De avibus	
X	5r–6r	*Unum autem nomen . . . quid nominarentur*	Is. Et. XII, 7, 1–9
		Sermo qualiter peccator deo placere valet	
XI	6v–7v	*Quocienscumque peccator . . . suam amisit*	see text
XII	7v	*Ergo agite . . . desit in nobis*	see text
	8r	**Incipit liber de naturis bestiarum . . .**	
		Bestiarum vocabulum . . . eo feruntur	Is. Et. XII, 2, 1–2
		De naturis leonum	
	8v	*Leo fortissimus*	see above

References to Honorius Augustodunensis, *De imagine mundi* (Hon. Aug.), and to Isidore, *Etymologiae* (Is. Et.) are to the editions given in the bibliography. Latin texts in bold are rubrics.

The first four leaves of M form a regular quire. Quire II is of four but wants the first leaf. Thereafter, the Bestiary is quired mainly in eights. It is plain from this, and from the text, that a leaf has been lost after f. 4v. This is indicated by the splitting of the table. It is important to try to reconstruct the content of this lost leaf but unfortunately R, which is otherwise identical to M, has lost not only this leaf but also the previous one, corresponding to f. 4 in M. The reconstruction must therefore be based on what remains, and is to that extent somewhat speculative.

Folio 4v, which precedes the lost leaf, ends with a complete passage from Honorius Augustodunensis. The last five words are squeezed onto an extra half-line below the ruling, indicating a pressing need to keep the next recto free of text. It could be argued, of course, that text from a different source was to follow, and that the scribe was eager to keep that separate. This kind of consideration, however, does not seem to have been particularly important to the compiler of M: we find the rubric for the sermon beginning '*Quocienscumque peccator . . .*' at the foot of f. 6r, while the relevant text starts at the head of the next page.

Folio 5r, which follows the lost leaf, begins midway through Isidore's introduction to Book XII of the *Etymologiae*, which justifies Isidore's own approach by the precedent of Adam, who named the animals according to their natures. Although f. 5r begins with a capital letter, Isidore is here part way through an argument about the usage of the word *pecus*, a herd. It is inconceivable that the text was meant to start at this point. If we go back to the beginning of this passage in Isidore, a passage which occurs in the prefaces to P and A, and regularly in Second Family Bestiaries, we find that 142 words are missing, not counting any rubrication. Now, f. 5r of M, comprising material entirely taken from Isidore and presumably having the same average word length as the missing passage, contains 150 words, and it is fair to assume from this that the missing text occupied a single side of the lost leaf. There is thus a strong likelihood that the recto of this leaf bore a full-page miniature of Adam naming the animals, similar to that which precedes the same text in P (plate 26). The presence of such a miniature would provide an explanation for the removal of a leaf from a book which is otherwise remarkably well preserved.[46]

The core of the preface is chapter 2 of Genesis, which was transcribed in its entirety, and around which the passages from Isidore and Honorius function as glosses, interpreting it as the basis of the encyclopedic approach that informs the body of the Bestiary text. Genesis 2 opens with an account of God resting on the seventh day, the work of creation finished. This signals an internal analepsis, beginning at verse 4: 'Iste sunt generationes celi et terra . . .', wherein the entire narrative of Genesis 1 is rewritten from a different viewpoint.[47] More precisely, the second chapter stands in relation to the first as a paralipsis, providing material of a kind systematically omitted from the earlier narrative. Chapter 1 gains much of its poetic force from its insistence on the power of speech as the agent of creation. In its repeated structure, every creative act is effected by the words Dixit Deus (God said). Chapter 2, in contrast, describes a mechanism of creation couched in anthropocentric terms: God is a gardener, making plants grow by watering them (vv. 5–6); or a sculptor, making man from dust (v. 7). Moreover, chapter 2 is concerned with names: most strikingly perhaps, with proper names, of which there are none in chapter 1, but for our purposes more importantly with the names of creatures. Here, however, the act of naming is not an act of creation, and is not performed by God but by Adam (Adam himself is named for the first time in v. 19, but not by God).

The texts from Honorius (I and II), and Isidore (III and IV), operate directly on the Genesis material. Section I deals with the name of the world, and II and III with its creation. In IV, the six days of creation are related to the six ages of world history, between Adam and the present. Next comes Genesis 2, which is followed by the Isidorean passage (VI) opening 'Homo dictus quia ex humo . . .': this is a gloss on Genesis 2, 7: 'Formavit igitur Dominus Deus hominem de limo terrae . . .'. The passages at VII & VIII concern the names of Adam and Eve, and their history. The texts before and after Genesis 2 can thus be seen to mirror one another closely in their treatment of the world and of man.

---

46. Apart from this leaf, M lacks only a single bifolium, which comes from the middle of quire X and could therefore be the result of normal wear and tear.

47. Genette (1986), 48–53.

In the original state of the book the long passage on Adam naming the animals (IX) was probably, as we saw, preceded by a miniature of the same subject. This passage is, of course, a gloss on Genesis 2, 19–20, as indeed is the whole of Book XII of the *Etymologiae*, which it introduces.

The last two texts in the preface (XI and XII) sit uneasily with the other material. They form a sermon on the spiritual healing of a sick soul, as a prerequisite of entry to the kingdom of heaven. I have not been able to trace an earlier example of their occurence, or to identify their author. They may indeed be a single text, rather than two: the opening of XII with '*ergo agite nunc fratres . . .*' (therefore live now brothers . . .) seems an unlikely beginning for any text, and acts as a corollary to the preceding argument. On the other hand, this passage is omitted in Bestiaries outside the Morgan group where XI appears,[48] and there is a telling change of tone. Whereas XI presents a general case, offering advice to a typical sinner, XII is addressed directly to a group of *fratres*, of which the author is a member:

Ergo agite nunc fratres aggrediamur iter vite revertamur ad civitatem celestem in qua scripti sumus et cives decreti
(Therefore live, brothers, so that we approach the journey of life as a return to the heavenly city where we are inscribed as citizens).

XII reads like an addition to XI, supplied to fill a specific purpose. It is comparatively short: only nineteen lines compared with the fifty-two of the main *Quocienscumque . . .* text. In this case, since the circumstances of the book's donation are known, the purpose is for once not merely a matter of speculation. I shall return to this question in chapter five.

Both James and White were at a loss to provide a convincing explanation for the inclusion of the *Quocienscumque . . .* sermon in the Bestiary.[49] This may be because both were principally concerned with the Second Family text of Cambridge University Library MS Ii. 4. 26, a book showing little trace in its organization of the *Physiologus* structure. Although M is organized along Isidorean lines for much of its content, there is still enough of *Physiologus* in the opening chapters for the meaning to remain legible. As we saw in chapter two, the B text operates to provide a guide to salvation with the aid of the spirit against the snares of the flesh, and this is just the message that the theorising of *Quocienscumque . . .* and the exhortation of the *Ergo agite nunc fratres . .* passage work to press home.

48. For a translation of the *Quocienscumque . . .* passage, see White (1954), 68–70.
49. James (1928), 14; White (1954), 68 n. 1.

The other two Bestiaries in the Morgan group, P and A, both begin with the text of the first two chapters of Genesis, although P now lacks the first leaf of quire I. Thereafter, both repeat texts VI to XI in the same order as M, only A repeating XII too.

The prefatory material in P occupies the whole of quire I, whose miniatures seemed, to Muratova, to be by a different hand from those in the rest of the Bestiary. From this she has concluded that the first quire is an addition to the manuscript and that this explains the origin of the addition of chapters from Genesis to the text.[50] One difficulty with this theory is that only the first four of the miniatures in the preface quire are stylistically different from those in the rest of the Bestiary. The fifth, showing Adam naming the animals (f. 5r) belongs with those in the body of the book (plate 26). Another problem is that the stylistic difference, while marked, does not necessarily imply a significantly different date of production. Morgan has pointed out that the artist of the creation scenes in the preface 'uses paint rather than line for his drapery systems',[51] but this in itself is no guarantee that the two artists were not working around the same time. Muratova's other point, that the preface occupies a quire on its own, also applies in substance to M, where it occupies the first two quires.

The only difference in the prefatory textual material between M and R on the one hand and P and A on the other, is the replacement in the latter pair of Genesis 1 for the extracts from Isidore and Honorius on the world and its creation and history. Significantly, the text of Genesis 1 is interrupted in both P and A by illustrative miniatures. It would appear that these general similarities between the prefaces of P and A imply that these two stand together in the same way as M and R. That this is not the case will become clear after a closer examination of the prefatory miniatures, and the main text and illustrations. In fact, so far as this group of four Bestiaries is concerned, P will be seen to stand on its own.

In both P and A, the text of Genesis 1 is interrupted by miniatures which precede the narrative of each day of creation. Table 10 shows the arrangement in both books. In the table, miniatures are indicated by upper case, and text by lower case characters.

TABLE 10. PREFACES OF ST PETERSBURG and NORTHUMBERLAND BESTIARIES

ST PETERSBURG (P)	**NORTHUMBERLAND (A)**
	f. 1v CREATION OF ANGELS
	/FALL OF REBEL ANGELS

---

50. Muratova (1984), 55.
51. Morgan (1982), 57.

1. Bourges (Cher) Cathèdrale Saint-Étienne, detail of Resurrection window. The Resurrection of Christ surrounded by two Old Testament types and two Bestiary subjects: the pelican, reviving her dead chicks, and the lion, breathing life into his cubs.

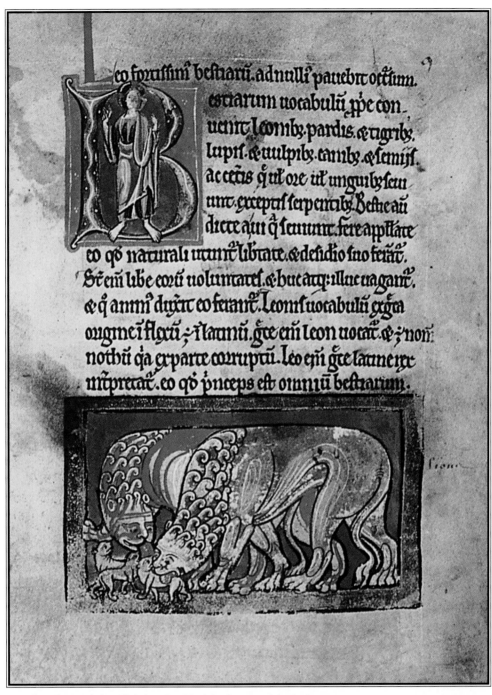

eo fortissimu bestiarum. ad nulliꝰ pauebit occursum. estiarum uocabulū ꝓꝑe conuenit leonibꝫ. pardis. & tigribꝫ. lupis. & uulpibꝫ. canibꝫ. & simiis. ac ceteris q̈ uel ore uel unguibꝫ seuiunt. exceptis serpentibꝫ. Bestie aū dicte aūt q̈ seuiunt. fere appellate eo qꝺ naturali utuntur libertate. & desiderio suo ferant̄. St eī libe eorū uoluntates. & huc atꝙ illuc uagant̄. & q̈ animꝰ duxerit eo ferunt̄. Leonis uocabulū grc̄ā originei flexū; i latinū. grc̄e eī leon uocat̄. & ꝫ nomꝭ nothū q̈a ex parte corruptū. Leo eī grc̄e latine īꝓ īꝑpretat̄. eo qꝺ ꝑnceps est omnīū bestiarum.

2. *St Petersburg, Saltykov-Shchedrin Q.v.V.1, f. 9r. Opening of the Bestiary text.*

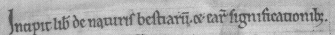

Incipit lib de naturis bestiaru & car significationib;.

Bestiarum uocabulum
pprie conuenit leonib;
pardis & tigrib;. lupis
& uulpib;. canib;. & simi
is. vrsib;. & ceteris que vt'
oreu'unguib; seuuunt ex
ceptis serpentib;. Bestie
autem dicte a ui qua se
uiunt. fere appellate
eo quod naturali utan
tur libertate. & desiderio suo ferant. Sunt
enim libere eaz uoluntates & huc atq; il
luc uagantur. Et quo animus duxerit;
eo feruntur . De naturis leonum.

3. New York, Pierpont Morgan MS M. 81, f. 8r. Opening of the Bestiary text.

4. St Petersburg, Saltykov-Shchedrin Q.v.V.1, f. 20v simia.

5. New York, Pierpont Morgan MS M. 81, f. 19v simia. *The hunter's arrow has been omitted.*

6. Westminster Abbey 22, f. 1v. The monstrous races.

7. *Oxford, St John's College 61, f. 103v* lapides igniferi *and the painted* ex-libris *of Holy Trinity, York.*

Ripes uocatur: quod sit animal pen
natum & quadrupes. hoc genus fera
rum in hiperboreis nascitur locis uel monti
bz. omni parte posteriori corporis leoni: alis
& facie aquilis simile. equis uehementer in
festum. nam & homines uisos discerpit.

St animal quod dr elephans in quo
non est concupiscencia coitus. Elephã

8. Oxford, Bodleian Bodley 764, f. 12r elephantus, *showing the arms of marcher lords on the shields and banner.*

9. Oxford, St John's College 61, f. 1v. Creation scenes.

ST PETERSBURG (P)

FIRST LEAF LOST

f. 1r CREATION OF PLANTS
Gen. 1, 9–13
f. 1v ” ctd.
CREATION OF SUN, MOON
& STARS
Gen. 1, 14–19
f. 2r ” ctd.
CREATION OF FISH & BIRDS
f. 2v Gen. 1, 20–23

CREATION OF ANIMALS &
ADAM & EVE
f. 3r Gen. 1, 24–31

NORTHUMBERLAND (A)
Gen. 1, 1–5
f. 2r CREATION OF FIRMAMENT
Gen. 1, 6–8
CREATION OF PLANTS
f. 2v Gen. 1, 9–13

CREATION OF SUN, MOON
& STARS
f. 3r Gen. 1, 14–19

CREATION OF FISH & BIRDS
Gen. 1, 20–3

f. 3v ” ctd.
CREATION OF ANIMALS,
EVE
Gen 1, 24–31
f. 4r ” ctd.
CHRIST IN MAJESTY

KEY

UPPER CASE: Miniatures.

lower case: Text.

Genesis 1, 9–13 describes the third day; the creation of the land and sea, and of plants. In both P and A, the creation of plants is shown, and the two compositions are extremely similar (plates 27 and 28). The treatment of the miniatures preceding Genesis 1, 24–31, on the other hand, differs significantly between the two manuscripts. Both show a group of animals in registers on the left, Christ as creator in the centre, and Adam and Eve on the right. In A (plate 29) the two humans stand side by side, holding hands. Christ addresses them while gesturing towards the animals. P, in contrast shows the creation of Eve from Adam's side, with the animals looking on (plate 30). The animals illustrated are very different in the two cases, and this is also true of the two miniatures showing the creation of fishes and birds. Finally, the minature of Christ in Majesty between four angels appears in A but not in P (plate 31). In general, while the two books are similar in including the text of Genesis 1 broken up by miniatures, the miniature cycles are so different that no connection at the production stage can be inferred.

Plate 26. St Petersburg, Saltykov-Shchedrin Q.v.V.1, f. 5r Adam naming the animals.

TEXTUAL VARIATIONS

The textual identity between M and R has already been noted. For the other two Bestiaries in the group, it is fair to say that A follows M and R closely, while P contains significant differences. Once again, it will prove valuable to compare the chapters on *leo* in P and M. The breakdown of P given below may be compared with that of M given above.

1.	*Leo fortissimus . . . occursum.*	[as M.1]
2.	*Bestiarum vocabulum . . . eo ferantur.* (Is. Et. XII, ii, 1–2)	[prefatory in M]
3.	*Leonis vocabulum . . . ignes magis.*	[as M.2]
4.	*Leo nature sue iii . . . consortium.*	[as M.3]
5.	*Phisici dicunt . . . in celis.*	[as M.4]
6.	*Donec missus . . . perierat.*	[as M.5]
7.	*Et hoc ignorans . . . temptare.*	[as M.6]
8.	*Etiam hoc . . . habere viderit.*	[as M.7]
9.	*Sic et dominus . . . vigilabat.*	[as M.8]
10.	*Sicut dicitur . . . vigilat.*	[as M.9]
11.	*Et in psalmo . . . suscitabitur.*	[as M.10]
12.	*Circa hominem . . . fame perimunt.*	[as M.11]
13.	*Pariter omnis . . . probat dentium.* (Sol. 27, 13–15)	[as M.12]
14.	*Adversi coeunt . . . leene.* (Sol. 27, 16)	[as M.16]
15.	*Fetu primo . . . in eternum.* (Sol. 27, 17)	[not in M]
16.	*Leo cibum . . . deficiantur.* (Amb. Hex. VI, 14)	[not in M]
17.	*Leo eger . . . sanari.*	[as M.13]
18.	*Leo gallum . . . veretur.*	[as M.14]
19.	*eo quidem . . . occiditur.*	[as M.15]
20.	*Leontophones . . . pedum usibus.* (Sol. 20)	[not in M]

Several points emerge from this analysis. First, it is not possible to establish the textual precedence of either P or M on the basis of comparisons with Stowe, since the Stowe text is itself so corrupt. In shared passages, P and M are always closer to each other than to Stowe. Next, P includes a great deal of material not found in M, but M contains nothing not found in P. From the point of view of production, this makes it extremely likely that M copied P, rather than the reverse. An examination of the long passage interpolated from Solinus (sections 13–16 in P) will make this clear. P quotes continuously a passage which is also continuous in Solinus. In the course of this copying, an error in punctuation led to a serious misreading. Solinus reads:

aversi coeunt (leones): nec hi tantum sed et lynces et cameli et elephanti et rhinocerotes et tigrides. leaenae fetu primo catulos quinque edunt . . .

Plate 27. St Petersburg, Saltykov-Shchedrin Q.v.V.1, f. 1r. The creation of plants.

Plate 28. Northumberland Bestiary, f. 2r. The creation of the firmament and creation of plants.

119

Plate 29. Northumberland Bestiary, f. 3v. The creation of the animals and God blessing Adam and Eve.

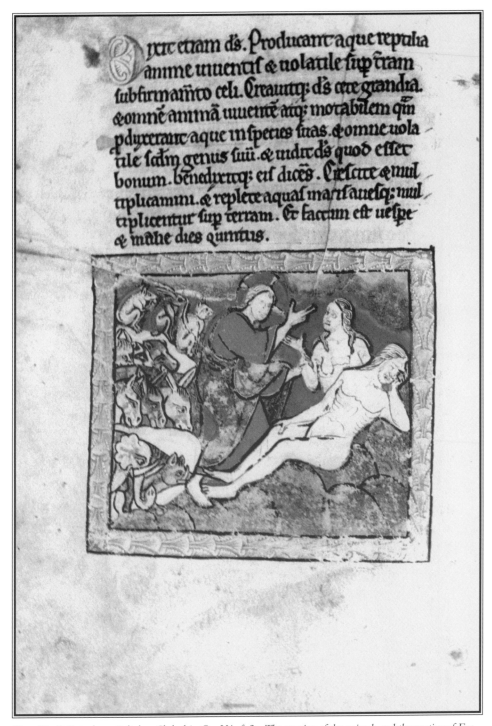

Plate 30. St Petersburg, Saltykov-Shchedrin Q.v.V.1, f. 2v. The creation of the animals and the creation of Eve.

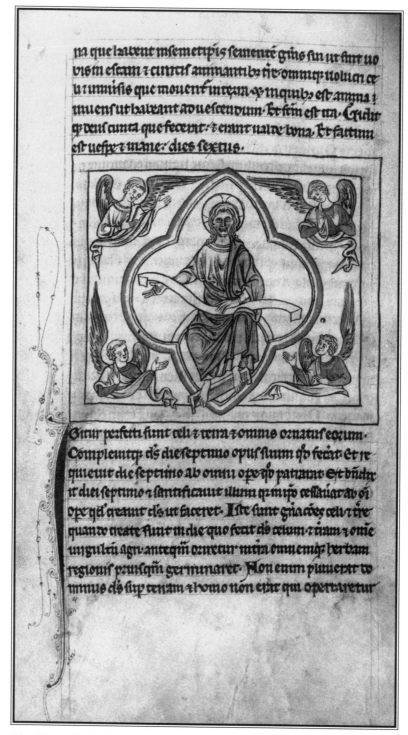

Plate 31. Northumberland Bestiary, f. 4r. Christ in majesty.

(lions copulate backwards, and not only lions but also lynxes and camels and elephants and rhinoceroses and tigers. Lionesses produce five cubs in their first pregnancy . . .).

In P, however, we read:

adversi coeunt (leones). Nec hi tamen sed et linces et cameli et elephanti et rinocerontes et
tygrides et leene. Fetu primo catulos quinque educant . . .
(lions copulate backwards, and not only lions but also lynxes and camels and elephants and rhinoceroses and tigers and lionesses. They raise five cubs in the first pregnancy . . .).

M not only repeats the error, it also alters the list of animals, omitting lynxes and rhinoceroses, and adding bears:

adversi coeunt leones. Nec hi tantum sed et cameli, ursi et elephanti, tigrides et leene.

Moreover, the passage beginning *Fetu primo* . . . (15 in P) is omitted from M, and what was a continuous passage in both Solinus and P has been split into two (P, sections 13–16: M, sections 12 and 16). This means, in effect, that while M could have been produced from P without the aid of Solinus (or any of the other sources), the reverse is not the case.

The opening leaves of the main Bestiary text of P and M are shown in colour plates 2 and 3. At first glance the two are practically identical, but an examination of the two texts in conjunction with the textual analyses of the two *leo* chapters given above, discloses an important difference. The opening quotation in P announces the start of a chapter on lions (line 1). This is followed, however, by material from Isidore's introduction to the section on *bestiae* in the *Etymologiae* (lines 2 to 10). Isidorean text specific to lions begins again part way along line 10, is interrupted by the lion miniature at the foot of the page, and continues on the verso. The text on this leaf is therefore a mixture of statements about lions in particular and wild beasts in general, and does not form a coherent block.

M, in contrast, opens with an incipit making clear that the text to follow is about *bestiae* (line 1). All the main text is from Isidore's introduction to *bestiae*, and the lion miniature, along with the *leo* text that begins on the verso, is introduced by a rubric. The corresponding leaves in R and A follow M rather than P (see plates 32 and 33).

Apart from minor textual variations, the only other notable type of deviation in the main Bestiary text between P on the one hand, and M, R and A on the other concerns material added from the *Cosmographia* of Bernardus Silvestris.[52] M, R and A all include verses on animals taken from the *Cosmographia* and added to the chapters on *canis* and *mustela*. No such added material is found in P.

MINIATURES

For the main body of miniatures shared by all four books, the animal illustrations – no two cycles can be attributed to the same workshop. Considerations of dating would, in any case, rule out this possibility except in the case of P and M. Most of the miniatures in these two Bestiaries are very close in composition but since I have been unable to examine P, it is not possible to make judgments about execution. Morgan, however, has stated that 'the two manuscripts are somewhat different . . . in their approach to composition and colour and in their handling of forms'.[53]

The lion miniatures in the four books (colour plates 2 and 3, plates 32 and 33) can be used to demonstrate the relationship between the illustration cycles. Here, as elsewhere, M is compositionally close to P, and A to R. One case where M and P show differences of detail provides corroborative evidence for the precedence of the latter. In the miniature illustrating *simia*, P shows the ape bearing its two young, pursued by a hunter who has just released an arrow. The bowstring is vibrating, and the arrow is lodged in the adult ape's arm. M has a practically identical composition but the arrow is nowhere to be seen (colour plates 4 and 5). Its omission could well be due to an error in copying.

SUMMARY

These four books appear to form an extremely coherent group. The miniatures in M are compositionally so close to P as to indicate direct copying. M and R are sister manuscripts of a type found only rarely, while A shares the Bestiary text of M and R, with miniatures compositionally identical to the latter.

SECOND FAMILY BESTIARIES

M.R. James's pioneering and invaluable census of forty-one Bestiaries,[54] involving their grouping into four textual families has proved so influential that it is unlikely to pass

---

52. Bernardus Silvestris, 109–10.
53. Morgan (1982), 57.
54. James (1928).

Plate 32. London, BL Royal 12.C.XIX, f. 6r. Opening of the Bestiary text.

Plate 33. Northumberland Bestiary, f. 8r. Opening of the Bestiary text.

wholly out of general use in the foreseeable future.[55] It is certainly no part of my approach to revise this structure, rather have I been at pains to unlace a residue of rigidity which has characterized much subsequent writing on Bestiaries, a legacy which James in no way intended to bequeath. The problems caused by McCulloch's adoption and subsequent revision of the First Family, and examined above, stem from an assumption that James's classification was much more clear-cut than he intended. A careful reading of his entries on individual Bestiaries makes it clear that, faced with so many texts, he only analyzed a handful in any great detail, and for the rest confined himself to looking at such keys to organization as the number of chapters, the subjects of the first two chapters, the opening of the first chapter and the main textual divisions.

Within his text, too, James acknowledged that the Bestiaries in his groupings exhibited varying degrees of resemblance: 'a few other copies (of First Family Bestiaries) show a text either quite or nearly identical with that of *Laud*'.[56] And again 'in fact, this Second Family shows all sorts of irregularities, which I am quite unable to reduce to order'.[57]

McCulloch, in contrast, was concerned to sustain the idea of an ordered pattern of family relationships, even where she was unable to identify it: 'an attempt has been made to group the following illustrated manuscripts of the Second Family according to iconographic resemblances, but since for a few of them written descriptions alone had to be relied upon, these groupings should not be judged as definitive'.[58]

She not only assumed that some order was there to be found but that it would be manifest in both text and miniatures. We have already seen, in the case of Laud and Stowe where similar drawings illustrate very different texts, and in the Morgan group where a complex network of textual and illustrative relationships subsists, that such an assumption cannot be justified. A major concern of the present work is to show that variations in content, particularly among late twelfth and thirteenth-century luxury Bestiaries, were often dictated by the needs of users and cannot simply be tied to considerations of textual recension, along with the associated assumption that the producers of Bestiaries simply copied whatever models they were familiar with, or happened to have to hand.

For the Second Family, there is a high degree of uniformity in the general structure of the main text. It would certainly be possible to subject the twenty-five or so

---

55. James's four families together with McCulloch's modifications form the basis of practically all subsequent art historical writing on Bestiary structure. Among the most recent examples are Morgan (1982), Muratova (1984, I and II), Sandler (1985) and Morgan (1988).
56. James (1928), 9.
57. Ibid., 14.
58. McCulloch (1960), 36.

surviving Second Family English Bestiaries to the kind of textual and illustrative analysis already undertaken for the Bestiaries of the Morgan group,[59] but such an analysis would be of little value in the present context, in view of the shortage of evidence of consumption available for most of these books. Instead I shall concentrate on describing a representative Second Family structure, and on relating this to Isidore's *Etymologiae* and to Bestiaries described previously, and attempt in chapter five to relate deviations from this artificial norm to known circumstances of use.

Book XII of Isidore's *Etymologiae* is divided into eight sections, each dealing with a division of the animal world. In general structure, the Bestiaries of the Second Family are very similar. Table 11 compares the structures of Book XII and London, BL MS Add. 11283, the earliest surviving Second Family book. Of the twelve sections in Add. 11283, seven correspond to sections in the *Etymologiae*: only Isidore's *minutis volatilibus* are omitted. Within the sections too, the general structure is often the same. Both tend to open with an introductory passage describing the etymologies proper to creatures within the division, to follow with a series of chapters on individual animals, and to close with general statements about their natures. In the case of the *vermes*, or worms, the entire section in Add. 11283 copies Isidore XII, 5. Even where the copying is not so slavish, the structure tends to be retained: the section on serpents begins with part of Isidore's introduction (plate 34), then devotes chapters to seventeen serpents (compared with Isidore's thirty), and closes with a series of generalizations synthesized from Isidore, Ambrose and the *Physiologus*.

After the sections on animals, Add. 11283 adds passages from Isidore on trees, on the nature of life and parts of the body, on the ages of man and the *Physiologus* chapter on the fire-stones. The sermon *Quocienscumque . . . suam amisit*, first found among the prefatory matter in the Morgan group, is placed between the last of the *bestiae* (*canis*) and the opening of the *pecora et iumenta*, or domestic beasts, a place it is to occupy regularly in those Second Family books where it appears.[60]

The chief difference between the general structures of Isidore, XII and Add. 11283 lies in the order in which the sections are arranged. While Isidore, as I have shown above, took as his organizing principle the food laws of Leviticus and Deuteronomy, Add. 11283 still retains traces of the *Physiologus* structure in that it opens with *bestiae* and promotes the *aves*, second most numerous of the *Physiologus* chapters, to fourth place, otherwise following the order of Isidore.

---

59. A project initiated in James (1928), 7–25.

60. It appears in the majority of Second Family books, but not in London, BL MS Harley 3244 and Cambridge, Gonv. & Caius Coll. MS 109, which form a pair; nor in Oxford, Bodleian Library MS Douce 88(I), Cambridge, Corpus Christi Coll. MS 53, New York, Pierpoint Morgan Library, MS 890, or Copenhagen, Royal Library Gl. kgl. S.1633, which are all late thirteenth or fourteenth-century books; nor in Cambridge, Gonville & Caius Coll. MS 384, which is otherwise an anomolous copy.

TABLE 11. ORGANIZATION OF *ETYMOLOGIAE* XII AND ADD. 11283

ETYMOLOGIAE XII	**ADD. 11283**
1. ***De Pecoribus et Iumentis***	1. *Leo fortissimus . . . occursum.*
Omnibus animantibus . . . et ovium.	*Bestiarum vocabulum . . . eo feruntur.*
5 chapters (*Pecora et Iumenta*)	30 chapters (*Bestiae*)
Industria quippe . . . dux gregis	
2. **De Bestiis**	2. *Quocienscumque . . . amisit.*
Bestiarum vocabulum . . . eo feruntur.	
26 chapters (*Bestiae*)	
3. **De Minutis Animantibus**	3. *Omnibus animantibus . . . et ovium.*
10 chapters (*Minutes Animantes*)	12 chapters (*Pecora et Iumenta*)
4. *De Serpentibus*	4. 6 chapters (*Minutis Animantibus*)
Anguis vocabulum . . . est locus.	
36 chapters (*Serpentes*)	
5. **De Vermibus**	5. *Unum autem . . . vocarentur*
Vermis est . . . aut vestimentorum	36 chapters (*Aves*)
22 chapters (*Vermes*)	
Proprie autem . . . perlabitur.	
6. **De Piscibus**	6. *Angius omnium . . . rectus.*
Pisci dicti . . . concipiunt ostreae.	17 chapters (*Serpentes*)
50 chapters (*Pisces*)	*Serpens vero . . . morte serpens.*
Animalium omnium . . . putrescunt.	
7. **De Avibus**	7. *Vermis est . . . aut vestimentorum.*
Unum nomen . . . nominarentur.	22 chapters (*Vermes*)
60 chapters (*Aves*)	*Proprie autem . . . perlabitur.*
Alites quae . . . vitri fragmenta.	
8. **De Minutis volatilibus**	8. *Pisces dicti . . . fluctuales.*
15 chapters (*Minutes Volatiles*)	22 chapters (*Pisces*)
	Animalium omnium . . . huic similia.
	9. *Arborum nomen . . . multitudinem.*
	19 chapters (*Arbores*)
	10. *Natura dicta . . . subiungamus.*
	11. *Gradus etatis . . . humum inicere.*
	12. *Lapides Igniferi.*

When we come to examine the text of Add. 11283 more closely, we find that its reliance on Isidore is extremely uneven. The section on *vermes*, we have seen, was appropriated *en bloc*, but within the *bestiae*, which have so far been our major concern, the direct importance of Isidore to the compiler seems much less certain. Table 12 shows the chapter orders of the *bestiae* in Add. 11283, the St Petersburg Bestiary and

Plate 34. London, BL Add. 11283, ff. 26v and 27r. Opening of section on serpentes.

the *Etymologiae*. Cambridge University Library MS Ii. 4. 26 is identical to Add. 11283 in this section except that it has lost sections of *autalops* and *unicornis*, and never included the chapter on *crocote* after *yena*.

TABLE 12. *BESTIAE* IN ISIDORE, ADD. 11283 and ST PETERSBURG

ISIDORE	ADD. 11283	ST PETERSBURG (P)
1. *Leo*	1. *Leo*★	1. *Leo*★
2. *Tygris*	2. *Tygris*★	2. *Antalops*★
3. *Pantera*	3. *Pardus*★	3. *Onocentaurus*
4. *Pardus*	4. *Leopardus*★	4. *Herinacius*
5. *Leopardus*	5. *Pantera*★	5. *Vulpis*★
6. *Rhinoceron* (Unicorn)	6. *Antalops*★	6. *Unicornis*★
7. *Elephans*	7. *Unicornis*★	7. *Castor*★
8. *Gryphes*	8. *Lincis*★	8. *Hyena*★

ISIDORE	ADD. 11283	ST PETERSBURG (P)
9. Chameleon	9. Grifes★	9. Hydrus
10. Camelopardus	10. Elephans★	10. Hydra
11. Lyncis	11. Castor★	11. Sirene
12. Castor	12. Ibex★	12. Caper★
13. Ursus	13. Yena★	13. Onager
14. Lupus	14. Crocote	14. Simia★
15. Canis	15. Bonnacon★	15. Satyrus★
16. Vulpis	16. Simie★	16. Pantera★
17. Simia	17. Satyros★	17. Elephas★
18. Cynocephali	18. Cervi★	18. Lupus★
19. Satyri	19. Caper★	19. Canis★
20. Leontophonos	20. Caprea (Pan?)	20. Cervus★
21. Hystrix	21. Monoceros [S]	21. Mustela
22. Enhydros	22. Ursus★	22. Formica
23. Ichneumon	23. Leucrota [S]	23. Ibex★
24. Musio	24. Cocodrillus	24. Lapides igniferi
25. Furo	25. Manticora★	25. Assida
26. Melo	26. Parandrus★	26. Tigris★
	27. Vulpis★	27. Pardus★
	28. Eale★	28. Leopardus★
	29. Lupus★	29. Lyncis★
	30. Canis★	30. Grifes★
		31. Aper
		32. Bonacon★
		33. Ursus★
		34. Manticora★
		35. Parandrus★
		36. Eale★

There are thirty chapters in this section of Add. 11283, compared with thirty-six in the corresponding section of St Petersburg. The two books share twenty-five chapters, asterisked in the table. The other five in Add. 11283 (plates 35 and 36) are 14. *Crocote*, the supposed offspring of a hyena and a lioness (source unknown), 20. *Caprea*, another type of goat (possibly from the *Pantheologus* of Petrus Londiniensis), 21. *Monoceros*, a single-horned animal much larger than the unicorn, and 23. *Leucrota* (both from Solinus) and 24. *Cocodrillus* (found among the *pisces* in both St Petersburg and Isidore).

Turning to the eleven chapters omitted from St Petersburg, we find nine of them elsewhere in Add. 11283. The two entirely left out, *sirene* and *onocentaurus* formed a double chapter in the original *Physiologus*, but are not found in Isidore. *Lapides igniferi*, also not in

Isidore, is added at the very end of the Bestiary. The remaining eight appear in the same sections in both Add. 11283 and Isidore. *Hydrus* and *hydra* are among the serpents, *onager* and *aper* with the domestic beasts, and *herinacius*, *mustela* and *formica* with the small animals.

As far as the chapter content of this section of Add. 11283 is concerned, then, nothing new is taken from Isidore, or anywhere else except the St Petersburg recension, Solinus, possibly the *Pantheologus*, and the unknown source of the chapter on *crocote*. The reliance on St Petersburg rather than Morgan is obvious from a close comparison of texts. We have seen that there are considerable differences between the *leo* texts of P and M, and here, as elsewhere, Add. 11283 follows P precisely apart from minor copying errors in single words. Likewise, the additions from Bernardus Silvestris found in M appear neither in P nor Add. 11283.

The order of chapters is more difficult to explain. The opening follows Isidore, but the correspondence is seriously disturbed after *unicornis* and never returns. Furthermore, none of the Isidore chapters after 17. *Simia* is used at all (the material in *satyros* is all from Solinus). The chapter organization is never very close to P, and while there are five chapters from Solinus between 21. *Monoceros* and 28. *Eale*, their order bears no relation to that of the *Collectanea*. All that can be said is that while Isidore is not followed especially closely, nothing else is followed at all.

THIRD FAMILY BESTIARIES

James's Third Family shows another recasting of the book.[61] It is known in only five copies, all from the thirteenth century, and many illustrated with dramatic miniatures (see plates 37 and 38):

Cambridge, Fitzwilliam MS 254 (*c.* 1220–30)
Cambridge University Library MS Kk.4.25 (*c.* 1220–40)
London, Westminster Abbey MS 22 (*c.* 1275–1300, from the Franciscan Friary in York)
Oxford, Bodleian Library MS Douce 88(II) (i.e., ff. 68–154 of Douce 88, *c.* 1240–60 from St Augustine's, Canterbury)
Oxford, Bodleian Library MS e Mus.136 (*c.* 1260–80)

These Bestiaries contain much of the same material as the Second Family books, but in a different sequence and with entirely different supplementary texts. The reorganization of text is so comprehensive and the added texts so unlike what has been associated with Bestiary material before that it is difficult to see how these Third Family books could have fulfilled the same functions as the Bestiaries described previously.

The five Bestiaries form an extremely homogeneous group, differing mainly in the

---

61. James (1928), 23–5.

material preceding the domestic beasts, and that added after the chapters on snakes and insects. The Westminster Abbey book is the most complete of the survivals, and an analysis of its structure will thus serve to represent the group.

TABLE 13. STRUCTURE OF WESTMINSTER ABBEY MS 22[62]

Sec.	Fol.	Rubric	Text	Miniature
I	f. 1r	*Iste liber vocatur bestiarium*	*Cum voluntas conditoris . . .* (Isidore on fabulous nations)	Monstrous races: 2 full-page mins
II	f. 4r	*De natura animantium*	*Omnium animantibus . . .* (Is. Et. XII,1)	Adam naming the animals
III	f. 4v		Bernardus Silvestris, *Cosmographia* extracts	
IV	f. 6v		Domestic beasts (18 chapters)	16 mins
V	f. 14r		Wild beasts (22 chapters)	26 mins
VI	f. 27r		Small animals (18 chapters)	15 mins
VII	f. 33v	*Explicit de bestiis Incipit de generibus avium*	Birds (47 chapters)	43 mins
VIII	f. 42r	*Explicit de avibus Et incipit de piscibus*	Fishes (30 chapters)	25 mins
IX	f. 46r	*Explicit de piscibus Incipit de serpentibus*	Snakes (31 chapters)	24 mins
X	f. 51r		Insects (22 chapters)	7 mins
XI	f. 52v		*Dicuntur quedam fabulosa portenta . . .* (Isidore on fabulous monsters) 5 chapters	3 mins
XII	f. 54r		*Lapides igniferi*	1 min
XIII		*De rota fortunae*	*Naturam diffinire . . .* (on the Wheel of Fortune)	1 min
XIV	f. 55r	*De remediis fortuitorum bonorum conferunt inter se Callio et Seneca*	*Callio: Dolor imminet. . .* (Seneca, *De remediis fortuitorum* extract.)	
XV	f. 57v	*De septem mirabilibus mundi*	*Primum de septem . . .* (On the seven wonders of the world)	
XVI	f. 58r	*Omnia vana esse et res ex fide sua*	*In creatoris prorumpis iniuram . . .* (John of Salisbury, Polycraticon extract)	
	f. 62r	*cuique respondere. Explicit liber de generibus hominum et bestiarum domesticarum, bestiarum ferarum, avium, piscium, draconum et serpentium, omniumque reptilium sine vermium, apium vel muscarium sive monstrinum, de morte. Et rota fortune, de divinationibus sortilegis et nigromanciis et duabus petris, Et de vij miraculis mundi.*		

---

62. Robinson and James (1909), 77–81.

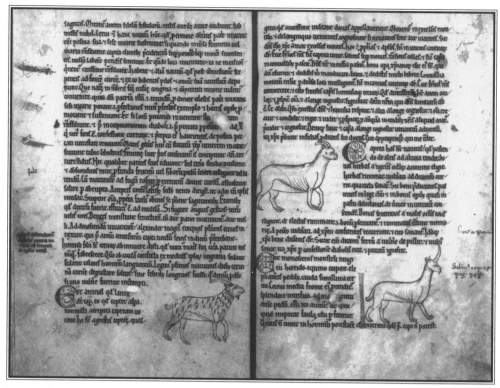

Plate 35. London, BL Add. 11283, ff. 6v and 7r caper, caprea, monoceros.

The completeness of the volume is attested by the opening and closing rubrics. Furthermore, the original contents page is now misbound in MS 23, and repeats in substance the list given in the closing rubric.[63] The same scribe was responsible for the entire volume, and none of the sections after the first begins on a new quire. We can therefore be quite certain that the book was designed as it now stands.

SUPPLEMENTARY MATTER

Ignoring for the moment the changes in organization of the animal chapters and the new sources of text, which will be examined in the next section, the Third Family contains a core of Bestiary material very similar to that found in the Second Family and the Morgan group. The main difference lies in the opening and closing texts and

---

63. Ibid., 81–2.

Plate 36. London, BL Add. 11283, ff. 7v and 8r ursus, leucrota, cocodrillus, manticora.

miniatures that provide the context in which this versatile material was intended to be read.

While the texts and miniatures preceding the Bestiary material in the Second Family and the Morgan group ensured that the chapters on animals would be read as a gloss on the Genesis creation myth, those found in the Third Family books suggest an entirely different interpretation. The closing rubric provides the key to this: it is a book of the species (*genera*) of humanity as well as of the animal world (colour plate 6): a concept which has no basis in scripture. The animals forming the core of the text are preceded by the monstrous races (section I) and followed by the fabulous monsters (section XI). Both of these sections are taken from Isidore, but it would be a mistake to see the Third Family books as just another step in the direction of the *Etymologiae*. For the section on domestic beasts (IV), for example, Isidore has been completely jettisoned.

Throughout the supplementary material there is a thread of the exotic. Where the Second-Family structure placed the animal world in a context of divine order, these Bestiaries juxtapose the divine system with images of pagan disorder. The justification for this is in the passage from Isidore which opens the book, where it is argued that monsters are not unnatural but the creations of God's will, following the divine scheme in ways that our limited understanding cannot comprehend.

The important difference between Isidore's use of the argument and its reiteration here is one of placing. In the *Etymologiae* it appeared towards the end of Book XI, when the teleology of humanity and the human body had been established. In the Third Family Bestiaries it is the opening text, calling into question from the outset the project of understanding the divine will. The monstrous races, the fabulous monsters, the Wheel of Fortune and the Seven Wonders of the World all work to disrupt the rigid teleology of the Second Family universe. It is not suggested that the disruption was deliberate. When the *Physiologus* was transformed via Laud Misc. 247, Stowe 1067 and the Morgan group into a different type of book, no revolution of ideas was involved. What was already present was gradually rearranged, and new material was added of a type related to that already there. The disruption was caused by the nature of the relation between the new material and the old. They had in common the natural world as their ostensible subject matter, but it had been appropriated by the *Physiologus* and by Isidore for different didactic purposes.

Something similar is at work here. In the Second Family Bestiaries, the familiar and the alien were represented as belonging to the same system. The addition of extra exotic material cannot be taken as a deliberate deviation, since the exotic is already present. What disrupts the message, as it did in the earlier transformation, is that the new material is not, and cannot be, incorporated into the old structure.

ORGANIZATION OF BESTIARY CHAPTERS

From the summary of contents given above it may be seen that the classes of the animal world are treated in a new order in the Third Family (plate 39). This differs from the Second Family structure in that domestic beasts now precede the wild, and fish follow immediately after birds.

Isidore's *Etymologiae* also opens with the domestic beasts, so this first change may be just what we would expect. When we come to examine the chapter order of the domestic beasts in the Westminster Bestiary, however, the first thing we notice is that it bears little relation either to Isidore or to the Second Family books (table 14).

second quire we cannot be entirely certain that other chapters have not been omitted as well. The last leaf before the loss, f. 12, follows the text of *cocodrillus* with the rubric *de vulpibus*; f. 13 begins in *lupus* and continues with *canis*. The normal order of chapters in this area is *cocodrillus, manticora, parandrum, vulpis, eale, lupus, canis*, and I know of no other case where *cocodrillus* is followed directly by *vulpis*. We cannot be absolutely sure that the missing leaf contained three chapters as well as the text of *vulpis* and the start of *lupus*, but apart from this small reservation we can be confident that the content, if not the order, of this section of Douce 88(I) is closer to that of the Third Family books than any other Second Family survival.

Folios 68–154 of Douce 88, here called Douce 88(II), constitute the Third Family Bestiary identified by Ker on the basis of its *secundo folio* as volume 870 in the 1491–7 catalogue of St Augustine's, Canterbury.[71] We thus have the Second Family Bestiary closest textually to the Third Family bound together with a representative of that family. The date when the two parts of the volume were brought together cannot be established. They were not bound together in the fifteenth century when the catalogue was made; they clearly were together when the volume received its present binding in the nineteenth century. It would be stretching coincidence too far to suggest that their juxtaposition is pure chance. A likelier hypothesis is that both Bestiaries came into the collection from St Augustine's and were bound together on account of the similarity of their contents.

Where does this get us? It is clearly not the case that Douce 88 contains both the source and the result of the Third Family reorganization. Both Fitzwilliam 254 and Cambridge University Library Kk.4.25 predate Douce 88(I) and (II) by twenty or thirty years. It does suggest, however, that both Bestiaries in Douce 88 shared the same model, possibly a defective Second Family text, and that this model was present at St Augustine's some time before 1230. More importantly, it suggests that the reorganization into the Third Family took place in that area, a conclusion substantiated by the heavy reliance on the *Pantheologus* which, as we shall see in chapter four, was used primarily in the south-east, and especially at Rochester.

71. Ker (1964), 46. See appendix three for the text of the St Augustine's catalogue entry.

PATTERNS OF CONSUMPTION

The changes in Bestiary structure described in the last chapter were presented as though they formed a linear temporal development, unrelated to geographical location or religious order. This was done in the cause of clarity but it is deceptive without qualification. The experiments leading to the recasting of the text along the lines of Isidore's *Etymologiae* can be dated, in Stowe 1067, as early as the second quarter of the twelfth century; and the earliest surviving Second Family Bestiary, Additional 11283, dates from the third quarter of the century. Nevertheless Bestiaries of the Laud type were still produced early in the thirteenth century in England (Bodley 602), and towards the end of that century in France (the two Malibu Bestiaries). This chapter will attempt to fit the structural changes to a geographical, temporal and social framework.

LOCALIZATION BY PRODUCTION AND CONSUMPTION

Before examining the evidence, however, a point must be made about the nature of the framework. Geographical localization based on such evidence as *ex-libris* inscriptions, heraldry or entries in medieval book lists will always relate to consumption – localization by script or scriptorium practices to production. Localization by pictorial style also relates to production, but such data must be handled with some care. It is only reliable when the artists involved can themselves be firmly localized. In the early part of the period covered by this study, up to about 1200, most high quality illumination seems to have been carried out in monasteries by travelling professional lay artists.[1] It is not until the thirteenth century that evidence of the acceptance of painters into guilds allows us to postulate fixed workshops.[2] In the early period too, it is often assumed that a monastic *ex-libris* implies internal production. That this is not always the case is demonstrated by Rodney Thomson's study of

---

1. Thomson (1982) I, 6.
2. Lehmann–Brockhaus (1955–60).

St Albans manuscripts in which a comparison of script and *ex-libris* inscriptions allowed him to conclude that 'there is enough evidence to suggest that St Albans produced books for "export", either as gifts or commissioned'.[3]

An early *ex-libris* is thus evidence only of use and not of production, but even if a book can be identified as a gift, it could still have been produced in the house it was given to. Henry of Eastry's early fourteenth-century catalogue of Christ Church, Canterbury, lists, according to M.R. James's interpretation, 1,831 volumes, of which 502 are grouped by subject and the rest by donor.[4] Furthermore, the gifts are listed chronologically, starting from Thomas Becket. The evidence of surviving books identifiable in the catalogue,[5] indicates that the books grouped by subject rather than donor predated the Becket books: they may have been arranged by subject because their donors were no longer known. This would indicate that gifts made up well over 70 per cent of the holdings, and that practically everything produced after the end of the twelfth century was classed as a gift. It is clear from this that to class a book as a gift did not necessarily mean that it was produced externally. On the death of a St Augustine's monk, for example, the customs of the abbey required that all the books he had in his possession, including those he had from the library, should be marked with his name and placed in the library.[6] The names marked in the volumes would then provide a convenient method of cataloguing them, but such evidence of the status of a book as a gift would imply nothing more than that it was in the possession of the donor when he died.

Evidence for the location of production of a manuscript, then, is only reliable when paleographic and codicological evidence can be amassed to connect it with a coherent corpus of books that can circumstantially be ascribed to a specific scriptorium. *Ex-libris* evidence, given the possibility of gifts and commissions, is not enough, and style locations are the most dubious of all, owing to the mobility of artists. For my purposes, since I am mainly concerned with the relation between changes in content and changes in use of the Bestiary, localization of consumption is far more valuable, and evidence for this, in the form of *ex-libris* inscriptions, heraldry and contents of surviving volumes, and of medieval book lists that allow the identification of centres of use even when the books themselves are lost or unidentifiable, is far more trustworthy.

3. Thomson (1982) I, 5.
4. James (1903).
5. Ker (1964), 29–39.
6. Ibid., xviii.

DATING OF SURVIVING BESTIARIES

Table 17 lists surviving Latin Bestiaries produced in England, together with French and German Latin Bestiaries for comparison, and some indication of their date of production.

TABLE 17. SURVIVING LATIN BESTIARIES

ENGLISH

Aberdeen	Univ. Lib. MS 24	*c.* 1200–10
ex-Alnwick Castle	MS 447	*c.* 1250–75
Cambridge	Corpus Christi MS 22	*c.* 1150–75
	MS 53	1304–21
	Fitzwilliam MS 254	*c.* 1220–30
	MS 379	*c.* 1300–25
	Gonv. & Caius MS 109/178	*c.* 1250–75
	MS 372/621	*c.* 1275–1300
	MS 384/604	*c.* 1275–1300
	Trinity MS R. 14. 9	*c.* 1275–1300
	Univ. Lib. MS Gg. 6.5	*c.* 1450–75
	MS Ii. 4. 26	*c.* 1200–10
	MS Kk. 4. 25	*c.* 1220–40
Canterbury	Cath. Lib. MS Lit. D. 10	*c.* 1275–1300
Copenhagen	Kongelige Bibl. MS 1633 Qto	*c.* 1400–25
London	B.L. MS Add. 11283	*c.* 1160–80
	MS Add. 24097	*c.* 1200–25
	MS Harley 3244	*c.* 1255–65
	MS Harley 4751	*c.* 1230–40
	MS Royal 2.C.XII	*c.* 1200–25
	MS Royal 6.A.XI	*c.* 1160–80
	MS Royal 10.A.VII	*c.* 1200–25
	MS Royal 12.C.XIX	*c.* 1200–10
	MS Royal 12.F.XIII	*c.* 1220–40
	MS Sloane 3544	*c.* 1240–60
	MS Stowe 1067	*c.* 1120–40
	Westminster Abbey Lib. MS 22	*c.* 1275–1300
New York	Pierpont Morgan Lib. MS 81	*c.* 1180–7
	MS 890	*c.* 1275–1300
Oxford	Bodleian Lib. MS Ashmole 1511	*c.* 1200–10
	MS Bodley 91	*c.* 1340–60
	MS Bodley 533	*c.* 1275–1300

ENGLISH

	MS Bodley 602	c. 1220–40
	MS Bodley 764	c. 1240–60
	MS Douce 88(I)	c. 1240–60
	MS Douce 88(II)	c. 1240–60
	MS Douce 151	c. 1340–60
	MS Douce 167	c. 1200–20
	MS Laud Misc.247	c. 1110–30
	MS e Mus. 136	c. 1260–80
	MS Tanner 110	c. 1240–60
	St John's MS 61	c. 1210–30
	MS 178	c. 1275–1300
	Univ. MS 120	c. 1300–25
Paris	Bibl. Nat. MS Lat. 3630	c. 1275–1300
	MS Lat. 11207	c. 1240–60
	MS Lat. 14429	c. 1250–75
	MS Nouv. Acq. Lat. 873	c. 1160–80
Rome	Bibl. Vaticana MS Reg. Lat. 258	c. 1200–10
St Petersburg	Saltykov-Shchedrin MS Q.v.V.1	c. 1175–85

FRENCH/FLEMISH

Brussels	Bibl. Roy. MS 8340(1031)	14c.
Cambridge	Sidney Sussex MS 100	c. 1260–80
Cambridge (Mass)	Houghton Lib. MS Typ. 101H	c. 1260–80
Chalons-sur-Saone	Bibl. Mun. MS 14	c. 1200–20
Douai	Bibl. Mun. MS 711	c. 1280–1300
Epinal	Bibl. Mun. MS 58(209)	12c.
London	BL. MS Sloane 278	c. 1280–1300
Malibu	Getty Mus. MS Ludwig XV3	c. 1260–80
	MS Ludwig XV4	c. 1277
Paris	Bibl. Nat. MS Lat. 10448	13c.
Valenciennes	Bibl. Mun. MS 101	c. 1230–60
Vienna	O.N.B., Cod. 1010	c. 1050–75

GERMAN

London	BL. MS Arundel 506	14c.
Munich	Bayern Staatsbibl. Clm. 2655	c. 1300
	Clm. 6908	14c.
New York	Pierpont Morgan Lib. MS 832	12c.

Only one English Latin Bestiary, Pierpont Morgan MS M. 81, provides a date which is a *terminus ante quem* for its production. In all other cases, evidence of script, codicology, initials and miniatures has been combined to give an estimate.[7] Only in one case where a surviving Bestiary appears in a medieval book list has additional evidence from the book list been considered in dating. The book in question is Paris, Bibl. Nat. MS Nouv. Acq. Lat. 873, identified on the flyleaf as a gift of Adam the sub-prior to St Augustine's, Canterbury. The fifteenth-century catalogue of the abbey library notes this volume as a gift of Adam (Item 758), and also allows us to extract twelve more of his books (including two more Bestiaries), which passed to the library, probably at his death.[8] The contents of the gift are listed in appendix one. In chapter five I shall consider how much this gift can tell us about Bestiary consumption, but for the moment I am concerned only with questions of date.

The gift, if it was made all at one time, must postdate the production of the latest work: in this case the *Tractatus Contra Curiales et Officiales Clerico* of Nigellus de Longo Campo, better known as Nigel Wireker, (described in the catalogue as *Epistola Nigelli*). This text is dateable between December 1192 and March 1194 by a reference to the captivity of Richard I in Germany.[9] This does not conflict with Emden's identification of Adam with a monk of the same name who, as chamberlain, acted for the abbot in the dispute over the manor of Preston in 1200 and 1201, and who was sacrist in about the year 1215.[10]

Neither does it confirm it: Emden's Adam is nowhere described as a sub-prior. Unfortunately, the St Augustine's library catalogue is incomplete, lacking the section on civil law which, had it also included gifts from Adam the sub-prior, would have provided circumstantial corroboration for the identification. Item 1836 in the catalogue, however, indicates at least an interest in canon law (see appendix one).

If Edmen's identification is accepted, then Adam was acting in a responsible position in 1200, and was still alive in 1215, but cannot have lived much beyond 1230–40, which must be taken as a *terminus ante quem* for the entire gift. Since the Bestiary could have been produced at any time before this, it is not surprising to find that the book itself provides evidence for a more precise dating. Both script and minor initials bear comparison with Pierpont Morgan MS M. 81, dated before 1187 by an inscription,

---

7. For script and codicology, primarily the unpublished notes, lectures and seminars of the late Professor Julian Brown. See also Ker (1960); Thomson (1969). For minor initials, see Patterson (1969). For miniatures, principally Kauffmann (1975); Morgan (1982) and (1988) and Sandler (1986).

8. James (1903).

9. The prose part of this work begins *Reverendo patri et domino Willelmo, Dei gratia Eliensi episcopo* . . . Boutemy (1959) gave several examples of the *Tractatus* referred to by the name *Epistola* in early catalogues, and there is nothing else among the known works of Nigellus that this could be.

10. Emden (1968), 5.

while the single column format and pricking in the outer margins make production after *c.* 1175 unlikely. There are no illustrations. A dating between *c.* 1160 and *c.* 1180 is therefore suggested.

LOCALIZATION OF SURVIVING BESTIARIES

Table 18 lists localized English Bestiaries. In every case but one, the localization is to a religious house, and the religious order is indicated in brackets after the name of the house. The basis of attribution to centres of use is shown by a letter in the evidence column of the table, according to the following code:

e – *ex-libris*

c – contents

p – provenance

m – miniatures

b – book lists

h – heraldry.

TABLE 18. LOCALIZED ENGLISH BESTIARIES

BESTIARY	HOUSE	ORDER	EVIDENCE
1. Cambridge, Corpus Christi 53	Peterborough?	B	c
2. Cambridge, Gonv. & Caius 109/178	Guisborough	AC	e[11]
3. Cambridge, Gonv. & Caius 372/621	?	F	e[12]
4. Cambridge, Trinity R. 14. 9.	Horsham St Faith?	B	c
5. Cambridge, Univ. Lib. Ii. 4. 26.	Revesby?	C	e[13]
6. London, BL Harley 3244	?	D	m
7. London, BL Royal 2. C. XII.	Gloucester	B	e[14]
8. London, BL Royal 6. A. XI.	Rochester	BCP	e[15]
9. London, BL Royal 10. A. VII.	Bardney	B	e[16]
10. London, BL 12. F. XIII	Rochester	BCP	e[17]

11. '*iste liber est dompni Ric.de Petro canonici de gysb*' (inside front cover).
12. '*Reverendo sacre theologie doctori Fratri Iohanni Zouch.*' (Fly at end) in s.xv hand. John Zouch was Provincial of the English Franciscans, and died in 1423 as Bishop of Llandaff.
13. James (1928) read 'Jacobus Thomas Herison,Thys ys ye Abbaye of Rev . . .' (f. 73r) in s.xvi hand, and concluded that it must refer to Revesby. The inscription is now practically illegible.
14. *Liber monasterii Sancti Petri Gloucestre* (f. 1r).
15. *Liber de claustro Roffensi H Monachi* (f. 1r).
16. *Constat liber iste monasterio de Bardenay* (f. 211v).
17. *Liber de claustro Roffensi R precentoris* (f. 3r).

BESTIARY	HOUSE	ORDER	EVIDENCE
11. London, Westminster Abbey 22	York	F	e[18]
12. New York, Pierpont Morgan M. 81	Worksop	AC	e[19]
13. New York, Pierpont Morgan M. 890	Fountains?	C	p
14. Oxford, Bodleian Bodley 91	Hyde Abbey?	B	c
15. Oxford, Bodleian Bodley 602	Newark, Surrey	AC	e[20]
16. Oxford, Bodleian Bodley 764	Mold?	S	h[21]
17. Oxford, Bodleian Douce 88(II)	Cant'bury, St Aug.	B	b
18. Oxford, Bodleian Tanner 110	Ramsey	B	e[22]
19. Oxford, St John's 61	York, Holy Trinity	B	e[23]
20. Oxford, St John's 178	Westminster	B	e[24]
21. Paris, BN Nouv. Acq. Lat. 873	Cant'bury, St Aug.	B	e,[25] b

Abbreviations

ORDER

AC Augustinian Canons
B Benedictines
BCP Benedictine Cathedral Priory
C Cistercians
D Dominicans
F Franciscans
S Secular use

EVIDENCE

b book list
c contents
e *ex-libris*
h heraldry
m miniature
p provenance

EX-LIBRIS INSCRIPTIONS

Ex-libris inscriptions were normally written on a flyleaf before *c.* 1300,[26] and hence when a book has been rebound and the old flyleaves discarded, the evidence is lost. Of the fifty English Bestiaries studied, only twelve, or perhaps thirteen, can be localized in this way. The

18. *Iste liber est de communitate fratrum minorum Ebor'* (f. 70v).
19. *Anno mclxxxvii Ab incarnatione dominum. In vigilia sancti Mathei apostoli. Philippus apostolorum canonicus Lincolniensis ecclesie Sancti Marie et Sancti Cuthberti de Radeford. Ad edificationem fratrum ipsius in perpetuum . . .* (f. 1v), for full text see chapter four.
20. *Iste liber pertinet domino Johannem Rosse chanonico de Newarke iuxta Guldeford (f. 1v); Johannes Rosse chanonicus de Newarke et Curatus de Weylde est possessor huius libri* (f. 13v).
21. Arms on miniature f. 12r, see text.
22. 'pertenyth to dane Rolande Sentyvys monke of Ramsey' (f. 1r).
23. *Liber Sancte Trinitate Eborencis* (f. 103v).
24. *Isti libri continentur in hoc volumine Beati Petri Westm(onasteriensis)* (f. 1r (fly)).
25. *De libris Sancti Augustini Cantuarensis G.vii.D.4* (f. 1r) and see text.
26. Ker (1964), xvii.

doubtful attribution is Cambridge University Library MS Ii. 4. 26. James read an inscription on f. 73 as 'Jacobus Thomas Herison Thys ys ye Abbaye of Rev . . .', and concluded that it must refer to Revesby since no other abbey begins with these three letters.[27] Unfortunately the inscription is now illegible, although it is clear enough in James's facsimile edition, and Ker has rejected the attribution,[28] which seems over cautious. One further Bestiary contains an *ex-libris* that suggests use by Franciscans, without identifying a particular house. Cambridge, Gonville & Caius Coll. MS 372 (621) contains the name of John Zouch, Provincial of the order, who died in 1423 while Bishop of Llandaff (plate 40).[29]

Most inscriptions date from a time when the entire contents of a library were marked. Those in the two Rochester Bestiaries, for example, follow the standard formula '*Liber de claustro Roffensi*' followed by an initial, and date from the fourteenth century. They thus provide no direct evidence of original or early use. In two cases, however, such evidence is provided by inscriptions. The first is the well-known case of Pierpont Morgan MS M81, which records the donation of the Bestiary, along with other books, in the following words.

Anno m.c.lxxxvii Ab incarnatione dominum. In vigilia sancti Mathei apostoli.

Philippus apostolorum canonicus lincolnensis ecclesie donavit deo et ecclesie sancti marie et sancti Cuthberti de Radeford. Ad edificationem fratrum ipsius ecclesie in perpetuum: Unum optimum psalterium glosatum et quatuor evangelistas glosatus in uno volumine elegantissimo et Genesim glosata et Meditationes beati Anselmi Cantuariensis Archiepiscopi et Bestiarium et mappa mundi. et ad petitionem ipsius Philippi. consensu Anchetum prioris et omnium fratrum excommunicati sunt candelis accensis et stolis acceptis ab omnibus sacerdotibus et canonicis. predicte ecclesie. quicumque aliquem de predictis libris elongaverit extra septa curie sancti Cuthberti commodaverit vel commodatum acceperit deposuerit vel depositum acceperit. pignori dederit vel acceperit: donaverit vel donatum acceperit: vel quocumque titulo alienationis alienaverit vel acceperit: vel vi vel clam abstulerit, vel precario cuiquam concesserit: noverit procul dubio se iram et indignationem omnipotens dei incursurum.[30]

---

27. James (1928), 35.
28. Ker (1964), 158.
29. As Provincial of the order, Zouch was not attached to a single house.
30. In the year 1187 after the incarnation of our Lord, on the vigil of St Matthew the apostle, Philip Apostolorum, canon of the church of Lincoln, gave to God and the church of St Mary and St Cuthbert at Radford, for the edification of the brothers of the church in perpetuity: one very fine glossed psalter and the four gospels in one most elegant volume, glossed, and a Genesis, glossed, and the Meditations of the blessed Anselm, Archbishop of Canterbury, and a Bestiary, and a map of the world. And at the request of the said Philip, with the consent of Prior Anchetus and all the brothers, whoever shall remove any of the aforesaid books out of the enclosure of St Cuthbert, shall be excommunicated by all the priests and canons of the aforesaid church with candles burning and stoles put on. Whoever gives or accepts it as a loan, deposits or accepts it as a deposit, gives or accepts it as a pledge, gives or accepts it as a gift, or by whatever title of alienation, alienates or accepts it, removes it either by force or by stealth, or yields it up for any plea: let him know for certain that he will incur the wrath and indignation of almighty God.

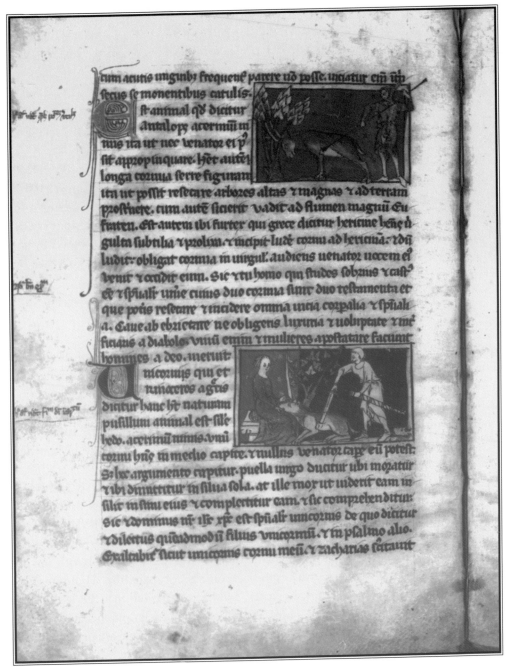

Plate 40. Cambridge, Gonville & Caius 372 (621), p. 10, autalops, unicornis.

Muratova's reading of this inscription as evidence for the production of illuminated Bestiaries promoted by 'a cultured elite centred on Lincoln and on its cathedral school',[31] has already been discussed in chapter one. In fact, there is strong circumstantial evidence of a lack of interest in Bestiaries in secular cathedrals in general. No surviving Bestiary can be localized to such a foundation, and the only reference found in a book list comes from Exeter (see appendix two). Neither the twelfth-century nor the fifteenth-century catalogue of Lincoln Cathedral includes a Bestiary.[32]

The other Bestiary which provides evidence of its first use is Oxford, St John's Coll. MS 61. There is a painted *ex-libris* at the foot of the last page of the book (f. 103v), immediately below the last miniature but painted before it, as the overlapping paint layers show (colour plate 7). It takes the form of a panel bearing the inscription *Liber Sancte Trinitate Eborencis* in majuscule letters, framed by two dragons painted by the artist of the miniatures, and thus indicates that this Benedictine house in York was the original patron of the book.

CONTENTS

In three cases some attempt at localization may be made with the aid of the textual contents of surviving volumes. Bestiaries themselves never include textual evidence of their place of use, in the way that Psalters sometimes do, and this kind of information is only available when other texts are bound up with the Bestiary. This can cause problems since, unless the original binding has not been disturbed or, failing this, quires are shared by the Bestiary and the localized text, there is no way of knowing when the texts came together.

A case in point is the so-called Peterborough Psalter and Bestiary (Cambridge, Corpus Christi Coll. MS 53). The manuscript contains a Psalter with kalendar, chronicles of England and of Peterborough Abbey, and a Bestiary. The inscription, *Psalterium fratris Hugonis de Stiucle: prioris* is written on a fly-leaf. In his 1921 study of the manuscript, M.R. James assumed that it was largely a unity, and with the aid of the *ex-libris*, the kalendar and the Abbey chronicle, localized the whole work to Peterborough.[33] In her 1974 study, however, Sandler established that the Psalter was originally for the use of Norwich, and that the additions relevant to Peterborough were made to the kalendar in a different hand.[34] The two chronicles were also

31. Muratova (1986), 120.
32. Woolley (1927).
33. James (1921), 13.
34. Sandler (1974), 123.

Peterborough additions.[35] The original Norwich part of the Psalter must post-date 1304 since the kalendar contains the dated obit of John, Earl de Warenne, in the first hand. The chronicle of the Abbey must have been originally written before 1321, since the first hand goes down to the death of William of Woodford in 1299, and the entry on his successor, Geoffrey of Croyland, who died in 1321, is an addition.

The Bestiary was bound up with the Psalter and chronicles by 1575, when the book was bequeathed to the college by Matthew Parker,[36] but it is unlikely to have been originally in this volume. The combination of Bestiary and service book is unique (although Queen Mary's Psalter has Bestiary illustrations in the margins), but apart from this it is written on separate quires from the rest of the book, and differs in ruling and script. Sandler's most recent opinion is that the Bestiary is earlier than the rest of the manuscript.[37] Hence, despite the quantity of evidence attached to other parts of the volume, there is nothing which allows a confident opinion about the location of the Bestiary before the sixteenth century.

The situation of the incomplete Bestiary in Oxford MS Bodley 91 is, if possible, even less clear-cut. The volume is composite, containing texts produced between the twelfth century and the fourteenth, of which the mid-fourteenth-century Bestiary is the latest.[38] Another text in the volume is a chronicle showing an interest in Hyde Abbey, Winchester, up to 1280, and an addition to the final text is a copy of the presentation of Walter Fyfyde to the king as abbot elect of Hyde in 1319. Two parts of the book as it now stands were therefore probably at Hyde before the Bestiary was produced, but once again the problem is a lack of information about when the various parts of the book came together.

A similar degree of uncertainty accompanies the suggested localization of the Bestiary in Cambridge Trinity Coll. MS R. 14. 9 (884) to the Benedictine priory of Horsham St Faith. The late thirteenth-century Bestiary now forms the last volume of a six-volume compilation of works dating between the twelfth century and the fifteenth. Another component of the manuscript is a chronology showing interest in Norwich, Ramsey and particularly Horsham St Faith, to which James attributed the entire work.[39] Again, lack of knowledge about the date when the parts came together makes the localization questionable.

---

35. Ibid., 126.
36. James (1921), 12.
37. Sandler (1986), II, 30.
38. Madan (1895–1953) II, pt. 1, 101–2.
39. James (1900–4). II, 291–7.

PROVENANCE

At the end of the Bestiary that is now New York, Pierpont Morgan MS 890 (plate 41) is the inscription 'Mr Merkynfeld owes this booke'. In the sixteenth century, one Thomas Markenfield of Markenfield Hall, only a mile from Fountains Abbey, married Isabel Ingilby. When the Ingilby library was sold in 1920, the Bestiary was in a vellum wrapper made from leaves of a missal and marked 'From Fountains Abbey' in a hand of the eighteenth century.[40] Some twenty other items in the Ingilby sale were identifiable by inscriptions as Fountains books. The assumption is that the Bestiary came to the Ingilby family, along with other books from Fountains, from the Markenfields in the sixteenth century.

MINIATURES

Like Gonville and Caius MS 372, the Bestiary in BL Harley MS 3244 (plates 42 and 43) can be linked to a religious order but not localized. In this case the evidence takes the form of a miniature of Christ blessing a Dominican friar which precedes a text of Peraldus's *Summa de vitiis* found in the same volume.[41] A fifteenth-century list of contents on f. 1v shows that the book contained the same works in the same order at that date, despite the rebinding of the book in the eighteenth century. Evans has shown, however, with the aid of quire numbers and catch marks, that although the present arrangement of works is not original, all the works contained in Harley 3244 were produced as part of a single, larger book,[42] and hence the Bestiary, as well as all the other works contained in Harley 3244, is a product of Dominican patronage.

BOOK LISTS

In only one case can a Bestiary be localized from a book list entry alone, although, as we have seen, a book list provided corroboration of the *ex-libris* inscription in Paris, Bibl. Nat. MS Nouv. Acq. Lat. 873. The volume that now forms Bodleian MS Douce 88 contains two complete Bestiaries and a fragment of a third. It is a composite volume made up of four or possibly five manuscripts written in the thirteenth and fourteenth centuries. The first Bestiary in the book, Douce 88(I), came from a different manuscript from the second Bestiary and the fragment Douce 88(II) (see previous chapter, table 16). Ker has identified folios 68–154 of the volume, containing Douce 88(II),

---

40. Sotheby's (1920), lot 17.
41. Evans (1982), 17 and Pl. 1a.
42. Ibid., 37–8.

Plate 41. New York, Pierpont Morgan 890 (formerly Cockerell's Bestiary), basiliscus.

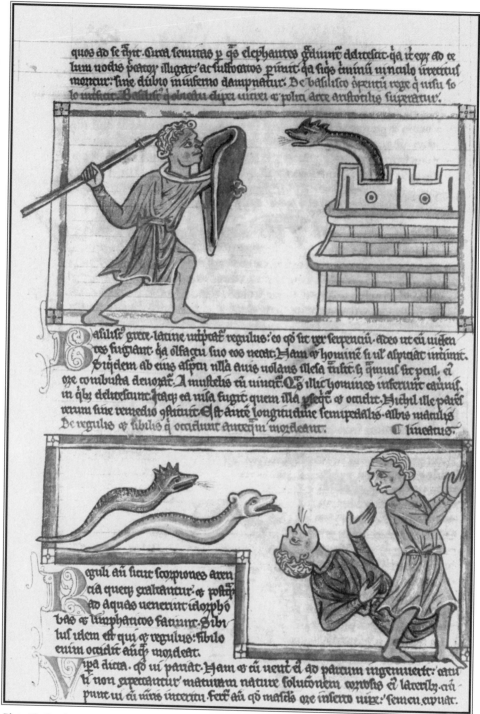

quos ad se thir. Circa semitas p̄ qs elephantos g̊dunt āderelat qa it egr̄ ad te
lum nodis potry. Migrat. ac suffocatos p̄unt qa siq̄ ēminu uinculo urtetur
moritur. sine dubio inuferno dampnatur. De basilisco ōrentu rege q̄ uisu so
lo interiat. Basilit ōoltrestu elyr utiner ar polin aere aristotlis superatur.

Basilise grete latine uterp̄et regulus. eo q̄ sit r̄r serpentu. adeo ut cu uiden
tes fugiāt qa olfacu suo eos necat. Nam oz homine si uel aspiciāt interimt.
Buidem ab eius aspiu ulla auis uolans illesa trāsit. sz q̄muis sit proul. eius
oze combusta deuozat. A mustelis tu uincit. Qz illic homines inseruit cauui̇s.
in q̄bz delitescunt. Itaq̄ ea uisa fugit quem illa p̄seqūz ar occidit. Nichil ille parit
rerum siue remedio gsistuit. Est aute longitudine semipedalis. albis maculis
De regulus ar sibilis q̄ occidunt anteq̄m mordeant.   C linestus.

Reguli aū sicut scorpiones aren
ria quep̄ exatuntur. ar postq̄
ad aquas uenerint idopho
bas ar limphaticos faciunt. Sibi
lus idem est qui ar regulus. sibilo
enim occidit auch mordeat.

Vipa dicta. q̄ ui pariat. Nam ar cu uenit es ad partum ingeminiert. catu
li non expectantur. maturam nature solutionem corpisis es lateribz eru
piunt ui cu uiis incertu. fert aū q̄ masalis oze inserto uirie. semen eripiat.

Plate 42. London, BL Harley 3244, f. 59v basiliscus, regulus.

158

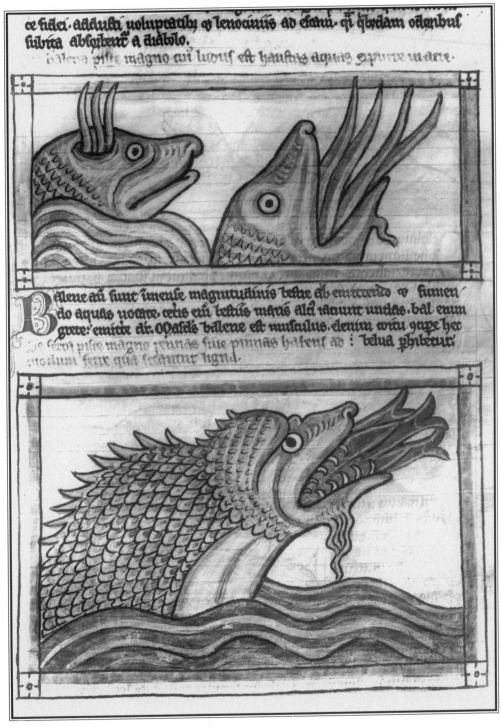

Plate 43. London, BL Harley 3244, f. 65r, balena.

with an item in the fifteenth-century catalogue of St Augustine's, Canterbury, partly from its contents but chiefly from the *secundo folio* recorded in the catalogue.[43] This localization has repercussions for Douce 88(I) since, as we saw in chapter three, these two Bestiaries share textual peculiarities which suggest that they were produced in the same area.

HERALDRY

All the evidence of localization considered so far concerns the use of Bestiaries in religious houses. In only one case has evidence of lay use been found. The Bestiary in question is Oxford, Bodleian MS Bodley 764, and the evidence takes the form of heraldic devices appearing in the miniature preceding the chapter on the elephant on f. 12r (colour plate 8).[44] Four identifiable coats of arms are shown, three on shields on the side of the tower on the elephant's back, and the fourth on a small pennant carried by a knight at the front of the tower. The most prominent, *azure, a lion rampant argent* on the central shield was borne by the Monhauts of Mold, Flintshire. When the Bestiary was made, *c.* 1240–60, it was carried by Roger de Monhaut (Lord of Mold 1232–60)[45] to whom it is attributed in Glover's Roll of *c.* 1253.[46] To the right of this shield appear the well-known arms of the Clares, Earls of Gloucester, *or, three chevronels gules.*[47] When the Bestiary was produced, the Earl was Richard de Clare (1230–60).[48] The arms on the pennant, *gules, a chevron argent*, were carried by the Berkeleys, lords of the manor and castle of Berkeley in Gloucestershire.[49] In the relevant period, Thomas de Berkeley (Lord, 1220–43) and his son Maurice (1243–81) were successive heads of the family.[50] The fourth coat, on the shield at the left of the tower, cannot be identified with certainty, but it is arguable that it was one of several coats used by the Earls of Hereford, the Bohuns.[51]

The patronage of Bodley 764 is thus fixed to a group of Barons of national or international importance based in the Welsh Marches, and specifically to Roger de Monhaut, whose arms are most prominently placed. These lords certainly did campaign together, although not, presumably, from the back of an elephant. Matthew

43. Ker (1964), 46. cf. James (1903), 290 (cat. 870).
44. Baxter (1987).
45. For biographical details, see Cockayne (1910–59) IX, 10–17.
46. Tremlett et al. (1967), 134, no. 98.
47. Ibid., 115, no. 5.
48. Cockayne (1910–59), V, 682–715.
49. Tremlett et al. (1967), 147, no. 167.
50. Cockayne (1910–59), II, 118–29.
51. Baxter (1987), 198–9.

Paris gives an account of a group of Marcher lords, including three of the four whose arms appear here, opposing a Welsh rising in 1244:

comes de Clare, comes de Herefort, Johannes de Munemue, Rogerus de Muhaut et alii marchisii potentes et praeclari.[52]

(the Count of Clare, the Count of Hereford, John of Monmouth, Roger de Monhaut and other powerful and famous Marcher Lords).

BESTIARIES IN MEDIEVAL BOOK LISTS

While surviving Bestiaries provide the only direct source of evidence about the period when this type of book was produced, and the number of survivals allow statistically significant conclusions to be drawn, the position is rather different with regard to localization. Original or early ownership can only be established for nineteen Bestiaries, fourteen with reasonable certainty. Such a small sample is no basis for generalizations about their distribution in the Middle Ages. Examining the various forms of surviving medieval book lists can provide more data (table 19).

TABLE 19. SUMMARY OF ENGLISH MEDIEVAL BOOK LISTS

HOUSE	ORDER	LIST	DATE	VOLS	BESTIARIES
1. Anglesey (Cambs)	AC	B	1314	23	0
2. Arundel	CC	I	1517	45	0
3. Bermondsey	Clu	C	1310–28	85	0
4. Bishop Auckland	CC	B	1499	48	0
5. Bordesley	C	G	1305	27	0
6. Bridlington (?)	AC	C	13c. (*in*)	127	1
7. Burton-on-Trent	B	C	post 1175	78	0
8. Bury St Edmund's	B	F	12/13c.	267	0
9. Canterbury, Christ Ch. 1	BCP	F	*c.* 1170	223	0
10. Canterbury, Christ Ch. 2	BCP	C	1284–1331	1831	3
11. Canterbury, Christ Ch. 3	BCP	G	1331	80	0
12. Canterbury, Christ Ch. 4	BCP	M	1337	73	0
13. Canterbury, St Aug.	B	C★	1491–7	1837	6
14. Coventry	BCP	S	*c.* 1240	16	0
15. Crowland	B	C★	13/14c.	92	0
16. Deeping	Bc	C	14c.	15	0

---

52. Matthew Paris IV, 358.

HOUSE	ORDER	LIST	DATE	VOLS	BESTIARIES
17. Dover	Bc	C	1389	449	2
18. Dover, St Radegund	Pre	C	c. 1300	254	0
19. Durham 1	BCP	C	12c. (ex)	337	0
20. Durham 2	BCP	C	1391–95	961	2
21. Durham 3	BCP	C★	1416	512	1
22. Evesham 1	B	G	1218	30+	0
23. Evesham 2	B	G	1229–36	25+	0
24. Evesham 3	B	G	pre 1392	86	0
25. Exeter 1	Cat	G	pre 1072	50	0
26. Exeter 2	Cat	I	1327	229	1
27. Exeter 3	Cat	I	1506	358	1
28. Exeter	F	G	1266	14	0
29. Farne	Bc	I	1451	13	0
30. Flaxley	C	C	13c.	79	0
31. Glastonbury 1	B	G	c. 1150	50	0
32. Glastonbury 2	B	C★	1247	340	1
33. Gloucester	B	G	13c.	6	0
34. Hulne 1	Car	C	c. 1365	79	0
35. Hulne 2	Car	F	1443	35	0
36. Ipswich	F	G	c. 1300 on	30+	0
37. Llanthony II	AC	C	14c.	486	0
38. Leicester	AC	C	post 1493	940	2
39. Leominster	Bc	C	13c.	130	0
40. Lichfield	Cat	C	c. 1622	79	0
41. Lincoln 1	Cat	C	1166–1200	95	0
42. Lincoln 2	Cat	C	15c.	109	0
43. Lindisfarne	Bc	I	1416	19	0
44. London, St Paul's	Cat	G	1313	126	0
45. London, St Paul's	Sch	G	1358	43	0
46. London	Cha	D	14c. on	38	0
47. London, Westminster	B	G	1376	94	0
48. Meaux	C	C	1396	465	6
49. Monk Bretton	Clu	C	1558	142	0
50. Newenham	C	G	1246–48	11	0
51. Norwich	BCP	B	1344–52	28	0
52. Norwich Priory 1	Bc	I	1422	34	0
53. Norwich Priory 2	Bc	I	1452–3	37	0
54. Oxford, Canterbury Col.	Col	C	1524	292	0
55. Oxford, Lincoln Col.	Col	C	1474–6	172	0

HOUSE	ORDER	LIST	DATE	VOLS	BESTIARIES
56. Peterborough 1	B	G	*c.* 970–84	20	1
57. Peterborough 2	B	G (16)	1222–1396	213	0
58. Peterborough 3	B	C★	12c. (*in*)	65	0
59. Peterborough 4	B	C	14c. (*ex*)	346	3
60. Ramsey 1	B	F	13c. (*ex*)	215	0
61. Ramsey 2	B	C★	14c. (*ex*)	600	0
62. Reading	B	C	12c. (*ex*)	228	1
63. Rievaulx	C	C	13c.	223	2
64. Rochester 1	BCP	C★	12c.	96	2
65. Rochester 2	BCP	C	1202	229	0
66. St Albans 1	B	G(5)	1077–1290	43+	0
67. St Albans 2	B	B	1420–37	56	1
68. Syon	Bri	C	1504–26	1421	1
69. Thorney	B	B	1324–30	51+	0
70. Titchfield	Pre	C	1400	224	2
71. Waltham	AC	C	13c. (*in*)	126	0
72. Welbeck	Pre	C	12c.	69	0
73. Wells	Cat	G	1425–6	10	0
74. Whitby	B	C	12c. (*ex*)	89	1
75. Winchester	Col	c	15c.	137	2
76. Windsor	RCC	I	1384–5	33	0
77. Witham 1	Cha	G	15c.	24	0
78. Witham 2	Cha	P	1474	44	0
79. Worcester 1	BCP	F	*c.* 1100	59	0
80. Worcester 2	BCP	C	1662–3	343	1
81. Worksop	AC	G	1187	5	1
82. Yarmouth	Bc	F	und.	22	0
83. York	AF	C	1372 on	646	1

Key to orders:

AC	Augustinian Canons	Cat	Cathedral
ACP	Augustinian cathedral priory	CC	Collegiate church
AF	Augustinian Friars	Cha	Charterhouse
B	Benedictine abbey	Clu	Cluniac
Bc	Benedictine cell	Col	College
BCP	Benedictine cathedral priory	F	Franciscan
Bri	Bridgettine	Pre	Premonstratensian
C	Cistercian	RCC	Royal collegiate chapel
Car	Carmelite	Sch	School

Key to lists:

B	borrowers' list		I	inventory
C	catalogue (* incomplete)		M	missing books
D	books sent elsewhere		P	books purchased
F	fragment of catalogue		S	scribe's list
G	gift (no. of donors)			

Here, too, are problems for the historian. First of all, the information is extremely patchy.[53] Of the great Benedictine foundations, Durham, the two Canterbury houses, Peterborough, Reading, Rochester and Dover all have reasonably full lists made at various times between the twelfth century and the late fifteenth.[54] Bury has three partial lists of *c.* 1200 and Glastonbury a fragment of 1247 and the record of a gift of fifty books made *c.* 1150. There is no comparable data from, for example, St Alban's, which provides only a few lists of donations by various abbots and a fragment of a borrowers' list; or from Ely, Westminster, Abingdon or either of the Winchester houses. Of the twelve richest houses according to Domesday,[55] we have some data from nine but full catalogues from only three.

Cistercian catalogues survive from Meaux, Rievaulx and Flaxley. The Augustinian canons are represented by Llanthony II and Leicester, and the Premonstratensians by St Radegund's and Titchfield. There is no complete catalogue from any Dominican or Franciscan friary, but a good one from the Augustinian friary at York. Secular cathedral catalogues survive from Exeter and Lincoln.

I have found no book list of any kind from any house of religious women. A good sixteenth-century catalogue of the Bridgettine double house of Syon survives, but the vast library it describes was probably in the hands of the brethren.[56]

Even where full library catalogues survive, the forms of the individual entries vary from house to house as well as tending to become more comprehensive later in the period. The Dover catalogue of 1389 not only lists the titles and first lines of every text in every book, together with the folio on which each text begins; it also gives *dicctiones probatorie* for each book. That is to say, the catalogue records the opening words of a specified page. Thus two volumes containing the same work could be distinguished. Furthermore, the whole catalogue is cross-referenced in a second list giving the titles and first lines of each text in the library. The entire collection was arranged by subject, and the catalogue gives the shelf mark of each volume. The Leicester catalogue of *c.* 1500 is similarly comprehensive.

---

53. Knowles (1955), II, 345–8.
54. References to the published sources of the book lists will be found under the name of the house in the bibliography.
55. Knowles (1963), 702.
56. Bateson (1898), xiii.

At the other end of the scale, early lists like the late twelfth-century catalogues from Lincoln and Durham give only short titles for each volume. In such cases, only the first or the main text in each book is listed, which may have been adequate for identifying books on the shelves of a small library, but cannot have served to find texts and is very deceptive for the present purpose. Short Bestiaries, such as First Family books or collections of extracts, were often bound with other works, and hence a library which, to judge from its catalogue, possessed no Bestiary, may well have housed several.

The major source for any investigation into medieval book lists is Gottlieb (1890), which gives references to catalogues published before that date. This was updated by Beddie (1930) for catalogues produced between 1050 and 1250. References to more recent publications of book lists are given by Knowles[57] and Ker.[58] Several more lists have come to light since the latter was last revized in 1964. A total of eighty-three lists were examined from sixty-two English houses, and the contents of these are summarized in table 19. The table does not aim to be comprehensive. It includes all the full catalogues and reasonably sized partial catalogues I have found, and every list of any kind containing Bestiaries. Such other lists as appear are intended to give an idea of the kind of material available. No lists of service books are included, and service books found in the lists examined have been excluded from the totals of volumes.

For comparison, I also examined 40 lists from 32 French houses and 266 lists from 108 German and Swiss houses.[59] Appendix two gives the full references to Bestiaries found in English medieval book lists, and table 20 gives a breakdown of the comparative data from England, France and Germany.

TABLE 20. BESTIARIES IN ENGLAND, FRANCE AND GERMANY

| | | | CATALOGUES | |
	SURVIVALS	HOUSES	LISTS	BESTIARIES
ENGLAND	50	61	83	41
FRANCE	12	32	40	5
GERMANY/ SWITZERLAND	4	108	266	3

---

57. Knowles (1955), II, 345–8.
58. Ker (1964), *passim.*
59. Data on French book lists was taken from Delisle (1874) and LePrevost (1855), and on German and Swiss lists from Lehmann (1918–32) and Gsell (1891).

PATTERNS OF CONSUMPTION BY TIME, PLACE AND RELIGIOUS ORDER

The evidence from surviving books and medieval book lists outlined above forms the basis of the three following sections, which examine the distribution of Bestiaries under the heads of time, place and order.

TIME

The surviving Bestiaries themselves offer the best evidence of the timespan over which the Latin Bestiary enjoyed its period of popularity in this country.[60] Figure 1 is a histogram of the production dates of surviving books in the period 1100 to 1500, extracted from table 17.

Bearing in mind the difficulties of dating, it was decided that a degree of precision more accurate than one-third of a century was impractical. Even so, it will be noted that the estimated dates of production given in table 17 do not always fall entirely within time periods specified on the histogram. In such cases the midpoint of the estimated dating range has been plotted on the histogram. Paris, Bibl Nat MS Nouv. Acq. Lat. 873, for example, is dated c. 1160–80, a dating that spans the second and last thirds of the century. The midpoint, 1170, falls in the last third, and this is where the book has been plotted. This unavoidable reduction in precision is unfortunate but acceptable in this case, since the purpose is to give an overall picture of the rate of production of Bestiaries over the period. If one or two books are misplaced, the shape of the histogram is not greatly altered.

Production of Bestiaries rose sharply to a peak in the early thirteenth century and declined more gradually thereafter. Almost three-quarters of surviving books date from the thirteenth century. The use of a sample (in this case the survivals) to represent the entire population (the total production of Bestiaries) is standard statistical practice, but there are three important points to be considered. First, the sample should be random, and in this case it clearly is not. It is reasonable to expect that more losses have been suffered among

---

60. Saunders (1928), I, 47 placed the Bestiary's period of popularity firmly in the twelfth century as part of an overall tendency to early dating on stylistic grounds, which labelled Royal MSS 12.C. XIX and 12. F. XIII as well as the two Harley Bestiaries as twelfth-century productions. James (1928), published in the same year, also dated early, but not so markedly (Royal 12. C. XIX and Harley 4751 were dated to the s.xii, Royal 12.F.XIII to s.xii–xiii, and Harley 3244 to s.xiii early). Overall, he concluded that 'the Bestiary may be reckoned one of the leading picture-books of the twelfth and thirteenth centuries in this country'. White (1954), 234, quoted this passage from James, but preferred the twelfth century to the thirteenth as the Bestiary's 'finest foliage in Latin prose'. McCulloch (1960) was prepared to accept James's datings. The tradition continued with her pupil, Willene Clark, who dated Harley 4751 to 'ca. 1200' as recently as 1982 (p. 73). Morgan (1982), 23, was aware of the problem, and favoured the later dating: 'In the older literature, many of these [Bestiaries] have been dated rather too early, to the late years of the twelfth century, whereas most of them were produced at a date well into the thirteenth century.'

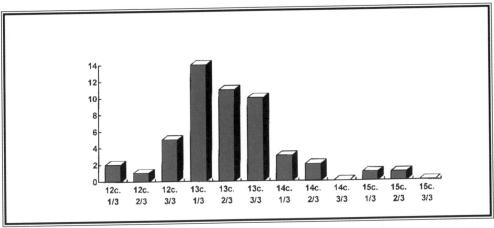

Figure 1. Production dates of surviving bestiaries based on the evidence of survivals. Bestiary production rose rapidly to a peak in the early thirteenth century, and gradually fell after 1300.

the earlier books. In the fragmentary Glastonbury (1247) and Durham (1416) catalogues, for example, the compiler has noted the condition of the books. A Bestiary in the latter is marked *modicum valet*, almost certainly a comment on its condition rather than its contents, and it is a short step from this to the scrapping or replacement of the book. The growth in Bestiary production was thus certainly less dramatic than the histogram would suggest. Evidence to confirm this is to be found in the oldest Peterborough list, which records a gift of twenty books including a *Liber Bestiarum* by St Aethelwold (d. 984).

The second point is that the sample should be large enough to represent the entire population. The question is not one of numbers, but of percentages: the higher the proportion of the whole represented by the sample, the more accurate is the picture that it gives.

It is extraordinarily difficult to come to a conclusion about the percentage of the total production of medieval books represented by the survivals. Various approaches to the problem are tackled in appendix three, where it is concluded that the survival rate probably falls within the range of 15 to 20 per cent, which would certainly be large enough to represent the population fairly if the criterion of random sampling applied.

Finally, while an adequate sample will give a good approximation of the mean of a population, it will tend to underestimate the variance. In this case, that means that the peak of production was, as shown in figure 1, in the early thirteenth century, but that the production was actually spread over a longer timespan than the survivals indicate. A standard statistical correction for this, Bessel's correction, can be applied (see appendix four), and this indicates that, judging from the data available, 99 per cent of Bestiaries were produced between the last third of the eleventh century and the middle third of the fifteenth, although, as we have seen, the bias of the sample is such that we must assume production to have begun before the earlier date in England.

The gift by St Aethelwold of a *Liber Bestiarium* to Peterborough[61] gives a *terminus ante quem* for the first appearance of Bestiaries in England. The *Physiologus* is known in two continental manuscripts of the eighth or ninth centuries, Bern, Burgerbibliothek MSS 233 and 318. The latter came to the library from the collection of Jacob Bongars, who had obtained it from the lawyer and philologist Peter Daniel.[62] Daniel, who lived in Orleans, acquired most of his books from the nearby abbey of Fleury and while there is no mark in the book to connect it with Fleury, the similarity of the miniatures to work of the Reims group of illuminators adds support to this theory.[63] The links forged with Fleury by Aethelwold are well known.[64] The house owned the body of St Benedict himself, and was the chief source of the monastic revival initiated by Aethelwold, Dunstan and Oswald in England. Aethelwold sent his disciple Osgar to Fleury in order to learn the ways of the monks there.[65] He became Archbishop of Winchester in 963 and at the synod that produced the *Regularis Concordia*, held there in about the year 970, were monks from Fleury and Ghent invited to give their advice.[66] Finding Peterborough in ruins in 966, Aethelwold undertook its rebuilding, which was completed four years later. The gift of church furnishings, land and books,[67] including the Bestiary, thus probably dates from the foundation in 970.

There is, then, a mass of circumstantial evidence connecting this Bestiary with Fleury. Such evidence can be no more than suggestive, but in the absence of anything harder it is tempting to see Fleury as the source and Aethelwold as the agent of the introduction of the Latin Bestiary into this country.

If this is so, it may be thought that the dates of surviving books set out diagrammatically in figure 1 indicate that Bestiaries were slow to gain popularity after their early introduction. One objection to this has already been argued: the disproportionate losses among early books. The other point which must be made is that the growth in Bestiary production coincides with the period of overall growth of monastic libraries. Referring again to table 19 we see, for example, that Durham book lists indicate a growth in holdings from 377 to 961 between the beginning of the twelfth century and the end of the fourteenth. Such comparative figures are rare for individual houses, but the information we have strongly indicates a considerable and general growth in the size of

---

61. Way (1863), 365, suggested that it may have been a copy of Bede's *De naturis bestiarum*. This seems improbable: the same gift included *Beda in Marcum* (citing the author).
62. Hagen (1875), 325.
63. See Woodruff (1930). Archbishop Ebbo of Reims was exiled to Fleury in 833. See Rocher (1865), 81.
64. See, e.g., Knowles (1963), 39–42.
65. Aelfric, 259.
66. *Regularis Concordia*, xxvii.
67. Given in full in Mon. Angl. I, 382.

book holdings, especially in the period up to 1300. If it were possible to express the production of Bestiaries as a proportion of total book production for each time period, therefore, we would see that their growth was much less steep than it appears in figure 1.

No such qualification is needed at the other end of the timescale. By 1300 the great age of Bestiary production was over and 90 per cent of our survivals had been made by then and 95 per cent by the middle of the next century. Investigation into the causes of this loss of popularity must wait until assessments of the uses of Bestiaries have been made in chapter five.

PLACE

Latin Bestiaries were above all English books. This fact is apparent from the evidence of both survivals (50 English, 9 French or Flemish, 1 German) and medieval book lists (36 Bestiaries from 32 English houses; 5 from 32 houses in France and 3 from 108 in Germany and Switzerland) given in table 20. The figures are too emphatic to need any statistical analysis to verify their significance.

Within England, information about centres of use can be obtained both from surviving books and from book lists. Before this is analyzed, however, the point should be made that the Bestiary was apparently not, despite the assumptions examined in chapter one, seen as an essential part of every monastic library.[68] Nor is it true to say that Bestiaries were only to be found in large libraries. Every surviving full catalogue made after 1300 and listing more than 500 volumes includes at least one Bestiary, but beyond that the picture is very varied. Llanthony II had no Bestiary in a collection of 486 books, while Meaux, with slightly smaller holdings, had 6. It is clear that constraints other than mere size were at work, and I hope to throw some light on these in this section and the next.

Attempts have been made before to locate centres important for Bestiary production, particularly for the lavishly illustrated books. James gave evidence of medieval ownership where he could find it[69] but was clearly exasperated at his inability to fix the provenance of the luxury books, and could go no further than a vague localization: 'I have an impression, which I cannot support with any cogent arguments, that the fine Bestiaries belong rather to the North of England than the South.'[70]

More recently, Xenia Muratova has made the assertion that:

---

68. See Knowles (1963), 525–7.
69. James (1928).
70. Ibid., 59. By 'the fine Bestiaries', he seems to imply the Ashmole and Aberdeen books, Pierpont Morgan MS M. 81, Royal 12. C. XIX, Harley 4751 and Bodley 764.

lo studio dei bestiari stessi, delle loro variazioni stilistiche e iconografiche, fa pensare all'esistenza di un solo centro di produzione[71]

(the study of these Bestiaries, of their stylistic and iconographic variations, suggest the existence of a single centre of production).

Her arguments in favour of Lincoln and her wider claims for the 'North of England' as the chief centre of Bestiary production have already been examined. I should only like to repeat that the available evidence does not lend itself to confident assertions about centres of production. If we move from these precarious constructions of cultural environments to the firmer ground of the mass of direct evidence offered by book lists and inscriptions in survivals, we will find direct pointers to centres of consumption.

The information provided by this approach must be treated with care, however. If two manuscripts are twins, then it is fair to assume that they were in contact at the production stage, either directly or through intermediaries. It is probable, however (in the case of Bestiaries), that they were not together in the consumption stage. While a religious institution might well need several identical psalters, it would probably not want two identical Bestiaries. The text and organization of the Bestiary were changing fast during the period under consideration, and different Bestiaries corresponded to different needs. When we can identify several surviving Bestiaries from a centre of use, we find textual and organizational differences between them. This is the case with the two Rochester Bestiaries, BL MSS Royal 6. A. XI and 12. F. XIII, and with the two St Augustine's Bestiaries, Bibl. Nat. MS Nouv. Acq. Lat. 873 and Bodleian MS Douce 88(II). Hence, when we find that BL MS Royal 12. C. XIX is identical with the Worksop Bestiary (New York, Pierpont Morgan MS M. 81), not only in the composition of the miniatures but textually, page for page and line for line throughout most of its contents, we must conclude that although the Royal manuscript is almost certainly a direct copy of the Morgan, it was probably not used at Worksop.[72]

Figure 2 is a map of England and Wales showing the locations where surviving Bestiaries and those mentioned in book lists were used. It is obvious from this map that while the overall spread of Bestiaries follows the general distribution pattern of religious houses, certain centres had a stronger interest in them. It is likely that these same centres of use were responsible for implementing the structural changes to the book described in the two previous chapters, and the aim of this chapter is to connect the two. In this, we are not confined to the evidence of survivals: it is sometimes possible to get some idea of

---

71. Muratova (1976.I), 178.

72. In the light of the compositional similarity of the Worksop Bestiary and Royal 12.C.XIX, 73 Muratova's assertion that, 'we shall never know what effect Philip's copyright had on the flourishing production of illuminated Bestiaries at the end of the twelfth century' (1986.I, 119) seems unduly pessimistic.

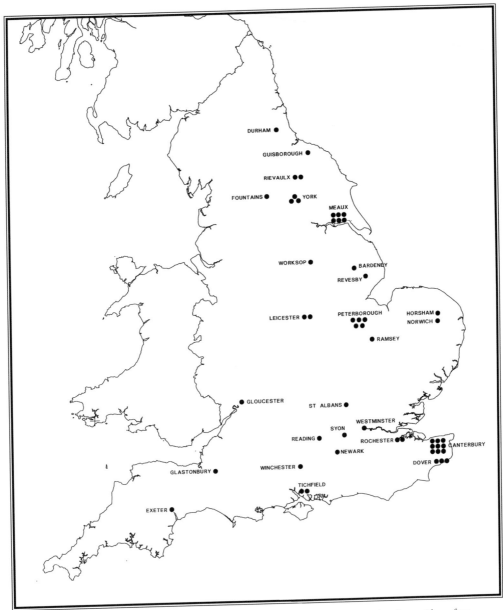

Figure 2. Bestiary distribution in England and Wales. Centres of Bestiary consumption based on evidence from survivals and booklists. Each dot represents one Bestiary.

the type of Bestiary referred to in entries in medieval book lists. All the organizational changes which took place involved modifications to the early part of the text: hence, when the *secundo folio* or better still, the *incipit* is given, the type of Bestiary can be estimated with some confidence. In the course of the following analysis of centres of Bestiary consumption, the reader will find it useful to refer to the map in figure 2, and to the Bestiary entries abstracted from medieval book lists in appendix two.

CANTERBURY AND DOVER

No surviving Bestiary can be firmly localized to Christ Church, although James tentatively placed both Laud Misc. 247 and Stowe 1067 there on the basis of script.[73] Henry of Eastry's Christ Church catalogue lists three Bestiaries, one bound with Gregory's *Dialogues* and two bound individually (see appendix two). Since the catalogue fails to specify *secundo folio* or *incipit*, there is no clue as to type. Some guide to dating, however, is given by the placing of the books in the catalogue (and hence on the shelves). The catalogue is divided into two great sections, called demonstrations. The *prima demonstratio* contained 782 volumes, of which the first 502 were arranged by subject. The *secunda demonstratio* began with the donations of Becket and Herbert of Bosham, and was entirely organized according to donor. The chronological sequence of donations extended throughout the second demonstration and ended with the space remaining at the end of the first demonstration (volumes 503 to 782). It is thus assumed that volumes 1 to 502 predate the Becket books, and represent the holdings of the library before records of donors were taken. Ker (1964) noted 105 survivals from these 502 volumes, of which only eleven or twelve post-date the twelfth century, so the assumption is largely justified. The three lost Bestiaries are found among the early books in the first demonstration, one among the works of Gregory, and the other two occupying successive positions in the Liberal Arts section. It is a fair assumption that they too were early books.

When we turn to St Augustine's, the picture becomes much clearer (plate 44). Two of the Bestiaries mentioned in the late fifteenth-century catalogue still survive, and the form of the entries allows us to deduce a good deal about the lost volumes.

Paris, BN Nouv. Acq. Lat. 873, as we saw, is a late twelfth-century Bestiary without illustrations, one of three given by Adam the sub-prior. The text follows Laud closely, while the chapter order, as we saw in chapter three, shows some regrouping towards the end in an effort to separate beasts from the rest of creation, a process that was also attempted in the first quire of Stowe. Adam's other two Bestiaries, 869 and 1557 in the catalogue, must predate his death, presumed no later than *c.* 1230, but may be considerably older: 869 was bound alone. The *secundo folio: deret in*, is probably a

---

73. James (1928), 7, 10.

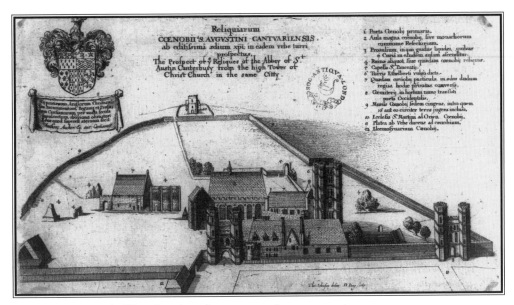

Plate 44. St Augustine's Abbey, Canterbury, from a seventeenth-century engraving

variant reading of *cum viderit in mare* from *serra*. It is worth noting that the *secundo folio* of Royal 2.C.XII, *cum viderit*, is from the same passage. The inference is that 869 must have been a Laud type Bestiary, or at least that it was not reorganized at the beginning in the way that Stowe was. Any such modifications to the early chapters would have moved the sea monster towards the end of the text.

Likewise the *secundo folio: feminas* in 1557 is probably from *lapides igniferi*, another chapter only found towards the start of Laud-type Bestiaries.

Douce 88(II), number 870 in the catalogue, is a mid-thirteenth-century Third Family Bestiary, now bound with the Second Family Bestiary, Douce 88(I). The textual evidence for the presence of both of these Bestiaries at St Augustine's has been given in chapter three, and the same evidence lends credence to the idea that the compilation of the Third Family organization took place in this area. Support for this is found in the heavy reliance on the *Pantheologus* in the Third Family recension. We shall see below that this uncommon text was popular mainly in the south-east, and above all at Rochester.

The two other Bestiaries in the catalogue, 650 and 1564, were both in composite volumes and since they did not open the volumes, the *secundis foliis* are no help to us. It is interesting to find that 1564 also included an Aviary. Willene Clark has traced ten combined Bestiaries and Aviaries of English origin,[74] and of these ten, seven belong to

74. Clark (1982), 73–4.

James's Second Family, one is Laud type, one Stowe type, and the last a book of extracts. The weight of statistical evidence implies that 1564 was likely to be a Second Family Bestiary but, in the absence of any indication of its date, this is of little value.

Further evidence for the placing of the Laud Bestiary at St Augustine's comes from an examination of the other contents of the book. It includes three texts related to Alexander: the life, the letter to Aristotle and the letter to Dindymus.[75] Nouv. Acq. Lat. 873 also includes the life and the letter to Dindymus,[76] while volume 870 in the catalogue included the two letters and probably the life too.

No Bestiary survives which can be identified with the cell of Christ Church at Dover. Nevertheless, the detailed entries in the catalogue of 1389 provide a good idea of the type of Bestiaries in use there, though not of their dates of production. Bestiary 132 began *Bestiarum vocabulum*, and could not have been Laud or Stowe type, or a Third Family book, but could have belonged to James's Second Family. Of surviving books, Royal 12. F. XIII, from Rochester; Douce 88(I), from St Augustine's; Sloane 3544; Bodley 533; Gonville & Caius 384/604; and Corpus Christi 53 (with Peterborough connections) all begin in this way. The Bestiary text of the Pierpont Morgan M81 group also starts like this but all four surviving manuscripts include prefatory material. The length of the Dover book, seventy-three leaves, also indicates one of these two types. Identification using the *dicciones probatorie, humani generis* is not easy in this case, since the words fall on f. 4. The phrase is found in *cervus*, but the chapter occurs too late in either recension. If it were a variant of *humanum genus*, from *pantera* this could indicate a Second Family book, in which *pantera* is usually chapter four, rather than one of the Pierpont Morgan 81 type where it appears much later in the text.

The other Latin Bestiary in the Dover catalogue, number 197, was only eleven folios long, and began *Leo quinque naturas*. As we saw in chapter three, this attempt to reconcile the described *naturas* with the phrase *Physiologus dicit tres naturales habere leonem* was a characteristic of the rewriting of the chapter found in Stowe, and particularly in Vat. Reg. Lat. 258, and Paris, B.N. Lat. 14429, both of which specify five natures. The abrupt opening of the text, and the title '*Tractatus de naturis animalium*', both point to a book of extracts rather than an organized Bestiary, as do the *dicctiones probatorie* (on f. 3) *et custodiant ple*, which are not found among the early chapters of any surviving Bestiary.

We have evidence, therefore, of early interest in Bestiaries at both the great Canterbury houses but particularly St Augustine's, which seems to have been the site of some of the twelfth-century recasting of the Laud text in the direction of Stowe. It

---

75. See Ross (1956), 127–32; Hahn (1980), 277.
76. This does not seem to have been noted by Ross or Hahn.

is tempting to see Adam the sub-prior as an agent of this transformation but it must be remembered that his surviving Bestiary, B.N. Nouv. Acq. Lat. 873, reorganizes chapters only towards the end, while in Stowe, which is approximately a quarter of a century older, the process begins at the start of the book, and is much more comprehensive. Nevertheless, James's ascription of Stowe to Canterbury, together with the undoubted involvement of St Augustine's and the cell at Dover in this particular transformation make up a strong case for localizing it in this region.

The evidence also points in the direction of St Augustine's as the site of the compilation of the Third Family recension. Indeed, the large number of Bestiaries of all types in the area around Canterbury, the Christ Church cell in Dover and Rochester indicates a continuing interest here which is far more significant than at Lincoln, for which more extravagant claims have been made.

OTHER SOUTH-EASTERN BOOKS

Bestiaries survive from Rochester Cathedral, Westminster Abbey, and the house of Augustinian canons at Newark (Sussex). No Bestiary is listed in the incomplete Rochester catalogue of 1202, although one of the two Rochester survivals, Royal 6. A. XI, was certainly produced before that date. The first text in the book, however, is erroneously rubricated *Ambrosius de divinis officiis*, and it may be identifiable with the *De divinis* that appears as 125 in the catalogue.[77] On the other hand, there is some doubt about whether Royal 6. A. XI was originally a Rochester book at all. The usual fourteenth-century *ex-libris* appears on f. 1r, but on f. 159v is an erased thirteenth-century inscription which looks as if it relates to another house. The Bestiary itself is abnormally entitled *Incipit exceptiones phisiologi*, and appears to be just that: an eclectic collection of thirty-five chapters from both the B and Y texts of the *Physiologus*, arranged in a unique order. The composition of the Bestiary and the other contents of the book offer valuable evidence of the use of the work, which will be considered in the relevant chapter, but it stands nowhere in the process of taxonomic reorganization described in the previous chapters.

Royal 12. F. XIII, the other Rochester Bestiary, is also an oddity. It belongs to James's Second Family, and the chapter order broadly follows the earlier Additional 11283, Ashmole and Cambridge University Library Ii. 4. 26. Bestiaries. The text, however, includes substantial insertions from the *Pantheologus* of Petrus Londiniensis, and the picture cycle is entirely unique. Petrus Londiniensis, otherwise Petrus canonicus or Petrus de Cornubia, was first a canon and later prior (1197–1221) of the Augustinian house of Christ-Church-within-Aldgate. In extant copies of the

---

77. Warner and Gilson (1921) I, 130–1.

Pantheologus, he is described as Petrus canonicus, or canonicus et archdiaconis, and thus the work presumably predates 1197. Five copies of the whole work, or parts of it, are known to me,[78] dating from *c.* 1200 to the fourteenth century. Two of these, both roughly contemporary with Royal 12. F. XIII, have a Rochester provenance. Another was produced for the Kentish house of Augustinian canons at Lessness, and was later in the hands of an archdeacon of Rochester.[79] A fourth belonged to St Albans,[80] and the latest bears no evidence of early localization.[81] Royal 12. F. XIII thus confirms what was already known about interest in Petrus Londiniensis at Rochester. The importance of the *Pantheologus* in the Third Family recension has been discussed in chapter three, where textual evidence was presented to make a case for the Canterbury region as the site where the recension was compiled. The popularity of the *Pantheologus* in the same area provides additional support for that case.

The Westminster book, Oxford, St John's Coll. MS 178, includes a late thirteenth-century Bestiary resembling Cambridge University Library MS Ii. 4. 26 in structure, but since it was produced almost a century later it is no help in localizing the site of the reorganization. The Newark book, Bodley 602, is similarly unhelpful, following Laud textually at a distance of a century.

We know from catalogues of the presence of two Bestiaries at Titchfield in 1400, one at Reading *c.* 1200, and one at Syon by 1526, but the catalogue entries are not detailed enough to allow identification of the type of Bestiaries involved.

PETERBOROUGH

Mention has already been made of Peterborough's association with the earliest recorded Bestiary in England: the *Liber Bestiarum* given by Bishop Aethelwold to the abbey, presumably either at its foundation in 970 or at Aethelwold's death in 984. Speculation about this lost book is largely futile but two points must be made. It was almost certainly an import, probably from Fleury and, it almost certainly contained additions from Isidore (otherwise it would have been called a *Physiologus*). In those respects, it presumably resembled Vat. Pal. Lat. 1074.

The only survival that can be associated with Peterborough is the fourteenth-century book, Cambridge, Corpus Christi 53, whose problematic provenance was discussed

---

78. London, BL Royal MSS 7.E.VIII, 7.C.XIII and 7.C.XIV form one complete copy made in the first half of the thirteenth century, from Rochester. Royal 7.F.IV is an incomplete Rochester copy of the second half of the century. Royal 6.E.VIII is another incomplete copy, from St Albans. Oxford, St John's Coll. 31 of *c.* 1200 is from the Augustinian house of Lessness in Kent. Oxford, Balliol LXXXII, of the fourteenth century, has not been localized.
79. Coxe (1852) II, MSS *Collegii S. Johannes Baptistae*, 10–11.
80. Warner and Gilson (1921) I, 159.
81. Coxe (1852), I, *MSS Collegii Balliolensis*, 25.

above. Neither this nor Aethelwold's Bestiary can be identified in the late fourteenth-century *Matricularium* of the library which, however, does include three other entries of interest. In no case are *incipits or secundis foliis* given, but the titles themselves provide some clues. Their form indicates in all three cases that the compiler of the catalogue was describing the contents to the best of his ability rather than copying rubrics. *Quedam metaphore sumpte a naturis bestiarum* (270.T.xii) was probably a book of extracts. *Tractatus de naturis bestiarum et volucrum* (55.L.iii) was presumably an organized Bestiary, although one cannot know what kind. *Quedam Summa de naturis animalium* (330.K.xv) could have been either or neither. The only conclusion to be drawn from the scanty evidence is that Peterborough was an early (though not necessarily the earliest) centre of Bestiary use, and retained its interest into the fourteenth century.

EAST MIDLANDS AND EAST ANGLIA

Of survivals from this region, arbitrarily limited to the north by the Humber, the Ramsey book, Bodleian Tanner 110, contains an unillustrated Bestiary in a mid-thirteenth-century cursive hand. In form it is a Second Family book but it contains only forty-one chapters, the remainder having been omitted, largely in blocks of up to ten chapters. The order of those that remain follows that of Cambridge University Library Ii. 4. 26, with the interesting additions of *passer* (the sparrow) and *milvus* (the kite), from Giraldus Cambrensis, and *merula*, (the blackbird) from Petrus Londiniensis; the three birds only found otherwise in Bodley 764 and Harley 4751, which both include many more additions from the same two sources. The Ramsey book is thus either a copy of a catastrophically defective Bestiary of the Harley 4751 type, or an imperfectly made copy of a complete model.

The other main centres of interest in the region are the Augustinian houses in Leicester and Worksop, and the Cistercian abbey at Revesby. If James's ascription of Cambridge University Library Ii. 4. 26 to Revesby is accepted, this becomes the earliest Second Family Bestiary that can be localized. Even so, the information is not of any great value since Additional 11283 predates it by some forty years.

The excellent post-1493 Leicester catalogue tells us that the two Bestiaries were bound in wooden boards with white covers, that one (480) was lavishly illustrated while the other (481) was not, and that the latter was among the twenty-one books found in *scriptoria*. The catalogue gives no *incipits* but does list *secundis foliis*. In both cases these imply introductory material from Genesis. *De operibus*, which opened f. 2 of 480, is found as a rubric preceding this material in the Bestiary formerly at Alnwick, as well as in such Second Family books as the Ashmole Bestiary, while *in principio creavit*, from 481, opens the Genesis material itself.

The case of the Worksop Bestiary, New York Pierpont Morgan 81, offers as we have seen, ample scope for speculation. Apart from its importance within the Morgan textual group, it also stands near the beginning of the 'early series of luxury Bestiaries'.[82] It will be as well to consider both groups separately.

I have suggested, in chapter three, that St Petersburg rather than Morgan is the earliest survivor of the textual group. Even if we speculate, from the similarity of the miniatures in the two books, that they were produced in the same area, if not the same workshop, we are still a long way from establishing this area as the origin of the textual group. If my calculations of survival rates are accepted (appendix 3), then the four books of the Morgan group could represent the remnant of a group of some twenty to thirty of this textual type, and it would be unreasonable to hope that P was the oldest member of this group, especially in view of the survival of Add. 11283, a Second Family book which certainly predates it and whose textual organization presupposes that of P. In other words, there must have been a Bestiary with the chapter order of P (but not necessarily the prefatory material) produced before 1170. This seriously weakens the case for Lincoln as an important centre of Bestiary production, where this textual reorganization may have taken place. Examination of the two Lincoln Cathedral library catalogues discloses no Bestiaries at all, in sharp contrast to the evidence of interest in them that we have found at centres like Meaux and St Augustine's, Canterbury.

The position of M as an early luxury Bestiary, a group which includes – as well as M, P and R – the Aberdeen and Ashmole books and Cambridge University Library Ii. 4. 26, is more interesting. M is valuable in this case, not because it is early, but because the circumstances of its consumption are known. Its high quality is associated with its status as a gift, as can be verified from the descriptions of other volumes in the list. More will be said on this subject in chapter five.

YORK

Two Bestiaries survive, one from the Benedictine priory of the Holy Trinity (now Oxford, St John's College MS 61), the other from the Franciscan convent (now Westminster Abbey MS 22). A third is known from the catalogue of the convent of Austin friars but its description gives no clue to its type. The St John's book, as we saw above, has an *ex-libris* painted by the artist of the miniatures (colour plate 7), indicating that the abbey was the original patron. It is a Second Family Bestiary of *c.* 1220, lavishly illustrated with ninety-six miniatures in full colour. The text, chapter order and miniature compositions are very close to Cambridge University Library MS Ii. 4. 26, produced ten to twenty years earlier. The two Bestiaries differ in the additional material at the beginning of the later book, and in the treatment of the miniatures. The St John's Bestiary opens (f. 1v) with a unique composition of four Creation scenes in a single miniature (colour plate 9),

---

82. Morgan (1982), 65.

followed by Adam naming the animals (f. 2r). The passage from Isidore beginning *Omnibus animantibus* . . . follows, and then a three-register illustration to *leo* (f. 3v). This is the point at which the Cambridge Bestiary begins, and apart from the inclusion in the latter of a second three-register illustration to *leo*, not found in the St John's book, the two correspond closely thereafter, even to the extent of the repetition of the *Omnibus animantibus* . . . passage before the section on domestic beasts in the St John's book.

This implies either that St John's 61 used elements of two exemplars, one organized like Ii. 4. 26, and the other with the Creation miniatures and the text and image of Adam naming the animals at the start, like the Ashmole Bestiary; or that the preliminary material not found in Ii. 4. 26 was introduced without an exemplar. Morgan seems to favour the latter alternative, certainly as far as the Creation scenes are concerned, on the grounds that the Temptation and Expulsion scenes included here are found in no earlier Bestiary.[83] The model he postulates: 'must have been of the style of the Aberdeen or Ashmole Bestiaries,' but, 'the iconography of this fully painted model was perhaps very similar to that of the drawings in the Cambridge Bestiary (i.e. Ii. 4. 26)'.[84] This does not solve the problem of the repeated text passage, which surely points to two exemplars. If one were organized like Ashmole and the other like Ii. 4. 26, the repetition would be explained, along with the stylistic and iconographic similarities noted by Morgan. The fact that no earlier Bestiary survives with exactly the same Creation scenes is hardly surprising in view of our expectations about survival rates.

Westminster Abbey MS 22, from the Franciscan convent, is a Third Family book, the latest of the five survivals I have found. One other is localized, as we saw above, Douce 88(II), from St Augustine's, Canterbury.

RELIGIOUS ORDER

The extensive search for Bestiaries in English medieval book lists, covering more than 15,000 volumes in 62 libraries, allows us to estimate the relative importance of Bestiaries to users in different types of institution. In table 21, a ratio of Bestiaries per thousand volumes has been extracted from the data in table 19. The results are striking but must, as always, be treated with caution. The high ratio associated with schools, for example, is based on a total sample of only 180 books, and the two Bestiaries both came from the same school library. This on its own is no sound basis for generalizations about the popularity of Bestiaries in schools. In many such cases there is insufficient data. In the following discussion, 'sufficient data' has been taken to mean a total of at least 500 volumes from at least 3 houses.

83. Morgan (1982), 90.
84. Ibid.

TABLE 21. USERS OF BESTIARIES FROM BOOK LIST ENTRIES

USER	HOUSES	VOLUMES	% OF TOTAL	BESTIARIES	BESTIARIES/ 1,000 VOLS
B/Bc	21	4,973	32.1	16	3.2
BCP	6	3,488	22.5	6	1.7
(All Ben.)	(27)	(8,461)	(54.6)	(22)	(2.6)
AC	6	1,707	11.0	4	2.3
AF	1	646	4.2	1	1.5
Bri	1	1,421	9.2	1	0.7
C	5	805	5.2	8	9.9
Car	1	79	0.5	0	0
Cat	5	682	4.4	1	1.5
CC	3	126	0.8	0	0
Cha	2	106	0.7	0	0
Clu	2	227	1.5	0	0
Col	2	464	3.0	0	0
F	2	44	0.3	0	0
Pre	3	547	3.5	2	3.7
Sch	2	180	1.2	2	11.1
TOTALS	62	15,495	100	41	2.6

Key to orders:

AC	Augustinian Canons	Cat	Cathedral
AF	Augustinian Friars	CC	Collegiate church
B	Benedictine abbey	Cha	Charterhouse
Bc	Benedictine cell	Clu	Cluniac
BCP	Benedictine cathedral priory	Col	College
Bri	Bridgettine	F	Franciscan
C	Cistercian	Pre	Premonstratensian
Car	Carmelite	Sch	School

The overall frequency of 2.6 Bestiaries/1,000 volumes is set largely by the Benedictine abbeys, priories and cathedral priories, which together supply more than half the books in the sample. Among the religious houses, only the Cistercian ratio of 9.9 significantly exceeds this. Although book lists from five houses were examined, all eight Bestiaries were from the two Yorkshire foundations of Rievaulx (plate 45) and Meaux, and on the face of it the unusual popularity of Bestiaries could thus be as much a Yorkshire as a Cistercian phenomenon. Fortunately book lists from four non-Cistercian houses in the county survive: Bridlington, Whitby, Monk Bretton and

Plate 45. Rievaulx Abbey (Yorks), abbey church and monastic buildings seen from the north-east.

York Augustinian friary (see table 19). The data from these libraries indicate a ratio of 3.0 Bestiaries/1,000 volumes: much closer to the national average than to the Cistercian figure. As long ago as 1956, Fr. Morson established the debt owed to the Bestiary by Cistercian sermons, particularly those of Aelred of Rievaulx.[85] The implications of his results will be examined in the next chapter. I only wish to suggest here that my statistical results provide a tool by which the results of textual analyses like Fr. Morson's can be evaluated and, belatedly in this case, justified.

85. Morson (1956).

CHAPTER FIVE

CONSUMPTION AND NARRATION

In the previous chapter, patterns of consumption of Bestiaries according to time, location and institutional user were established. This final chapter aims to take the story a step further by attempting to answer the following two questions. What kind of books were Bestiaries to their owners? How, and in what circumstances, were Bestiaries read?

WHAT WERE BESTIARIES?

The analysis of changes to text, image and organization which occupied chapter three suggests that no single answer can be given to this question. It has been assumed throughout the enquiry that changes in the content of the book were dictated by changing conditions of use and as a corollary of this, that different versions of the Bestiary, even when present in the same library at the same time, were used for different purposes.

Past attempts to define Bestiaries have usually involved some variation on the theme of 'moralized natural history', with varying degrees of emphasis being placed on the two components of the definition.[1] There are two kinds of problem involved in definitions of this type. First, they take no account of changes in Bestiary structure and second, they take as their basis a concept that had no meaning to the original users of the books. Thinking of Bestiaries in anachronistic terms is to some extent unavoidable. There is no way we can repeat Evans-Pritchard's methods of research into the Azande, by going to live for a time among our subjects.[2] On the other hand, it would be a

---

1. Allen (1887), Bond (1910) and to some extent Druce emphasized the moralizations in the sense that they used them to read theological symbolism in animal imagery wherever they found it. At the same time we find in Evans (1896) criticisms of the moralizations as poor theology. On the other hand, Druce's speculations on the identities of the animals he wrote about spurred later investigators (e.g., George (1968)) into venturing down the same treacherous byways. There is no doubt that the physical descriptions of animals and their behaviour in Bestiaries are much more understandable and entertaining to modern readers than the moralizations. This was recognized in New York (1960) and Boase (1953) where the moralizations were omitted from quoted Bestiary chapters. White (1954) repeatedly presented Bestiaries as serious works of natural history. James (1928), perhaps wisely, did not commit himself.
2. Evans-Pritchard (1937). See also the discussions on his work by Winch and MacIntyre in Wilson (1970), 78–111 and 112–30.

mistake to assume, as he did, that our 'common-sense' or 'scientific' approach to other cultures can be justified by the assertion of some privileged access to an objective reality on our part.[3]

To label the Bestiary 'natural history', a term which did not begin to acquire its present meaning until the middle of the seventeenth century,[4] could only be justified if we were able, through the exercise of an objectivity unavailable to its original users, to state that this is what it really was. Since we cannot, the use of the label puts us in a position of discussing the Bestiary in terms of a concept foreign to both its medieval consumers and to any notion of objectivity. Foreign also, it seems to me, to modern scientific thought, since choosing the term 'natural history', as did James (1928) and White (1954), rather than 'zoology', like Allen (1887), looks suspiciously like deliberate archaism.

An opposition occasionally employed specifically by modern writers, but more significantly incorporated into the classification systems of modern libraries, is one which identifies Bestiaries as 'secular' books as against such 'religious' works as saints' lives and homilies.[5] Any Bestiary, whether composed largely of *Physiologus* material like Laud Misc. 247, or organized along Isidorean lines like Ashmole 1511, was informed by a motive of Christian didacticism (the provision of sermons or exemplars in the one case: the exegesis of part of the Genesis creation myth in the other). Moreover, however, much 'zoological' material was added, enough of *Physiologus* always remained to remind us that we are not in any sense dealing with zoology.

BESTIARIES IN THEIR INSTITUTIONAL CONTEXT

One method of assessing what kind of book medieval users considered Bestiaries to be is to examine the institutional and personal contexts in which they were situated. Where Bestiaries were repeatedly bound with texts of a particular type, or where they were located in sections of the library devoted to a particular class of book, then it is reasonable to assume that Bestiaries were considered to share characteristics with these other texts and volumes. Likewise, though less objectively, when Bestiaries are among the books associated by borrowing or donation with a particular user, some kind of context can be established from the other works in which the user was interested. My answer to the question of what Bestiaries were, therefore, will consist of building up a corpus of textual material to which Bestiaries were seen to relate.

---

3. See Winch in Wilson (1970), 78–111.
4. Foucault (1974.I), 128–32.
5. Kauffmann (1975), pp. 16–17 specified Psalters, Bibles and saints' lives as religious, and classical, scientific, medical and astrological manuscripts as secular. Bestiaries were included among the scientific books. Likewise, the Conway Library of the Courtauld Institute of Art organizes its collection of photographs of manuscripts in this way.

As usual there are pitfalls involved. Dealing with individual users is a speculative though rewarding undertaking, and each instance must be judged on its own terms. At the end of this section I shall present three studies of Bestiary users. In the case of mixed volumes, it is vital to be sure that the collection was together in the Middle Ages, if not originally. Original bindings are a guarantee of this, as is scribal uniformity, but both of these are relatively rare. Furthermore, even when texts were bound together, it is not certain that they were intended to be read together. Texts may have been bound together to suit the needs of a particular reader, or simply because they were in quires at the same time and happened to be of the right length to compose a volume of reasonable size. Finally, a limitation of the method is that it can only be applied to texts that are short enough not to fill a volume on their own, and this is largely true only of First Family books and collections of extracts.

In handling mixed volumes, we are on much surer ground when dealing with entries in medieval book lists. Of course, such information is only available where the catalogues are detailed enough to list every text in each volume, and this is rare in early catalogues, though fairly common after the middle of the twelfth century. Another problem with catalogues is that unless they are detailed enough to give *incipits* or *secundis foliis* we have no way of knowing what kind of Bestiary we are dealing with. As compensation, book lists have the advantage over surviving mixed volumes in that we can be sure that the texts they list were together when the list was compiled. It is for this decisive reason that my analysis of texts associated with Bestiaries will be based on catalogue entries rather than on surviving volumes, although the latter will be used as corroboration when it is reasonable to assume that their contents have remained undisturbed.

THE BESTIARY AS A SUBJECT IN MEDIEVAL LIBRARIES

Where catalogues are arranged by subject and not by chronological order of accession or by donor, then, according to the broadness of the subject categories employed, the cataloguer has had to take a view of the general type of book a Bestiary was. This is the broadest of classifications, and it is here that my analysis will begin.

It will be seen from table 19 that complete or partial catalogues or inventories including one or more Bestiaries survive from eighteen houses. In the following discussion of the way Bestiaries were classed in these houses, the catalogue entries listed in appendix two may be found useful by the reader. The bibliography gives references to the published catalogues under the names of the houses concerned.

The two Bestiaries in the fifteenth-century catalogue of Winchester College were both in mixed volumes, and in neither case was the Bestiary treated as the main text for cataloguing purposes. The same applies to the Bestiaries from the catalogues of

Glastonbury, Peterborough (4), Rievaulx, Reading, York, Worcester, Syon and Durham. For the last named, however, there is useful evidence to be gained, albeit mostly negative. The catalogues of 1391–5 and 1416 both recorded the locations of books within the monastery along with their contents. Thus in 1391–5, books were kept in three places: in the Spendement, in cupboards in the cloister, and in a cupboard by the entrance to the infirmary for reading in the refectory. The Spendement was a room divided by an iron grating with a door in it, the inner part being the Treasury where records were kept. Through the grating, wages were paid to the employees of the house. Book cupboards were housed in both inner and outer rooms. The inner room clearly had more space for books, and here were kept Bibles, glossed books of the Bible including Psalters, ecclesiastical histories, works of the Fathers and other theological writers, sermons, saints' lives, chronicles, classical authors, poetry, philosophy, logic, medicine, grammar and episcopalia. The three copies of Isidore's *Etymologiae* were to be found here among the theological books.[6] In the outer room were law books and unglossed (i.e., liturgical) Psalters. The books in the monks' cloister cupboards were very similar in content to those in the inner Spendement (which may have functioned as a reserve collection), but one cupboard was set aside for novices, and the books it contained give a guide to the kind of reading considered suitable for them. It contained no Bestiary. Bestiaries likewise did not appear among the thirty-six volumes sent from the cathedral to Durham College, Oxford, for the use of monks sent there for academic study, nor were they read in the refectory.

The Bridlington list is not a great deal of help to us. It begins as an author catalogue, with rubrications indicating *Libri Gregorii*, *Libri Ambrosi* and *Libri Hugonis*, but this only takes us to volume 32. Thereafter, the books are arranged in no discernable pattern.

Both the Bestiaries in the 1400 catalogue of Titchfield are found in section N, labelled *voluminum de mixtis*. This title tells us little since the mixture is so diverse. Between the two Bestiaries on the shelves (N.X and N.XVII) for example, we would have found a treatise on the black monks (N.XIII), an exposition on the mass (N.XI) and a Virgil (XIV). The late twelfth-century Whitby catalogue and the 1396 catalogue of Meaux are similarly loose in their organization.

The 1327 inventory of Exeter Cathedral includes a *Liber bestiarum et alii plures* . . . among the *Libri Istoriarum*. This section contains eleven volumes and is something of a miscellany. The other sections are organized by author or by donor, except for the books of canon and civil law, which form a section of their own. Among the history books, however, we not only find Josephus *Magnus* and *Parva*, Egesippus and Sydonius, but also the ecclesiastical histories of Eusebius and Orosius; Pliny's *Natural History*; the

---

6. Durham catalogue, 21.

military manual of Vegetius; works of Solinus and and an unidentified *Liber moralium Epistolarum*.

Although both Bestiaries in the Dover Priory catalogue are the opening texts of the volumes they occupy, only one (132) is classified as a Bestiary in the catalogue. The other is only some eleven leaves long, and the volume is classified according to the sermons that form its major part (197). The library was arranged in nine distinctions (bookcases), each divided into seven grades (shelves). Bestiary 132 was shelved at D.III.2, the second book on the third shelf of bookcase D and, according to James's reading of the system, distinctions C, D and E were devoted to 'Sermons and other Theological books', while works on 'Logic, Philosophy, Rhetoric, Medicine, Chronicles and Romances', where we might expect to find 'natural history', and indeed do find *Aristotilis de natura animalium*, were shelved in distinction H.[7] On the same shelf as the Bestiary we find meditations and works of mystical theology, such as Bonaventure's *Itinerarium mentis in deum* (136).

Henry of Eastry's catalogue of Christ Church, Canterbury, lists three Bestiaries, two of which occupy entire volumes. It is helpful for our purposes that these two appear among the earlier accessions – arranged by contents – rather than among the later ones, which were arranged by donor. Both Bestiaries (numbers 483 and 484) appear among the medical books, between the herbals (480–2) and the lapidaries (485–6).[8]

The catalogue of St Augustine's Abbey, Canterbury, is not only arranged by subject, but an attempt has also been made to cross-reference the texts in mixed volumes so that while the main entry is given under the first text in the volume, brief entries for the other texts also appear in their place in the sequence, referring to the main entry. Hence, after the two books containing Bestiaries as their first or only text (869 and 870), we are told that there is another in a *Penitentiali Reymundi* and a fourth in *collectionibus cum H*. The former is no. 650. As for the latter, there are no *collectiones cum H* containing a Bestiary, although there are Bestiaries in *collectiones cum B* and *cum A* (1557 and 1564, see appendix three). The *H* must be a misreading, either by the scribe of the book list or by James in preparing his edition. There were also two other Bestiaries which seem to have escaped the notice of the cataloguer when cross-referencing (see appendix two). Nevertheless, this system of cross-reference serves to identify unambiguously the place in the catalogue where Bestiaries were intended to go. Unfortunately, there is no rubrication to help us assign a name to the category of books in which they were included, so we must rely on the contents of neighbouring volumes in the series to give us a context.

---

7. James (1903), xcii.
8. Ibid., 59.

According to James, the broad outlines of the classification system would place the Bestiaries among the works of 'Natural History', which follow the 'ascetic Theology' and precede the 'history' sections.[9] Such a label is, as we have seen, of no help, because 'natural history' in its present sense had no meaning in the fifteenth century. When we look at the titles themselves, we find a series on the monastic life (855–62) followed by works described as *de proprietatibus rerum* or *de naturis rerum* or *speculum naturalis* (863–8). The two Bestiaries and cross-references to others come next (869–70), and then a copy of Nigellus de Longo Campo's *Speculum stultorum*, Peter Damian and three copies of the *Ysagogue* on moral philosophy (871–6) before the history books begin. The Bestiaries are thus to be found among works on the monastic life, rather than in a 'natural history' section of their own.

The catalogue of the Leicester Augustinians is another extremely workmanlike document. Like the St Augustine's list, it is arranged by subject and copiously cross-referenced. The two Bestiaries (480 and 481) are found in a section headed *volumina de diversis materiis* covering volumes 469–98 of the catalogue. Within the general organization of the books, this section falls between the penitentials and sermons (415–68) on the one hand and the *specula* (499–511) on the other. Within the *volumina de diversis materiis* we find several volumes containing a large number of diverse texts (469–75, 479, 485), but the remainder are books containing one or two theological texts which do not fit readily into any of the rubricated sections. There are, for example, three martyrologies (482–4); two treatises on vice and conscience (477–8); a volume of *exemplis sacrae scripturae* (494); and two treatises on the instruction of novices (496–7). The Bestiaries were thus firmly placed within the institutional context as theological works, related most closely to sermons, penitentials and *specula*; and useful alongside martyrologies, treatises on vice and works on the instruction of novices.

Apart then from the compiler of Henry of Eastry's catalogue, all the librarians who imposed a subject classification on the books in their care treated Bestiaries as works of theology and shelved them alongside sermons, penitentials and works of moral philosophy.

BESTIARIES IN MIXED VOLUMES

In turning to mixed volumes containing Bestiaries, the possibility that texts may have been juxtaposed by chance or to suit the varied interests of some user means that we must proceed with care. It is not reasonable to place too much weight on the contents of individual books, whether surviving or known from catalogues. Only when

---

9. Ibid., lix.

Bestiaries are repeatedly found with some other type of text can any reliance be placed on the association.

Appendix two lists the complete entries from medieval book lists of all volumes which contain a Bestiary. At first sight, Bestiaries seem to be combined with a bewildering variety of other texts, but a closer examination reveals that certain types predominate. There are forty-two volumes in the appendix, and twelve of these include no other named material. For the remaining thirty, the following types of associated text are the most common (table 22).

TABLE 22. TEXTS COMMONLY ASSOCIATED WITH BESTIARIES

ASSOCIATED TEXT	PROPORTION (%)
Virtues and vices, penance, heresy	9/30 (30%)
Sermons	8/30 (27%)
Lives of Saints, exemplary lives	8/30 (27%)
Miracles, marvels and visions	4/40 (13%)
Biblical narratives	3/30 (10%)
Lapidaries	3/30 (10%)
Medical texts	3/30 (10%)

The percentage total exceeds 100, of course, since in many cases Bestiaries are combined with texts of more than one type. Some explanation of these classes of text is called for. It is also striking that there are only two examples of Bestiaries combined entirely with non-theological texts. One is a *Liber Catonis cum bestiario* from Glastonbury, the other a late medical compendium from Syon, on which I shall have more to say below.

VIRTUES AND VICES, PENANCE AND HERESY

Most religious writing, apart from ontology or teleology, is in some way concerned with virtue and vice. In table 22 I have only included texts which examine the subject as their main concern. Such treatises were combined with Bestiaries by all the orders for which I have data. An example from the Benedictine abbey of Peterborough (330.K.xv) includes Augustine's *de conflictu viciorum*; the *Formula honestae vita*, a treatise on the four virtues by Martinus Pannonius; and a *Libellus de quattuor virtutibus cardinalibus*. Similar combinations can be found in Cistercian (Meaux and Rievaulx) and Premonstratensian (Titchfield) houses. Among surviving books, the Brussels *Physiologus* also includes the *Psychomachia* of Prudentius. Harley 3244, a volume produced under Dominican patronage *c.* 1255, is a compendium of penitential writings containing, alongside the Bestiary, the *Liber penitentialis* and the *De sex alis cherubim of*

Alanus ab Insulis, the *Summa de vitiis* of Peraldus, Grosseteste's *Templum Domini* and an anonymous treatise on confession.[10] Royal 6. A. XII, which was at Rochester in the fourteenth century, includes the *Liber de virtutibus et viciis* of Alcuin.[11]

Heresy is included in this section as the vice *par excellence*. The *Physiologus* has been shown (chapter two) to be a treatise on virtue and vice itself, and the issue of heresy is treated explicitly in *formica* and *fulica*, and implicitly in chapters like *columbae, arbor peredixion, aspis* and *unicornis*, which combine the rehearsal of issues of dogma with exhortations to remain in the Catholic and Apostolic church.

SERMONS

All the orders for which we have evidence combined Bestiaries with sermons. Examples are found in the catalogues of the two Benedictine houses at Canterbury, and the priory of Christ Church at Dover; of the Cistercian abbeys of Rievaulx and Meaux, the Premonstratensian abbey of Titchfield and the convent of Austin friars in York. Among the survivals, Harley 3244 contains sermons of Bernard of Clairvaux as well as a collection of 124 *exempla* and the *Ars dilatandi sermones* of Richardus de Thetford.[12] Royal 10. A. VII includes *sermones de tempore* as well as sermon material in the form of the *distinctiones* of William of Lincoln, which form the main text, distinctions on the Psalms, and a *summa*, arranged alphabetically.[13] Bodl. MS Lat. Th. e. 9, probably from the Augustinian priory of Flanesford, includes Bestiary extracts along with sermons on the eucharist.[14]

EXEMPLARY LIVES

The most striking example of this kind of collection is to be found in the Bestiary in section L of the 1395 Durham catalogue, which survives, minus its Bestiary text, as Oxford, Bodl. MS Rawl. D. 338.[15] This includes the *Libri de viris illustribus* of Jerome, Gennadius and Isidore. Three of the Meaux Bestiaries contained saints' lives, and Peterborough 330.K.xv included a life of the Virgin. Oxford, Bodl. MS Bodley 602, which may have been at the Benedictine alien priory of Hatfield Regis, includes a *vita sanctorum*.[16] In this section, I have also included volumes containing Alexander

---

10. Evans (1982).
11. Warner and Gilson (1921), I, 130–1.
12. Evans (1982).
13. Warner and Gilson (1921), I, 304–5.
14. Madan (1895–1953), no. 32710.
15. Mynors (1939), no. 126; Macray (1893) V, III, cols 171–2.
16. Madan (1895–1953), no. 2393.

material, found in two of the St Augustine's catalogue entries (758 and 870 – both surviving) and in Oxford, Bodl. MS Laud Misc. 247, which also includes a life of Charlemagne, and in Cambridge University Lib. MS Kk. 4. 25.

MIRACLES, MARVELS AND VISIONS

Such texts, like the Alexander material, seem to have been especially popular at St Augustine's (758 [Bibl. Nat. MS nouv. acq. Lat. 873], 870, 1564), although Peterborough 55.L.iii provides a *Visio Baronte Monachi*, a text not familiar to me.

BIBLICAL NARRATIVES

Exemplary stories, adapted from the Bible or from non-canonical sources, were often associated with material of the type described in the previous two sections. An example is the *Narratio Josephi de S. Maria Magdalena*, found in Peterborough 55.L.iii and in the section of Douce 88 not found in volume 870 of the St Augustine's catalogue.[17] Part of Douce 88 was certainly at St Augustine's in the fifteenth century, and it was here above all that Biblical *exempla* were found collected with Bestiaries (870 includes a *Narratio qualiter [Ihesus] fuit sacerdos in templum*, 1557 an *Accusatio duorum Judicum in Susannam*).

LAPIDARIES AND MEDICAL TEXTS

Evax super lapidarium, as recorded in Titchfield N.X, is a version of the *Carmen de lapidibus* of Marbod, a treatise on the medical properties of stones, which is frequently accompanied by two letters purporting to be from Evax, King of Arabia to the Emperor Tiberius. The same is found in a French prose version in Royal 12. F. XIII and the *Carmen de lapidibus*, along with the two letters in both Latin and French in Paris, Bibl. Nat. MS Nouv. Acq. Lat. 873. The St Augustine's catalogue entry for this volume makes no mention of Marbod or Evax, describing the collection as a *Lapidarius tripliciter versifice latine et gallice*. Both of the St Augustine's volumes containing lapidaries and medical texts were Adam the sub-prior's books, and we shall have the opportunity to examine the interests of this Bestiary enthusiast in a user study below. The only other catalogue entry of a medical compilation containing a Bestiary is found in the 1504–6 Syon book list (B.24). The donor was John Bracebrigge, one of the largest benefactors of the library and recorded as a brother of

17. Ibid., no. 516. For the contents of Douce 88, see appendix 2.

Syon in 1428.[18] The compilation is thus very late. A key to the inclusion of a Bestiary in such a volume may be provided by the librarian's explanation that it was provided *cum quorundam animalium formis in pictura*. It may be, however, that the treatise in question was not a Bestiary at all, but something like the *Liber de virtutibus bestiarum in arte medicina* ascribed to Sextus Placitus, or the similar text in Bodl. MS Bodley 130, which contains medical recipes requiring the use of twenty-six animals, and gives a coloured illustration of each.[19]

Surviving volumes provide several examples of Bestiaries combined with lapidaries. The justification for this was provided by the frequent relegation of the chapter on *lapides igniferi* to the end of the Bestiary texts. Thus in Aberdeen University Library MS 24, a late thirteenth-century supplement to the text adds further *Physiologus* chapters on stones, originally omitted (*adamas* and *mermecoleon*), then a tract on the Twelve Stones (i.e. a commentary on Revelation 21, 19–20), and a prose version of Marbod.[20] A different treatise on the Twelve Stones is to be found in Rome, MS Vat. Reg. lat. 258, preceding the Bestiary chapter on *lapides igniferi*. Likewise the French Marbod in Royal 12. F. XIII was added after *lapides igniferi*.

BESTIARIES IN CONTEXT

It remains to investigate this statistical association, and some of this work has already been done. The analysis of the *Physiologus* text in chapter two established the status of the Bestiary as a treatise on virtue and vice, and although the changes and additions to the text described in chapter three disrupted the structure of that particular treatise, the individual lessons it contained were to remain intact. Analyses of both mixed volumes and medieval libraries agree in placing Bestiaries in a user context alongside works on virtue and vice, penitentials, and sermons and sermon material in the form of *distinctiones*, *summae* and instructions to preachers. Their statistical association with exemplary lives, miracles and Biblical narratives, and lapidaries is exactly what we would expect if they were in use as a source of sermon *exempla*. Welter's exhaustive analysis, based on Migne, of the *exempla* used in sermons between the eleventh and thirteenth centuries indicates that it was precisely those kinds of texts with which preachers used to colour their teaching.[21] Peter Damian, for example, drew his illustrations from the Bible, the profane history of Greek and Latin antiquity, current affairs, visions, prodigies, animal stories and personal experience.[22]

18. Bateson (1898).
19. Madan (1895–1953), no. 27609.
20. James (1928), 57.
21. Welter (1927), 9–64.
22. Ibid., 32.

Guibert de Nogent's widely distributed handbook on preaching, the *Liber quo ordine sermo fieri debet*, recommended as material suitable for use as *exempla*, the Fathers, especially Gregory and St John Cassian, as well as:

moralites . . . sicut de lapidibus, de gemmariis, de avibus, de bestiis, de quibus quidquid figurate dicitur[23]
(moralizations . . . for example from stones, gems, birds, beasts, from anything at all spoken figuratively).

Examples could be multiplied to illustrate this point, but this would involve nothing more than rehearsing Welter's researches. As far as Greek and Latin antiquity was concerned, Alexander was, as we might have suspected, the commonest source of *exempla*.[24] The case of medical texts has been examined above, and is probably not significant. Other associations are relatively rare.

Morson's work on the use of Bestiary material in Cistercian sermons has already been mentioned in connection with the significantly high occurence of Bestiaries in Cistercian libraries (chapter four). His approach was to search the sermons of three Cistercian writers – Aelred of Rievaulx, Gilbert of Holland and Baldwin – for material connected with the Bestiary. He used six Bestiary texts for comparison with the sermons: Pitra's Greek text; Stowe 1067 as a representative of James's First Family; Cambridge University Library MS Ii. 4. 26, the textually similar Additional 11283, and the Cockerell Bestiary (now New York, Pierpont Morgan Library MS 890) as members of the Second Family; and the French verse paraphrase of Philippe de Thaun found in Cotton Nero A.V.

What he was looking for in the sermons was not direct quotation from the Bestiary texts but for passages that seemed to be reliant on Bestiary material. Such an approach could, of course, be dangerously misleading if applied to a small number of extracts, but Morson's statistical treatment of a large volume of material ruled out the possibility that his writers were using the Bestiary as a second-hand source. He discovered a total of forty-six passages in sermons by the three writers which used Bestiary material. Of these, thirty-two were in Aelred, twelve in Gilbert and only two in Baldwin. Morson took into account the possibility that these writers were using Isidore rather than any Bestiary as a source but discounted it on the grounds that while most of the passages could have been taken directly from Isidore, nine of them could not; whereas all forty-six could have come from a Bestiary. Among the six Bestiary texts he used, he took

23. Ibid., 35, note 2.
24. Bourgain (1879), 258.

Cambridge University Library MS Ii. 4. 26 as his main source of comparison, supplementing it from Additional 11283 to fill gaps in the text caused by missing leaves. Pitra's Greek text was used to identify passages from the *Physiologus*, and the three other Bestiaries simply to identify textual variations. In other words, all of the Bestiary passages he identified in the Cistercian sermons could have had their sources in a Second Family text.

What is interesting in the present context is that it was not only *Physiologus* material that found its way into sermons but also text added to the *Physiologus* from Ambrose, the *Pantheologus* of Petrus Londiniensis, and especially Isidore. This opens up the exciting possibility that changes made to the text and organization of the Bestiary transformed it from a structured treatise on virtue and vice into a *summa* of sermon material arranged, neither alphabetically like the *Summa Abel* of Peter the Chanter (d. 1197) nor chronologically, according to the relevance of its material to the liturgical year, like the anonymous *Proprietates rerum naturalium adaptate sermonibus de tempore per totius anni circulum*, dating probably from the late thirteenth century,[25] but instead according to a framework defined by the account of creation in Genesis. I would not argue that this was invariably the case: simply that for many users, the Bestiary could be employed in this way.

THREE USER STUDIES

In questioning the information available about Bestiary use in England during and after the twelfth century, my approach has been largely statistical. Statistical methods find their justification in a desire to avoid generalizing about consumption from individual examples which may or may not be representative. They tend, however, to be rather dry. More importantly, if the investigation were to stop there, it would lack the specific relationship to people and events which distinguishes statistics from history.

In the course of the analysis, three cases of Bestiary consumption have been uncovered which are well enough documented to serve as specific examples. They may perhaps be odd and uncharacteristic but this is probably true of all individual cases. The first concerns the gift of a Bestiary, among other books, to the Augustinian Priory of Radeford (later Worksop), Nottinghamshire in 1187. The second, a monk at St Augustine's Abbey, Canterbury in the early part of the thirteenth century, who took a particular interest in Bestiaries. The third, a luxury Bestiary produced under baronial patronage in the mid-thirteenth century.

---

25. But known only in a fifteenth-century copy in Munich, Staatsbibliothek cod. Lat. 18141. See Thorndike (1958).

USER STUDY 1: A GIFT OF BOOKS TO RADEFORD PRIORY

The inscription on f. 1v of New York, Pierpont Morgan Library MS 81 has already been mentioned several times. The text is given in full in chapter four. In chapter one, I considered Muratova's reading of the inscription as evidence for the presence of a centre of Bestiary production in Lincoln. I am more concerned here to discover what it can tell us about the expected use of this Bestiary at Radeford Priory. The inscription opens by recording the precise date of the gift (the vigil of the feast of St Matthew, 1187); the identity of the donor (Philippus Apostolorum, canon of Lincoln); the beneficiaries (God, and the Church of SS Mary and Cuthbert in Radeford); and the purpose of the gift (the spiritual improvement (*edificatio*) of the brothers). It then describes the six items making up the gift, and ends with a threat of excommunication for anyone removing any of the books from the precincts of the house, couched in the form of an agreement between Philip, on the one hand, and Prior Anchetus and the brothers of Radeford on the other.

Legal terms are used to specify particular acts which would constitute removal. These are: lending or accepting as a loan (*commodaverit vel commodatum acciperit*); depositing or accepting as a deposit (*deposuerit vel depositum acciperit*); giving or receiving as a pledge (*pignori dederit vel acciperit*); donating or receiving as a gift (*donaverit vel donatum acciperit*); or anything else under any other name which involves alienation of the books from the house, either temporarily or permanently (*vel quocumque titulo alienationis alienaverit vel acciperit vel vi vel clam abstulerit vel precario cuiquam concesserit*).

Muratova understood this anathema to be a form of medieval copyright, which it is not.[26] There is nothing in it which forbids copying, so long as it takes place within the precincts of the house. As we have seen, the Bestiary at least was certainly copied some fifteen to twenty years after the gift was made. The legal form of the anathema is certainly unusual, as is the presence of a specific date (even royal letters were not systematically dated before the accession of Richard I in 1189),[27] but precedents do exist. A manuscript of Augustine from Buildwas was dated 1167 by its scribe,[28] while anathemas were commonly used at Bridlington, Lessness, Newark, Reading, St Alban's, Southwick, Waltham, Winchester, and in the earlier Llanthony and Rochester inscriptions,[29] though not at Lincoln or Radeford.

26. Muratova (1986), 119.
27. Clanchy (1979), 237.
28. Ker (1964), 15.
29. Ibid., xvii.

It is possible that the unusual legal precision of the inscription in the Bestiary was connected with the luxury status of the books themselves, of which much is made in their description. There was a most beautiful (*optimum*) glossed Psalter; a most elegant (*elegantissimo*) Gospel book and a *mappa mundi* which must have been illustrated. The Bestiary itself, a copy of the Meditations of Anselm, and a glossed Genesis are listed with no descriptive adjectives, but the first is certainly a luxury book, provided with more than a hundred miniatures, most of them on a gold ground, and written in an attractive *formata* script.

The form of the inscription as an agreement between Philip and the prior and canons of Radeford makes it clear that this was not a testamentary bequest: indeed, Muratova's research into Philip's life shows that he was still living as late as 1203.[30] What kind of gift are we dealing with in this case? Five books, at least three of which were luxury items, and all of which were single texts, and a *mappa mundi*. The fact that the inscription is in the hand of the scribe of the Bestiary text indicates that this book at least was new when the gift was made and this, alongside the unusual inclusion of a precise date in the inscription, reinforces the impression of a commemorative function, as opposed to a gift from the Lincoln Chapter to a dependant house of, for example, volumes which it no longer had any use for.

Unfortunately, no records of Radeford Priory survive which would allow us to identify the event commemorated by the gift. The priory was founded in 1103, but the church was rebuilt some time later, in a style described by Pevsner as, 'a "Baroque" late phase of Norman, one is tempted to say, just before the new classicity of the Early Gothic became the ideal'.[31] The present nave (plate 46) belongs to this campaign, and the sculptural decoration, including a great deal of nailhead ornament and capitals with stylized leaves, indicates a date at the end of the twelfth century, around the time of the gift of luxury books from Lincoln.

USER STUDY 2: ADAM, SUB-PRIOR OF ST AUGUSTINE'S

As we noticed in chapter four, the 1491–7 catalogue of St Augustine's Abbey, Canterbury, disclosed the existence of a monk with a particular interest in Bestiaries. The evidence for the dating of his gift and his activities in the abbey to the early part of the thirteenth century have already been examined. If, as seems reasonable, we accept Emden's identification, we are in a position to make a thumbnail sketch of the man and his interests.[32]

---

30. Muratova (1986), 123.
31. Pevsner (1951), 211–14.
32. See also Baxter (1991).

Plate 46. Worksop Priory Church (Notts), interior of nave.

We first encounter Adam in 1200, acting for the abbot in a dispute over land. At this time he was chamberlain of the abbey: the official with overall responsibility for the provision of clothing, bedding and baths for the brothers.[33] By 1215 he had become sacrist, in charge of the service of the altar, the vestments and, to some extent, the fabric of the church itself. When he died, he was sub-prior, third in command of the abbey after the abbot and the prior. Following the customs of the abbey, all the books in his possession at his death were marked with his name and placed in the library (plate 47).[34] When the library was catalogued at the end of the fifteenth century, the librarian noted the records of ownership he found in the volumes. Hence the catalogue allows us to identify the contents of the volumes Adam owned, even when the books themselves are lost. These catalogue entries are given in appendix one.

33. Knowles (1963), 430–1.
34. Ker (1964), xviii, note 3.

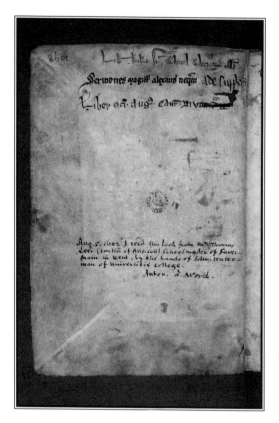

Plate 47. Oxford, Bodleian Library Wood empt. 13, flyleaf. Adam the sub-prior's name (ade supprioris) was written in the book when he died (top right). The third line of text (Liber sci. aug' cant followed by a pressmark) dates from the cataloguing of the library in the fifteenth century.

That his gift of books betrays no evidence of his interest in civil law (apart, perhaps, from Macrobius's commentary on the dream of Scipio from Cicero's *Republic* in volume 1114) is explained by the fact that the St Augustine's catalogue is defective to the extent that it contains no civil law at all. However, 1836 indicates an interest in canon law.

In many ways, 1557 is the most interesting volume. So far as dateable writings are concerned, it is certainly the latest, containing, in Adam's own collections, works by the Christ Church monk Nigel Wireker and Walter Map, contemporaries of Adam himself. Both Wireker and Map were strongly critical of religious orders, the former attacking almost every order except the Gilbertines: the latter reserving a cynical and bitter hostility for diatribes against the Cistercians. We also find a *computus*, a *Physiognomia*, two Bible stories, an assortment of proverbs, a lapidary and a copy of Aesop's fables as well as a Bestiary.

Elsewhere in the gift we find confirmation of the tendencies revealed in this volume. In the light of 758 (which includes tracts about bleeding), 1207 (Hippocrates and Galen) and the *Physiognomia* in 1557, Adam must have had some pretensions to being a physician, a useful accomplishment while he was chamberlain, since the medicinal bleeding of the brothers was carried at the time of their regular baths. The passages on the causes and avoidance of disease in the *Timaeus* provide a philosophical background to medicine similar in form to that provided by Macrobius for the law, and it is perhaps significant that both texts were in the same volume (1114).

The only theology in the gift is of the practical pastoral variety. Adam's interest in the satirical works of Wireker and Map is legible as part of the serious preoccupation with the responsibilities of those entrusted with the care of souls indicated by Gregory on pastoral care (405). The preponderance of sermons (675, 692, 1556) points to an active involvement in this kind of work, and the three Bestiaries (758, 869 and 1557) as well as the works on symbolism (304 and 772) and on virtue and vice (1556), the Bible stories (1557), miracles (758), proverbs and Aesop's Fables (1557) could well have provided *exempla*.

What is striking about the Bestiaries, of course, is that there were three of them. Unfortunately, only 758 has survived (Paris, BN MS Nouv. Acq. Lat. 873) but that, as we saw in chapter three, is of great interest because it shows some attempt to isolate the *bestiae* from the other classes of creation. The book was produced towards the end of the twelfth century, and may thus be contemporary with Adam or slightly earlier. We have no indication that he was involved in its production – it is not marked in the catalogue as his own *collectiones* – but whether he was or not, the textual reorganizations it embodies were by no means anything new at the time. Stowe 1067 had taken the process much further some fifty years before.

It would be a mistake, then, to connect Adam's medical and astronomical activities with a proto-scientific interest in the natural world. We have seen that the contents of books described as Bestiaries could vary considerably, supplying moralizing stories from a wide variety of textual sources. It is this variety which explains the usefulness of three copies for the compiler of sermons.

USER STUDY 3: THE MONHAUT BESTIARY

The evidence for ascribing Oxford, Bodleian Library MS Bodley 764 to the patronage of Roger de Monhaut, or at least to one of a group of men of baronial status, based in the Marches of Wales in the mid-thirteenth century, has been discussed above.[35] It should be emphasized again that the ownership of a Bestiary by a layman appears to be unusual. This is the only demonstrable example, and every other Bestiary whose

---

35. See chapter four and Baxter (1987).

ownership is known belonged to a religious house. What remains to be examined is whether unusual features of the Bestiary can in any way be explained by the requirements of the patron.

Bodley 764 is a luxury manuscript, written in a high-grade script on good quality membrane. The miniatures are skilfully drawn and painted in rich colour with the liberal use of gold leaf, much of it tooled. If we accept Clanchy's argument that heraldry was a system of signs peculiar to the knightly class, alternative to the letters that were the clergy's way of asserting their superiority,[36] then the identification of figures by shields rather than written rubrics in the elephant miniature (colour plate 8) becomes a statement of baronial aspiration.

For a secular reader, the organization of this Second Family book, based on Isidore's expanded exegesis of the Genesis Creation myth, could easily be read in another way. The hierarchy of the animal world finds its counterpart in the organization of human society in which the barons, on their elephant, are firmly placed in the highest class. Taken alone, this might not be particularly convincing, but Bodley 764 also contains textual peculiarities in the shape of additions from the *History and Topography of Ireland* of Giraldus Cambrensis. This was a work by a member of a Welsh Marcher baronial family who was continually at odds with the crown over Henry II's tyrannical treatment of Becket[37] and his, and King John's, repeated thwarting of Gerald's ambition for the see of St David's.[38] Gerald described Henry as a polluter of the Church[39] and he was equally critical of Hubert Walter, who in combining the offices of Chief Justiciar of England and Archbishop of Canterbury between 1193 and 1198, was at once the head of the justiciary and of the established church.[40] In Gerald, the barons had a writer of their own status, who was estranged both from the king and from the established church: a powerful image of baronial independence.

The final piece of the puzzle is provided by the added text itself. The chapter on *melota*, the badger (plate 48), which opens the third main textual division, the *minutis animantibus*, was taken from Giraldus Cambrensis and may be translated:

the badger . . . is an unclean animal and tends to bite, frequenting rocky and mountainous places. Scraping and digging with its feet it makes for itself holes under the ground as places of refuge and defence. Some of them are born to serve by nature. Lying on their backs, they pile on their bellies soil that has been dug by others. Then

36. Clanchy (1979), 230.
37. Giraldus Cambrensis autobiography, 215–17.
38. Ibid., *passim.*
39. Ibid., 111.
40. Ibid., 129–36.

Plate 48. Oxford, Bodleian Library Bodley 764, f. 50v melota. *Badgers digging their tunnel.*

clutching it with their four feet, and holding a piece of wood across their mouth, they are dragged out of the holes by others who pull backwards while holding on here and there to the wood with their teeth. Anyone who sees them is astonished.

The parallel with human society is striking. For the Marcher barons, the image of places of refuge and defence in inhospitable surroundings could easily refer to their own situation, holding the border against the troublesome Welsh. Likewise, the same nature that ordered animal society so that some badgers were only fitted for use as wheelbarrows was also responsible for human society, which represented the baronial patron and his class as innately superior to their tenants. For this group of powerful men, who traditionally claimed a high degree of autonomy from central government, and who aspired to the kind of superior status claimed by the church, on account of the secular power its members now enjoyed, employing their traditional literacy in influential government posts, Bodley 764 was a potent ideological work.

NARRATION: THE PERFORMANCE
OF THE BESTIARY

We are at last in a position to return to Gerard Genette's distinction of three senses of the word *récit*, which I have translated, following Lewin, as 'narrative'.[41] In chapter two, I examined the *Physiologus* text and the drawings in the Brussels *Physiologus* from the viewpoints of the first two senses: the text (*récit*), verbal and visual, of the manuscript itself; and the story (*histoire*) comprising the sequence of events and cast of characters. The third sense, that of narration (*narration*), or performance of the narrative, I have postponed until now since it is bound up with the question of consumption and could not properly be addressed before the broad lines of ownership and use had been established.

The main question at issue is whether Bestiaries, in their various manifestations, were intended to be read aloud to an audience, or consumed inwardly by a silent, lone reader. It would seem that for the vast majority of Bestiaries in monastic hands the answer has already been given. Since they provided material for sermons, they must, to some extent, have been compiled with oral performance in mind. As always, matters are not quite so straightforward. Morson's analysis of English Cistercian sermons revealed that while Bestiaries were the source of a great many stories, it was by no means usual for the preacher to adhere blindly to the Bestiary text. Moreover, even if we find Bestiary *exempla* verbatim in sermon texts, there is no guarantee that the written texts are an accurate account of what the preacher actually said on a specific occasion and to a particular audience. In fact, it is more than likely that the written sermons were compiled before or after the event, with the written textual *exempla* to hand.

In order to address this question at all, therefore, we must turn to the Bestiary texts themselves, looking for signs of oral or written patterning. Walter Ong has identified characteristics which he found typical of oral thought and expression,[42] but his aim was not to search for indications of oral narration in written texts, but the larger enterprise of investigating the differences in habits of thought between orally based cultures and those rooted in writing. In a primary oral culture, one with no knowledge of writing, or even of the possibility of writing, knowledge is strongly dependent on memory. A fact, once forgotten, can never be recovered since it cannot be written down.[43] It is easier to remember thoughts formulated (as spoken words) if they follow patterns of rhythm, alliteration and repetition, if they use standard thematic settings and roles and if they rely on proverbs and familiar set expressions.

41. Genette (1986), 25, note 1.
42. Ong (1982), 36–57.
43. Ibid., 32–6.

Our problem is somewhat different from Ong's. We are not dealing with primary oral cultures but looking for signs of oral performance of texts in cultures that knew some literacy but carried a massive oral residue. Some of the characteristics of orally based thought, however, apply equally to effective oral performance before an audience which may have been illiterate, and it is for those signs that I shall examine our texts.

NARRATION OF THE *PHYSIOLOGUS*

It has been amply demonstrated in chapter two that the *Physiologus* text is structured around a set of characters, which I called actantial functions, recurring in different guises in story after story. The audience, of course, would not recognize Greimas's categories of 'sender and receiver' or 'subject and object', but they would certainly respond to the repeated formulae of quest, hunting and predation, and to the types of role enacted by animal, human and superhuman actors in these scenarios.

Turning from story to text, we notice in chapter after chapter of the *Physiologus* that sequences of events are described in a series of additive clauses linked by the repeated conjunction *et*. This example is from *caladrius*.

> . . . *intendit faciem eius caladrius, et assumit omnes infirmitates eius intra se, et volat in aera solis, et comburit infirmitates eius, et dispergit eas, et sanatur infirmus*
> (. . . the *caladrius* turns its face towards him, and it takes all his infirmities into itself, and flies in the air towards the sun, and his ailments burn, and he disperses them, and the sick person is made well).

Oral discourse simply does not need the elaborate grammar and syntax of written discourse, which lacks such contextual clues, provided by a speaker, as emphasis and gesture.[44] The best known example of this type of construction, the residue of an oral culture retaining grammar and syntax largely unchanged through translations into Hebrew, Greek, Latin and even English writing because the very words of the text were sacred, is, of course, Genesis 1, 1–5.

Redundancy, in the form of repeated parallel phrases, is another oral characteristic common in the *Physiologus* text. Faced with a written text, the reader can re-read passages missed owing to distractions, or those whose significance was not fully appreciated at first. The listener has no such recourse, and must proceed slowly, kept on the track by repetitions.[45] Hence, the Peredixion Tree, '*cuius fructus dulcis est nimis et valde suavis*',[46] or

---

44. Ibid., 37–8.
45. Ibid., 39–40.
46. Whose fruit is very sweet and most pleasant.

the salamander which puts out the flames '*si casu undecumque inciderit in caminum ignis vel in fornacem ardentem*',[47] or the extended description of the sirens luring sailors to their deaths:

> *et musicum quoddam ac dulcissimum melodiae carmen canunt, ita ut per suavitatem vocis auditus hominum a longe navigantium mulceant et ad se trahunt, ac nimia suavitate modulationis prolixae aures ac sensus eorum delineates in somnum vertant. Tunc diende, cum viderint eos gravissimo somno sopitos, invadunt eos et dilaniant carnes eorum, ac sic persuasionis vocis ignaros et insipientes homines decipiunt et mortificant sibi.*
>
> (and they sing tunes of a certain music and the most pleasant melody, so that by the sweetness of their voices they lure men sailing far away and draw them to themselves, and by the very great sweetness of the music they lull their seduced and willing ears and senses into sleep. Then, when they see them slumbering in the deepest sleep, they attack them and tear their bodies to pieces, and thus by their enticing voices they deceive unsuspecting men and kill them.)

Five occurences of words for music or singing; four for sweetness and three for sleep; all in the space of a few lines of text.

The basic strategy of a text like the *Physiologus*, that of using the behaviour of animals, even if they were unfamiliar to the audience, as a way of explaining abstract concepts, is characteristic of oral performance. In primary oral societies all knowledge must be conceptualized with more or less close reference to the human world.[48] In the kind of oral performance to an illiterate or semi-literate audience that I am suggesting characterized the narration of the *Physiologus*, some kind of connection with the human world was essential to an effective presentation. This reflection illuminates a paradox at the heart of the *Physiologus* text. If the things of this world have no importance in comparison with those of the spirit, an opposition central to the structure of the text, what can be their value in teaching genuine truths? The answer, of course, is that for such an audience nothing could be taught save by reference to what was known. It may even be the case that the didactic use of animals, of which nothing was known except by report, was an attempt to resolve this paradox.

A final clue pointing to oral performance of the *Physiologus* is provided by passages in the text which are phrased as if speaking directly to a listening subject. One such form is *Bene itaque Physiologus asseruit (de vulpe)*,[49] occuring, usually at the end, in four chapters.[50] Another is the form of rhetorical questioning found in *caladrius*.

---

47. If for any reason it falls in a fiery furnace or a burning oven.
48. Ong (1982), 42–3.
49. Indeed, *Physiologus* spoke truly (of the fox).
50. At the ends of *vulpis*, *unicornis* and *caper*, and part way through *arbor peredixion*.

sed fortisan dicis quia caladrius immundus est secundum legem: certum est; sed . . .
(but perhaps you say that the *caladrius* is unclean according to the law: this is true,
but . . .).

A third is the exhortation to listen, found in *turtur*.

Audite itaque, omnes animae fidelium, quanta castitas in modica avicula invenitur;
quicumque tamen personam turturis in vultu animae portatis, huius castitatem imitemini
(Hear then, all of a faithful soul, how chastity is found in a little bird; if you carry
the image of the turtle-dove in your soul, you will imitate her chastity).

An admonition to practise chastity is also found, appropriately enough, in *castor*, the
beaver, providing at last the key to the type of audience for which the performance of
the *Physiologus* was principally intended. Among the eight examples of direct appeals to
the audience we find at least five which seem to imply that the hearers were monks or
novices.[51] *Autolops, castor, turtur* and *lapides igniferi* all encourage chastity, the last in a
phrase strongly suggestive of a monastic audience.

unde et vos, homines dei, qui istam vitam geritis, separate vos longe a feminis
(whence you too, men of God, who live this life, keep well away from women).

Finally *formica* urges the avoidance of heresy, following this with a list of heresies so
comprehensive that it could only benefit those with a thorough grounding in doctrine.

THE ILLUSTRATED *PHYSIOLOGUS*

If the text of the Latin *Physiologus* was intended for oral performance, what was the
purpose of illustrating it? First, it was by no means usual to do so. Of the three
manuscripts edited by Cahier and Martin, the oldest, Bern Burgerbibliothek MS
233, is unillustrated. Bern Burgerbibliothek MS 318 is fully painted and Brussels
10074 contains the first fourteen drawings of an uncompleted cycle. Texts unnoticed
by Cahier and Martin include Rome, Vatican MS Palat. Lat. 1074; Rouen, Bibl.
Mun. MS 638; and London, BL MS Royal 6. A. XI, none of which is illustrated.[52]

---

51. The three chapters that include direct appeals without implying a specifically monastic audience are *ibis, herinacius*
and *aquila.*
52. Sbordone (1949), 248–50.

We may take it that a *Physiologus* manuscript was illustrated when there was a need for it, and that the nature of its intended use governed the kind of illustrations chosen.

In the case of the Brussels *Physiologus*, we have seen that the drawings were subordinated to the text, first by being placed after rather than before the chapter they referred to, and then by their rubrication which ensured that they could only be read in the same way as the text (chapter two). Furthermore, the fact that the planned cycle of drawings was never completed argues that the book could function perfectly well without them. An examination of the rubrics themselves leaves a strong impression that they, like the main text, were meant to be read aloud. The three episodes in the narrative of *aquila* (plate 14) are all rubricated in a similar form:

ubi aquila comburit alas suas ad radios solis.
ubi trina vice se fonte mergit.
ubi aquila renovata sede in arbore.[53]

Likewise the scene of baptism in the same drawing:

ubi renovatur homo per baptismum sicut aquila.[54]

This drawing, like many others, also shows Christ preaching, and he does so using direct speech to his audience of three. Both of these forms appear designed for oral didactic performance. In the first, the narrator guides his hearers around a complex narrative sequence: in the second he takes the role of Christ, paraphrasing the lesson he has just read from the text.

NARRATIONAL IMPLICATIONS OF CHANGES TO THE *PHYSIOLOGUS*

FIRST FAMILY BESTIARIES

In First Family Bestiaries the bulk of the text is just as amenable to oral performance as the *Physiologus*. The only textual changes are additions from Isidore at the end of some of

---

53. where the eagle burns its feathers in the rays of the sun; where it dives three times in the well; where the renewed eagle sits in a tree.
54. where a man is renewed by baptism like the eagle.

the chapters: the *Physiologus* text itself is not systematically amended. The added Isidore material, however, is by no means suitable for oral narration. It is not formulaic. On the contrary, it avoids assigning roles to the creatures described, since to do so would defeat the main thesis of the work – that each animal is individually and uniquely represented by the name given to it by Adam. Neither does it rely on additive clauses or repetitive phrases. While it deals with the world of experience, it doesn't use it analogically as a method of teaching moral lessons. Finally, it never addresses its audience in the second person. In fact this added text is a dense mass of unrelated and unrepeated information, usually in the passive voice, which could never be digested aurally. The First Family books, therefore, present a mixture of material designed for reading aloud and material which could only be absorbed by using reading skills like backlooping.[55]

The illustrations, where they occur, are of little or no didactic value. Those in Laud Misc. 247, for example, could not be used in the same way as those in the Brussels *Physiologus*. Their only value, apart from decoration, would be as a 'finding aid' for a solitary reader looking for a particular chapter (see chapter three).

STOWE 1067 AND RELATED BOOKS

We saw in chapter three that the production of Stowe 1067 involved both the addition of extra text from Isidore and elsewhere, and reorganizations both of the order of chapters and of the text within each chapter. Text from the *Physiologus* and Isidore were integrated with additional material found for the first time in this Bestiary. Furthermore, the *Physiologus* text itself was heavily modified, and a glance back to chapter three, where the text of *leo* is given in full, will quickly show that these changes were in the direction of paraphrase. The text was made suitable for private consumption rather than oral narration.

A single example will serve to illustrate this point. Lines 30–2 of Stowe read as follows:

Cum leena parit suos catulos: mortuos gignat; et custodet tribus diebus donec veniens pater eorum in faciem eorum exalet vivificentur.
(When the lioness gives birth to her cubs: she bears them dead; and looks after them for three days until their father comes and breathes into their faces and they are revived.)

They paraphrase the following lines of the *Physiologus* B text found, for example, in Laud:

55. Ong (1982), 39–40.

cum laena peperit catulum, generat eum mortuum, et custodit eum tribus diebus; donec veniens pater eius die tertia, insufflat in faciem eius et vivificat eum.

(when the lioness gives birth to a cub, she produces him dead, and looks after him for three days; until his father, coming on the third day, breathes in his face and brings him to life.)

The differences are slight but significant. The Stowe version contains twenty words, five less than the *Physiologus*. Savings have been made by omitting the pronoun *eum* and the second *et*, and by not repeating the reference to the third day. All these were features of the original text designed to make it easier for a listener to follow an oral performance. The revised version is more concise but assumes private consumption.[56]

THE MORGAN GROUP AND THE SECOND AND THIRD FAMILIES

The immediate basis for the Morgan group was not the *Physiologus* or Laud but the modified text represented by Stowe. Additions made to this text all came from Isidore or from other sources equally designed for private reading (Solinus and Ambrose). Subsequent rearrangements forming the Second and Third Families took the process further: more material was added of a type entirely unsuitable for oral performance. More than this – as this extra text was added, the themes of hunting and quest, which had allowed listeners to assimilate new information by presenting it in familiar forms, were progressively diluted and rendered ineffective. The conclusion is that the sequence of changes we have traced resulted in Bestiaries intended for private reading.

CONCLUSIONS

We are faced, then, with a text called *Physiologus*. A treatise on virtue and vice which, as it stood, was designed for reading aloud to an illiterate or semi-literate audience of monks or novices. A small enough audience, at least in the case of the Brussels *Physiologus*, for the narration to be accompanied by a directed reading of the illustrations under the finger of the narrator.

By the time the text arrived in England it had undergone some changes. The earliest record we have is of Aethelwold's gift to Peterborough which was described not as a *Physiologus* but a *Liber Bestiarum*. The oldest survival already has additions from Isidore

---

56. This is not so apparent in the translation, where attempts have been made to make the text understandable.

appended to many of the chapters, and the chapter list preceding the opening of the text is headed *Incipit capitula libri bestiarum*. In short, although there seems little textual difference between, for example, Laud and the Brussels *Physiologus*, to their users they were different books with different titles.

The various modifications to the text all had three things in common. They structured the chapters in increasingly legible orders to users familiar with the Genesis myth and with the most popular encyclopedia of the early Middle Ages. They added extra information about creatures already represented and chapters on new creatures. Finally they made it more of a reference book and less of a lecture script. All of this is compatible with the evidence of monastic context which places Bestiaries among material used as sermon *exempla* alongside *summae* and *distinctiones*.

This is no place to start yet another hare, but the intimate textual and contextual relationships between Bestiaries and *distinctiones* call for some comment. Bestiaries provided a good deal of the material for *distinctiones*, the difference being that the latter were organized in ways more useful to sermon compilers: alphabetically, like the *distinctiones* of Peter of Limoges;[57] by moral topics, like Nicholas Gorram's collection;[58] or following the liturgical year, like the anonymous *Proprietes rerum naturalium adaptate sermonibus de tempore per totius anni circulum*.[59] It cannot be entirely coincidental that the compilation of such collections by Mendicant preachers began in the mid-thirteenth century when Bestiary production was at its height and gained momentum during the very period that Bestiary production was falling.

57. Rouse and Rouse (1974), 35.
58. Ibid., 34.
59. Thorndike (1958).

CHAPTER SIX

A RETURN TO THE DISCOURSE

We began with a discourse, tracing its origins and development from the nineteenth century, and summarizing its various strands in a list of five propositions. We are now in a position to address these propositions with confidence, and to deny them all.

Assertions of the currency over a certain timespan, and of the universal availability of Bestiaries were found to be simply untrue.[1] These very propositions had already come under attack, by James and by Muratova, from within the discourse itself. It was only by standing outside the discourse, on the more solid foundations provided by textual criticism and bibliography, that it was possible to address and to discredit its more firmly rooted assumptions: that the Bestiary was a textbook of zoology, representing the sum of medieval knowledge on the subject, and that its imagery carried symbolic meaning even when divorced from the text.

The analysis, however, is not simply destructive. It is now possible to situate Bestiaries within other discourses, in which we may have greater confidence because they are more closely tied to what is known of medieval institutions and individuals.

The treatment of Bestiaries as iconographic guides for animal imagery in wood and stone lies outside the realm of manuscript books on which this study is focused. To be satisfied that Allen and his followers were right, we would have to be sure that the carvers of misericords and capitals invariably followed an iconographic programme, rather than simply using Bestiary imagery transferred to model books. In the absence of documentation we can never be sure, but the unusual example of the south doorway of Alne clearly merits special study.[2] In this case we would like to know what the archivolt meant to the twelfth-century users of the church. We would need, therefore, to identify a congregation, and to assess the extent to which its members could have connected the carvings with the Bestiary chapters they normally illustrate. Two qualifications were required by members of this congregation. First, they must have

---

1. Compare the opinions of J. Anderson in Allen (1903), xli, accepted by e.g., Saunders (1932), 63, M. Anderson (1938), 11, Stone (1960), 245, note 6, and McCulloch (1960), 44, discussed in chapter one, with the conclusions reached in chapter four.
2. See Allen (1888), Druce (1912), Collins (1940), Boase (1953), 239 and Stone (1955), 80. Their shared assumption that it constituted a legible iconographic programme are discussed in chapter one.

had some familiarity with the Bestiary stories. This could perhaps be established by an investigation into the sermons they heard, or the preachers who read them. In either case the trail would lead back to the prime reason adduced in this thesis for the proliferation of Bestiaries, namely the production of sermons.[3] It is arguable in any case, that the occasional use of Bestiary imagery for a didactic purpose was, if it happened at all, nothing more than a by-product of this activity.

The second qualification concerns the literacy of the congregation at Alne. They would have needed some Latin to read the inscriptions on the *voussoirs*, since without these many of the carvings are not sufficiently discursive to permit identification of the animals from a knowledge of the stories alone. This minimal qualification of literacy would seem to rule out the lay congregation we would expect to find at a provincial parish church.[4]

At first glance, it might seem that to treat Bestiaries as monastic zoological textbooks and Bestiary consumers as primitive zoologists, has much to recommend it. After all, if we could ask, say, Adam the sub-prior of St Augustine's to tell us all he knew about lions, his reply would probably depend largely on Bestiaries. But to label this 'zoology' would be misleading. His account would include a few observations which could be broadly classed as zoological, mainly those taken from Isidore, but the bulk of it would be of no interest to modern zoologists at all. If, on the other hand, we ask, 'Where was medieval zoology practised, and by whom?', we get answers leading away from the monastic institutions which were the prime consumers of Bestiaries, to the court of Frederick II perhaps,[5] or, stretching a point, to the unique activities of Giraldus Cambrensis.[6]

There is a sense in which the project of placing Bestiaries or any other medieval books in the context they occupied to their original consumers may seem misguided. Although the zoological discourse established by Allen and his successors has here been rejected on the grounds that the Middle Ages possessed no category of zoology, it may be objected that, whether medieval monks knew it or not, Bestiaries really *were* a form of primitive zoology.

It is of interest to us to understand how Bestiaries relate to modern science, and it is certainly true that without the scientific tools of classification and evaluation we would

---

3. See chapter five.
4. For a useful discussion of the knowledge of Latin among non-churchmen, see Clanchy (1979), 186–91.
5. The well-known story of Frederick's investigation of Gerald of Wales's account of the origin of the Barnacle Goose is to be found in Wood and Fyfe (1961), 51–2.
6. Gerald's account of the activities of beavers (Giraldus Cambrensis Wales, 174–7) must be largely based on his own observations. These were not always reliable (he reports, for example, that they have no tails to speak of) but were clearly undertaken to satisfy his curiosity, and are embellished with no moralizations. Nevertheless he also adds the Bestiary story of the beaver's self-mutilation, an activity he attributes to beavers in Eastern countries, citing Cicero, Juvenal and St Bernard as his authorities.

be unable to judge the medieval position. This is not to say, however, that medieval beliefs about the natural world are better understood in our terms than in theirs. At root it is we who want to know about them, and not the reverse.

Much the same point has been made by Winch in discussing MacIntyre's criticisms of Evans-Pritchard's work on the Azande,

> since it is we who want to understand the Zande category (of magic), it appears that the onus is on us to extend our understanding so as to make room for the Zande category rather than to insist on seeing it in terms of our own ready-made distinction between science and non-science.[7]

I have pointed out that the Middle Ages had no category of zoology, and that by placing Bestiaries in this category we are impeding our understanding of them. What is more important to emphasize is that we no longer possess the medieval category into which Bestiaries fell. It has been my intention in this study to reconstruct that category by situating Bestiaries within the social framework of their consumption.

---

7. Wilson (1970), 102.

ADAM'S GIFTS TO ST AUGUSTINE'S, CANTERBURY

304. *Interpretaciones nominum Hebraicorum et in eodem libro*
Allegorie diccionum per alphabetum

405. *Pastoral' Gregorii*

675. *Sermones Alexandri Necquam*

692. *Sermones*

758. *Expositio misse*
Mirabilia que sunt in britannia
de naturis Bestiarum et avium
Exposicio super Apocalypsum
Miraculum quoddam quod contigit in ecclesia Sancti Magni Martiris
Miraculum de duobus militibus quod contigit in alemania
Gesta Alexandri
de pulsibus Venarum cognicio
lapidarius tripliciter versifice latine et gallice
Quibus oris vena aperienda

772. *Liber orationem*
letania magna
Exposicio dominice orationis pluribus modis
Simbolum fidei et quedam alia

869. *Bestiarium*

1114. *Macrobius de sompno scipionis*
documentum spere
plato in timeo

1207. *ysagoge Iohannisii ad tegm' Galieni*
amphorismorum ypocratis
liber prognosticorum ypocratis
tegm' Galieni

1406. *Malchus*

1556. *xxiiij sermon' excerpt' de omelis greg'*
veritates theolog' subtilissime
alleg' super pm Regum
Summa Warnerii de allegg' diversorum vocabulorum
secundum greg' lib 4
quidam tractatus de elemosina et oratione
summa de fallaciis que incidunt in theolog'
distinctiones et diffinitiones viciorum et virtutum
divisio scientiarum

1557. *Collecciones eiusdem [i.e., Ade supprioris] cum b in quibus continentur*
tractatus de naturis bestiarum
Item phisonomia
Relatio de Ioseph et asenech
Compotus Brandani
proverbia undecunque collecta
Accusatio duorum Iudicum in susannam
dissuasio Valerii de uxore ducenda ad ruffinum
versus flaviani ad quintillianum de curia vitanda
ffabule esopi
lapidarium
epistola Nigelli
speculum stultorum et alia

1836. *Pars cuiusdam tractatus qui dicitur speculum iuris canonici*
Quedam alie constitutiones de theologica

BESTIARY ENTRIES IN MEDIEVAL BOOK LISTS

BRIDLINGTON, Aug. priory of B.V.M.

List of *libri magni armarii*, s.xiii in.

127 vols, 1 Bestiary:

61. *Bestiarium; opuscula Anselmi.*

CANTERBURY, Ben.cath.priory of Holy Trinity or Christ Church.

Henry of Eastry's catalogue (1284–1331)

1831 vols, 3 Bestiaries:

151. *Dialogus beati Gregorii, libri iv. In hoc volumine cont. Moralia de naturis quarundam avium et bestiarum.*

483. *Liber de naturis bestiarum,* i.

484. *Liber de naturis bestiarum,* ii.

CANTERBURY, Ben.abbey of St Augustine.

Incomplete catalogue of 1491–7

1837 vols, 6 Bestiaries:

650. *Penitentiale Reymundi et in eodem libro/Bestiarium/vitas patrum et/ principale magistri Odonis de Ciretune.*   *2. fo. penitens*

758. *Expositio misse et in eodem libro/Mirabilia que sunt in britannia/Expositio missae versifice/de naturis Bestiarum et avium/Expositio super Apocalipsum/Miraculum quoddam quod contigit in ecclesia sancti Magni Martiris/Miraculum de duobus militibus quod contigit in Alemannia/Gesta Alexandri/de pulsibus venarum cognitio/lapidarius tripliciter versifice latine et gallice et/Quibus oris vena aperienda. sit Ade supprioris.*   *2. fo. Cantore*

(758 = Paris, BN Nouv. Acq. Lat. 873)

869. *Bestiarium Ade supprioris.*   *2. fo. deret in*

870. *Bestiarium et in eodem libro/prognosticationes/Quedam mirabilia Indie/Quedam de rege Alexandro/Expeditiones eiusdem in Iudica/versus Sibille de diecem iudicii/Narratio qualiter [Ihesus] fuit sacerdos in templo/de xii abusionibus seculi/Sermo Augustini in quo describit que sit vera penitentia/Ymago mundi/Epistola Alex' ad Aristotelem de situ Indie/Epistola bragmanorum ad Alexandrum/versus de Roma/ versus de proprietatibus arborum/versus de proprietatibus herbarum/de verbale/et versus de Susanna. Henr' de Burgham.*   *2. fo. enim greco*

(870 = Oxford, Bodl. Douce 88(II))

1557 *Colleciones eiusdem [i.e., Ade supprioris] cum b.in quibus continentur tractatus de naturis bestiarum/Item phisonomia/Relacio de Ioseph et asenech/Compotus Brandani/proverbia undecunque collecta/Accusatio duorum Judicum in Susannam/dissuasio Valerii de uxore ducenda ad ruffinum/versus flaviani ad quintillianum de curia vitanda/Fabule esopi/lapidarium/epistola Nigelli/speculum stultorum et alia.*   *2. fo. feminas*

1564. *Colleciones Joh' pistoris cum A in quibus continentur de natura quarundam avium cum suis moralitatibus/Item de naturis bestiarum et avium cum suis moralitatibus/Item sermones per totum annum/Expositio orationis dominice/Item tractatus de etate et statura resurgentium/Item de 4 miraculis in celo/Item de illusione nocturna/Item epistola cuiusdam monachi ad abbatum suum que incipit 'Augustie mihi undique'/Item equinoctus magnus a magistro matheo Wyndonic' (Vindocinensi) composita et/quidam sermones.*   *2. fo. amat*

DOVER, Ben.priory of B.V.M. and St Martin. Cell of Canterbury.
Catalogue of 1389

449 vols, 2 Bestiaries

132. *Bestiarius eadmundi. Incipit. 'Bestiarum vocabulum'. 73 fols. dicciones probatorie 'humani generis', loca probationum 4.*   *D.III.2.*

197. *Tractatus de naturis animalium. Inc. 'Leo quinque naturas' [starts f. 1r]. Liber sermonum. Inc. 'Que est ista' [starts f. 12r]. 90 fols. loca probationum 3, dicc. probatorie 'et custodiant ple'.*   *E.III.6.*

DURHAM, Ben. cath. priory of St Cuthbert.
Catalogue of 1391–5

961 vols, 2 Bestiaries

In commune armariolo . . . infra spendimentum. 1391

D.   *RICARDUS DE SANCTO VICTORE de Contemplacione, sive de xii Patriarchis. Libellus de NATURA ANIMALIUM ET AVIUM. Quaedam glosa super LIBROS SENTENTIARUM, in uno quaterno.*   *2. fo. Quodammodo*

In communi armariolo . . . in diversis locis infra claustrum 1395.

L.   *Liber JERONOMI de viris Illustribus. Catholigus GENNADII de Viris Illustribus. Catholigus YSIDERI Episcopi de Viris Illustribus. Liber CASSIODORI Senatoris de Institucionibus Divinarum Scripturarum. Epistola Decretalis GELASII PAPAE, et aliorum LXX. Episcoporum, de recipiendis vel non recipiendis Scripturis extra Canonem conscriptis. Interpretacio NOMINUM APOSTOLORUM et LIBER BESTIARUM.*   *2. fo. lxxi Maltheon*

(in librarium)

(Now Oxford Bodl. Rawl D.338, but lacks Bestiary)

DURHAM, Ben. cath. priory of St Cuthbert

Partial catalogue of 1416 (covers *Cancellaria* (Spendment) only)

512 vols, 1 Bestiary

D. *RICARDUS DE SANCTO VICTORE* . . . as above, now marked *Modicum* valet.

EXETER, Cath. of St Peter

Catalogue in 1327 inventory with additions

229 vols (omitting service books), 1 Bestiary

Liber bestiarum et alii plures in uno volumine: 'De tribus naturis . . .'   5s 0d

EXETER, Cath. of St Peter

Catalogue in 1506 inventory First text only given.

358 vols (omitting service books), 1 Bestiary

Liber Bestiarum,   2. fo. Dicuntur

GLASTONBURY, Ben. abbey of B.V.M.

Incomplete catalogue of 1247 including notes on condition.

c. 340 vols, 1 Bestiary

Liber Catonis cum bestiario. bon.

LEICESTER, Augustinian abbey of B.V.M. de Pratis

Catalogue of *c.* 1500 (post–1493)

c. 941 vols, 2 Bestiaries

480. *Liber vocatus Bestiarium in pulcro volumine et bene illuminatus.*

2. fo. de operibus

Described in cross-reference as *Bestiarium solempne in ass(eres) cum alb(o)*

2. fo. [blank]

481. *Bestiarium aliud non illuminatum nec figuratum.*   *2. fo. in principio*

Described in cross-reference as *Bestiarium aliud non figuratum in ass. cum albo.*

2. fo. in principio creavit

MEAUX, Cistercian abbey of B.V.M.

Catalogue of 1396

465 vols, 6 Bestiaries

Passio Sancti Thomae Cantuarensis compilata: in quo, libellus de naturis bestiarum et piscium.

Formula honestae vitae; in quo Gregorius de conflictu vitiorum et virtutem; Beda de arte metirica; Jeronimus de voti solutione; Interrogationes Orosii et responsiones Augustini; De naturis bestiarum; et principium de vitis Patrum.

Explanatio Remigii; in quo, Augustinus ad Macedonium; Augustinus ad Januarium; Ambrosius de sacramentis; Augustinus de baptismo parvulorum; De naturis animalium.

De sex verbis Domini in cruce; in quo Infantia Salvatoris; Salutationes Bernardi; Vita Sancte Elizabeth; Templum Domini; Sermones super 'Ave Maris Stella'; Bestiarium, De naturis bestiarum; et Lucas glosatus.

De naturis bestiarum; et alia.

PETERBOROUGH, Ben. abbey of SS Peter, Paul and Andrew.

Gift of Bishop Aethelwold, *c.* 970–84.

20 vols, 1 Bestiary

20. *Liber Bestiarum*

PETERBOROUGH, Ben. abbey of SS Peter, Paul and Andrew.

Catalogue (*Matricularium*) of late s.xiv.

346 vols, 3 Bestiaries

55.L.iii. *Visio Baronte Monachi; Narracio Iosephi de S. Maria Magdalena; Tract. de naturis bestiarum et volucrum*

270.T.xii. *Quedam metaphore sumpte a naturis bestiarum; versus de Penitentia; Tract. de Pentitentia; Versus de operibus vidierum; Errores Originis*

330.K.xv. *Aug. de conflictu viciorum; Aug. de ecclesiasticis dogmatibus; Libellus de quattuor virtutibus cardinalibus; Aug. de verbis Domini; Meditt. Aug; Meditt. Bernardi; Formula vite honeste; Regula B. Basilii; Vita B. Virginis; Tract. B. Bernardi de lamentacione; B. Marie in morte filii eius; Quedam Summa de naturis animalium.*

READING, Ben. abbey of B.V.M.

Catalogue of s.xii ex/ s.xiii

228 vols, 1 Bestiary

Petrus alfunsi contra judeos in uno volumine, ubi est etiam bestiarius.

RIEVAULX, Cistercian abbey of B.V.M.

Catalogue of s.xiii.

c. 223 vols, 2 Bestiaries

Augustinus contra mendacium, et ad Renatum de origine anime contra libros Vincentii, et ad Petrum contra libros eiusdem Vincentii, et ad Vincentium Victorem, et contra perfidem Arrianorum, et contra Adversarios legis et prophetarum, et liber bestiarum, et epistolae Anselmi in uno volumine.

Liber sermonum; et quedam excerpta de libros Justiniani, et bestiarium, in uno volumine.

ST ALBANS, Ben. abbey of St Alban

Borrowers' list of 1420–37

56 vols, 1 Bestiary

20. *Item bestiarium cum aliis contentis ex dono Roberti Maynolf supprioris.*

SYON, Bridgettine abbey of St Saviour, B.V.M. and St Bridget

Catalogue of 1504–26

1421 vols, 1 Bestiary

B.24.   *Bracebrigge. Libellus de flegbothomia; Breviarium de Signis, Causis et curis morborum divisum in quinque particulas cum suis Rubricis fo. 6; Dermaciones et efficacie quorundam nominum medicinalium fo. 62; Item de diversis dia(etis) cum aliis medicinis fo. 64; Bestiarium hugonis de Sancto Victore de naturis rerum cum quorundam animalium formis in pictura fo. 118; Antidotarium Nicholai in cuius medio inseruntur medicine in minoribus quaternis fo. 151; Libellus de Flegbothomia cum aliis medicinis fo. 167; Magister Ricardus de Urinis et earum significationibus fo. 170; Item alie medicinae fo. 175.*   *2. fo. vel quia non*

TITCHFIELD, Premonstratensian abbey of the Assumption

Catalogue of 1400

224 vols (omitting service books), 2 Bestiaries

N.X.   *Bestiarium in quaterno / Lapidarium / Evax super lapidarium / Tractatus / De floracio remigii autisiodorensis super missam / Tractatus de Baptismo / Augustinus de conflictu viciorum atque virtutum / Sermones et Notabilia diversa et significacio misse / Gesta salvatoris / Methodius de principio et fine seculorum et regno gencium.*

N.XVII.   *Liber bestiarum, volatilium, serpentium et lapidum / Liber de sensu et sensato / Tractatus de substancia orbis / Liber compendii logicis / Liber de animacione / Concordancie decretalium et decretorum / Ars computandi secundum algorismum / Regule ad cognoscendum quot pollices et pedes aera terre continet et practica mensurandi diversi / Fractiones et proportiones de arte algorismi / Tabula capitulorum et literatum in omnibus libris moralium beati Gregorii / Concordancie de moralibus beati Gregorii / Sermo beati Augustini de fide sancte trinitatis / Tractulus de dilectione proximi et inimici.*

WHITBY, Ben. abbey of SS Peter and Hilda

Catalogue of s.xii ex

c. 89 vols, 1 Bestiary

Natura Bestiarum

WINCHESTER, College of B.V.M.

Catalogue of s.xv in – ex.

137 vols (omitting service books), 2 Bestiaries

Item, liber moralium Gregorii abbreviatus 2. fo. 'molem subvehi' cum certo Chronico Regum Angliae, et liber cum moralizationibus volucrum et bestiarum vocato Bestiario, ex dono Roberti Colpays.

Item, liber continens Hugonem de Sancto Victore de sacramentis, cum tractatu de naturis Bestiarum, et Chronicis Merlini. 2. fo. 'danae', Pret' vj.s viij.d.

WORCESTER, Ben. cath. priory of B.V.M.

Patrick Young's 1662–3 catalogue

343 vols, 1 Bestiary

23. *Aug contra quinque haereses/symbolum Nicaenum et aliae confessiones fidei ut Greg. Nyss/de naturis quorundam animalium videtur Epiphanii, 'Physiologus leone' est initium/Disputatio regalis Pippini juvenis et Alcuini. Initium 'Quid est litera? R. Custos historiae. quid est verbum? proditor animi' et caet. 8vo. vet.*

WORKSOP, Augustinian priory of B.V.M. and St Cuthbert

1187 gift

5 vols, 1 Bestiary

et Bestiarium

YORK, Augustinian friary

Catalogue of 1372 with additions to s.xv.

646 vols, 1 Bestiary

611. *Sermones anni in dominicis et precipuis festivitatibus tam super epistolas quam evangelia. 2. fo. 'esse transitorii'. bestiarium.*

SURVIVAL RATES OF BESTIARIES

Any estimate of the proportion of the total production of manuscript books that has survived to the present day must involve assumptions and generalizations that would horrify any statistician. The two approaches presented below are unjustifiable for different reasons, which will be spelled out in due course, but they seem to me reasonable guesses given the data available. In the event, the two estimates provide a range within which the answer may lie, since the first is certainly too low and the second probably too high.

METHOD 1

Since we are concerned particularly with Bestiary survivals it may seem reasonable to base our approach on these alone: to discover directly the size of the original population of which our fifty survivors are the remnant. Survival, after all, is not merely a matter of chance, and it may be that Bestiaries are more or less likely to have survived than the average medieval book. A case could be made out for either alternative. On the one hand, Bestiaries were no longer produced much after 1300, and it is possible that existing copies were scrapped and their leaves used in the binding of other volumes. On the other hand, it is arguable that picture books were more likely to escape destruction, particularly at the Dissolution. Whether Bestiaries usually were picture books is hard to assess: the majority of the survivals are illustrated, but they may have escaped destruction for precisely that reason.

If it were possible to estimate with any confidence the total number of manuscript books in English monastic libraries in, say, 1300, it would be an easy matter to assess the number of Bestiaries, given the mean frequency of 2.6 Bestiaries per thousand volumes occurring in medieval library catalogues (see table 12). Unfortunately, such an estimate is not readily available, and so the argument must take a more indirect route.

For nine of the fifteen houses with full library catalogues made after 1300, Knowles and Hadcock (1971) gives estimates of the maximum size of the religious community based on documentary evidence, as follows:

HOUSE	MONKS	BESTIARIES
Canterbury, Christ Church	100	3
Canterbury, St Augustine's	90	6
Durham	70	1
Llanthony II	50	0
Leicester	40	2
Meaux	60	6
Peterborough	64	3
Titchfield	18	2
York (Aug. Friars)	46	1
TOTAL	**538**	**24**

In the last column of the table, I have listed the number of Bestiaries in each house. Totalling each column gives figures of 24 Bestiaries for 538 brothers. Assuming that this ratio was the norm, and accepting Knowles and Hadcock's estimate of 14,279 as the mean total of male religious between 1216 and 1350, we can make the following calculation:

Total number of Bestiaries	$= 14{,}279 \times 24/538$
	$= 637$
Number of survivals (Table 17)	$= 50$
% survival rate	$= 50/637 \times 100$
	$= 7.85\%$

There are strong reasons to believe that this figure is too low. It is based on data from only nine houses of which four, St Augustine's, Meaux, Peterborough and Titchfield, were important centres of Bestiary use and housed more Bestiaries than other houses of comparable size. (They account for 17 of the 24 Bestiaries but only 232 of the 566 brothers.) This results in an overestimate of the total number of Bestiaries, and a consequent underestimate of the survival rate. Of course, these houses could be omitted from the calculation, and the estimated survival rate would be higher (in fact it more than doubles to 17 per cent), but with a sample of only seven Bestiaries from six houses, we are stepping outside statistics and into the realm of pure guesswork. Paradoxically, it is useful to have a figure that we know is too low, since this sets a limit to our estimated range.

METHOD 2

The problem with method 1 is that the sample is much too small. By focusing on Bestiaries alone, we have limited it to the point when the omission of a few houses from our calculations more than doubles the estimated survival rate. The sample size can be increased easily enough, but only at the expense of the specific concentration on Bestiaries. In other words, we can calculate with more confidence the overall survival rate of medieval books, but we would still not know whether Bestiary survivals exceeded or fell short of the norm, and by how much.

For those houses where a full catalogue survives, the total number of books in the library when the catalogue was compiled can be counted. In most of these cases, the compilation of the catalogue was accompanied by the writing of *ex-libris* inscriptions and shelf marks in the books themselves. These have been noted in Ker (1964). We are thus in a position to compare the original contents and the survivals of a number of libraries. The figures are summarized in the table below, survivals have only been counted when they were produced before the compilation of the catalogue, and when press marks were apparently systematically written in the books.

HOUSE	ORIG. VOLS	SURV. VOLS	% SURVIVING
Canterbury, Christ Church	2,100	335	16
Canterbury, St Aug.	2,000	260	13
Dover	449	24	5.3
Durham	1,000	560	56
Exeter	373	142	38
Llanthony II	500	180	36
Lincoln	110	92	84
Titchfield	224	9	4.0
TOTAL	**6,756**	**1,602**	**24**

The first point to be made is that the pattern of survivals is extremely variable. It is only to be expected that those houses which remained or became cathedrals in 1540 and 1541 should have been more fortunate than the average, since their guardians were not expelled at the Dissolution. This is certainly true of Lincoln (eighty-three of whose ninety-two survivals are still in the cathedral library), Exeter and Durham. It is not, however, true of Canterbury, nor, according to Ker (1964), of Wells, York, Lichfield, Coventry or Carlisle.

Examining the sample, we notice two obvious sources of error: a preponderance of large houses and a disproportionate number of cathedrals. The first is easy to explain: only houses with large libraries would have felt a pressing need for a catalogue. In the case of the second, cathedral catalogues, like cathedral books in general, were more likely to survive. It is difficult to judge whether survival rates were likely to be higher among larger houses than among small ones, and perhaps it doesn't matter too much given the high proportion of medieval books originally concentrated in relatively few houses. The bias towards secular cathedrals is more worrying, especially given that Bestiaries were never very common in this type of institution. If we ignore the figures from Lincoln and Exeter, however, the overall survival rate only drops to 22 per cent.

SUMMARY

The 8 per cent rate arrived at by the first method is much too low, both as an estimate of Bestiary survival and as an overall figure. It is useful for two reasons, however. It sets a lower limit to the range of survival rates we may feel happy to accept, and it implies that Bestiary survival is probably lower than the average, if only because Bestiaries were never popular in secular cathedrals, where survival rates are high. For a general figure, we may feel that 24 per cent is rather too high, but not by much. I would be confident in estimating a survival rate among Bestiaries certainly of 12–22 per cent, and probably of 15–20 per cent.

THE TIMESCALE OF BESTIARY PRODUCTION

As explained in chapter four, the use of a sample to represent an entire population of data will, if it is random and large enough, give an accurate approximation of the population mean but will underestimate the variance, or spread. The application of Bessel's correction is intended to rectify this. The analysis which follows owes much to Moroney (1982), 226–7.

In this case, our sample is the set of estimated dates of production of surviving English Latin Bestiaries; and the population they represent is the set of dates of production of all English Latin Bestiaries. The sample is thus some 15–20 per cent of the population (see appendix three), although it cannot be considered random. Each Bestiary in the sample has been dated to one third of a century, as described in chapter four. The sample data are shown in the form of a histogram in figure 1 in that chapter.

Taking the year 1100 as our starting point, and calling one third of a century one time unit, then the mean of the sample (**m**) is given by:

$$\mathbf{m} = \Sigma \mathbf{tf}/\mathbf{n}$$

Where **f** is the frequency, or number of Bestiaries produced in each time unit, **t** is the number of time units after 1100, and **n** is the total number of Bestiaries in the sample.

In this case:

$$\mathbf{m} = 252/50 = 5.04$$

In other words, the mean time of production of the sample, the time when exactly half the Bestiaries had been produced, was 5.04 time units after 1100. In terms of dating, this corresponds almost exactly with the midpoint of the fifth time unit (1233–67), or to the year 1251. Within the limits of accuracy of our dating, however, we cannot do better than to place the mean time of production in the second third of the thirteenth century.

The sample variance (**s²**) is calculated according to the following formula:

$$s^2 = \Sigma(t-m)^2/n$$

$$= 200.08/\ 50$$

$$= 4.0016$$

Applying Bessel's correction to give the population variance (σ^2), we get:

$$\sigma^2 = (n/n-1)\ [x]\ s^2$$

$$= 50/49 \times 4.0016$$

$$= 4.0833$$

This means that 95 per cent of the population would fall within 2 standard deviations of the mean, i.e., in the range:

$$5.04 + 2\ \sqrt{4.0833}\ \text{to}\ 5.04 - 2\ \sqrt{4.0833}$$

or between 1 and 9.08 time units after 1100 (1117–1386, or within our dating limits, early twelfth century to late fourteenth).

It also indicates that 99 per cent of the population would fall within 3 standard deviations of the mean, which translates to 1049–1453, or within our dating limits, mid-eleventh century to mid-fifteenth.

To summarize, bearing in mind the warnings about sampling error given in chapter four, we can conclude that the time distribution of surviving Bestiaries itself implies that they were produced at least fifty years earlier than the oldest survival.

GLOSSARY

Aviary

An instructional work for monks, or possibly for lay-brothers, written by Hugo de Folieto (*c.* 1110–*c.* 1174). Hugo (also known as Hugues de Fouilloy) entered the religious life as a Benedictine, perhaps *c.* 1128–30, at Saint-Laurent-au-Bois at Heilly, near Amiens. The priory came under Augustinian rule in 1148, and Hugo was elected prior in 1152, remaining in this position until his death. Clark (1982) dates his composition of the *aviary*, variously known as *De avibus*, *De columba argentata*, *De tribus columbis*, and *Ad Ranierum* (after the knight to whom the work was dedicated turned religious), to the 1150s or early 1160s. The book is closely modelled on Bestiaries, in containing some sixty chapters on birds synthesized from various sources including the *Physiologus*, Isidore, Hrabanus Maurus and Gregory's *Moralia in Job* as well as the Bible. In comparison with Bestiaries, however, it is much more explicitly directed towards teaching monks how to live. Some twenty-five copies are known, almost all dating from the thirteenth century, and often combined with Bestiaries.

Catch words

In codicology, the first word or words of a quire written at the foot of the last verso of the previous quire, as an aid to the binder.

Computus

A treatise designed to teach useful calculations, such as the dates of the moveable feasts of the liturgical year.

Dicctiones probatorie

The first words of a specified page in a book, noted in some medieval library catalogues as an aid to identifying the precise volume referred to.

Distinctiones **(distinction books)**

A class of book used by preachers from the late twelfth century onwards to help them compile sermons (see Rouse and Rouse (1974)). The books list terms for use as *exempla (qv)*, originally from scripture but later also from the natural world, and distinguish various senses or levels of meaning. For example, in the article on birds in Maurice of Provins' *Distinctiones Mauricii* (*c.* 1248), scripture and observation are used to show how the bird can represent Christ, the Devil, a sinner, a religious man, and the vices of luxury, gluttony and anger. In early distinction books, the chapters are organized by the subjects of the *exempla*, and often alphabetically, like a dictionary. From the late thirteenth century onwards there was a tendency to reverse the process and group *exempla* together by the moral topics they covered, like a thesaurus. Many distinction books were called *summae*, for example the *Summa Abel* of Peter the Chanter, an alphabetical work that took its name from its first entry.

Episcopalia

A collection of works useful to bishops.

Exemplum

A story used to teach a moral lesson (see Welther (1927).

Herbarium (herbal)

A manuscript containing accurate illustrations of plants and listing their medicinal uses. Although Bestiaries and herbals have often been grouped together, as medieval books which deal with animals and plants respectively, herbals were quite different in intention, being designed above all as practical aids to medicine.

Incipit

The opening words of a text or volume.

Lapidarium (lapidary)

A treatise on the medical properties of stones, generally a version of the *Carmen de lapidibus* of Marbod, which is frequently accompanied by two letters purporting to be from Evax, King of Arabia, to the Emperor Tiberius.

Martyrologium (martyrology)

A collection of saints' lives.

Penitential

A book detailing the penances appropriate for offences in the monastery, usually fasting or dietary restrictions for a specified period, although penances could also involve excommunication, saying a specified number of Psalms (some Psalters are organized with this use in mind), periods of silence or beatings. For serious offences like murder or unchastity, periods of exile or pilgrimage were sometimes prescribed (see McNeill and Gamer (1938)).

Pressmark
A series of letters and numbers written on the flyleaf of a book to indicate where in the library it is to be shelved. Usually the contents of a library were all marked with pressmarks at the same time as the library was catalogued.

Secundo folio
The opening words of the second leaf of a book, sometimes recorded in library catalogues as an aid to identifying a specific volume.

Speculum
Literally a mirror, in which the reader is urged to examine himself from various viewpoints. In the most celebrated of these books, Vincent de Beauvais's thirteenth-century *Speculum Maius*, the plan was to study four mirrors: nature, science, morals and history. The work thus forms a great encyclopedia, but each of its sections is written from the viewpoint of human redemption. Thus the description of the natural world is structured according to the account of Creation in Genesis; the Liberal Arts described in the Mirror of Science are presented as a preparation for the appearance of the Redeemer; the Mirror of Morals treats virtues and vices, building on the Liberal Arts which are revealed to be no more than the groundwork for living a moral life; finally the Mirror of History, like Augustine's *City of God*, traces the history of the church from Abel onwards as the story of a series of virtuous men whom the reader should emulate.

The *Speculum Maius* is probably the most encyclopedic of these works: most were much more restricted in their ambition, as in the *Speculum Ecclesiae* (Mirror of the Church) written by St Edmund of Abingdon, *c.* 1240, a devotional treatise containing meditations on the life of Christ, but all share an element of self-examination.

Summa
See *distinctiones*.

BIBLIOGRAPHY

Aelfric. 'Vita S. Aethelwoldi auctore Aelfrico', *Chronicon Monasterii de Abingdon*, 2 vols, Rolls Series, 1858, II, appendix 1.

Alexander, J. and Binski, P. (eds). *Age of Chivalry: Art in Plantagenet England 1200–1400*, London (Royal Academy), 1987.

Allen, J.R. *Early Christian Symbolism in Great Britain and Ireland before the Thirteenth Century*, London, 1887.

——. 'The Norman Doorways of Yorkshire: Alne', *The Reliquary*, I (N.S.), 1888, 167–75.

——. *The Early Christian Monuments of Scotland, with an Introduction (being the Rhind Lectures for 1892)* by Joseph Anderson, Edinburgh, 1903.

Anderson, M.D. *The Medieval Carver*, Cambridge, 1935.

——. *Animal Carvings in British Churches*, Cambridge, 1938.

Anglesey catalogue. Hailstone jun, E. 'The History and Antiquities of the Parish of Bottisham', *Cambridge Antiquarian Society Octavo Publications*, XIV, 1873, 247.

Arundel catalogue. St J. Hope, W.H. 'On an Inventory of the goods of the Collegiate Church of the Holy Trinity, Arundel, taken 1 October, 9 Henry VIII.(1517)', *Archaeologia*, LXI, 1, 1908, 61–96.

Barfield, S. 'Lord Fingall's Cartulary of Reading Abbey', *English Historical Review*, IX, 1888, 113–25.

Bateson, M. *Catalogue of the Library of Syon Monastery, Isleworth*, Cambridge, 1898.

Baxter, R. 'A Baronial Bestiary. Heraldic evidence for the patronage of Bodley 764', *Journal of the Warburg and Courtauld Institutes*, L, 1987, 196–200.

——. 'A Monk of St Augustine's', *Medieval World*, 2, Sept./Oct. 1992, 3–10.

——. review of D. Hassig, *Medieval Bestiaries: Text, Image, Ideology*, Cambridge 1995, in *Burlington Magazine*.

Beddie, J.S. 'The Ancient Classics in the Medieval Libraries', *Speculum*, V, 1930, 3–20.

Bermondsey catalogue. Denholm-Young, N. 'Edward of Windsor and Bermondsey Priory', *English Historical Review*, XLVIII, 1933, 437–43.

Bishop Auckland catalogue. Howden, M.P. (ed.), 'The Register of Richard Fox, Lord Bishop of Durham, 1494–1501', *Surtees Society Publications*, CXLVII, 1932, 93–6.

Boase, T.S.R. *English Art 1100–1216*, Oxford History of English Art, III, Oxford, 1953 (corrected impression 1968).

Bond, F. *Wood Carvings in English Churches: 1. Misericords*, Oxford, 1910.

Bordesley catalogue. Blaess, M. 'L'abbaye de Bordesley et les livres de Guy de Beauchamp', *Romania*, LXXVIII, 1957, 511–18.

Bourgain, L. *La chaire française au XIIe siècle*, Paris, 1879.

Boutemy, A. *Nigellus de Longchamp dit Wireker*, Paris, 1959.

Bridlington catalogue. Omont (1892), 203.

Burton-upon-Trent catalogue. Omont (1892), 200–1.

Bury St Edmunds catalogue. James, M.R. 'On the Abbey of St Edmund at Bury', *Cambridgeshire Antiquarian Society 8vo Publications*, XXVIII, 1, 1895, 23–32.

Butler, H.E. (ed. and trans.). *The Autobiography of Giraldus Cambrensis*, London, 1937.

Cahier, C. and Martin, A. *Mélanges d'archéologie, d'histoire et de litterature*, II–IV, 1851–6.

Canterbury, Christ Church catalogues. James (1903), 7–12 (1); 13–142 (2); 143–5 (3); 146–9 (4).

Canterbury, St Augustine's catalogue. James (1903) 173–406.

Carmody, F.J. 'De Bestiis et Aliis Rebus and the Latin Physiologus', *Speculum*, XIII, 1938, 153–9.

——. *Physiologus Latinus. Editions préliminaires, versio B*, Paris, 1939.

——. *Physiologus latinus, versio* Y, University of California Publications in Classical Philology, XII, 1941, 95–134.

Clanchy, M.T. *From Memory to Written Record. England 1066–1307*, London, 1979.

Clark, W.B. 'The Illustrated Medieval Aviary and the Lay-Brotherhood', *Gesta*, XXI, 1, 1982, 63–74.

Cockayne, G.E. *The Complete Peerage*, 13 vols in 14, 2nd edition, London, 1910–59.

Collins, A.H. 'Some Twelfth-Century Animal Carvings and their Sources in the Bestiaries', *Connoisseur*, CVI, 1940, 238–43.

Coventry catalogue. *Monasticon Anglicanum*, III, 186.

Coxe, H.O. *Catalogus Codicum MSS. qui in Collegiis Aulisque Oxoniensis hodie adservantur*, 2 vols, Oxford, 1852.

——. *Catalogi Codicum Manuscriptorum Bibliothecae Bodeianae*, 3 vols, Oxford, 1853–8.

Crowland catalogue. H. Boese, 'Ein mittelalterliches Bücherverzeichnis von Croyland Abbey', *Bibliothek, Bibliothekar, Bibliothekswissenschaft* (J. Vorstius Festschrift), Leipzig, 1954, 286–95.

Deeping catalogue. *Monasticon Anglicanum*, IV, 167.

Delisle, L. *Le Cabinet des mss de la bibliothèque nationale*, II, 1874, 427ff.

Derrida, J. *Of Grammatology*, trans. G.C. Spivak, Baltimore, 1976.

——. *Margins of Philosophy*, trans. A. Bass, Chicago, 1982.

Douglas, M. *Purity and Danger: An analysis of concepts of pollution and taboo*, second edn, London, 1978.

Dover catalogue. James (1903) 407–96.

Dover, St Radegund's catalogue. Sweet, A.H. 'The Library of St. Radegund's Abbey', *English Historical Review*, LIII, 1938, 88–93.

Dronke, P. (ed.)., *Bernardus Silvestris, Cosmographia*, Leiden, 1978.

Druce, G.C. 'The Symbolism of the Goat on the Norman Font of Thames Ditton', *Surrey Archaeological Collections*, XXI, 1908, 110.

——. 'The Symbolism of the Crocodile in the Middle Ages', *Archaeological Journal*, LXVI, 1909, 311–68.

——. 'The Sybill Arms at Little Mote, Eynsford', reprinted from *Archaeologia Cantiana*, London, 1909.

——. 'The Amphisbaena and its Connexions in Ecclesiastical Art and Architecture', *Archaeological Journal*, LXVII, 1910, 285–317.

——. 'Notes on the History of the Heraldic Jall or Yale', *Archaeological Journal*, LXVIII, 1911, 173–99.

——. 'The Caladrius and its Legend, Sculptured on the Twelfth Century Doorway of Alne Church, Yorkshire', *Archaeological Journal*, LXIX, 1912, 381–416.

——. 'Some Abnormal and Composite Human Forms in English Church Architecture', *Archaeological Journal*, LXXII, 1915, 135–86.

——. 'The Elephant in Medieval Legend and Art', *Archaeological Journal*, 1919, 1–73.

——. 'Legend of the Serra or Saw-Fish', Proc. Soc. Antiquaries of London, 2nd Series, XXXI, 1919, 20–35.

——. 'The Mediaeval Bestiaries and their Influence on Ecclesiastical Decorative Art, Part 1', *Journal of the British Archaeological Association*, New Series XXV, 1919, 41–82.

——. 'The Mediaeval Bestiaries and their Influence on Ecclesiastical Decorative Art, Part 2', *Journal of the British Archaeological Association*, New Series XXVI, 1920, 35–79.

——. 'An Account of the Mermecolion or Ant-Lion', *Antiquaries Journal*, III, 1923, 347–64.

——. '"The Sow and Pigs" a Study in Metaphor', *Archaeologica Cantiana*, XLVI, 1934.

——. 'The Lion and Cubs in the Cloisters', *Canterbury Cathedral Chronicle*, XXIII, April 1936.

——. 'Queen Camel Church bosses on the chancel roof', *Proceedings of the Somersetshire Archaeological and Natural History Society*, LXXXIII, 1937, 89–106.

Dugdale, W. *Monasticon Anglicanum*, new enlarged edition by J. Caley, H. Ellis and B. Bandinel, 6 vols, in 8, London, 1817–46.

Durham catalogues. 'Catalogi veteres ecclesiae cathedralis Dunelm', *Surtees Society Publications*, I, 1838, 1–10 (1); 10–84 (2); 85–116 (3).

Eco, U. *Art and Beauty in the Middle Ages*, trans. H. Bredin, New Haven and London, 1986.

Edwards, E. *Memoirs of Libraries*, 1859.

Emden, A. B. *Donors of Books to St Augustines Abbey*, Canterbury, Oxford, 1968.

Evans, E.P. *Animal symbolism in Ecclesiastical Architecture*, London, 1896.

Evans, M. 'Peraldus's *Summa* of Vice', *Journal of the Warburg and Courtauld Institutes*, XLV, 1982, 14–68

Evans-Pritchard, E.E. *Witchcraft, Oracles and Magic among the Azande*, Oxford, 1937.

Evesham catalogues. *Chronicon Abbatiae de Evesham*, Rolls Series, XXIX, 1863, 267–9 (1). Monasticon Anglicanum, II, 5 (2); II, 7 note d (3).

Exeter Cathedral catalogues. (1) Monasticon Anglicanum, II, 527. (2) Oliver, G. *Lives of the Bishops of Exeter*, Exeter, 1861, 301–10, 317–19. (3) Ibid. 366–75.

Exeter Franciscan convent catalogue. Oliver, G. *Monasticon diocesis Exoniensis*, Exeter, 1846, 332–3.

Exh. Cat. Hayward (1984). Zarnecki, G., Holt, J. and Holland, T. (eds). *English Romanesque Art 1066–1200*, London (Arts Council of Great Britain), 1984.

Farne catalogue. Raine (1852), 353.

Flaxley catalogue. Omont (1892), 205–7.

Foucault, M. *The Order of Things: An archaeology of the human sciences*, translator unacknowledged, London, 1974.

——. *The Archaeology of Knowledge*, trans. A.M. Sheridan Smith, London, 1974.

Fraeys de Veubeke, A-C. 'Un catalogue de bibliothèque scolaire inédit du XIIe siècle dans le MS. Bruxelles, B.R.9384–89', *Scriptorium*, XXXV, 1981, 23–38.

Gardner, A. *English Medieval Sculpture*, Cambridge, 1951.

——. 'The East Anglian bench-end menagerie', *Journal of the British Archaeological Association*, XVIII, 1955, 34–41.

Gaspar, C. and Lyna, F. *Les Principaux Manuscrits à peintures de la Bibliothèque Royale de Belgique*, 2 vols, Paris, 1937 and 1945.

Genette, G. *Narrative Discourse*, trans. Jane E. Lewin, Oxford, 1986.

George, W. 'The Yale', *Journal of the Warburg and Courtauld Institutes*, XXXI, 1968, 423–8.

Giraldi Cambrensis Opera, Rolls Series, XXI, 8 vols, 1861–91.

Glastonbury catalogues. (1) Hearne, T. (ed.), *Adami de Domerham, Historia de rebus gestis Glastoniensibus*, Oxford, 1727, 317–18. (2) Williams (1897), 55–78.

Gloucester catalogue. *Monasticon Anglicanum*, I, 537.

Gottlieb, T. *Ueber Mittelalterliche Bibliotheken*, Leipzig, 1890.

Greimas, A.J. *Sémantique Structurale: Recherche de Méthode*, Paris, 1986.

Gsell, B. (ed) *Xenia Bernardina*, Vienna, 1891, III, 112.

Hagen, H. *Catalogus codicum bernensium*, Bern, 1875.

Hahn, T. 'Notes on Ross's Check-List of Alexander Texts', *Scriptorium*, XXXIV, 1980, 275–8.

Hassig, D. *Medieval Bestiaries: Text, Image, Ideology*, Cambridge, 1995.

Heider, G. 'Physiologus nach einer Handschrift des XI. Jahrhunderts', *Archiv fur Kunde Osterreichischer Geschichts-Quellen*, III, 2, 1850, 541–82.

Henkel, N. *Studien zum Physiologus im Mittelalter*, Tubingen, 1976.

Hommel, F. *Die Aethiopische Uebersetzung des Physiologus*, Leipzig, 1877.

Honorius Augustodunensis. *De Imagine Mundi*, P.L.172, cols 115–88.

Hugo of Saint Victor. *De bestiis et aliis rebus*, P.L.177, cols 15–164.

Hulne catalogue. 'Catalogi veteres ecclesiae cathedralis Dunelm', *Surtees Society Publications*, I, 1838, 131 (1); 128 (2).

Ipswich catalogue. Anon. 'A Mediaeval Manuscript of Ipswich Interest', *Ipswich Library Journal*, XLVI, 1939, 14–17.

James, M.R. *The Western MSS in the Library of Trinity College*, Cambridge, 4 vols, Cambridge, 1900–4.

——. *Ancient Libraries of Canterbury and Dover*, Cambridge, 1903.

——. *A Descriptive Catalogue of the MSS in the Library of Gonville & Caius College*, 2 vols, Cambridge, 1907–8.

——. *A Descriptive Catalogue of the MSS in the Library of St John's College*, Cambridge, 1913.

——. *A Peterborough Psalter and Bestiary*, Oxford, 1921.

——. *The Bestiary*, Oxford, 1928.

Kaimakis, D. *Der Physiologus nach der ersten Redaktion*, Meisenheim, 1974.

Karneev, A. *Materiali i samietki po literaturnoi istorii Fisiologa*, St Petersburg, 1890.

——. 'Der Physiologus der Moskauer Synodalbibliothek', *Byzantinisches Zeitschrift*, III, 1894, 26–63.

Kauffmann, C.M. 'Romanesque Manuscripts 1066–1190', *A Survey of MSS Illuminated in the British Isles*, ed. J. Alexander, vol. 3, London, 1975.

Ker, N.R. *English Manuscripts in the Century after the Norman Conquest*, Oxford, 1960.

——. *Medieval Libraries of Great Britain: A list of surviving books*, 2nd edn, London, 1964.

Knowles, D. *The Religious Orders in England*, 2 vols, Cambridge, 1955.

——. *The Monastic Order in England*, 2nd edn, Cambridge, 1963.

Land, J.P.N. 'Physiologus Leidensis' and 'Scholia in Physiologum Leidensem', *Anecdota Syriaca*, IV, 1875, 31–98 and 115–76.

Lanthony II catalogue. Omont (1892), 207–8.

Lauchert, F. *Geschichte des Physiologus*, Strassburg, 1889.

Lehmann, P. *Mittelalterliche Bibliothekskataloge Deutschlands und der Schweiz*, 3 vols, Munich, 1918, 1928, 1932.

Lehmann-Brockhaus, O. *Lateinische Schriftquellen zur Kunst in England, Wales und Schottland vom Jahre 901 bis zum Jahre 1307*, Munich, 1955–60.

Leicester catalogue. James, M.R. 'Catalogue of the Library of Leicester Abbey', *Transactions of the Leicestershire Archaeological Society*, XIX, 1936–7, 118–61, 378–440; XXI, 1939–41, 1–88.

Leominster catalogue. Barfield (1888), 123.

LePrevost, A. (ed.), *Ordericus Vitalis Historiae Ecclesiasticae V*, 1855, viiff.

Lincoln catalogues. Woolley (1927), v–ix (1); x–xv (2).

Lindisfarne catalogue. Raine (1852), 93–8.

Lindsay, W.M. (ed.). *Isidori Hispaliensis Episcopi: Etymologiarum sive originum. Libri XX*, Oxford 1911 (repr. 1985).

Litchfield catalogue. Ker, N.R. 'Patrick Young's catalogue of the Manuscripts of Lichfield Cathedral', *Medieval and Renaissance Studies*, II, 1950, 151–68.

London, St Paul's Cathedral catalogue. Emden, A.B. *Biographical Register of the University of Oxford to AD1500*, III, 1959, 2147–8.

London, St Paul's School catalogue. Rickert, E. 'Chaucer at School', *Modern Philology*, XXIX, 1932, 257–74.

London, Charterhouse catalogue. Thompson, E.M. *The Carthusian Order in England*, London, 1930, 325–6.

Luard, H.R. (ed.). *Matthiae Parisiensis, Chronica Majora*, 7 vols, London, 1872–4.

McCulloch, F. *Medieval Latin and French Bestiaries*, Chapel Hill, 1960.

Macray, W.D. *Catalogi Codicum Manuscriptorum Bibliothecae Bodleianae* (Quarto catalogue), Oxford, 1893.

Madan, F. et al. *A Summary Catalogue of Western Manuscripts in the Bodleian Library at Oxford*, 7 vols in 8, Oxford, 1895–1953.

Mai, A. 'Excerpta ex Physiologo', *Classici Auctores*, VII, 1835, 589–96.

Mâle, E. *L'art religieux du XIIIe. siècle en France*, 3rd edn, Paris, 1910.

Manitius, M. 'Geschichte der lateinische Literatur des Mittelalters', *Handbuch der Klassischen Altertumswissenschaft*, IX, 2, sec. 1, Munich, 1911.

Mann, M.F. 'Der Bestiar Divin des Guillaume le Clerc', *Franzosische Studien*, VI, 2, 1–106.

Marr, N. *Fisiolog, armiano-grusinskii isvod*, St Petersburg, 1904.

Maurer, F. *Der altdeutsche Physiologus*, Tubingen, 1967.

Mayhoff, C. (ed.). *Naturalis Historiae libri XXXVII*, 5 vols, Leipzig, 1892–1909.

McNeill, J.T. and Gamer, H.M. *Medieval Handbooks of Penance*, New York 1938 (repr. 1990).

Meaux catalogue. *Chronica Monasterii de Melsa*, Rolls Series XLIII, 1866–8, 3, lxxxiii–c.

Migne, J.P. (ed.). *Patrologia Cursus Completus, Series Secunda (Latina)*, Paris, 1844–64.

Monk Bretton catalogue. Hunter, J. *English Monastic Libraries*, London, 1831, 1–7.

de Montault X. Barbier. *Traité d'iconographie chrétienne*, Paris, 1890.

Morgan, N.J. *Early Gothic Manuscripts* (1) 1190–1250, A Survey of MSS Illuminated in the British Isles, ed. J. Alexander, vol. 4 (i), London, 1982.

——. *Early Gothic Manuscripts* (2) 1250–85, A Survey of MSS Illuminated in the British Isles, ed. J. Alexander, vol. 4 (ii), London, 1988.

Moroney, M.J. *Facts from Figures*, 2nd edn, Harmondsworth, 1953, repr. 1982.

Morson, J. 'The English Cistercians and the Bestiary', *Bulletin of the John Rylands Library, Manchester*, XXXIX, 1, Sept. 1956, 146–70.

Muratova, X. 'L'iconografia medievale e l'ambiente storico', *Storia dell'Arte*, XXVIII, 1976, 171–9.

——. 'The Study of Medieval Bestiaries. Problems, Enigmas, Quests', Symposium paper 'The Bestiary in Art', London, *Society of Antiquaries and Linnaean Society*, 1976.

——. 'Adam donne leurs noms aux animaux', *Studi Medievali*, XVIII, 2, 1977, 367–94.

——. 'L'arte longobarda e il Physiologus', *Atti del 6 Congresso Internazionale di studi sull'alto medioevo*, Milan, 1978, publ. Spoleto, 1980.

——. 'The Decorated manuscripts of the bestiary of Philippe de Thaon (the MS 3466 from the Royal Library in Copenhagen and the MS 249 in the Merton College Library, Oxford) and the problem of the illustrations of the medieval poetical bestiary', Third International Colloquium, *Beast Epic, Fable and Fabliau*, Munster 1979, publ. Cologne/Vienna, 1981, 217–46.

——. 'Problèmes de l'origine et des sources des cycles d'illustrations des manuscrits des bestiaires', *Épopée Animale, Fable, Fabliau*, Actes du 4e Colloque de la Société Internationale Rénardienne, Evreux, 1981, publ. Paris, 1984, 395–7.

——. *The Medieval Bestiary*, Moscow, 1984.

——. (with Poirion, D.) *Bestiarium. Facsimile du manuscrit du Bestiaire Ashmole 1511, conservé . . . la Bodleian Library d'Oxford*, Paris, 1984.

——. 'Bestiaries: an Aspect of Medieval Patronage', *Art and Patronage in the English Romanesque*, ed. Macready, S. and Thompson, F.H. *Society of Antiquaries Occasional Paper*, NS, VIII, London, 1986, 118–44.

Mynors, R.A.B. *Durham Cathedral Manuscripts from the Sixth to the Twelfth Centuries*, Oxford, 1939.

Newenham catalogue. Russell (1936), 65.

Norwich Cathedral catalogue. *Giraldus Cambrensis*, V, xxxix note 2.

Norwich Priory catalogues. Bensly, W.T. 'St Leonard's Priory, Norwich', *Norfolk Archaeology*, XII, 1895, 190–6, 208–10 (1); 210, 216, 224–6 (2).

Offermanns, D. *Der Physiologus nach der Handschriften G und M*, Meisenheim, 1966.

Omont, H. 'Anciens Catalogues de Bibliothèques Anglaises', *Centralblatt fur Bibliothekswesen*, IX, 5, May 1892.

Ong, W.J. *Orality and Literacy: The Technologizing of the Word*, London, 1982.

Oxford, Canterbury College catalogue. James, M.R. (1903), 165–72.

Oxford, Lincoln College catalogue. Weiss, R. 'The Earliest Catalogues of the Library of Lincoln College', *Bodleian Library Quarterly Record*, VIII, 1937, 343–59.

Patterson, S. *Paris and Oxford University Manuscripts in the Thirteenth Century*, Bachelor of Letters thesis, Oxford, 1969.

Perkins, C.C. *Italian Sculptors*, London, 1868.

Perry, B.E. 'Francesco Sbordone: Physiologus, Milan, 1936' (book review), *American Journal of Philology*, LVIII, 1937, 488–96.

Peterborough catalogues. James, M.R. 'Lists of MSS formerly in Peterborough Abbey', *Bibliographical Society Transactions Supplement*, V, 1926.

Pevsner, N. *The Buildings of England. Nottinghamshire*, Harmondsworth, 1951.

Physiologus. Carmody (1939), Mann (1888).

Pitra, J.B. *Spicilegium Solesmense*, III, Paris, 1855.

Prior, E.S. and Gardner, A. *An account of medieval figure-sculpture in England*, Cambridge, 1912.

Propp, V.I. *Morphology of the Folktale*, trans. L. Scott, Austin Tx and London, 1958.

Raine, J. *The History and Antiquities of North Durham*, 1852.

Ramsey catalogues. *Chronicon Abbatiae Rameseiensis*, Rolls Series LXXXIII, 1886, lxxxv–xci (1); 356–67 (2).

Randall, R.H. (ed.). *A Cloisters Bestiary*, New York, Metropolitan Museum of Art, 1960.

Reading catalogue. Barfield (1888), 113–25.

Regularis Concordia. *Monasticon Anglicanum*, I, xxvii–xlv.

Rievaulx catalogue. Edwards (1859), I, 333–41.

Rimmon-Kenan, S. *Narrative Fiction: Contemporary Poetics*, London, 1983.

Robinson, J.A. and James, M.R. *The Manuscripts of Westminster Abbey*, Cambridge, 1909.

Rocher, J.N.M. *Histoire de l'Abbaye royale de Saint-Benoît-sur-Loire*, Orleans, 1865.

Rochester catalogues. (1). Coates, R.P. 'Catalogue of the Library of the Priory of St. Andrew, Rochester, from the texts of the Textus Roffensis', *Archaeologia Cantiana*, VI, 1866, 120–8. (1); (2). Rye, W.B. 'Catalogue of the Library of the Priory of St Andrew, Rochester, A.D.1202', *Archaeologia Cantiana*, III, 1860, 47–64.

Ross, D.J.A. 'A Check-List of MSS. of three Alexander Texts', *Scriptorium*, X, 1956, 127–32.

Rouse, R.H. and M.A. 'Biblical Distinctiones in the thirteenth century', *Archive d'Histoire Doctrinale et Litteraire du Moyen Age*, XLI, 1974, 27–37.

Russell, J.C. *Dictionary of Writers of thirteenth-century England*, London, 1936.

St Albans catalogues. (1). *Gesta Abbatum Monasterii Sancti Albani*, Rolls Series, 28 (1), 1867, 58, 70, 94, 233, 483. (2). Hunt, R.W. 'The library of St Albans', *Medieval scribes, manuscripts and libraries: essays presented to N.R. Ker*, ed. M.B. Parkes and A.G. Watson, London, 1978, 273–7.

Sandler, L.F. *The Peterborough Psalter in Brussels and other Fenland Manuscripts*, London, 1974.

——. *Gothic Manuscripts 1285–1385*, A Survey of MSS illuminated in the British Isles, 2 vols, vol. 5, Oxford, 1986.

Sauerlander, W. and Hirmer, M. *Gotische Skulptur in Frankreich 1140–1270*, Munich, 1972. English translation by J. Sondheimer as *Gothic Sculpture in France 1140–1270*, London, 1972. French translation by J. Chavy as *La Sculpture Gothique en France 1140–1270*, Paris 1972.

Saunders, O.E. *English Illumination*, 2 vols, Florence and Paris, 1928.

——. *A History of English Art in the Middle Ages*, Oxford, 1932.

Sbordone, F. (ed.). *Physiologus*, Milan, 1936.

——. *Richerche sulle fonti e sulla composizione del Physiologus greco*, Naples, 1936.

——. 'La tradizione manoscritta del Physiologo latino', *Athenaeum*, N.S. XXVII, 1949, 246–80.

Schenkl, C. (ed.). *Ambrose, Hexaemeron*, Corpus Scriptorum Ecclesiasticorum Latinorum, XXXII, 1, Vienna, 1937.

The Septuagint Version of the Old Testament, with an English Translation, London (Samuel Bagster & Sons), 1879.

Silvestre, H. 'A propos du Bruxellensis 1066–77 et de son noyau primitif', *Miscellanea codicologica F. Masai dicata*, Ghent, 1979, 131–56.

Sotheby's sale catalogue, London, 21.10.1920.

von Steiger, C. and Homburger, O. *Physiologus Bernensis*, Basel, 1964.

Stone, L. *Sculpture in Britain: The Middle Ages*, Pelican History of Art, Harmondsworth, 1955.

Syon catalogue. Bateson (1898).

Theobaldus. Rendell, A.W. (trans.). *Physiologus a Metrical Bestiary of Twelve Chapters by Bishop Theobald*, London, 1928.

Thomson, R.M. *Manuscripts from St Alban's Abbey 1066–1235*, 2 vols, University of Tasmania, 1982.

Thomson, S.H. *Latin Bookhands of the Later Middle Ages 1100–1500*, Cambridge, 1969.

Thorndike, L. 'The properties of things of nature adapted to sermons', *Medievalia et Humanistica*, XII, 1958, 78–83.

Thorney catalogue. Humphreys, K.W. 'Book distribution lists from Thorney Abbey, Cambridgeshire', Bodleian Library Record, II, 1948, 205–10.

Thorpe, L. (trans.). *The Journey through Wales and The Description of Wales*, Penguin, 1978 (repr. 1980).

Titchfield catalogue. Wilson, R.M. 'The Medieval Library of Titchfield Abbey', *Proceedings of the Leeds Philosophical Society* (Literary & Historical Section), V, 1938–41, 150–71, 252–76.

Tremlett, T.D., London, H.S. and Wagner, A.R. *Rolls of Arms Henry III*, London, 1967.

Tychsen, O.G. *Physiologus Syrus, seu Historia animalium XXX in SS. memoratorum syriace*, Rostock, 1795.

Waltham catalogue. James, M.R. 'MSS from Essex Monastic Libraries', *Transactions of the Essex Archaeological Society*, N.S.XXI, 1933, 38–41.

Warner, G.F. *Queen Mary's Psalter*, London, 1912.

Warner, G.F. and Gilson, J.P. *Catalogue of Western MSS in the Old Royal and King's collections*, 4 vols, Oxford, 1921.

Way, A. 'The Gifts of Aethelwold, Bishop of Winchester (AD 963–84), to the Monastery of Peterborough', *Archaeological Journal*, XX, 1863, 355–66.

Welbeck catalogue. James, M.R. (1913), 11–13.

Wellman, M. 'Der Physiologus: ein religionsgeschichtlich-naturwissenschaftliche Untersuchung', *Philologus*, Supplementband XXII, 1, 1930, 1–116.

Wells catalogue. Church, C.M. 'Notes on the Buildings, Books, and Benefactors of the Library of the Dean and Chapter of Wells', *Archaeologia*, LVII, 2, 1901, 210.

Welter, J-Th. *L'exemplum dans la littérature religieuse et didactique du moyen âge*, Paris, 1927.

Westminster catalogue. Robinson and James (1909), 4–7.

Whitby catalogue. *Whitby Cartulary, I*, Surtees Society Publications LXIX, 1879, 341.

White, T.H. *The Book of Beasts*, London, 1954.

Williams, T.W. *Somerset Medieval Libraries*, Somerset Archaeological Society, Bristol, 1897.

Wilson, B.R. (ed.). *Rationality*, Oxford, 1970.

Winchester College catalogue. Gunner, W.H. 'Catalogue of books belonging to the College of St Mary, Winchester, in the reign of Henry VI', *Archaeological Journal*, XV, 1858, 62–74.

Windsor catalogue. *Monasticon Anglicanum*, VI, 1362–3.

Witham catalogues. Thompson, E.M. *The Carthusian Order in England*, London, 1930, 316–20 (1); 320–1 (2).

Wittkower, R. 'Marvels of the East', *Journal of the Warburg and Courtauld Institutes*, V, 1942, 159–97.

Wood, C.A. and Fyfe, F.M. (trans. and eds). *The Art of Falconry (being the De Arte Venandi cum Avibus of Frederick II of Hohenstaufen)*, Stanford, 1961.

Woodruff, H. 'The Physiologus of Bern', *Art Bulletin*, 1930, 226–53.

Woolley, R.M. *Catalogue of the MSS of Lincoln Cathedral Chapter Library*, Oxford, 1927.

Worcester catalogues. (1). Bannister, H.M. 'Bishop Roger of Worcester and the Church of Keynsham, with a List of Vestments and Books possibly belonging to Worcester', *English Historical Review*, XXXII, 1917, 387–93. (2). Atkins, I. and Ker, N.R. (eds). *Catalogus Librorum Manuscriptorum Bibliothecae Wigorniensis*, Cambridge, 1944, 31–59.

Wright, T. *Popular Treatises on Science during the Middle Ages*, London, 1841.

Yapp, B. 'The birds of English Medieval Manuscripts', *Journal of Medieval History*, V, 1979, 315–48.

——. *Birds in medieval manuscripts*, London, 1981.

Yarmouth catalogue. Beeching, H.C. and James, M.R. 'The Library of the Cathedral Church of Norwich', *Norfolk Archaeology*, XIX, 1917, 78.

York catalogue. James, M.R. 'The Catalogue of the Augustinian Friars at York', *Fasciculus Ioanni Willis Clark dicatus*, Cambridge, 1909.

Zarnecki, G., Holt, J. and Holland, T. (eds). *English Romanesque Art 1066–1200*, London (Arts Council of Great Britain), 1984.

INDEX